ANIME WONG

ANIME WONG

FICTIONS OF PERFORMANCE

Karen Tei Yamashita

Edited with an afterword by Stephen Hong Sohn

 COFFEE HOUSE PRESS :: 2014

Copyright © 2014 by Karen Tei Yamashita
Afterword © 2014 by Stephen Hong Sohn
Cover and book design by Linda Koutsky
Cover illustration by Ronaldo Lopes de Oliveira
Author photo by Carolyn Lagattuta

Coffee House Press books are available to the trade through our primary
distributor, Consortium Book Sales & Distribution, cbsd.com or (800)
283-3572. For personal orders, catalogs, or other information, write to:
info@coffeehousepress.org.

Coffee House Press is a nonprofit literary publishing house. Support from
private foundations, corporate giving programs, government programs,
and generous individuals helps make the publication of our books possible. We gratefully acknowledge their support in detail in the back of this
book. To you and our many readers around the world, we send our thanks
for your continuing support.

Visit us at coffeehousepress.org.

Library of Congress CIP information
Yamashita, Karen Tei, 1951–
[Plays. Selections]
Anime Wong : fictions of performance /
By Karen Tei Yamashita ;
Edited with an Afterword by Stephen Hong Sohn.
pages cm
ISBN 978-1-56689-340-4 (pbk.)
I. Title.
ps3575.a44a55 2014
812'.54—dc23
2013003665
Printed in the U.S.A.
First edition | First printing

CONTENTS

for Jane Tei & Jon (& Mary & Salie)

KUSEI
ENDANGERED SPECIES

A Short Film

Written by Karen Tei Yamashita, Ronaldo Lopes de Oliveira, and Karen Mayeda

■

Directed and produced by Karen Mayeda

■

Queen: Michelle Umemoto
805.AJA: Chris Tashima

Camera Assistant: Joan Morisaki
Still Photographer: Mark Williams
Boom: Neal Steiner
Alien's Voice: François Chau
Special thanks to: Abe Ferrer, Roy Mayeda, Ann Wei,
Benjamin Wey, Miles Hamada, John Esaki

■

Funded in part by the
National Endowment for the Arts
Expansion Arts Program
and Community Donations

■

Filmed in Super 8 and under the instructions of
John Esaki, Visual Communications

CHARACTERS

QUEEN

Awarded title of Miss Gardena. Gives an interview in the beginning at a marketplace, is struck by an explosion during her venture into the freezer section to retrieve her reward (ice cream), and is found frozen in the same spot 250 years later. Last surviving Japanese American female, selected to preserve her near-extinct species.

805.AJA

A clone of Kenji, the QUEEN's childhood friend. Last surviving Japanese American male, ninth generation (Kusei), destined to be paired with the QUEEN to continue their species.

ALIEN VOICES

Narrate during the QUEEN's encounter with 805.AJA. Given the mission of preserving Japanese American heritage.

TWO SCIENTISTS

Who find the QUEEN frozen at the marketplace.

ALSO HOODED AND CAPED FIGURES

Who push a cart loaded with cloned, Barbie-like figurines in glass containers.

On a white screen, the count of "1" appears. Black typed lines appear, saying:

> ISSEI
> 1st generation Japanese
> In America

Followed by the count of:

> "2"
> NISEI
> 2nd generation . . .

Then the count of:

> "3"
> SANSEI
> 3rd generation . . .

The count goes on from "3" to:

> "4"
> YONSEI

Then from "4" to:

> "5"
> GOSEI
>
> "6"
> ROKUSEI
>
> "7"
> HICHISEI
>
> "8"
> HASSEI

And last, a reversed figure of "6":

> "9"
> KUSEI
> 9th generation . . .

Screen turns dark. Soon the background turns white again. Opening music (mechanical, techno-style) and introductory caption appears:

> A Car Pool Production
> Presents
>
> KUSEI
> Endangered Species
>
> Director of Photography
> Stan Nakazono
>
> Assistant Director
> Kaz Takeuchi
>
> Edited by
> Denise Okimoto
>
> Directed and Produced by
> Karen Mayeda

Screen turns black again. An indistinct shot of unidentifiable body parts appears. Again screen returns to a black backdrop, followed by a white background with a black caption:

> the year 1994

Music ceases.

The next scene is an Asian American teenage girl, QUEEN, *in a gown and a crown, holding a trophy and flowers in her hand. She is standing in front of a partial shot of a white building with a white truck stationed in its rear. Lighting is constantly flickering.*

QUEEN: I'm very proud to be chosen as Miss Gardena. First I'd like to say hi to my boyfriend Brandon. (*raises her hand*) Hi Brandon! Um, (*pulls up the right sleeve of her dress*) I want everybody in the City of Gardena to know that I'm very proud to be a Japanese American. As Miss Gardena, I will do my best to serve the city. As a token of my appreciation, I would like to donate half (*hesitation*) or maybe not half, um, "some" of my new supply of Häa-gen-Dazs ice cream that I was given for being Miss Gar-dena. (*reads from a sheet of paper held in her hand*) Um, with this gesture, I hope to newly begin my struggles, toward the peace and prosperity of mankind, and the universe. (*constantly beaming*) Thank you. (*gracefully waves her gloved hand/arm*)

Music resumes, a slow melody with strong beats. Screen goes white again, with the following words appearing.

2244 . . . Meiji Market Ruins

Screen blacks out again.

Shot of a woman with long wavy hair, SCIENTIST 1, *following another woman wearing a white shirt and headband,* SCIENTIST 2, *through an aisle of stacked boxes. Music gradually fades.*

SCIENTIST 1: What are we looking for anyway?

SCIENTIST 2: A perfectly preserved Japanese American girl from the twentieth century.

SCIENTISTS *approach a steel door, hesitate as they come closer.*

SCIENTIST 1: What is all this stuff?

SCIENTIST 2:   Oh gosh, I don't know. (*turns around and looks at other as if consulting; is wearing goggles and holding a pick*)

SCIENTIST 1:   Oh wait, I'm starting to get a reading.

SCIENTIST 2:   This way. (*tries to pry open the door with pick*)

SCIENTIST 1:   Yes, behind this door. Get in.

Door does not easily open.

SCIENTIST 2:   Hey . . . (*enters*)

SCIENTIST 2:   Oh god.

Angle changes. Ahead is a frozen figure of a girl, QUEEN, *dressed in a cheerleading outfit.* SCIENTISTS *approach, pulling on gloves.*

SCIENTIST 1:   There she is! Is she alive? (*produces an unidentifiable device and makes a diagnosis*) She is! Let's get her out!

SCIENTISTS *place frozen cheerleader/*QUEEN *on a cart and push her toward the camera.*

SCIENTIST 2:   My god she's heavy.

They push her out into the aisle, through vinyl curtains. Scene changes, showing static. Screen goes black, then slowly lights up. Sound of water bubbling.

ALIEN VOICE: Subject female.

View of QUEEN's *body from the side, a black wire device slowly moving along the front.*

ALIEN VOICE: Blood life indicates pure third-generation Japanese American, also known as sansei. Age: nineteen standard Earth years. Height: five foot one inch and two decibel millimeters. Weight: three thousand fifty caligrams.

Camera gradually pulls back, revealing QUEEN *lying in a vinyl, coffin-like container, still in her cheerleading costume.*

ALIEN VOICE: No substantial water loss during radiation, frost, sublimation; now scanning brain.

Wired device moves toward QUEEN's *head.*

ALIEN VOICE: Voted best looking in graduating class of 1992. B+ average. Went to Silver Bells dance with Kevin Kimura. Key Club Sweetheart and Interact Club.

Device lingers near her head.

ALIEN VOICE: Favorite food: Häagen-Dazs ice cream, and when I get married I want a guava angel cake from Ishigo Bakery for my wedding cake.

Device moving away from head to lower body.

ALIEN VOICE: Subject is now gaining dream sequence consciousness.

Camera pulls away. Close shot of QUEEN's *head, now moving.*

QUEEN: Don't, Kevin (*shaking her head*). Don't (*jerks her shoulders*). Besides, we're here in your cramped Celica. What do you mean people can't see through tinted windows?

Scene changes to show a young man, 805.AJA, *standing against an ivory wall with a white pipe shooting up toward the ceiling.* 805.AJA, *wearing a rectangular device on the side of his head, lifts a dumbbell with one arm. Shadowed backs of the heads of the* ALIENS *observe him.*

ALIEN VOICE: This is our male specimen. He is the last of his species.

Camera closes in on 805.AJA's *arm, particularly the biceps moving as he continues to exercise with the dumbbell.*

ALIEN VOICE: In fact, he is the only one that survived the return trip from the planet Topanzanar.

Camera stops, focused on the biceps.

ALIEN VOICE: He is a direct descendant of those Japanese Americans—

Camera abruptly pulls back to show a table in front of 805.AJA, *with jars of food and a brown paper bag placed on the surface.* 805.AJA *hurriedly puts the dumbbell down.*

ALIEN VOICE: —who were relocated during the Ford-Mitsubishi Wars.

805.AJA *looks at a watch and begins to stuff the objects on the table into the bag.*

ALIEN VOICE: The Topanzanees have succeeded in maintaining a pure line of nonintegrated generations.

805.AJA *finishes putting the objects into the bag, picks up the watch again, and gazes into it.*

ALIEN VOICE: He represents the ninth generation of Japanese Americans. He is the Kusei.

805.AJA*'s face shows an expression of enlightenment.*

Scene changes to show 805.AJA *sitting in front of the table, eating.*

ALIEN VOICE: Just think. We've been able to bring the platypus and the weenie dog back from extinction.

Camera closes in on the food on the table: tubes labeled "tempura," "okazu," and so on; a bowl of rice and a jar of soy sauce. 805.AJA *squeezes contents of the tubes onto a dish.*

ALIEN VOICE: Surely we can save this species of humans from extinction.

Back to a wider shot of 805.AJA *and his food.*

ALIEN VOICE: This male specimen is part of our peace-saving link.

805.AJA *pours soy sauce on food.*

ALIEN VOICE: Only this male and—

Camera returns to QUEEN *in her vinyl container.*

ALIEN VOICE: —this female preserve in themselves the cultural mix-
                tures of two races without being threatening to either.

Camera returns to 805.AJA. *Food and other objects are cleared from the table,
and he stands in front of a traditional Japanese taiko, holding the drumsticks
in his hand. He lifts up his arms and begins to drum, grand gestures verging
on a formal performance.*

ALIEN VOICE: Ah, yes, the drums. It is the beginning of the mating rit-
                ual.

Camera returns to QUEEN. *Drum sounds are supplemented by more percussion music.* 805.AJA *approaches the girl and slowly opens the container.*

ALIEN VOICE: Wait, what's he doing?

Close shot of QUEEN'*s face.*

ALIEN VOICE: Ah, yes, he's removing the transparent sticky tapes on her
                eyes.

805.AJA *removes the tapes.*

ALIEN VOICE: It's working. It's the ancient ritual of divestment. After
                being frozen for two hundred and fifty years, maybe her
                eyelids will double permanently.

Camera shows a full shot of QUEEN'*s body. She jerks and finally sits up. She
checks her trophy, touches her crown, and continues to give her interview.*

QUEEN: I'd like to thank everyone for voting for me. And I'm very proud to accept this award as Miss Gardena. Thank you.

Wearing a broad smile, she gracefully waves her hand. Suddenly she realizes the peculiarity of her situation, looks at her hand in surprise, and begins to look around. She locates 805.AJA, and brightens up with recognition.

QUEEN: Ah, haven't I seen you from somewhere?

Camera moves to 805.AJA, a shot of his face against the wall.

805.AJA: Probably so. Did you know Brian Kenji Masaoka from 2108? I was patterned after his sociophysio makeup. But you can call me 805.AJA.

Camera returns to QUEEN's face, wearing a baffled expression.

QUEEN: (*slowly repeating his words*) 805.AJA?

Camera returns to 805.AJA's face, close-up.

805.AJA: Yes, (*expressionless*) there were some slight modifications made on his behavioral patterns. We didn't all want to be exactly the same. But it has been a successful clone model. At least most of the females indexed at the two hundred level have been attracted to the AJA model.

Camera returns to QUEEN, still puzzled.

QUEEN: What are you talking about? (*expression of a certain understanding*) Wait a sec. I did know a Brian Matsushita in fifth grade. But he went to Cerritos and his parents had a flower business. And then I saw him again driving his delivery truck, (*brightening up*) and he even delivered two dozen roses to me when I got this award. Can you imagine that? (*reminiscing*) After not seeing him for ten years.

Camera returns to 805.AJA, who looks serious.

805.AJA: You remind me of model number 222, modeled after Nicole Toshiko Kamiyama. She was a rather popular choice back in 2200. In fact the female handwriting was patterned after hers.

QUEEN: (*sitting on the container, her hands gathered on her knees, still puzzled*) Handwriting? What handwriting?

805.AJA *hands her a sheet of paper. Close shot of the paper shows the following handwritten inscriptions.*

> Japanese American
> alphabet
> a b c d e f g h i
> j k l m n o p q r s
> t u v w x y z
> 1 2 3 4 5 6 7 8 9 10

Camera returns to QUEEN, *who looks suspicious.*

QUEEN: What's that thing on the side of your head?

Close shot of 805.AJA's *head from the side. A metal device contains colorful lights, constantly blinking.*

805.AJA: My pocket memory. I probably have to expand to two pockets, but it's rather clumsy. Single drives are sufficient for us AJAs. Where's yours?

805.AJA *fumbles with the device, then returns to a rigid posture, facing ahead.*

805.AJA: (*as if reciting from a script*) Memory code 009066-B. History of Japanese American Citizen's League being relocated in 1995 to planet Topanzanar.

QUEEN's *face: confused, lost.*

805.AJA: One hundred and three Japanese American citizens were shipped with five copies of the *Pacific Citizen* . . .

Shot of front page of a newspaper, Pacific Citizen, *folded in half.*

805.AJA: . . . and *Rafu Shimpo* . . .

Shot of newspaper, Rafu Shimpo, *followed by two books,* The Quiet American *and* Years of Infamy.

805.AJA: . . . copies of historical pieces such as *The Quiet American* . . .

Camera shifts to videotapes, with titles: Hiroshima Mon Amour *and* Hiroshima Book I.

805.AJA: . . . and videos of Hiroshima and other implements, such as . . .

Shot of bags of rice and shoyu.

805.AJA: . . . a five-pound bag of Cal Rose rice and bins of shoyu.

Camera returns to QUEEN.

QUEEN: (*recovering from her reverie, talking with note of understanding*) Wow, how'd you do that? You know, I don't understand any of this. The last thing I remember, I was in the new Meiji Market taking a queen's tour in the freezer section. That's where my prize was being stored. You know I won a year's supply of Häagan-Dazs ice cream? (*frowning*) And anyways, there was this big explosion . . .

Camera returns to 805.AJA.

805.AJA: That's right, you've been stiff in the freezer for two hundred and fifty years. You're the last Japanese American female. And I'm the last male of the one hundred and three who were relocated. Over the years we were unable to fight our eventual extinction. Our cloning devices were antiquated on Planet Topanzanar. But now with you (*a note of excitement*), we're given a chance!

805.AJA *approaches the girl, who looks mystified, and stands beside her.*

805.AJA: The scanner has found your appropriate natural habitat, shown by decoding your experience.

805.AJA *takes* QUEEN's *hand, and she dismounts the container.*

805.AJA: So just relax. Come with me.

They look into each other's faces and suddenly vanish from the scene, leaving the empty container behind. Scene changes to a bare concrete wall with a car, a convertible Toyota sports car, circa 1986, parked in front. 805.AJA *and* QUEEN *suddenly appear beside the car.*

805.AJA: This ancient vehicle should reestablish your sensual stimulation in familiar surroundings.

QUEEN: (*letting go of his hand, looking around the car*) Wow, what a rad car.

Camera on 805.AJA's *face.*

805.AJA: It's all yours. Get in. (*opens the door*)

QUEEN: (*jumping into the driver's seat*) Wow, this is cool!

805.AJA: (*closing the door*) Memory code, 1986 version. Car means moving in for a good time; (*looks into the window at* QUEEN *and pulls out a pair of sunglasses*) stimulates libido.

QUEEN *puts on the sunglasses and looks up at* 805.AJA, *smiling.*

805.AJA: Hey baby, let's cruise! (*in a rather awkward tone*) We can

do it Sea and Ski! Let's trip on out to Twenty-Second
Street in Hermosa. Let's swing up to Mammoth for
some gnarly skiing!

805.AJA *runs around the car to join* QUEEN, *who excitedly gets ready to start
off. Shot of the two sitting side by side,* QUEEN's *face brightening with recognition.*

QUEEN: Wait, I do know you. Didn't you used to be a boxer boy
                    at Food's Company?

805.AJA: (*smiles mischievously*) How did you know?

They start the car and drive away from the scene.

ALIEN VOICE: We've done it. We've retrieved the species from extinc-
                    tion.

*Scene changes to a corridor, showing the back of two figures wrapped in capes
and hoods, pushing a cart with doll figurines in glass tubes.*

ALIEN VOICE: Congratulations are in order, and just in time. The mem-
                    ory of the female queen will be waning in a few minutes.
                    The freezing process has never been known to preserve
                    the memory, therefore keeping cultural and social func-
                    tions intact. In about twenty-one minutes, her brain will
                    be a sociocultural vacuum.

ALIEN VOICE: But she can always be reprogrammed. Nicole Toshiko
                    Kamiyama, number 222, has perfect handwriting skills,
                    permanent double eyelids, and a competitive taste . . .

*Sound of bubbling water resumes. Shot of three doll figurines, encased in glass
tubes. Screen blacks out. Music.*

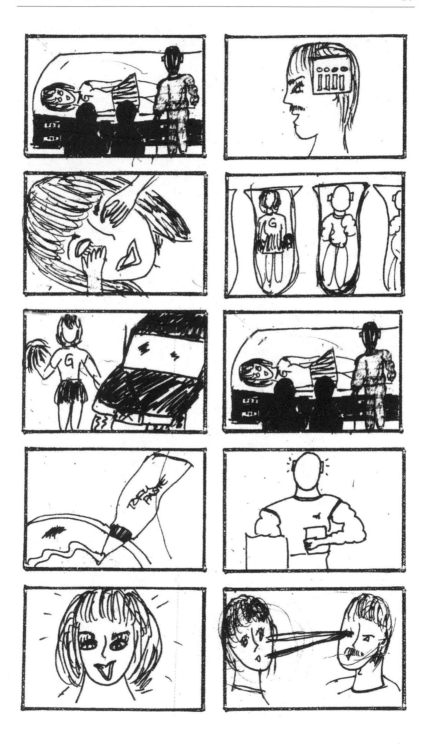

                                                              PAGE 1
FADE IN:

EXT. IN FRONT OF MEIJI MARKET. VIDEO OF MICHELLE ACCEPTING NISEI-WEEK
QUEEN'S CROWN IN FRONT OF A MEIJI MARKET TRUCK.

HIROSHIMA AND OTHER DIASTER FOOTAGE.

VIDEO OF THE QUEEN'S RESCUE FROM THE FREEZER.

INT. LAB

THE ROOM IS DARK WITH AN ISOLATION CHAMBER AND ELECTRONIC COMPONENTS
BLINKING IN THE BACKGROUND. THE ISOLATION CHAMBER CONTAINS THE NISEI
QUEEN. THE CHAMBER IS A DEFROSTING UNIT. IT IS MISTY (DRY ICE).

C.S. QUEEN'S EYES IN ISOLATION CHAMBER. (SHOT THROUGH THE PLASTIC)
      SLOW ZOOM TO REVEAL A SCANNER MOVING ACROSS THE CHAMBER, LEFT TO   1.
      RIGHT, LEFT TO RIGHT.

                      VO COMPUTER SCANNER
            Height 5'1" and 2 decibel minimiters. Weight 3050
            caligrams. No substantial water loss during radiation
            frost sublimation. Now, scanning brain..defrosting
            memories from surface folds. First indention indicates:
            voted best-looking in graduating class of 1995 . B+
            average, Silver-Bells Queen, Key Club Sweetheart and
            Interact club. Favorite food - Haagen Daz Icecream.
            and when I get married I want a Guava Angel Cake from
            Ishigo Bakery for my wedding cake. Subject is now
            gaining dream sequence consciousness.

C.S. QUEEN'S FACE WITH CLOUDY BACKGROUND (MISTY)   2.

                          QUEEN
            (MUMBLES) Don't Kevin. Don't! Besides we're all
            squashed here in your celica. What do you mean
            people can't see through the tinted windows?

NEXT TO FIRST ISOLATION CHAMBER IS ANOTHER CHAMBER. THERE IS A BARRIER
BETWEEN THE QUEEN AND THE GUY. IN FRONT OF THE 2ND CHAMBER IS A
VIEWING -WINDOW FOR THE SCIENTIST TO OBSERVE.

O.S.S. OF SCIENTIST. SLOW DOLLY INTO OBSERVATION CHAMBER. WE SEE
GUY STAND UP AND PICK UP DUMB-BELLS. HE STANDS AND STARTS PUMPING
THE WEIGHTS   3.

                      VO SCIENTIST #1
            This is our male speciman. He is the last of his
            species. In fact, he is the only one that survived the
            return trip from the planet Topanzanar. He is a direct

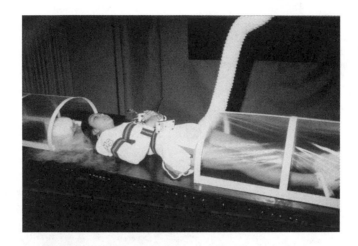

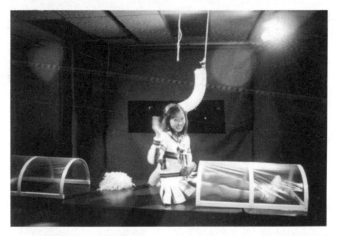

T.ransitions ◆

1987 Asian Pacific American International Film Festival
Presented by the
UCLA Film & Television Archive
and Visual Communications
April 4, 5, 7, 21, 25, 26, 28, and May 2
Melnitz Hall Theater, UCLA

Saturday, April 4 7:30 P.M.
Pak Bueng On Fire (1987)
by Supachai Surongsain
My Country: In Desperate Straits
(Bayan Ko: Kapit sa Patalim) (1984)
by Lino Broka

Sunday, April 5 3:00 P.M.
Yuki Shimoda: Asian American Actor (1985)
by John Esaki and Amy Kato
IN PERSON: Director John Esaki
and Producer Amy Kato

ASIAN AMERICAN ACTORS SYMPOSIUM
with Kim Miyori (John and Yoko: A Love Story),
Rodney Kageyama (Gung Ho), and James
Shigeta (The Crimson Kimono, The Yakuza)
MODERATED BY: Actor/Director Mako
FREE ADMISSION

7:30 P.M.
The Crimson Kimono (1959) Directed by
Samuel Fuller. With James Shigeta, Glenn
Corbett, Victoria Shaw

Tuesday, April 7 8:00 P.M.
**PIONEERING VISIONS, A SELECTION OF
ASIAN AMERICAN SHORT FILMS**
The Boat People (1986) by Bua Chau
No Vacancy (1986) by Naomi Hirahara
Renewal (1986) by Kaz Takeuchi
Chisai Samurai (1986) by Chris Tashima
Yamaguchi Sensei (1986) by Roland Hazama
Dribble (1986) by Allison Kurumta
Kusei: Endangered Species (1986)
by Karen Mayeda, edited by Chiyen Yee
Grasshoppers (1986) by Denise Okimoto
Lotus (1987) by Arthur Dong (work-in-progress)

Tuesday, April 21 8:00 P.M.
ASIAN AMERICAN WOMEN FILMMAKERS
Co-presented by the Asian Pacific Women's Network
To Live Or Let Die (1982) by Freida Mock
Conversations: Before The War/After The War
(1986) by Robert Nakamura. Written and
produced by Karen Ishizuka
Made in China (1985) by Lisa Hsia
Broken Rainbow (1985) by Tom Tysona &
Victoria Mudd (excerpts will be screened)
IN PERSON: Directors Lisa Hsia (schedule
permitting), Freida Mock, Karen Ishizuka, and
Victoria Mudd (schedule permitting)

Saturday, April 25 7:30 P.M.
AN EVENING WITH LINO BROKA
Jaguar (1979) by Lino Broka
IN PERSON: Director Lino Broka

Sunday, April 26 7:30 P.M.
TWO BY ALLEN FONG
Just Like Weather (1986)
Father and Son (1981)

Tuesday, April 28 8:00 P.M.
**DREAM VISIONS AND STAR GAZERS:
AN EVENING OF ANIMATION AND ZEN TALES**
How To Become A Fascinating Speaker
by Fu-Ding Cheng
Acapulco Gold by Arnie Wong
Kabuki Suite by Laureen Burger
Etharo by Fu-Ding Cheng
Don Giovanni by Marilynn Yamada
Little One Inch by Kelly Takemura
Mochi Monster by Troi Pang
Tough Talk by Abraham Ferrer
Lion Dance, Sleep Sounds, Peep Show
by Mar Elepano
Karma II by Arnie Wong
Mental Block by Doug Chiang, Arnie
IN PERSON: Fu-Ding Cheng, Arnie
Mar Elepano and Doug Chiang

Saturday, May 2 7:30 P.
**ASIAN AMERICANS IN HOLLYW
THE EARLY YEARS 1915 - 1944**
Including a special tribute to A

Clip show and slide presenta
Narrated by actress Kim Mi

TICKETS: $4.00 (general), $2.50 (st
except where indicated FREE AD
available at the door on the day
prior to showtime.

MELNITZ THEATER is locate
the UCLA campus, near the
and Hilgard Ave.

PARKING is available for
to Melnitz Theater. Free c
east of Hilgard Ave. on C

For more
(213) 68

DEBUT SCREENINGS—Receiving certificates of completion in graphic filmmaking and narrative filmmaking courses as part of Visual Communications' Asian Pacific Filmmaker Development Program at a special screening were (left to right, back row) Kelly Takemura, Chris Tajima, Jose De Vega, Karen Mayeda, Stuart Iwasaki, Abraham Ferrer and Kent Hirohama; (left to right, front row) course instructors John Esaki and Mar Elepano, and course participants, Kaz Takeuchi, Denise Okimoto, Yachiyo Mattox and Evangeline Galicia.

NEW FILMMAKERS HOLD SCREENINGS

Several new Asian American filmmakers, who took part in the Filmmaker Development Program of Visual Communications, marked the beginning of their careers at a public screening held on Saturday, July 12, at the Japanese American Cultural and Community Center in Little Tokyo.

Animation was first on the program with Kent Hirohama's "Seeds," documenting the history of a Japanese American family viewed through a series of photographic stills.

Next up...

was the theme for Yachiyo Mattox's "Over The Edge."

Abe Ferrer's "Tough Talk" was a powerful filmic discourse on the need for social protest.

Even politically relevant films were not without a lighter side as 13-year-old Troi Pang's "Mochi Monster" shows that even a rice cake is not immune to the effects of nuclear waste.

The dramatic portion of the program begins... Chris Tashima's ... a film about a ... 's fantasy of ... samurai who re... distress.

... science fiction ... parodies a ... queen who is ... ed in time and ... cell in cultural ... generation ...

... without its ... er, as Kaz ... "Renew... takes that an

chiefly Filipino undergoes just to renew his driver's license.

And finally, Jose De Vega's moving portrait of a young Japanese American dancer who must spend her rehearsal time in a Japanese relocation camp during World War II is highlighted in his poignant film, "Harusame."

A selection of these films will be screened at the Pioneering Visions Japan America Theatre. For further information about this event, call (213) 680-4462.

8e Festival International du Film Super 8 + Vidéo du Québec.

PRÉSENTÉ PAR L'ASSOCIATION POUR LE JEUNE CINÉMA QUÉBÉCOIS

Montreal, February 16, 1987

RE: KUSEI: ENDANGERED SPECIES

Dear friend,

Firstly, I would like to thank you for having participated in the 8th Quebec International Super 8 Film and Video Festival by registering your film.

Unfortunately, despite its qualities, your film could not be selected for the official competition. We received over one hundred international films and videos from which only twenty were chosen.

We hope that you will continue your work as a filmmaker and that you will not hesitate to participate again in the Festival. Until we meet again, I remain,

Sincerely yours,

Jean Hamel
Director

HANNAH KUSOH

AN AMERICAN BUTOH

A Performance in Six Senses

Written by Karen Tei Yamashita

Choreography and Direction by Shizuko Hoshi

Video and Slides by Karen Mayeda

Music by Vicki Abe

Scene/Lighting and Tech by Ronaldo Lopes de Oliveira,
Chris Tashima, and Steve James

Ensemble: Victor Chew, Tim Dang, Linda Igarashi,
Sala Iwamatsu, Mimosa Iwamatsu, Susan Nakagiri

■

Originally staged at the Japanese American Cultural and Community Center,
Little Tokyo, Los Angeles, and Highways, Santa Monica

PART 1: THE SNEEZE—THE SENSE OF SMELL

KOAN: *In a single sneeze, millions of germs are released into the air.*

PART 2: THE JAPANOPHILE—THE SENSE OF TOUCH

KOAN: *Nice Caucasian boy looking for nice Asian girl.*

PART 3: THE EYES—THE SENSE OF SIGHT

KOAN: *The only things Japanese about me are my name and my eyes.*

PART 4: TOROZUSHI/EROTICA EXOTICA—THE SENSE OF TASTE

KOAN: *Toro is the fat underbelly of the tuna. In sushi, it is the best part, like the thighs of a woman.*
or
A hundred million miracles are happening every day!

PART 5: MADAME BUTTERFLY—THE SENSE OF SOUND

KOAN: *Tienti la tua paura, io con sicura fede lo aspetto—*
Keep your fears; I, with secure faith, wait for him. (Last lines from *Madama Butterfly* aria)

PART 6: THE SIXTH SENSE—THE SENSE OF INTUITION

KOAN: *You've got to be kidding.*
or
Hey, like, go with the flow, man; go with the flow.

PART 1: THE SNEEZE—THE SENSE OF SMELL

MUSIC: Piece with mixed cultural instruments: koto, shakuhachi, marimba, bagpipes, or some other sansei invention of a multicultural nature.

SCENE: There is an enormous half mask (nose and eyes) on stage, possibly ukiyo-e in design, but probably Japanese. The nose part of the mask allows for the entrance and exit of dancers. The eyes, which may blink, open and shut, house large video monitors. Mask coloring is effected with the use of slides/lighting. Changes in mask may create Kabuki-like makeup; red, white, and blue highlights; and so on. Slide material over white mask is effective.

DANCE: A sneeze begins the music/dance. Five dancers (three women, two men) in bags fall out of the nostrils. The bags are of different colors/materials and should be stretchy in nature: green (the first bag), kimono material, khaki camouflage, and so on. Possibly one stretchy type of material can be airbrushed into different possibilities. The bags roll, splat, fall over, congregate, stick to each other, expostulate, ruminate, and so on. Possibly film projection over bags.

SMELLS: There is a flow of smells directed into the audience: hibachi, teriyaki, incense, chili, marijuana, takuan, cherry, and so on.

VIDEO/SLIDES: Eyes are closed. Footage of atomic bomb at the flutter of eyes during the initial sneeze. Scenes of Hiroshima post–A-bomb destruction. Then, Japanese America scenes of the concentration camps, early farming and urban pioneers, with movement to present day—Little Tokyo, Gardena, festivals, family life, daily life.

PART 2: JAPANOPHILE—THE SENSE OF TOUCH

MUSIC: Chinese dance from the *Nutcracker*.

DANCE: A large finger appears. Feet push through each bag. Some
                    feet wear sneakers; others put on geta, tabi, or heels. The
                    chase begins. Some bags get stuck to the finger. Some of
                    the bags get pushed against the wall. Some run back into
                    the nose. The finger rubs the nose. The bags escape
                    through the opposite nostril. Some bags produce fingers;
                    some bags produce bare feet. Other bags produce mas-
                    saging aids. One bag has an electric massager, which jit-
                    ters like crazy. The bags massage the finger until it flees,
                    the bags running the finger up into the nose.

VIDEO/SLIDES: Sansei discussing her blind date with a Japanophile. This
                    may be broken up into several women telling the same
                    story. Narrative over photographs from family albums
                    and old film footage showing a sansei girl growing up in
                    America.

VIDEO NARRATIVE:

                    Listen, I never do this, but I figure I'd do this for my
                    friend. She's says, "Listen, this guy has money, and he
                    loves Asian women, but none of the women he dates are
                    fun like you. He oughta date an Asian woman who
                    knows how to have fun, you know what I mean? Listen,
                    I think you'll really hit it off."

                    Well, I shoulda known better, but, after all, they're all
                    Japanophiles out there. They just manifest themselves in
                    different forms.

                    I drive out to meet this guy at his place. I'm like driving
                    through this nice area, so I figure I'm going to get treated
                    to a nice dinner. When I get to his place, he like lives
                    behind this Japanese gate with Japanese kanji painted on
                    the doorway. I get let in the gate, and this place is a total

Japanese garden. My parents live in Gardena, but they don't have a garden like this. I mean it is out of *Japan Home Gardens*. It's like a setting for a Japanese restaurant. There's this koi pond and a little red lacquered bridge and all this bonsai and this moss and rocks. I never been in Japan, but I swear to myself, like I'm totally in Japan.

So then I get to his house, and he's got this marble entranceway and these shoes all left at the doorway. He meets me at the door, and he is this hakujin guy who's shorter than me. He looks me over, and you know I was prepared for this big evening, so I came in black stockings and heels and my black leather miniskirt and big shoulder-padded leather coat. I was really looking wonderful, but I'm towering over him so I take my heels off at least.

I say, "Wow. You got a nice place. I never seen anything like it." He looks surprised you know.

He shows me around. He's got scrolls everywhere and screens here and there. He's got these big dead branches built up into giant arrangements next to white walls. He's got a big red silk kimono hanging on his bedroom wall with all these prints of Japanese women with their kimonos falling off. And get this, he sleeps on tatami mats, and he takes a bath in a sunken tub. All the time he's got this koto and flute music playing on his compact disc.

I ask him if he lives there all by himself. And he says, "Yeah." This is sort of his retreat that he's made for himself. And I say, "Yeah." Then I ask him whether he's got anything to drink. He says he's got some fine tea. I ask him if he's got anything stronger. He says he doesn't drink, but he's got this bar for guests, so I help myself.

Then he goes off to get something, so I snoop around and open all his closets. And he's got these Playboy foldouts of all these Asian nudes in the closets.

Then he comes back with this apple cut up on a Japanese plate, and he says it's a Japanese apple. I try this apple, and it tastes like an apple, so I say, "So what is this, a Japanese grew it?" He says something about intensive agriculture, and I say, "Oh yeah, my grandfather used to do that."

Then he shows me his newest acquisition, some antique Japanese furniture that's sitting there on the tatami. He says it's a something or other sort of dressing table from the fourteenth century and he paid a fortune for it. I remember the Japanese nudes in the closet, so I say, "Yeah, but you need a midget to use it."

By now I'm really hungry. Japanese apples don't do anything for me. Besides, I really feel like I need to return to L.A. He says, "Where would you like to eat?" I suggest _____. Well, he says he's heard of that place, and isn't it a little expensive? So I suggest another place, and he doesn't like Italian. He doesn't like Thai. He doesn't like Tex-Mex. He doesn't like this or that or this is too expensive. He says, "Don't you like Japanese food?" Well, I tell him Japanese food is no big deal. If I want it, I can get it at home. "Do you cook Japanese?" he asks. I say, "Of course not; my mom does." He looks confused. But all he wants to eat is Japanese, so we end up going to a Japanese family restaurant on Sawtelle. Can you imagine? I'm dressed for _____, and he takes me to a teriyaki place. I can't believe it.

Then, get this. He orders everything in Japanese. Seriously. Japanese. He orders all that disgusting gooey stuff like salmon eggs and quail eggs. Me, I order tekkamaki and some California rolls.

He knows the owner, and they spend the whole dinner talking in Japanese. He never even talks to me. Just to really freak him out, I ask for a fork and spoon and pour shoyu all over my rice.

So I take him back to Japan on the Westside and leave him there at the gate. I say, "Well, I don't know what you're looking for in the way of a date, but the only things Japanese about me are my name and my eyes," and I drive off.

PART 3: THE EYES—THE SENSE OF SIGHT

MUSIC: Aperture (piece originally composed by Vicki Abe)

DANCE: Heads and arms, covered in white chalk, push out of the
                  bags. The legs are further exposed. Faces emerge in dark
                  glasses. Eyeball earrings. Mouths encase tiny lights; as
                  the dancers open their mouths in little Os, lights flash
                  on and off. Eyes might be patched underneath glasses
                  with painted-on almond eyes; on one dancer's eyelids are
                  inscribed a *3* and an *M*. Candy almonds are passed out to
                  the audience after dancers remove patches. Dancers use
                  mirrors and paint eyes extravagantly and formally on
                  stage. All dancers then display rolls of Scotch tape, which
                  may be torn in long pieces and applied to parts of the
                  body. Bodies and faces move together, positioning the
                  eyes dramatically. Ongoing demonstration of latex appli-
                  cation to create Asian features.

ONSTAGE DIALOGUE:

> Quotations from various sources about eyes:
>
> A: Medical
> B: Makeup/Special Effects
> C: Biblical/Shakespearean
> D: Poet
> E: Scholar/Reporter

C: You see her eyes are open. (*Macbeth*)

D: Ay, but their sense is shut. (*Macbeth*)

E: It is probably futile to claim that most Japanese eyes are not
                  slanted—especially in a work on Japanese prints, whose
                  artists adopted the pleasing sensation that they were . . .
                  (*The Floating World*, Michener)

D: I met a lady in the meads
Full beautiful, a faery's child;
Her hair was long, her foot was light,
and her eyes were wild.
(*La Belle Dame San Merci*, Keats)

C: Lust not after her beauty in thine heart; neither let her take thee with her eyelids.
(Proverbs)

A: Westernization of the Asian eyelid has become a topic of considerable interest in the Western world in recent years due to the increasing number of surgeons being consulted to perform this procedure. This demand is attributable to the great influx of Asian immigrants, who are influenced by Western culture, design and esthetics. After performing over two thousand cases of westernizing Asian eyelids, I have developed a method of surgically creating a *double eyelid* as well as a method for removing the epicanthal web. The techniques result in a marked improvement of the narrow, puffy Asian eye and greater patient satisfaction.
(Ronald S. Matsunaga, DDS, MD, FACS)

C: Behold, I show you a mystery; we shall not all sleep, but we shall all be changed, in a moment, in the twinkling of an eye . . .
(Corinthians)

B: Instructions for the makeup artist.
Number 24: Oriental Makeup.
Materials: One pair of Oriental eyelids . . .
(*Makeup for Theater, Film & Television*, Lee Baygan)

A: The goal . . . is to surgically create a supratarsal fold, commonly referred to as a "double eyelid" of the typical Asian to a more esthetic and cosmetically larger eyelid characteristic of the occidental. The newly created eyelids can be further enhanced by proper cosmetic application, resulting in greater self-image and confidence.

B: Black eyebrow pencil shapes and defines brows at the arch. For natural effect, blend color well with cotton swab. Apply honey-brown eye shadow from crease to brow, smokey olive shadow on lid. Blend out, extending color under lower lashes.
("Beauty Center," *Good Housekeeping*)

C: Did not the heavenly rhetoric of thine eye,
'gainst whom the world cannot hold argument,
Pursuade my heart to this false perjury?
(*Love's Labour's Lost*)

A: In the Asian eye, there is a congenital absence of the supratarsal fold with excessive preorbital septal fat extending down to the ciliary margin along with the obicularis oculi muscle, causing a puffy, narrow *slit eye.*

C: Life for life. Eye for an eye . . .
(Exodus 21:23)

B: 1. Oriental eyelids must be large enough to cover the area from your eyelashes to your eyebrows . . .
2. Place the eyelid latex piece so you can look straight ahead easily . . .
3. Powder heavily . . .

E: She's got eyes like Jezebel, teeth like pearls, gosh or gee, she's out of this world.
(Folk song)

A: The epicanthal web in Asians is a normal ethnic occurrence and is not due to an abnormal position of the orbits or canthal elements.

E: Is life more enjoyable with Caucasian eyes? Is visibility greater?

B: Using a small piece of foam rubber sponge, apply liquid latex . . .

5. Dry with a hand hair dryer . . .
6. Powder . . .
7. Apply rubber mask grease . . .
8. Blend foundation . . .
9. Powder the entire face . . .

E: Can you see when you laugh?

A: 1. A curvilinear line is marked with gentian violet solu-
        tion on the upper eyelid five to ten millimeters above
        the ciliary margins of both eyelids simultaneously . . .

B: 10. With the proper clothes and mannerisms . . . you can
        achieve a believable Oriental appearance. Remember
        that the highlight and shading used [must be] suited
        to [the] actor's bone structure. If you have a very
        healthy, full face, changing it to a thin one with high
        cheekbones and shading will not be easy—you might
        simply wind up with a dirty face. (Remember, too,
        that not all Orientals are thin!) Do the best you can
        with your face and stay away from stereotypes.

E: Police are on the lookout for an Asian male, age twenty-
        five, medium height, short black hair, and surgically
        Westernized Asian eyes.

C: Take, oh take those lips away,
        that so sweetly were forsworn;
            and those eyes, the break of day;
        lights that do mislead the morn.
        (*Measure for Measure*)

A: 2. Local anesthesia of 1 percent lidocaine hydrochloride
        with 1:100,000 adrenaline is injected . . .

D: Or if thy mistress some rich anger shows,
        Imprison her soft hand and let her rave,
        And feed deep, deep upon her peerless eyes.
        (*Ode to Melancholy*, Keats)

E: Mariko fanned herself . . . "What is the lady, your wife
            like?"

A: "She's twenty-nine. Tall compared with you. By our
            measurements, I'm six feet two inches, she's about five
            feet eight inches, you're about five feet . . . Her hair's . . .
            fair with a touch of red. Her eyes are blue, much bluer
            than mine, blue-green . . ."
            (*Shogun,* Clavell)

            (sung) Don't it make my brown eyes
            Don't it make my brown eyes
            Don't it make my brown eyes
            Don't it make my brown eyes blue?
            ("Don't It Make My Brown Eyes Blue," lyrics by Richard
            Leigh)

C: If thine eye offend thee, pluck it out, and cast it from
            thee: it is far better to enter into life with one eye, rather
            than having two eyes to be cast into hellfire.
            (Matthew 18:9)

            (in Japanese) Okome o somatsu ni suru to me ga tsubu-
            reru.

A: 3. The skin incision is made . . .

D: Her eyes were deeper than the depth
            of waters stilled at even . . .
            (The Blessed Damozel, Rosetti)

E: I can sort of see that [this alien being] had a bald, rather
            largish head for someone that size. And that its eyes are
            slanted, more than an Oriental's eyes . . .
            (*Communion,* Whitley Strieber)

C: Why beholdest thou the mote that is in thy brother's eye,
            but considerest not the beam that is in thine own eye?
            (Matthew 7:3)

A: 4. Pretarsal subcutaneous dissection is carried out to remove all orbicular oculi muscle and fat . . .

D: Beauty is in the eye of the beholder.
(Margaret W. Hungerford)

E: It is only with the heart that one can see rightly; what is essential is invisible to the eye.
(*The Little Prince*, Saint-Exupéry)

D: The light that lies
in women's eyes,
has been my heart's undoing . . .

My only books
were women's looks
and folly's all they taught me.
(*Tho Time I've Lost in Wooing*, Thomas Moore)

C: Fie, fie upon her!
There's language in her eye . . .
(*Troilus and Cressida*)

A: 7. Final closure of the incision line is performed with a running subcuticular 6–0 polyester suture . . .

C: For where is any author in the world
Teaches such beauty as a woman's eye?
(*Love's Labour's Lost*)

E: The look of love is in your eyes,
a look your smile can't disguise.
The look of love is saying so much more
than just words could ever say;
and what my heart has heard,
well, it takes my breath away.
("The Look of Love," lyrics by Burt Bacharach and Hal David)

A: 8. Ointment and dry sterile dressing is applied over the incision line . . .

VIDEO/SLIDES: Eyes on screen. Possibly painting of eyes, application of Scotch tape and thick black pencil and mascara. Shiseido/Maybelline commercials. Possible video of eyelid plastic surgery. Before and after slides of surgery. Cuts from movies where Caucasian actors have had their eyes Asianized (Alex Guinness, Marlon Brando). Ukiyo-e eyes. Also a myriad of Asian eyes, all, in fact, quite different from one another.

PART 4: TOROZUSHI/EROTICA EXOTICA—THE SENSE OF TASTE.

MUSIC: Japanese folk songs similar to "Miracles" from *Flower Drum Song* or something from *The Mikado.*

DANCE: All of the bodies, heavily powdered in white chalk, are finally removed from the bags—a sort of butterfly emerging act combined with a striptease. Sensuous, despite the fact that their tongues hang out most of the time (or some other permanent facial expression). As they emerge, inflatable wings and body parts (muscles, breasts, extra appendages) inflate. They all don lace aprons.

All dancers then lug bottles of shoyu and sake and five-pound bags of rice. They bear these things like burdens. Dancers pour sake and shoyu into buckets and then draw out raw fish and squid and octopus.

Five microwaves are rolled onstage. The microwaves obviously hum and ding. Dancers stuff the microwaves with instant Japanese foods: Top Ramen and other packaged foods, packages and all. Sushi miraculously appears from the microwaves. Dancers stuff their faces with sushi and disappear into the nose.

FACIAL/PHYSICAL EXPRESSION:
Permanently cute.

ONSTAGE DIALOGUE: (*split among the actors as they go about their business, cooking and so on*) When I first came to this country, I worked for my relatives in a Japanese restaurant. It was not a fancy restaurant. It was family restaurant on Sawtelle. At first, I could not speak any English, so I started working in the kitchen. I washed dishes and I cut vegetables. I filled shoyu containers. I also watched noodles boiling. Then I got better in my English, so I started to serve tea and to clear the tables. Now I am waitress.

Customers always tell me how good my English is, but if I make mistake or forget something, they always talk among themselves and complain about service. They say nobody in L.A. speaks English anymore.

Then, of course, there are these Americans who have been to Japan. They like to tell you about the ryokans they have been to and going to Kamakura to see big Buddha and how expensive everything is in Japan.

Before, my relatives tell me that only Japanese Americans and Japanese business people come to eat at our restaurant. Now, you only see Americans. They say they get the same amount of business but that they have double their profits because Americans eat more, maybe twice as much as the Japanese.

Mostly we make money from the sushi bar. In Japan, sushi is very expensive. Maybe if you go to the sushi bar, you eat a few sushi and some sake or beer. It's just a food to eat with a little sake or make the sake go down better. Only the salaryman on a business account can afford to eat so much.

But Americans want to have a big dinner. They eat and drink and eat and drink, and they can't help themselves. Someone is explaining to me that the Americans are eating big steak dinners with big potato, and you cannot expect them to eat like us Japanese.

They want to try everything, and they want to try everything twice. Americans like to have salad before their meals, so we make a special salad and a special soup. Then, they like to try halibut or tuna sashimi or maybe sea bass. Most often they order two or three servings all at once so we have to pile all the sashimi together. I don't think this is very aesthetic, but they tell us we are very inexpensive.

Then they ask for a long list of sushi, and we put maybe twenty pieces on a big platter for one person. Once I saw a man eat one hundred pieces of sushi. He said sushi is very healthy for you. He said he discovered sushi. I was thinking this was strange. He said he even discovered our restaurant. I surprised that the Americans like sushi.

In the beginning, I see some people cry, but usually we tell them that the wasabi kills germs. I surprised that American eat so much raw fish. Even some Japanese don't like raw fish. One man only eat sea urchin. Eat ten to twenty pieces of sea urchin every time and leave. I wonder he don't get sick.

Usually an American comes in for the first time with a friend. This friend they call "the sushi aficionado," I think. This friend sits at the sushi bar and talks with the sushi maker. He says maybe to Ichiro, "Ich, I'll have the regular." Ichiro very professional. He remember one sushi aficionado out of hundreds. If Ichiro don't remember the regular for this customer, he say, "I got something different for you today." Something like that. This is very impressive to the new customer. Pretty soon, the new customer is sushi aficionado himself, coming with his new friends and saying, "Ich, I'll have the regular."

But sometimes there are Americans who can speak Japanese. There is a guy like this who comes all the time. He say to Ichiro in Japanese that he only likes Japanese women. Ichiro like to agree and say that when a man marries, he marries an old-fashioned cute Japanese girl, but American type is only for playing around. Ichiro says that American-type woman don't make a good marriage. You gotta get a woman who don't ask questions and stay at home and cook and do whatever you want. You know, "Oi kimi, get this, get that."

The American guy ask Ichiro to make an arranged marriage with a nice Japanese girl for him. Maybe he is joking but I don't think so. He keep looking at me. When he leaves, Ichiro says that this guy has gone to a lot of trouble to get a Japanese wife, speaking Japanese, building a Japanese house, learning everything Japanese. Of course, he's not Japanese; only Japanese can be Japanese, but it would be a very shame if he didn't marry a Japanese girl.

So I very surprised one day when this American guy comes with a sansei girl in black leather. Sansei girl don't know how to use ohashi. She don't know what the American guy and Ichiro are talking about. When I go to the kitchen, I know they are talking about me. Ichiro tell the guy that I will do anything to stay in America. Ichiro and the guy laugh.

The sansei girl, she's bored so she get up and go to the bathroom and telephone her friend. I hear her talking on the telephone. She say, "This Japanophile's a jerk." I don't know what she mean, "Japanophile," but I think Ichiro is a jerk too.

VIDEO: Cuts of Japanese commercials about Japanese food products, fishermen cutting up fish, Americans eating Japanese food, the nape of a geisha's neck, the kimono suggestively falling off the shoulder and other suggestive cuts. Food and sex get mixed up. Flashes of ukiyo-e prints of courtesans, erotica. Also repetitive narrative, "A hundred million miracles are happening every day!" and "The way to a man's heart is through his stomach."

PART 5: MADAME BUTTERFLY—THE SENSE OF SOUND

MUSIC: Puccini's *Madama Butterfly*

DANCE: Women reappear from nose in long unorthodox kimonos
                of recycled and unconventional matter (Styrofoam
                balls/popcorn, nori, mini-blinds, shimmering transpar-
                ent plastic, crazy eyes, and so on). Footwear may be var-
                ied (high heels, boots, and traditional). Fog flows out of
                the nose with the emerging dancers. Wigs hang from
                nylon strings above. Women move under and into wigs,
                moving about each other until the wigs tangle and pop
                off.

                One dancer sings Puccini (karaoke-style) into a mic.

                Meanwhile, dancers all partake of long wet noodles/
                spaghetti, some with enormous chopsticks and some
                with enormous forks. The noodles flicker this way and
                that, get draped in their hair and over their bodies. Some-
                one might have some permanent plastic noodles that are
                permanently held up in the air. Dancers brandish chop-
                sticks in a sort of breast-beating, bizarre, ritualistic fash-
                ion, threatening suicide. It never happens.

FACIAL/BODILY EXPRESSION:
                Probably permanently wild/hysterical/distressed. Could
                be changing, evolving, but all women must have exactly
                the same expression. All mouths hang open, all eyes are
                crossed, all have Kabuki-esque movements.

VIDEO: Deep red lips sensuously reciting a long list of Japanese
                words: ohiyogozaimasu, benjo, bakatari, sushi, teriyaki,
                obachan, hakujin, gaijin, Toyota, bonsai, Honda, sukoshi,
                hi, hi, moshimoshi, Suzuki, konichiwa, konbanwa, korewa,
                sorewa, arewa, gohan, ohashi, chawan, niku, ojoosan, ari-
                gato, obachan, sansei, nisei, issei, manju, banzai, samurai,
                ninja, sushi, origami, sake, ocha, biru, Sapporo, Kirin,

ringo, kaki, sashimi, wasabi, shoyu, ajinomoto, udon, boya, unchi, zori, nori, ikebana, tatami, doodesuka, harakiri, yakuza, gyoza, gaysian, hiragana, katakana, kanji, hoppi coat, happa, sukiyaki, kimono, bonsai, karate, judo, Mitsubishi, Sumitomo, Mazda, Sony, National, Sharp, Toshiba, Akai, Kenmore, Fujinon, Nikon, Kumon, Suzuki violin, Daihatsu, Nissan, Subaru, Lexus, Cressida, Celica, Sankaijuku, Dairakudakan, Danjuro, Kabuki, Noh, Bunraku, Gagaku, terebi, Sado, Tokyo, Nikko, Nagasaki, Hiroshima, Osaka, Akihito, Hirohito, Yamashita, Abe, Mayeda, Hoshi, sembei, snowcones, Gardena, Meiji, Marukai, Little Tokyo, Big Tokyo, 22nd Street, Rafu Shimpo, JACL, Topaz, Manzanar, Heart Mountain, JAL, Kawabata, Mishima, Oi, Kurosawa, Mifune, Oshima, Panasonic, Bridgestone, hamubaga, Japanophile, kohi, miruku, hachimaki, sakura, koto, shakuhachi, hichiriki, shamisen, enryo, Yamaha, katana, Edo, ukiyo-e, daruma, Utamaro, Sharaku, Issumboshi, Dodesukaden, Urashima Taro, Momotaro, Ran, Shogun, Tokugawa, onibaba, geisha, My Geisha, rikisha, Teahouse of the August Moon, Hiroshima Mon Amour, Godzilla, The Barbarian and the Geisha, Majority of One, Sayonara, Love Is a Many Splendored Thing, Hinomaru, MacArthur, Admiral Perry, Pacific Overtures, Mako, Ohara, Karate Kid, Pat Morita, Jack Soo, Acura, Dark Shadow, Snow Country, Yoko Ono, Kenzo Tanji, Kenzo, Marimekko, Waseda, Todai, Keio, Shinjuku, ichi, ni, san, shi, go, roku, hichi, hachi, ku, ju, redress, corum nobis, Fujica, Casio, Canon, futon, habakari, makura, maguro, uni, saba, ikura, takenoko, hamachi, ika, ochazuke, furikake, tenegui, ofuro, obento, shinkansen, onigiri, mogusa, shiatsu, ochanoyu, sumo, beisubaru, karaoke, manga, Gung Ho, shabushabu, kabucha, tamagogohan, tempura, oshogatsu, bon odori, namuamidabutsu, transformers, soroban, ichiban, tsukudani, yen, salaryman, Pacific rim, the Nikkei, kaisha, Tennoheika, kamikaze, Showa, Heisei, bushido, kao, me, mimi, hana, kuso, sayonara.

PART 6: THE SIXTH SENSE—THE SENSE OF INTUITION

MUSIC: Synthesized gagaku

DANCE: Women discard and step from kimonos. Something con-
                temporary underneath (maybe white Indian pants on
                powdered bodies). All dancers pick up hair blowers, Dep
                and blow-dry their hair in extreme angles. "Hey, like, go
                with the flow, man; go with the flow" and "You gotta be
                kidding."

FACIAL/PHYSICAL EXPRESSION:
                Permanent laughter, then serene.

VIDEO: Shapes, odd forms from nature, close-ups of ordinary
                things seen from another perspective; nothing is quite
                recognizable, but all are clearly something you have seen
                somewhere.

Credits and the End/Owari. Eye winks at end.

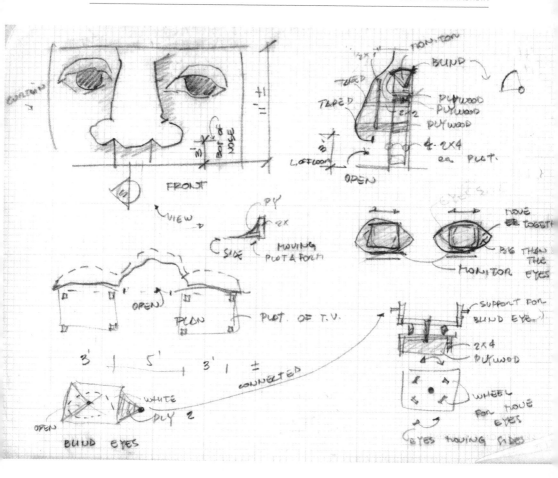

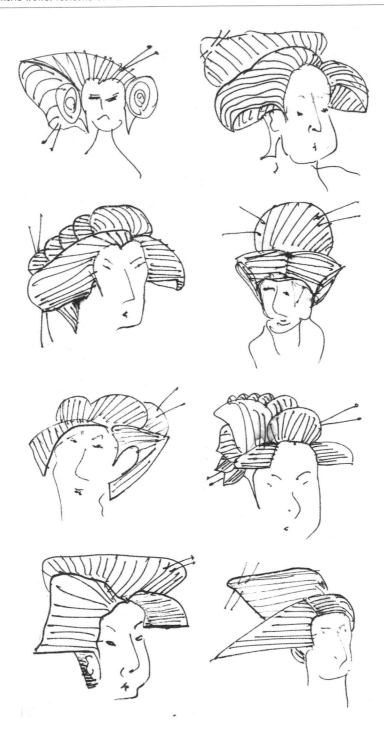

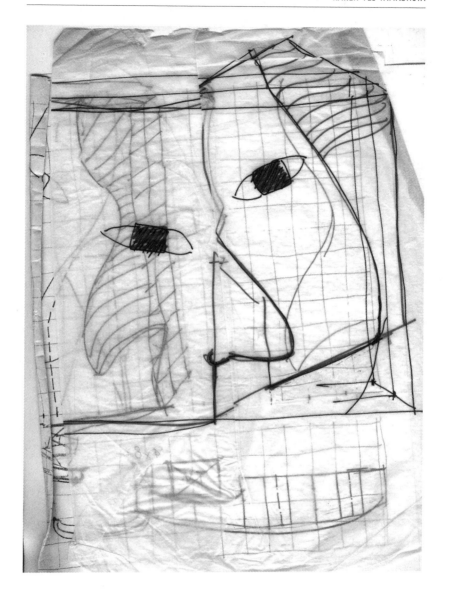

We pr   a special collaboration of dance,
theat١   ٮ٠ and music, and using the Japanese art form,
Butoh, as a structural and artistic basis, to explore and
satirize Western perceptions of the Japanese woman. Our
proposal is for research and development of a new work,
HANNAH KUSOH: AN AMERICAN BUTOH.

HANNAH KUSOH is divided into six parts or "six senses": 1.
The Sneeze: The sense of smell. 2. Japanophile: The sense
of touch. 3. The Eyes: The sense of sight. 4. Torozushi/
Erotica Exotica: The sense of taste. 5. Madame Butterfly:
The sense of sound. 6. The Sixth Sense: The sense of
intuition. Each part is marked by a modern koan of sorts and
a synthesized arrangement of music, much of it harkening back
to Western examples enthused at their creation by Asian
traditions: the Chinese dance from the Nutcracker Suite, The
Mikado, Flower Drum Song and Madame Butterfly. Simultaneous
video will carry narrative, commentary and character
delineations. Choreography and movement will draw from
Japanese dance and theatre and, in particular, from Butoh.

Butoh is a dance-theatre art form evolved in the 1960s by
Tatsumi Hijikata and Kazuo Ohno as a post-war expression,
linking the ancient cultural traditions, such as Kabuki and
Noh, to a new generation of Japanese dancers. Sankai Juku, a
representative troupe of Butoh, was first introduced to the
United States during the Olympic Arts Festival in 1984. Last
year, 1987, the UCLA Center for the Performing Arts sponsored
a second visit by Sankai Juku as well as the performance by
another Butoh troupe, Dai Raku Kan.

The recent interest by Americans in Japan has been extensive,
beginning notably with sushi and other culinary habits along
with the absorption of Japanese commercial and technological
design and extending toward a sophisticated knowledge of
Japanese traditional arts, ceremony, society and business
practices. The result has been that things Japanese, once
enjoyed or acquired only within the boundaries of the
Japanese-American community, have suddenly been absorbed by
an all-inclusive and ever-evolving American culture.

The consequences for Japanese-Americans, born and raised in
America, of this influx of Japanese culture into the
mainstream is not clear. Certainly the acceptance of raw
fish in America is a major achievement. The absorption of
Japanese culture into American life must, at some level,
force Americans to pause when considering, as in World War
II, the incarceration of American citizens of Japanese
descent without due process and solely on the basis of race.
It is, of course, debatable whether the "California roll"
might have, in 1941, prevented this injustice.

For the Japanese-American woman, the influx of Japanese
culture into the American has had its own particular

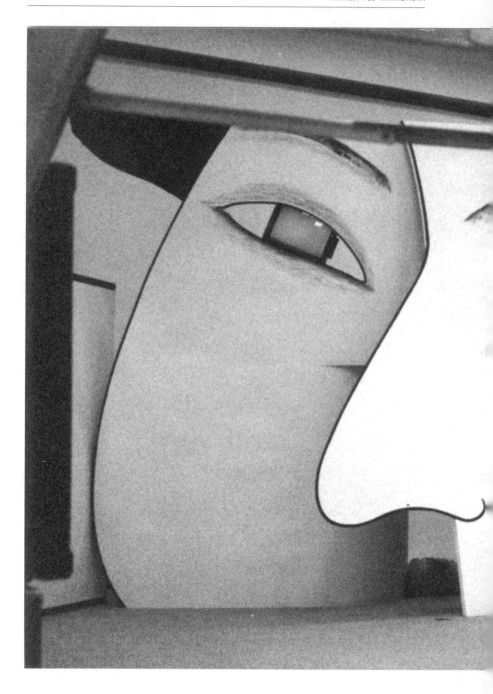

HIGHWAYS

P R E S E N T S

HANNA KUSOH

AN AMERICAN BUTOH
March 28, 29 & 30, 1990

HIGHWAYS IS A GALLERY FOR NEW VISUAL AND PERFORMANCE WORKS BY
ARTISTS AND A CENTER FOR INTERCULTURAL COLLABORATION.
1651 18TH STREET, SANTA MONICA, CA 90404 · 213-453-1755

A PERFORMANCE IN SIX SENSES:

Part 1: THE SNEEZE: The sense of smell

Koan: "In a single sneeze, millions of germs are released into the air."

Part 2: THE JAPANOPHILE: The sense of touch

Koan: "Nice Caucasian boy looking for nice Asian girl

Part 3: THE EYES: The sense of sight

Koan: "The only thing Japanese about me are my name and
my eyes."

Part 4: TOROZUSHI/EROTICA EXOTICA: The sense of taste

Koan: "Toro is the fat underbelly of the tuna. In sushi, it is the
best part, like the thighs of a woman," or

"A hundred million miracles are happening every day!"

Part 5: MADAME BUTTERFLY: The sense of sound

Koan: "Tienti la tua paura, io con sicura fede paspetto."
(I, with assured faith, trust that you will return.)
(Last lines from Madame Butterfly aria.)

Part 6: THE SIXTH SENSE: The sense of intuition

Koan: "You've got to be kidding." or "Hey, like, go with the
flow, man; go with the flow."

This performance is part of the "Sex, God and Politics" performance festival at HIGHWAYS, which is supported in part by a grant from the National/State/County Partnership, a cooperative program among the National Endowment for the Arts, the California Arts Council, the L.A. County Music and Performing Arts Commission, and by a grant from the City of Santa Monica.

HANNA KUSOH: AN AMERICAN BUTOH
Despite years of rejection, the celebrated Japanese - American female icon is
given her satirical due.

PROGRAM:

Ensemble:

Victor Chew
Linda Igarashi
Sala Iwamatsu
Mimosa
Susan Nakagiri

Written by: Karen Tei Yamashita
Director/Choreographer: Shizuko Hoshi
Original Music: Vicki Abe
Video Artist: Karen Mayeda
Artistic Consultant: Mako
Producer: Keone Young

Stage Manager: Chris Tashima
Set Design & Construction: Steve James, Ronaldo L. Oliveira & Chris Tashima
Costume Design: Desi Griffin & Lainie Oda Mann
Flyer: Lainie Oda Mann
Videotape Operator: Steve Kindernay

Acknowledgements for Hannah: Chris Aihara, Duane Ibata, Gail Matsui/JACCC - Esther Abe -
Evelyn Abe/CREATIVE CUTS - Michael Bernard - Jane Tomi Y. Boltz - Linda Burnham, Jill
Burnham, Tim Miller/HIGHWAYS - Darlyne Dandridge - Joanne Funakoshi - Nobel Gordon -
Teresa Iizuka/ANTON'S - Kathleen Imanishi - KEYBOARD TECHNOLOGIES INC. - Dan
Kwong - Roy & Eileen Mayeda - Aaron Paley/CARS - Reyes Rodriguez - Than Silverlight/WEST
LA MUSIC - Chizu Togasaki - Laura Uba - YAMAHA INTERNATIONAL -Asako Yamashita

JACCC Community Programs presents

Contemporary Performances in the Gallery
September 9 & 10, 15 & 16

The premiere of an original multi-media theatre work

"HANNAH KUSOH:
An American Butoh"

**An imaginative mad brainstorm of four
Japanese-American female artists**

A celebrated Japanese-American female icon is given an appropriately satrical debut. "Hannah" displays her versatility through dance, tactile theatre, drama, insightful video, synthesized sound and intuitive audience participation. Broadly employing the Japanese art form *butoh*, "Hannah" exposes the often cruel stereotyping of Japanese-American women.

Written by:	**Karen Tei Yamshita**
Directed by:	**Shizuko Hoshi**
Original Music:	**Vicki Abe**
Video Artist:	**Karen Mayeda**
Ensemble:	**Victor Chew, Tim Dang, Mimosa Iwamatsu, Sala Iwamatsu**

**Saturday, September 9, at 8 pm &
Sunday, September 10, at 2 pm
$10 General Admission**

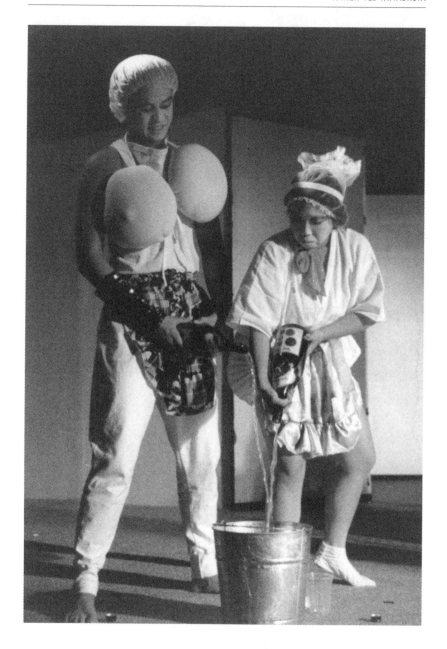

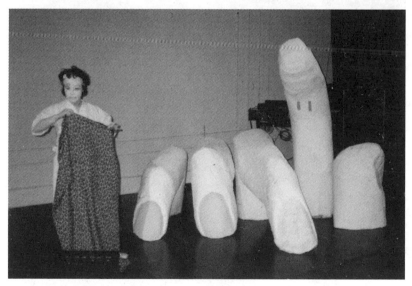

MADAMA B

(Based on a True Story)

Written by Karen Tei Yamashita

MADAMA B
(BASED ON A TRUE STORY)

> *Tienti la tua paura, io con sicura fede lo aspetto.*
> (Keep your fears; I, with secure faith, wait for him.
> —LAST LINES FROM *MADAMA BUTTERFLY* ARIA

THE FACTS IN THIS TRUE TALE have all been embellished, but none of the names have been changed to protect anyone, especially not the innocent.

It's been a few years now, but we used to have a chicken in the backyard. The chicken's name was Madame Butterfly. The kids called her Madame. I called her DaDami (an invented Italian-Japanese equivalent) because it sounded ridiculous, living in the middle of a working-class L.A. suburban neighborhood, especially in a predominantly Asian American one, to chase after a chicken yelling, "Madame! Madame! Madame Butterfly! Butter-fly!"

As chickens come and go, Dame Butter was an elegant one, her red-and-golden plumbs settling about a supple body, her eyes alert beneath a stylish comb. She was, I'm told, a Barnette-Hatch from a careful line of bred chickens, the sons of whom were fighting cocks. If parentage in chickens means anything, this chicken had a pedigree.

In the beginning, however, it wasn't Dame Butter who was coming to live with us. It was just the sound byte. The idea was to synthesize the song of a chicken and to reproduce the sound operatically. The bright performance proposal was to have Puccini's famous aria sung by a chicken. I admit this was my idea, but when I announced this to the composer, Vicki said, "We'll need a chicken."

"Chicken?" I said. "Haven't you got a tape with farm sounds? You know, a moo moo here. A neigh neigh there."

"That's what I mean. It's all mixed up. I need that ka ka ka kaa. It's a kind of flourish that peaks to match the aria when it does its thing."

"Ka ka ka kaaaa . . ." I tried to sing it myself.

"Yeah, well, I need to isolate that sound."

"I see." I thought about this. Oh well. How hard could it be to record a bunch of chicken noises?

We live in Gardena; it used to be all strawberry patches, cow pastures, and probably chickens around here. No chickens now. But Gardena High School—I figure they still have a farm there. I write a note to the farm instructor at the high school: "I realize this is a strange request, but would it be possible to tape your chickens squawking?" I never get a reply. It's true; maybe I don't deserve one. Maybe if I had explained about synthesizing Puccini's opera, but maybe not.

"The high school doesn't return my calls," I complain, "but I heard there's a community college in Van Nuys with an ag section. We're going to check it out this Saturday."

We go out to the Valley on the pretext of buying the college's co-op corn. We pretend to make a wrong turn and proceed to take the dirt road up into the school's farm. Nobody flags us down. Maybe it's because there's nothing up there. No animals. No chickens. Maybe there were chickens, but no chickens today. We put the tape recorder back in its case.

Someone suggests the county fair in Pomona. "They got all kinds of chickens. They got these little red ones with big green poofy hats and then they got these fluffy white ones that look like Vegas dancers with feathers coming out of their feet. Fair opens in September. Yeah, you gotta wait till September."

Or, "How about over there at Alondra Lake? Oh no, those are ducks, aren't they." And the beach has seagulls.

"You know, Hill's Pet sells Easter chicks around that time."

"East L.A. Yeah, somebody's got to have them in their yard."

"Hey, how about the Koreans? Are they into chickens?"

By now, we carry a tape recorder with us wherever we go. You never know when you're going to meet up with a chicken in L.A.

Finally someone says, "Chinatown. You can get a live hen there for soup." This is obviously the tip-off we've been hoping for. We drive down to Chinatown and cruise around, looking for some sign, hopefully in a language we can read, that says, "Live Chickens!" Maybe the markets hide them in the back of the stores. Nope. All dead. Fresh though, with the head and feet and everything. A grocer says, "Down the street. Go right. Then left. Near the corner. You see live ones. They kill for you."

When we get there, it's too late. A man in rubbers is hosing down the lot. White feathers, droppings, and blood scoot along with the gush of water from the hose. The odor of yellow chicken fat rises from the damp asphalt. One very big, very ugly dirty white hen is pecking around near a tall wall of cages. I approach her with my tape recorder, and she saunters off heavily, without a sound. The man in the rubbers looks back at me and says, "Too late. All gone today. Come back tomorrow."

I ask, "Do they make a lot of noise?"

"Hah? Butcher go home. Come back tomorrow!"

I look back at the tough old hen wandering stupidly about. I say to my husband Ronaldo, "Maybe he'll let us have that chicken. We can keep it awhile to record sounds, then put it in a stew." Ronaldo is a Brazilian farm boy sort; he's twisted a chicken neck or two in his day. But even he looks at this chicken with some trepidation. It's huge, the size of a turkey. Lot of meat there. Times like this, Ronaldo doesn't say much—his wife is crazy, and this is the ugliest chicken he has ever seen. He just says, "How many hours are you going to cook it?" I look at the dirty white feathers dragging about, the limp red comb and the fading eyes. It's probably deaf. Will that make a difference? Well, maybe it's dumb. Enough said. We leave.

I talk to Vicki on the phone. She says, "I borrowed another sound library. This one's on CD. Lot of roosters, but no hens."

I think about Vicki out there in Santa Monica in a glass building in a cubicle in front of her computer monitor. The Santa Monica sunlight wafts through tinted windows, brightens the air-cooled flourescent atmosphere. The elevators vipt and vapt open and shut. There's a coded entry to every floor. Other computer programmers saunter with coffee down the carpeted hallways. There's a high-tech binary intensity suggesting a real world within a spatial vacuum. Whatever that means. No chickens there.

Chickens on CD. There must be a way.

Ronaldo once had an idea for a kind of terrorist theater experience. The audience would be invited into a dark theater. High above the audience, unknown to anyone, would hang several poles heavy with roosting hens, all dozing silently in the dark theater. At some appointed moment, the poles would suddenly be removed, and the hens would tumble chaotically into the audience. This performance would be called *Rain of Chickens*. And his wife is the crazy one.

My friend Mikey, who does impersonations of everything, comes by with his chicken imitation. Right there, before my very eyes, Mikey transforms himself into a chicken. He gets his elbows up and prances around in agitation. "Pluck pluck pluck squawk. Squawk. SQUAWK! Pluck pluck pluck PLUCK!" My tape recorder never leaves my side. I tape Mikey. What the hell. I tape everyone's imitations. Even my kids volunteer chicken noises. I send the tape to Vicki. "Surprise!" I write on the tape, intimating victory.

Vicki calls me back. "What's this? A baritone chicken?" Damn. She wasn't fooled.

"What about the kids? They aren't baritones."

"Yeah, well, they aren't chickens either."

It was the Hawaiian Chicken Man who finally made it happen. The bro came by one day and said, "I heard you looking for chickens. What is it? You like chickens? Hey, chickens my life, man."

It's true. Chickens are Johnny's life. We go to Johnny's place in Sun Valley, a nice big plot of land wedged up in the hills where there are horses and where you can keep chickens. And there are chickens everywhere. But what you notice are the roosters—beautiful deep emerald-green, burnished brown, and shimmering black creatures, perched and crowing arrogantly. Each of them is restricted by a line, which is tied to one leg. "Fighters," nods Johnny. "Gotta keep 'em tied or they kill each other. That's their nature. I don't fight 'em here. I take my birds 'cross the border or Hawaii, where it's legal. Guys who do it illegal give us a bad name. Here, everything is clean." He picks up one of his favorites and holds it near. We can feel the muscular tension beneath the shining feathers. "Now that's a champion. Yeah, that's beautiful," purrs Johnny with satisfaction.

We walk around admiring the birds, pushing the tape recorder up to cages and under pecking beaks.

Johnny continues, "You want chicken noises? I got chicken noises. But I tell you it's not noise. It's music. I gotta have this music, you know what I mean? Can't live without it." He points to the tape recorder. "You wanna hear something? Here." He picks up a chicken, holds her with firms hands around her wings and chest. "They go crazy with this." Suddenly he tosses the chicken up into the air. We watch her grapple and flap hysterically, flying awkwardly over the roosters, who all ruffle their feathers, press out their chests, and crow like crazy. The tape recorder is rolling. The cacophony is incredible. Johnny smiles. "See what I mean?"

Yeah. I turn the tape over. Thirty minutes and more, but who's counting. If these aren't chicken sounds, what are chicken sounds?

We go over to Vicki's studio and watch her pull up sound bytes on her computer screen. The sound is translated into a graphic wave on the screen. She can mouse in and cut and paste the wave, make it bigger, stretch it out. We watch her tamper with the sound. She plays back the chicken tape. "I thought we could use this section here, but the hiss in the machine is too loud. I could use a little here, but I still need a more isolated sound without all the crowing." She fast forwards. "This was perfect, but hear that hiss?"

I think about the *Madama Butterfly* aria. Lately I play it over and over again, just to have it under my skin at any moment, ready to merge with the singing chicken I am going to find. Then I think, what are we, crazy? This is only one piece in the entire performance, one obsessive, decadent, avant-garde moment, obscured by video and slide images, lights and writhing dancers.

Hiss in the recording. Isolate the chicken.

Johnny says, "No problem. You wanna chicken? I give you a chicken."

"Would you mind if we ate the chicken, or do you want it back?"

"I gotta get rid of some birds. You know how to twist their necks? Good eating. Barbecue. You can't eat that stuff in the stores after you eat my birds. That's real meat. Hey, I get you some eggs too, yeah?"

Next day Johnny comes in with a big cardboard box and sets it on my desk. I peek in, look at the chicken sitting in the dark box. "She's okay. Don't worry. I give you some feed. Last you a week. Here's a water bowl. You get a mayonnaise bottle, yeah? Fill it up, screw it on here. That's it." He puts the box behind my desk. "I send my birds to Hawaii all the time; hey, this one's just going to Gardena. She's fine right there."

But I'm thinking all the time, there's a chicken in this office in the middle of Hollywood. I go back to my typing. I pretend it's a normal workday in the life of any secretary. I can't stand it. I call up Ronaldo. I speak to him in Portuguese so no one can understand. "Ganhei uma galinha, viu. We're gonna need a cage or something. And don't tell the kids yet; we're not going to get attached to this thing. It's not a pet. First we get the sounds, then we're going to eat it."

"Okay, okay," Ronaldo agrees.

I hang up. I can hear the chicken shuffling and scratching in the box. Then there's this very low squawking. On no. Be quiet, I mentalize my command to the chicken, but Lorenzo, the graphic artist, comes in to use the copier. He's trying to enlarge something. It's going to take a while. And then my boss, Hal, emerges from his office. He comes around to one side of my desk to finger through some files in an open cabinet. I think to myself: Hal never does this; he always just asks for what he wants.

"You need something, Hal? Can I help you?"

Outwardly, Hal is stern and grumpy with a thin line of a smile across his lips that suggests he's right, you're wrong. The residue of a career in the military never washes away. But despite everything, over the years Hal got used to me, leftist ethnic American politics and all, which only goes to prove that good secretaries are hard to come by.

By now the chicken is squawking in a sort of continuous low drone. Squawwwwk. Squawwwwwk. Squawwwwk.

Hal looks up from the files at me. I shut my eyes and think maybe he'll think it's my stomach. He looks over at the box behind me. Squawwwk. Squawwwwk. Squawwwwwk.

Lorenzo keeps looking around from the copier, looking around the room. I roll my eyes. Lorenzo says, "You know, you oughta check that out. I think it's your drive. That disk drive of yours is going."

At which Hal says, "It's more than her goddamned disk drive that's going!"

I give up. By now the squawking is really loud, and I would even say somewhat exuberant. I think these were the sounds Vicki wanted to isolate. I should have recorded it all then and there. We look in the box. The chicken is absolutely and implacably pleased with herself, clucking and squawking and strutting around—enough isolated chicken noises for ten performances. And there, in one corner of the box, is an egg.

I drive the chicken and her egg home. I sing Butterfly's aria all the way home. When I drive up to the house, there's Ronaldo and his cousin Evandro in the garage. There's chicken wire and nails and boards and even asphalt shingling everywhere. "What are you doing?" I ask, carefully taking the box out of the back of the car.

Everyone crowds around the box and looks in at the chicken and her egg. My kids touch her feathers, hold the precious egg in their hands. "Is it going to hatch? Let's not eat it. Maybe she's going to be a mother." It's love at first sight.

Ronaldo and Evandro go back to their pounding and sawing. They pound and saw late into the night. By midnight, they make me go into the backyard with a flashlight. I look at the chicken house, which by some standards is a chicken castle, complete with nesting box, feeding trough, and sleeping perch. "A little much, isn't it?" I look at the chicken on her perch staring at me in the dark. "We can't keep her, can we?" But I already know the answer. By now, her name is Madame Butterfly.

Now the problem is to record her. Every morning around five we wake to the chicken clucking in her cage under our window. Every morning I jump out of bed and run out in my pajamas with the tape recorder. Every morning the chicken hears me coming with my tape recorder, becomes quiet, and jerks her head around, staring at me with one eye and then another, as if to say, "Well, what is it?"

We devise another scheme. We wrap the tape recorder in plastic and wire it to the cage outside. Then we pull an extension cord from the recorder and through the window. The record/play button is pushed. Everything is ready to go. When the chicken starts her song and dance in the morning, we can simply reach over and push the plug into the socket and continue to sleep.

Morning one: "Ronaldo! She's making noises. Quick. Put the plug in." Ronaldo fumbles with the plug, but the chicken ceases to cluck.

Morning two: I fumble with the plug and activate the recorder. Again, nothing.

Morning three: We try again. Again she quits making any sounds. I walk out in my pajamas to see what's the matter. I see the chicken jerking her head around, staring at the whirring recorder, first with one eye and then the other, as if to say, "What is it?"

I call Vicki. "I think chickens are social animals. You can't isolate sounds because they can't be isolated. Besides, lately this chicken is actually silent. I think we traumatized her. She just sits there in her nest all day. She never moves. Maybe trying to tape her has been too much for her poultry-type psyche."

But Johnny says, "Naw, she's setting. What's she sitting on?"

"Nothing."

"Got no egg under her?"

"No, we ate it."

"You got a plastic egg?"

"Plastic egg?"

"She's gotta have something under her. A plastic egg'll do."

I go home and rummage through my kids' toys. Plastic eggs from the last Easter egg hunt. Fine. They're scattered everywhere; the problem is to find two matching halves. Mismatched halves? Purple and blue? Will the chicken know? I guess not.

Johnny says, "Still sitting on that plastic egg, yeah? How long she been there? That long, huh? Stuck there real good, yeah?"

Next day, Johnny brings me a carton of eggs. I look inside; there's maybe nine eggs. "You put these under her easy like this, with this end tilted like this and your hand covering them like this. You say she's stuck there good, yeah?"

"It's been three weeks! I don't think she even eats."

"She eats. You watch. Every day, she gets off, stretches her legs. She'll take some feed and water, and then she'll take a nice big dump, yeah? Then you see her get down and take a dust bath. You got some grass in your yard? That's good. Grass is good for her."

Twenty-one days. In junior high school, every year someone had a science project like this one. It's Saturday; every kid in the neighborhood is playing in our backyard because it's got everything: a tree house, a dirt hole, a sand pile, tall weeds, buried treasure, thousands of pill bugs. Nothing is pruned or cultivated or even remotely like a Japanese American garden. It's truly an embarrassment to my upbringing. Not that we don't have plans, but for now, our house is a Hollywood set; only the front has the aspect of suburban cultivation.

I call out to the kids, "Today's the day! See any chicks?"

My daughter looks in the direction of the nesting chicken and shrugs. My son says, "Nah." They've grown bored of the chicken's version of pregnancy. "She just sits there," they complain.

I go out to take a look. Peeping out from under her wings are tiny dark chicken faces. They are absolutely quiet and camouflaged by the black-and-red coloring of their mother. The kids run back and forth and never notice the chicken's secret. I stare in astonishment at the chicken and her new babies, and suddenly we are mothers together, bonded in a state of grace.

A couple more days and the chicken pushes the chicks out of the nest. We notice the plastic egg with the mismatched halves is still there. When Ronaldo picks it up, it's heavy, and there's a real egg inside of it. "She was always rearranging her eggs. It's like those Russian dolls inside Russian dolls. She must have somehow pushed it apart and together. Poor chick!" Ronaldo inspects the egg; there are little pecks where the chick attempted to emerge. "Oh!" I want to cry.

"It's alive!" Ronaldo announces. He pecks the shell from the outside and peeks in at the poor soggy chick. We put the chick still in its shell near the chicken, but she ignores it. She's too busy showing her other eight babies how to scratch for food. Ronaldo picks up the helpless chick still stuck to its shell and brings it in the house. He rummages in the medicine cabinet and makes a nest with a box of sterile cotton balls. Sterile cotton balls? This is not a third-world Brazilian chick, I can see. Then he puts the nest behind the refrigerator, where the motor makes a cozy place for the chick. I think to myself that that pig Wilber in *Charlotte's Web* maybe had it this good.

By nighttime, the chick is starting to lose its soggy appearance. Ronaldo peels the pieces of shell away, and the thing sort of falls over on its face, its little limp wings outstretched in a sorry heap. "I don't know," I say. "Are we going to have to raise it? I mean really. Where's Vicki at a time like this?"

Then at midnight, we hear it, and it gets louder and louder. The helpless chick behind the refrigerator in an exclusive and expensive nest of sterile cotton balls is peeping like crazy. No one can sleep. Ronaldo goes to comfort it, but nothing works. "Peep peep peep poep PEEP PEEP PEEEEP PEEEEEPPPPP!" I think, too bad it's not a mammal; then maybe I'd know what to do.

My daughter comes out of her room, rubbing her eyes. She wanders into the kitchen and says, "I think it wants its mommy," and wanders back to bed.

We take the helpless chick with the big mouth (and a great future in the avant-garde opera) to the chicken castle and stuff it with the others under the hen. Suddenly no peeping. We go to bed.

It's weeks later, but finally I can call Vicki and say, "I chased the chicken around the yard with the tape recorder. The loud pecking you hear is her trying to destroy the machine. She was really mad. You wanna touch her babies; she'll claw your eyes out. I risked losing her friendship, but I got everything. Screeching, cackling, peeping chicks. You name it. I got it. This tape's in the bag."

"All right! Mission accomplished."

But now we have this happy family in the backyard. And we have no bugs. The thousands of pill bugs? All naturally exterminated. Weeks go by. Baby chicks grow into adolescent chicks. Even the runt in the plastic egg grows up.

Johnny asks, "So how many males you got? How many females?"

"They all look the same. How am I supposed to know?"

"Well, you turn 'em over, see, and the male's got this male thing."

"Do I look like a chick sexer?"

"I'm just kidding. But you gonna know soon."

Well soon it happens. I sit up in bed one morning. Never heard this chicken sound. I run out back, and there is this little black chicken puffing out his little chest and trying out this pitiful crow. So this is where they got the idea that roosters say cockadoodledoo. "Ronaldo," I run back in. "They're turning into roosters. Pretty soon they'll be Johnny's breed of killer roosters, and this place will be a battlefield."

We put the grown-up chicks in a box and drive out to Johnny's place and leave them there in the big farmyard. When we come home, the chicken is wandering around the yard by herself. "Maybe we should've kept one for company," I say.

"We've got to get started on the back room addition. The chicks would be in the way," Ronaldo reminds me. "Don't worry. She'll start laying again soon."

But I miss all the peeping and the mothering. Once again the yard becomes quiet. I feel her loss personally; maybe it wouldn't be so bad if she could just, well, return to her career. "Maybe we could incorporate the chicken into the performance itself. Remember that Butoh group, Sankaijuku? They had a peacock walking around on stage, spreading that incredible fan under the lights. Well, we'll have a chicken. Just let her wander around the stage."

Nobody likes my idea. They're afraid of chickens. "What if she attacks the audience? What if she poops on the floor? Dancers won't like that. Besides, what's the point?"

What's the point? This is abstract theater! This is satire! This is the point at which a chicken meets technology. I think about Madama B, the chicken, staring with one eye at the recorder in silence. Now what was that opera again? A Japanese woman kills herself because her white lover leaves. The chicken stares at the recorder with her other eye. Yeah, so what is it?

Meanwhile the chicken hops around the construction materials that crowd the yard, pouncing on roaches and observing the frame to our back room go up. When the rafters are set in place, she takes to sleeping in the roof. She must think the back room addition is her new house.

Talk about a chicken castle. Every morning she flies down from the rafters to greet me. Sometimes, she brazenly comes into the house, cackling until I provide her with special scraps of bread and veggies. But one day the back room addition gets doors and windows, and Madame has to sleep outside. A few days later, we can't find her anywhere.

We walk out into the backyard, parting the tall weeds, looking under the house, calling everywhere, "DaDami! Madame? Madama Bee! Madame Butterfly! Butter-fly!" We leave food. Her favorite stuff. We look into the neighboring yards that border ours. We walk around the block, hoping to see a chicken decimating someone's flowerbed. We look anxiously in the street, fearing to find a dead chicken with tire marks running down her back.

"She got mad. Felt lonely without her babies. Went into a deep depression. Are chickens suicidal?"

"Give me a break. She flew away."

"Do chickens fly south? How far could she get?"

"Will she become a wild chicken? Will she be the predecessor for a wild breed of Gardena chicken? Will there be a rogue gang of fighting cocks wandering through the alleys and parking lots of our mini-malls?"

A few weeks later, I happen to talk to a man who lives four houses down from us. He says, "Strangest goddamned thing. I got a chicken living in my plum tree out back."

We take Madame B back to Sun Valley and let her out into Johnny's chicken world again. She hops out, joins her species without even a nod or a notice to the stupid humans who housed her for her song. Pretty soon she's mixed into the crowd, and we don't know which one she is. Just another chicken in the flock.

A week later our performance opens. The chicken aria is just one piece in the entire performance, one obsessive, decadent, avant-garde moment, obscured by video and slide images, lights and writhing dancers. Tienti la tua paura, io con sicura fede lo aspetto. Some people mistake it for a broken disk drive. A byte of sound.

GILAREX
OR GODZILLA COMES TO LITTLE TOKYO

■

A Musical

Story by Karen Tei Yamashita

Lyrics by Vicki Abe and Karen Tei Yamashita

Music by Vicki Abe

Originally staged at the Northwest Asian American Theater, Seattle

Given a staged reading at the Japanese American Cultural and Community Center,
Little Tokyo, Los Angeles

CHARACTERS

MANZANAR "RINGO" MURAKAMI

An old homeless Japanese American man in his late fifties. Lives on the streets of Los Angeles near Little Tokyo. Claims to be the first sansei born in the camps. "The first sansei born in captivity."

EMI YAMANE

A rebellious fifteen-year-old Japanese American girl who has run away from home. Has no Japanese identity and is interested to discover that she is a "rock-say" (rokusei). Say what?

DR. GARY YAMANE

A famous paleontologist and father of Emi Yamane. A widower. Workaholic. A man with a sense of Earth's past but no personal cultural past.

MRS. SALLY OGATA

A very active member of the Japanese American Preservation League, a league for preserving Japanese Americans.

STEVE MARTIN

A sensationalist on-the-scenes television news reporter.

DR. EUGENE PATRICK, PHD

A jingoistic researcher-in-residence in the Department of Pacific Rim Affairs of a prominent university, considered a specialist in the field.

THE SERIZAWA BROTHERS—ICHIRO, JIRO, SABURO

Japanese businessmen and owners of Serizawa Enterprises, currently involved in a joint venture with the City of L.A. to build a super structure called the L.A. Colossus over the Harbor Freeway. Serizawa Enterprises is also a front for a ninja operation. They all wear patches over their eyes.

MIMI AND MINI MOTHRA
Twin Presidents of the Los Angeles Chapter of the Society for Living Art Performance (SLAP).

THE HONORABLE MS. JANE OLVERA
Mayor of Los Angeles.

ITCHIE (ICHIRO)
A nisei senior citz, widower who lives in the Little Tokyo Towers.

RAD MAN
Drives a black Cadillac with a car phone up and down the Harbor Freeway, looking for love.

LOVELY LADY
Drives a white Mercedes while putting on her makeup and driving up and down the Harbor Freeway, looking for love.

UDEMAE-SAN
A sushi maker.

GILAREX
A dinosaur from the Cretaceous period who reemerges from under the Manzanar concentration camp.

W. EDWARDS DEMING
Ghost-like and fearful, the famous theoretician of business appears to exact an epiphany of self-realization by Dr. Eugene Patrick, PhD.

SENIOR CITZ (SENIOR CITIZENS)
SUSHI BAR CLIENTS
CAMERA CREW
MEMBERS OF THE JAPANESE AMERICAN PRESERVATION LEAGUE
MEMBERS OF SLAP
MAYOR'S TASK FORCE MEMBERS
KIDS WITH DINOSAUR T-SHIRTS
CITY PLANNERS AND SURVEYORS

GILAREX/SONGS

ACT I

OVERTURE: *Dawn over LA*, Concerto No. 22 in D Major
The Mind of Music
Harbor Freeway Lovin'
First Sansei Born in Captivity
The Monster in Me
Pacific Rim
Solo
The Water and the Power
En Gard! The Avant-Garde
The Dollar versus the Yen
Mutant Gila Monsters
The Reality on TV

ACT II

The Reality on TV (continued)
A Simple Citizen
Our Lady of Angels
Fossils in Our Past
The Monster in Me/Loathing in L.A.
Subtleties of Sushi
Out of Crisis (The Dollar versus the Yen continued)
You Can Learn from the Past
Homogeneous Collective Culture
Back to the Cretaceous Period
Song for Sally
The Monster in Your Dreams
The Performance of Life
Closing

ACT I

Turn-of-the-century Los Angeles. Voice and/or talking head video of DR. GARY YAMANE *speaking in academic tones about a paleontologist's vision of the past, dinosaurs, the Cretaceous era, the Earth, and so on. A high-tech prologue. Perhaps this is an ongoing/repeating video that greets the audience in the lobby or while being seated from the get-go, or perhaps it is on video in piecemeal throughout the first act.*

GARY YAMANE: Beyond the obvious danger to existing fault alignments and inciting the movement of molten rock beneath the earth's crust, I have found evidence indicating that underground nuclear testing generates a kind of rejuvenating heat. For the layperson, this can be compared to reheating food in a microwave oven. This Los Alamos Gila monster (*shows live Gila monster*) was discovered in a dormant state buried along with prehistoric remains some fifteen feet below a desert terrain. As you can see, it is quite revived, although this particular species lived some five thousand years ago. The study of this animal may provide answers to questions scientists have been asking about prehistoric extinction.

Some of my colleagues in the field have theorized that the dinosaurs faced mass extinction because of a cosmic catastrophe. Luis Alvarez has proposed that a giant meteorite some ten kilometers in diameter collided with Earth, causing an explosion that threw massive quantities of dust and vapor into the air, blocking the sun's rays. Other theories encompass the idea of gradual climatic change where the movement of the continents and volcanic activity caused the earth to cool.

Whatever the truth of these theories, we know that dinosaurs emerged two hundred and twenty-five million years ago in the Triassic, and flourished in the Jurassic and Cretaceous periods. These creatures existed on Earth for one hundred and sixty million years and then some sixty-five million years ago became extinct.

By comparison and in the history of Earth, human existence to date can be considered very brief, as brief as a single song in your lifetime.

SCENE 1

Background L.A. skyline, possibly done in expanding mylar. Possible backdrop screen that receives images by means of slides and film. The scene moves to Los Angeles at dawn, a grand panorama of the city and downtown, passing over scenes on the streets of Little Tokyo and blooming into the early morning rush hour, hovering over the gridlock on the Harbor Freeway. In front of this backdrop, an overpass is raised over the movement of cars (possibly toy miniatures).

MANZANAR, *an old, disheveled homeless person, walks along the overpass carrying a sort of wooden stand by a handle. He stops in the center of the overpass and looks over at the flow of traffic below. He nods approvingly. From a compartment of his suitcase he produces a shiny baton. He presses back his disheveled hair and straightens his torn and dirty coat. He steps up onto his podium and faces the traffic. Lifting his baton, he begins to conduct.*

Overture—*Dawn over L.A.*, Concerto No. 22 in D Major

Traffic sounds emerge, some of them isolated—the skid of cars, the beep of horns, the clamor of people, radios, the crash of an accident—sounds that are all slowly translated into their separate and equivalent instruments in a symphony orchestra as MANZANAR *brings everything to musical life.* EMI YAMANE *is walking by over the same overpass with all her possessions in a backpack, a television-radio, and an electric guitar. She pauses with her TV–boom box turned up to full volume to watch* MANZANAR, *looking over the overpass at the traffic and back at* MANZANAR, *who is disrupted by the sound from her machine.* MANZANAR *brings his symphony to a dramatic close and begins to pack up his baton.*

EMI: Hey, wha- what are you doing with that stick?

MANZANAR: What are you doing on my overpass?

EMI: Okay, could be wrong, but it looks like conducting.

MANZANAR: Is that so? Then, what are you doing up here disrupting my concert?

EMI: I'm sorry. Okay. I didn't know it's your overpass.

MANZANAR: How 'bout it, you got some change?

EMI: Listen, I only pay for music I can hear, okay?

MANZANAR: And I never charge the deaf.

EMI: (*looks confused*) Yeah, well what's there to conduct?

MANZANAR: *Dawn over L.A.*, Concerto No. 22 in D Major.

EMI: Classical? Does the Philharmonic know about this? Hey, you're not Seiji Ozawa, are you?

MANZANAR: You're not Midori, are you?

EMI: Okay, so what's *Dawn over L.A.*?

MANZANAR: I wrote it myself. What did you think?

EMI: Think?

MANZANAR: The string section was a little weak today. The violas were off. It's this damn outside lane! They think they can take that turnoff at sixty miles an hour. They ruin everything. It's slow. It's lilting. I keep telling them, but they never listen. You think conducting under these circumstances is easy, but it's not! (*silence*) Did you notice the cymbals? (*makes a motion with a crashing sound*)

EMI: Fresh! You mean when that Porsche rammed into the
                Cad? What a bumper crunch!

MANZANAR: Yes. The timing was perfect! (*begins to hum everything
                over again while conducting*) This part is so sweet. Listen.
                This part here.

EMI: Cars, horns, screeching tires. So?

MANZANAR: You're not listening.

EMI: You really hear music?

MANZANAR: *Song*
                "The Mind of Music"

                Everything on Earth is music to my ear,
                but the music of the freeway is a special sound to me.
                You hear solitary people thinking,
                reflecting on their day,
                the energy of their contemplation,
                the anger of their frustration.
                The mind of the music to me.
                The mind of the music to me.
                Hear the laughter in their voices.
                You can hear the suffering in their hearts.
                You can hear the questions, the anticipation,
                so many hopes, so many fears, so many dreams,
                The mind of the music to me.

                Everything on Earth is music to my ear,
                but the music of the freeway is a special sound to me.
                The energy of their contemplation,
                the anger of their frustration.
                The mind of the music to me.
                The mind of the music to me.
                You can hear the pools of workers,
                words of hate,

heat of love.
The mind of the music to me.

(*Coda*)

Everyone brings music to the freeway.
Who can be deaf to this symphony of sound?

(*looks over overpass*)

Well, there you have it. All that life just waiting in line to
get to work. But, if you think about it, there's a lot of trust
out there. A lot of trust to get on the freeway and trust
that everyone will be going at the right speed and in the
same direction. With animals it's instinct, but with people it's blind trust. Some people look at this, but what do
they see?

EMI: Millions of dollars in car and accident insurance.

MANZANAR: Hey, there's _____. Always late, every morning.

EMI: I'm sure that's his name.

MANZANAR: Written right there on the license plate.

EMI: What a heap!

MANZANAR: That's what I mean. You're late. Later the hour, cheaper
                the car. The early birds are executives rushing in to talk
                with New York: Mercedes, Lexus, BMW. (*shakes head*)
                Used to be cars had real names: Mustang, Cougar,
                Impala, Puma, Wombat . . .

EMI: Wombat? That one's asleep.

MANZANAR: Nah, just on automatic . . . look there. Finally happened.

EMI: What?

MANZANAR: That one. His wife left him. Yeah. Look how he's driv-
                ing.

EMI: I'm sure.

MANZANAR: Comes home late every night, usually with this other
                female. The wife found out.

EMI: But how do you know?

MANZANAR: He's driving the old station wagon. She took the
                Corvette. Now if he were a pigeon in a monogamous
                relationship, never woulda happened.

EMI: That lady's doing her makeup.

MANZANAR: Mating behavior. Does it every day, twice a day during
                the rush hour. Gotta be the thickest traffic to do it. Get
                those eyebrows straight.

EMI: Twice a day?

MANZANAR: Yeah, coming and going. I don't think she even goes to
                work some days. Some days, she just cruises the freeway
                to do her makeup.

EMI: Yeah, right.

MANZANAR: Don't believe me? It's true. There's people who get on
                this freeway just to be on the freeway with other people.
                Loneliness is a hard thing. People cruising, going up and
                down looking for something, something they lost, some-
                thing they can never find, somebody out there. Trouble is
                they're often going the wrong way. Got culture but no
                instinct.

                Song
                "Harbor Freeway Lovin'"

(*with* RAD MAN *in the black Cad and the* LOVELY LADY *in the white Mercedes*)

See this great river of life before you,
two opposing currents of cruising humanity,
careening down a fast lane to destiny.
Where is it they are all going?
When will they return?
Who is the person behind the wheel?

RAD MAN: So I'm on the phone,
lookin' for my baby;
yeah, she'll be that lovely lady
in the white Mercedes.
Gonna find that lady,
jus' like me, (Lovely Lady)
lookin' for love,
lookin' for love.

*'Cuz every day, I'm cruising.
I'm cruising.
Every day, I'm cruising this scene,
lookin' for love,
lookin' for love.

LOVELY LADY: While I'm makin' my face,
lookin' for my man;
yeah, he'll be that radical man
in the black Cad sedan.
Gonna find that man,
jus' like me, (Rad Man)
lookin' for love,
lookin' for love.

*repeat

MANZANAR *picks up his suitcase and starts to walk away.*

EMI: Hey, where're you going?

MANZANAR: Little Tokyo Towers. It's Wednesday. Tempura udon.

EMI: Huh? Tempra dawn? This another concert?

MANZANAR: (*walking away*) Food.

EMI: Food. Ohhh.

Without looking back, MANZANAR *waves* EMI *to come along.* EMI *grabs everything and runs after him.*

SCENE 2

Little Tokyo Towers. It's lunchtime for the senior citizens.

MANZANAR *and* EMI *get in line with a crowd of* SENIOR CITZ *with their trays, sit down, and eat.* EMI *has some difficulty eating noodles with chopsticks; as she's famished, she manages to eat everything and some of* MANZANAR's *lunch as well.*

ITCHIE: Hey, Ringo. How ya doing, buddy? Figures you'd be here today. Tempura udon like always. Hey, you stood me up yesterday. I been waiting a whole hour at Tokyo Gardens with two plates gyoza. That's a lotta cholesterol for one body. What's my doctor gonna say?

MANZANAR: You're tough. I should know. I can hear your heart beating. Besides, I been working on some new stuff.

ITCHIE: That's right, buddy. Keep it up. You're lucky. You're old, but still you're sansei. Can afford to be a little crazy. Nisei like me don't get no opportunity to be artists. Dream a little. It don't hurt.

EMI: (*to* MANZANAR) He said you're crazy.

ITCHIE: Hey, Ringo knows me. You know what I mean. I used to play the sax. I know music. This man's a musical genius.

EMI: You mean you can hear his music too?

ITCHIE: Sure. I used to be like you. I see a guy sitting on a bench, tapping his foot, snapping his fingers, and I think to myself, he's a little off, but one day, I catch myself tapping my foot, snapping my fingers. I hear music. Eh, Ringo, isn't that right? (*looks around*) Hey, Sally's been looking for you. Here she comes. Here she comes.

SALLY OGATA: Manzanar! There you are.

MANZANAR: (*to* EMI) Check it out. I'm the focus for a lot of shame.

SALLY OGATA: Manzanar, who's your young friend? Is she yours? I didn't know you had a granddaughter. You're not going to try to make her homeless too? (to EMI) Who are your parents? I would like to have a word with them, leaving this poor man on the street. Do you know what oyakoko is?

MANZANAR: (*to* ITCHIE) Do you know what baka is? . . . Sally, she's not my granddaughter. I don't have any family. You know that. She's—(*aside to* EMI) What's your name?

EMI: You think I'm gonna tell you that?

MANZANAR: This is Kristi. Yeah, Kristi Yamaguchi.

SALLY OGATA: Hello, Kristi. (*to* MANZANAR) Where were you yesterday? Mrs. Sato was waiting for you to come by for your bath. She missed her ikebana classes waiting for you.

MANZANAR: I don't like taking baths at Mrs. Sato's. She makes me undress in the hallway. Last time she put my clothes in a garbage bag, dumped them in the chute, and made me wear her dead husband's stuff.

SALLY OGATA: She was only trying to help. She's one of the Preservation League's most active members. She makes wonderful homemade chirashizushi from an original issei recipe.

MANZANAR: Her husband was shorter than me.

SALLY OGATA: Shorter? Really, now.

MANZANAR: And fifty pounds lighter. I'm a conductor! And you wanna put me in a straitjacket?

SALLY OGATA: Oh, you're exaggerating. Mrs. Sato said you looked so handsome. Oh, I almost forgot. There's another apartment vacant upstairs here in the Little Tokyo Towers.

ITCHIE: Sad Shimo just passed away. Very sudden. We nisei are dropping like flies.

SALLY OGATA: But, as I was saying, you're at the top of the list again— I always put you back on—and as your social worker, I strongly suggest you take Sad's place. You're not getting any younger, and besides you are—

ITCHIE: You're ruining Sally's reputation is what.

MANZANAR: I don't want Sad's place.

SALLY OGATA: You wouldn't have to be there all the time. Just sleep there, at least.

MANZANAR: Sad lived next to Mrs. Sato, didn't he?

SALLY OGATA: As a matter of fact.

MANZANAR AND ITCHIE:
              Poor bloke. Did him in.

SALLY OGATA: Well, you think it over.

MANZANAR: I don't want Sad's place!

SALLY OGATA: Oh, you're impossible. (*turns to* EMI) Now, why aren't you in school? We do have services for runaway youth.

MANZANAR: (*defends* EMI) Kristi here is a rokusei.

EMI: What the—

SALLY OGATA: A rokusei?

MANZANAR: Yes, the last genuine living rokusei.

EMI: Say what?

SALLY OGATA: My my. This is very important. You know, it is our business, the business of the Japanese American Preservation League, to set up proper credentials for people like you and to preserve and follow up on your progress. Well, I must make a note of this, and we must gather all the pertinent information.

EMI: What's she talking about? What's a rock-say?

SALLY OGATA: Oh my my. Another cultural illiterate. Ro-ku-sei. Sixth-generation Japanese American. (*to* MANZANAR) Haven't you explained this to her?

MANZANAR: Kristi's not familiar with the terminology, Sally.

EMI: Stop calling me Kristi! And what does she need with pertinent information?

SALLY OGATA: You mean you've never heard of the Japanese American Preservation League? Well, let me tell you about our fine organization. Our purpose is to find and preserve Japanese

Americans. You are a very rare species, you know. Do you know that I am responsible for discovering this man—Manzanar "Ringo" Murakami, the first sansei to be born in the camps. He was named after and born in the Manzanar concentration camp on February 28, 1942, just as his mother arrived.

ITCHIE: Ringo here was the first sansei born in captivity!

EMI: Captivity?

SALLY OGATA: My poor, rootless child. A cultural orphan. Manzanar's family were fishermen on Terminal Island, out there in the L.A. Harbor. When the war broke out, his father and grandfather were suspected of being spies and they were taken away to prison.

EMI: Spies?

SALLY OGATA: All lies of course, and then his poor mother was put on a transport and sent away to the Manzanar concentration camp.

EMI: Concentration camp. That's the second time she said that. What concentration camp?

SALLY OGATA: How could she be a rokusei? She doesn't know anything.

MANZANAR: Give her a break, Sally. By the sixth generation, it was all a long time ago.

SALLY OGATA: And there was Manzanar's mother, pregnant, homeless, all alone, separated from her husband (*to* EMI) and not much older than you. All she had was a bundle of her belongings and that heavy burden in her belly. She walked away with the soldiers and left everything behind forever.

Stark mountain backdrop of eastern Sierras behind the Owens Valley man-made desert. Noh-style music and performance, in the sense that ghosts from the past retell this tale.

> *Song*
> "The First Sansei Born in Captivity"
>
> Sleep dear child,
> safe in your innocence,
> protected by those great snowy peaks.
> Beyond those towers in the distance—
> hope as far as this desert is wide,
> love as deep as this sky is blue,
> a future as sure as a people have pride.
>
> Wandering in the swirling dust of the Owens Valley,
> fishermen lost in a desert sea,
> there are no apple orchards here.
> Only a bitter cider brewed of human tears
> to wet my mouth, parched dry
> as the withered remains of my lost liberty.
>
> When will I know your love again—
> the sweet taste of freedom on our lips?

ITCHIE: Sleep dear child,
> strong in resolution.
> Remember that you come from the sea,
> freedom—the fisherman's great passion.
> One day I'll return. Till then, take
> courage to ride this passing storm;
> net the good catch, leaving truth in your wake.
>
> Wandering in the swirling dust of the Owens Valley,
> fishermen lost in a desert sea,
> there are no apple orchards there.
> Only a bitter cider brewed of human tears
> to wet your mouth, parched dry as the
> withered remains of our lost liberty.

When will I know the sea again—
drink deep the salt spray of your black hair?

MANZANAR: Sleep dear mother.
Sleep dear father.
Peace be with your memory.

SALLY OGATA: Protected by those great snowy peaks—

ITCHIE: Remember that I came from the sea—

MANZANAR: I will not forget your story.

SALLY OGATA: Hope as far as this desert is wide—

ITCHIE: One day I'll return. Till then, take—

SALLY OGATA: Love as deep as this sky is blue—

ITCHIE: Courage to ride this passing storm—

ALL: A future as sure as a people have pride.
Net the good catch, leaving truth in your wake.

When will we know our love again?
When will we know the sea again?
When will we know?

MANZANAR: Hey, I gotta go! I'm late!

EMI: Hey, wait, where are you going?

MANZANAR: I've got a concert to do in fifteen minutes.

SALLY OGATA: (*to* EMI) Now young lady, let me get some pertinent statistics on you. Who are your parents and where are you from?

EMI: (*looks frantically around only to see* MANZANAR *leaving the lunchroom*) Uh, well ah, I've got a concert to listen to in fifteen minutes.

SALLY OGATA: (*still following* EMI *around*) I'm concerned about having a Japanese American minor like you roaming the streets.

EMI: (*to* MANZANAR) Hey, wait for me! (*runs after* MANZANAR)

SALLY OGATA: It's shameful enough to have him out there . . .

SCENE 3

MANZANAR *and* EMI *walk back toward the overpass.*

EMI: What did she mean Japanese American? I'm not Japanese American. I'm American. And what was that chewy stuff with the sweet beans in it? And what's this rock-say stuff? And stop calling me Kristi.

MANZANAR: Well, what is your name?

EMI: Emi. My name is Emi Yamane.

MANZANAR: Yamane. Yamane. I seen that name somewhere. Who's that?

EMI: Dr. Gary Yamane, world-famous paleontologist.

MANZANAR: That's right. Dinosaurs. Your dad, huh?

EMI: I have nothing to do with him. It's just a coincidence.

MANZANAR: So you run away, hum?

EMI: Who you calling a runaway? Do I look like a runaway?

MANZANAR: What you wanna look like?

EMI: Like I belong out here.

MANZANAR: Runaway's a species that belongs out here.

EMI: (*silence*) I'm not running away. There's nothing to run from. You see some monster coming for me? Everything back there is dead, wiped out, gone.

MANZANAR: Suburbia?

EMI: The past is over, done with. I'm not going back!

                Song
                "The Monster in Me"

                Everything I need is right here with me.
                You got a problem with that?
                No monster past is coming after me.
                No monster future is waiting down the road.
                The monster is living in me.
                Death is inevitable.
                Life is suicidal.
                In your face.
                You got a problem with that?

MANZANAR: It's been awhile since I been on hormones. Scary what they can do to you.

As they approach the overpass, three Japanese businessmen, the SERIZAWA BROTHERS, *are talking to the Mayor of Los Angeles,* JANE OLVERA. *They are rolling out street plans and pointing in several directions. An entourage of assistants and the press surround them.*

MAYOR OLVERA: This is a historic moment in the history of Los Angeles. The city of Los Angeles is proud to announce that we have completed negotiations with the very reputable firm of Serizawa Enterprises in a joint venture to build the L.A. Colossus: an indoor sports stadium seating crowds up to twenty-five thousand, a ten-story convention center, hotel, shopping, and business complex, all intertwined by a two-and-a-half-mile high-speed tubular automotive race track, metro systems, people movers, and biospheric landscaping. The L.A. Colossus will be a literal statement of Los Angeles's commitment to the new century as the most technically sophisticated and futuristic creation ever built anywhere in the world, and it will literally hover over our freeways!

STEVE MARTIN *and his cameras are there to record everything.*

STEVE MARTIN. (*to the cameras*) Mayor Jane Olvera has just announced the finalization of the controversial plans to build the L.A. Colossus in the air over the Harbor Freeway. We are told that Serizawa Enterprises has indeed built similar structures in Japan, but until now nothing of such grand dimensions. As you know, the city council has spent months in debate over the question of selling a grandiose chunk of the L.A. air. After considerable discussion, the council voted unanimously to approve the venture, which will give Los Angeles the distinction of having a sports coliseum in the air and above its endless freeway system. Critics of this plan point out that in-depth studies of zoning the L.A. airspace have yet to be made, although no one questions the safety of such structures in the case of earthquakes. (*to* MAYOR OLVERA) Your Honor, what about the comment made this morning in the *Times* that you consider this a viable process by which pollution can be recycled into usable real estate—a sort of redevelopment plan for the air? Isn't it true that this deal is just the city's way of ignoring the problem of enforcing clean-air laws and bringing L.A.'s air up to any standards at all?

MAYOR OLVERA: Steve, you know as well as I do that concerted efforts to reduce this traffic below us have been made, but until we can reduce the number of vehicles on the road, we can't begin to tackle this problem of bringing the air up to standards.

STEVE MARTIN: But Your Honor, won't projects like this attract more traffic into the city?

MAYOR OLVERA: Every day we are making progress on this question. We know alternative vehicles and transportation are even now being developed. After all, we are on the brink of a new era, and we in Los Angeles must seize this moment.

STEVE MARTIN: I heard Dr. Eugene Patrick, famous author of *The Dollar versus the Yen*, has come out in severe opposition to this plan.

MAYOR OLVERA: On the contrary, Steve. I've personally invited Dr. Patrick as a consultant to this project. The Serizawa brothers are an example of our strong alliance with our brothers on the Pacific Rim. Together, we will make Los Angeles the capital of this new era.

> *Song*
> "Pacific Rim"
> (*with the* SERIZAWA BROTHERS)
>
> Welcome to the Asian-Pacific century
> with its capital in L.A!
> Welcome to the doorway
> of an economic renaissance!
> An Asian angel of radiance
> rising from the smog.
> Coppertone tans with hotdogs!
>
> *What can L.A. do for Asia?
> What can Asia do for L.A?

See the future in our skyline.
Marketing pollution is the solution.
A pacific future from rim to shining rim.

Welcome to the Asian-Pacific century
with its capital in L.A!
Welcome to a screenplay
cast in immigrant entrepreneurs,
a workforce of ethnic consumers
laboring in the sun,
riding these concrete waves to fortune.

Roller coast on to our future.
Sit with L.A. on the high-tech edge.
Building the world of tomorrow.
Catch a ride on the L.A. Colossus!

Welcome to the Asian-Pacific century
with its capital in L.A.!
Welcome to the consumer freeway,
free trade and investment expertise,
center for cultural diversities.
Mixing rock 'n' roll,
guacamole on a California roll.

*repeat

As the MAYOR *and the* SERIZAWA BROTHERS *leave,* PLANNERS *and* SUR-VEYORS *cordon off the overpass, push out and block* MANZANAR's *way.*

MANZANAR: But I've got a concert to do! This is important!

PLANNERS AND SURVEYORS:

> Hey, who is this guy?
> Get him out of here!
> I know him! He's that crazy guy who conducts the traffic.
> He's harmless. Leave him alone.
> Call the cops on him!

STEVE MARTIN's *camera crew is capturing the whole mad ruckus.*

> Hey, they're filming. Er, (*to* MANZANAR) sir, the city has designated this area off-limits. You'll have to leave.

MANZANAR:

> I'm not leaving. You can drag me away, but I'll be back here. This overpass belongs to the public. I'm the public. I use this overpass. You can't push me around!

EMI:

> Yeah! You can't push him around!

BYSTANDERS:

> Who's she?
> Leave the poor man alone! What's one more day?
> Let him conduct if he wants!
> You got your air! Let him have his!

MANZANAR *sits in the middle of the overpass and refuses to move.* EMI *decides to join him.* STEVE MARTIN's *crew keeps filming.*

STEVE MARTIN:

> Well, we seem to have a new development here, a homeless human-interest story. (*to a* PLANNER/SURVEYOR) What does the city propose to do? What will happen to the hundreds of homeless who find refuge in the bushes and tunnels of the freeway system?

PLANNERS AND SURVEYORS:

> This, this man cannot stand in the way of progress.

STEVE MARTIN:

> But he does have a point. This is public property. He has a right to be here.

EMI: That's right!

PLANNERS AND SURVEYORS:
Who is this kid? Hey, this your granddad? Take the old man home.

EMI: This is his home. Our home.

PLANNERS AND SURVEYORS:
There are laws. Laws about loitering and juveniles.

EMI: Who're you calling a juvenile?

PLANNERS AND SURVEYORS:
And we'll be back to make them stick. You can be sure of it.

STEVE MARTIN: Once again that unanswered question: what of the homeless? A homeless man has laid claim to a freeway overpass—the only home he knows—to confront a monstrous handshake between government and business: the L.A. Colossus. All through the city, however, we sense a tenuous peace and an underlying unrest among the disenfranchised and destitute. Will this be the incident that finally ignites the passions of the masses?

SCENE 4

MANZANAR *and* EMI *camp out on the overpass. It grows dark.* EMI *is watching her miniature television.*

MANZANAR: Hey, why don't you go home? You oughta go home. You got a famous dad. A real home. Some people wander all their lives looking for home.

EMI: I don't have a mom. She died.

MANZANAR: What about Dr. Yamane?

EMI: Yeah, well, he doesn't have much time to be around. He's too important. Workaholic and proud of it. When he does things for me, he calls it quality time. It's just bullshit. He probably hasn't even noticed I'm gone.

MANZANAR: I don't know nothing about kids. What is it that you do all day anyway?

EMI: He makes me go to school.

MANZANAR: Yeah, but what is it you do?

EMI: Do?

MANZANAR: Yeah, I do this. I compose music. Conduct. You need to find something you do.

EMI: I can play that thing. (*points at case with electric guitar*) Sort of.

MANZANAR: (*nods*)

EMI: You don't believe I can play it, do you?

MANZANAR: Does it run on batteries too?

EMI: Yeah, but they're dead. Besides, I need speakers.

MANZANAR: Big deal. Let's hear it.

EMI: I said you need speakers. To hear. Get it? To hear.

MANZANAR: So?

EMI: Oh, that's right. You're crazy. Look, I can't play. It's bullshit. I never could.

MANZANAR: I don't believe you. (*raises air guitar and strums a silent strum*) Hum, how about that. Nice tone. Hum. (*more dramatic; grimaces*) Listen to that.

EMI: Oh. (*looks uncertain; then, with* MANZANAR's *insistence, plays and performs, first with hesitation and then as a true rocker*)

Solo
(*maybe musical rendition of "The Monster in Me"*)

Slowly, from nowhere, but starting with the intensity of MANZANAR *as audience, we begin to hear the music that Emi wants so much to hear as well.*

MANZANAR: So that is what you do. I'm no critic of rock music, but it's well conceived. Well conceived.

EMI: I wish I could really play.

MANZANAR: Human's a funny sort of animal. Not happy with hootin' and chatter. Only one that wants to sing like a bird. (*thoughtful*) You know, my mother died too. When I was born. She died in that concentration camp I got named after.

EMI: My mom died two years ago. (*takes photograph out of backpack*) This is her.

MANZANAR: And this must be Dr. Yamane himself. He certainly looks Japanese American.

EMI *grabs photo away.*

When my dad got out of jail, heard he came to Manzanar. Probably didn't know what to do with a newborn baby. The nurses at the camp hospital took care of me. Then the war was over. I was three or four. I got left behind in an orphanage. Dad went off with his dad to find work—probably picking fruit, going here and there. Poor fishermen—traded the sea for the land, became nomads, huntin' and fishin'.

Almost as soon as I could walk, took up nomading myself. When I was your age, I was already in Africa, following a herd of white rhino over the grasslands with a naturalist from the Smithsonian.

EMI: Really? My dad took me to Cairo. I didn't see much.

MANZANAR: Cairo is at the end of the Nile. You start at Lake Victoria and travel up the White Nile through the Sudan into Egypt. Six great cataracts. The pyramids. Now that was a great adventure.

EMI: You did that?

MANZANAR: Of course. It took awhile, but I pretty much walked all around the earth. When I got to China, I walked around the Great Wall, then went up into Mongolia, crossed the Bering Strait.

EMI: Why'd you do it?

MANZANAR: Some people have the wandering bug. Start and then you can't stop. You get somewhere and say, hey, I wonder what's over there, but all the time you're hoping it's home. One day I walked all the way back to Manzanar—only home I ever knew. Lived out in that manmade desert in the Owens Valley for maybe ten years, wandering around. I knew every stick and bramble in that desert terrain.

EMI: How'd you end up here?

MANZANAR: When you're in the desert and you're thirsty, you get to thinking about water. I had a theory that it connects things together. Connects past to present. Maybe I could get back to the sea, where my folks came from. So I followed the water. L.A. Department of Water and Power. There's an aqueduct that sucks the water right on out through the desert. Starts up at Mono Lake and winds down through tunnels and canyons. I must've followed it for more than three hundred miles. And it all ends up right here.

Song
"The Water and the Power"

They say the water comes from pristine places,
snowcapped peaks that nature graces,
but I'm a desert fisherman
who knows the water and the power,
tracking water through a wasteland
and traffic through a city,
looking for an ocean,
found a people in commotion.
I know the source is muddy.
I know the past is cloudy.
Three hundred miles, it keeps on coming,
never mind who's thirsty on the way,
this water's got appointments with L.A.

EMI:

They say the water comes from pristine places,
baby tears down crying faces,
but I'm a California brat
who knows the water and the power's
not enough to put out fires.
Sleeping in the music
looking for a reason
in a time so out of season.
I'm looking for a dream,
I'm searching for a memory.
Three hundred miles, it keeps on coming.
So many thirsty for a way
this water's time has come to heal L.A.

MANZANAR AND EMI:

>Now I lay my head upon this overpass,
>cradled by these silent monoliths
>bridging this wide river of human troubles
>and sleep to dream
>and dream to wake
>and wake to find a friend.

EMI *falls asleep in* MANZANAR's *lap. Hesitantly, he puts his arms around her and looks out at the skyline, where tones of orange and purple melt across the twilight sky.*

SCENE 5

Next day: Protestors from the Japanese American Preservation League, headed by MRS. SALLY OGATA, *are on the overpass in full force. Twins* MIMI *and* MINI MOTHRA, *representing the Society for Live Performance Art (*SLAP*) are also there with their members protesting the removal of the overpass, as they have declared that* MANZANAR *is "living performance art."* STEVE MARTIN *and his camera crew are there to film everything live.*

STEVE MARTIN: Overnight this downtown freeway overpass, recently des-ignated to be replaced by the first structural wonder of the new century—a Los Angeles City joint enterprise with the well-known Japanese entrepreneur group, Ser-izawa Enterprises, to build the so-called L.A. Colossus—has suddenly become the focus of protest and preservation. The single linchpin in this controversy seems to be one homeless man named Manzanar, er, My-ura-cammie. (*to* SALLY OGATA) Is that right?

SALLY OGATA: Mr. Murakami is not a homeless person. He is simply an eccentric man who has always lived in the open. I repre-sent the Japanese American Preservation League, whose concern is to look after Japanese Americans whom the League has designated under preservation.

STEVE MARTIN: Yes, but what is Mr. Mura-kakami's connection to this overpass? Why does he refuse to leave?

SALLY OGATA: Why don't you ask him yourself? The purpose of the Preservation League is to make sure that Manzanar Murakami is not harassed and to ensure that his civil liberties are protected.

STEVE MARTIN: Mr. Murakami, just what is it that you hope to accomplish here?

MANZANAR: This is the overpass from which I have conducted for the past six years. Before I accepted this overpass, I made a careful study of the city. Look. There is the city hall, First Street, the New Otani, the JAC-C-C! Through there, Olvera Street, Chinatown, and Chavez Ravine! And that way the L.A. River, and beyond, East L.A., where the sun rises straight through the Arco Towers and reflects brilliantly off the Bonaventure. And here, below, there is no other sight like it from any other overpass. It is a full orchestra at its best. Listen to the depth and the richness of the sound, the variety of tone, the clarity of each single instrument, and yet the vitality of life flowing there.

STEVE MARTIN: I see.

MIMI MOTHRA: No, you don't see at all. Manzanar is living performance art! He is, in Los Angeles, the predecessor for all live public art! What Stuart, Huang, or even Torres are doing today was inspired by Manzanar Murakami.

MINI MOTHRA: That's right. If this overpass and Manzanar are removed, the city will be destroying one of its finest examples of continuing art performance.

STEVE MARTIN: And just who are you?

MIMI AND MINI MOTHRA:
                 We are the twin Presidents of the Los Angeles Chapter

of SLAP, the Society for Living Art Performance. A society for the living and performing avant-garde!

MIMI MOTHRA: Manzanar Murakami has a right to his performance.

MINI MOTHRA: A right to this overpass.

MIMI MOTHRA: A right to rebellion.

MINI MOTHRA: Yesterday, he was but one human being against the L.A. Colossus.

MINI AND MIMI MOTHRA:
               Today he is three!

EMI: Four!

               Song
               "En Garde! The Avant-Garde"

MIMI MOTHRA: Performance begins at birth,
               a living pageant from the first.
               I was the first to cry.

MINI MOTHRA: I was the first to cry.

MIMI MOTHRA: I was the first to cry.

MINI MOTHRA: En garde! The avant-garde—
               always before my time!

MIMI MOTHRA: Always before the crowd—
               the progressive edge,

MINI MOTHRA: the artistic wit,

MIMI MOTHRA: for sex, God, and the body politic.

MINI MOTHRA: I was the first to smile!

MIMI MOTHRA: I was the first to walk!

MINI MOTHRA: I was the first to talk!

MIMI MOTHRA: En garde! The avant-garde—
                always before my time!
                Always before the crowd—

MINI MOTHRA: the progressive edge,
                the artistic wit,
                for sex, God, and the body politic.

MIMI MOTHRA: I was the first to kiss a boy!

MINI MOTHRA: I was the first to kiss a girl!

MIMI MOTHRA: I was the first to—(!)

MINI AND MIMI MOTHRA:
                *En garde! The avant-garde—
                always before our time!
                Always before the crowd—
                the progressive edge,
                the artistic wit,
                for sex, God, and the body politic!

MIMI MOTHRA: I was the first to play a Stradivarius in the nude.

MINI MOTHRA: I was the first to read my poetry from the rusting carcass
                of a '78 Ford at a public dump site in Detroit.

MIMI MOTHRA: I was the first to make the symbolic pilgrimage from
                Salinas to the Silicon Valley with a computer strapped to
                my back.

EMI: I was the first to, to . . . reconstruct the skull of a duck-
                bill out of Legos from an actual fossil carbon-dated at
                about 64.5 million years old.

MINI, MIMI, AND EMI:

>*En garde! The avant-garde—
>always before our time!
>Always before the crowd—
>the progressive edge,
>the artistic wit,
>for sex, God, and the body politic!

SCENE 6

In the MAYOR's *offices overlooking the overpass and the city.*

The MAYOR, EUGENE PATRICK, *and the* SERIZAWA BROTHERS *are in conference.*

EUGENE PATRICK: The city called me in to give my opinion, and I have done so. I have told you and told you again that you are making a big mistake, but you haven't been willing to listen.

MAYOR OLVERA: Dr. Patrick, may I remind you that the city council has made its decision, and now that we are in the final negotiations, it behooves all of us to work together for the best possible results. That is why we have called upon you, who have studied the Pacific Rim for years, to work with the Serizawas on ironing out the fine points.

EUGENE PATRICK: I won't do it! Selling our airspace to the Japanese is the beginning of the end! Already the Japanese and Chinese own most of the downtown area. The Koreans own the outskirts, and Southeast Asians are flooding into the crevices. The city council simply caved in to Asian special interests.

ICHIRO SERIZAWA:

Dr. Patrick, as you must know, we are involved in a joint venture. We are bringing necessary capital and technology to this project. We are not buying anything.

JIRO SERIZAWA: We approached Mayor Olvera because Los Angeles is the new center for Pacific Rim commerce, but there are many other cities in the u.s. that have been more than interested in our projects.

SABURO SERIZAWA:

We have accomplished similar projects in Tokyo, which you know is overpopulated and lives in fear of earthquakes, and where space is an expensive and precious commodity.

EUGENE PATRICK: But this isn't Tokyo! This is L.A! We are precisely a sprawling metropolis. We don't need to build up. If we are going to build, let's look to the great desert, the Owens Valley for example. Space that boggles the mind. We owe it to that desert community to bring forth civilization. But this L.A. Colossus is an expensive and unnecessary undertaking that only puts money into the hands of the Japanese.

Song
"The Dollar versus the Yen"

Read my book:
The Dollar versus the Yen.
It's all right here in Chapter Ten.
Give 'em an inch and they'll take a mile.
A long-term vision, they may take awhile,
but, reinventing capitalism,
beating us at our own game—
the end result is all the same:
a yellow peril,
a poison arrow,
straight to the heart
of the American dream.

The trade deficit? Unemployment?
Poor management? Poor production?

Inferior quality? The national debt?
Junk bonds? The recession?
The failure of the S & L's?
Crooks and liars in government and business?
Selling arms to Iran?
Funding illegal wars and funneling cocaine?
It's all their fault!

This is your dollar!
Spend it on the American dream!
This is our dollar!
Spend it on the American dream!

SERIZAWA BROTHERS:

Read his book:
The Dollar versus the Yen.
It's all right here on page eleven.
Take off your shoes, remember to smile;
a good business sense, knows where it's fertile,
can delve into the Oriental mind,
drink until the contract's signed,
then take a hot bath to unwind.
A change of tactics
in order to compete,
conserve the heart
of the American dream.

Cheap labor and foreign goods?
Korean cars and VCRs?
Argentine leather and Indian cotton?
Brazilian shoes and orange juice?
Chilean fruit? Mexican vegetables?
Toys from Taiwan? TVs from Japan?
French wine and water?
German beer and Finnish furniture?
Chinese silk and Australian wool?
It's all their fault!

This is your dollar!
Invest it in the American dream!
This is your dollar!
Invest it in the American dream!

EUGENE PATRICK AND THE SERIZAWA BROTHERS:
This is your dollar!
Spend it on the American dream!
This is your dollar!
Invest it in the American dream!
This is your dollar!

(*NOTE:* EUGENE PATRICK *sings "This is our dollar!"*)

SCENE 7

STEVE MARTIN *has taken his cameras to another site, the site of the Manzanar concentration camp in Owens Valley, Inyo County, where* MANZANAR *was born. He interviews* MRS. SALLY OGATA.

STEVE MARTIN: We're here between Lone Pine and Independence off Highway 395 in the Owens Valley at the foot of California's eastern Sierras. Behind me is a monument with the inscription "Memorial to the Dead," built by the former Japanese American inmates of the Manzanar war relocation camp during World War II. It was here in this desolate setting that Manzanar Murakami, named after the camp itself, was born on February 28, 1942.

SALLY OGATA: There's nothing here now but this gravesite and that guard gate. You can see some of the old foundations where the barracks were.

STEVE MARTIN: Yes, but about Manzanar Murakami?

SALLY OGATA: Manzanar's mother was one of the first people to arrive here. She was nine months pregnant to the day. There weren't any medical facilities awaiting her. The trauma of losing her home and seeing her husband taken away to jail, of not knowing where he had been taken, must have been too much. She died while giving birth to Manzanar.

STEVE MARTIN: Now you also mentioned that Manzanar Murakami, until about six years ago, lived out here in the open in this desert terrain.

SALLY OGATA: That's right. For some reason he returned to this place and roamed around here for many years.

STEVE MARTIN: There's nothing out here, and I'm told that temperatures in the summer get up to a hundred and ten and down to zero in the winter. Now what is that activity over there? (*points over the barbed-wire fence; cameras follow to* DR. GARY YAMANE *working in a pit*) (*addresses* GARY YAMANE) Sir, excuse me. What is happening here?

GARY YAMANE: This is a dig.

STEVE MARTIN: Are you digging for the remains of the old residents of the Manzanar camp?

GARY YAMANE: I'm a paleontologist, not an archaeologist. My studies don't encompass the human past. What we're studying here are fossils from the Cretaceous era.

STEVE MARTIN: Aren't you the famous paleontologist Dr. Gary Yam-aguchi?

GARY YAMANE: Yamane. The name is Gary Yamane. Now if you'll excuse me, I'm very busy. We're under a very tight deadline.

STEVE MARTIN: Why is that? You'd think fossils from the Cretaceous era have waited millions of years to be unearthed—with all due respect Dr. Yamane, what's a little five-minute interview?

GARY YAMANE: This area is slated for construction in the next few months. Tract housing, condominiums, and a shopping mall. (*looks up*) There he is. Dr. Eugene Patrick. Why don't you direct your questions to him? He's one of the partners in this development plan.

STEVE MARTIN: Dr. Patrick, how interesting to find you here. Watching your investment, I suppose.

EUGENE PATRICK: This is an American venture. It will be totally financed by and for Americans. Every piece of material from the cement to the steel beams will be American. And when this place is teeming with American life, there'll only be American cars for that matter.

SALLY OGATA: I'm an American, and this place used to be teeming with American life! Bashing Japan will not make up for the treachery of people like you, and to turn this into a shopping mall is treachery. Japanese Americans have considered this area sacred ground for years since the war. This is a sacrilege!

EUGENE PATRICK: That was a long time ago, and may I add, it was for your own good. Wartime necessity. Now there's nothing out here but a family of Gila monsters. Mrs. Ogata, there'll be a nice plaque. You'll be able to shop at Sharper Image, get a Mrs. Field's cookie, and come see your memorial plaque.

SALLY OGATA: (*to* GARY YAMANE) Are you going to let this happen? What are we going to do about this? It's despicable! (*to* EUGENE PATRICK) You are despicable!

Song
"Mutant Gila Monsters"

Years of shame.
Years of infamy.

A lone heart for a desert jewel.
An apple orchard for your mutant Gila monsters.
Hatred to fill a castle.
Fear to drive a Hearst.
How are your lies any different
from the yellow peril
spewed by those dragons of the past?

I was a young girl then.
What did I know of race?
What did I know of war?
What did I know of spies?
I went to prison for a bunch of lies.
Lies lies lies.

And people at the top,
people who knew the truth
but no conscience to say stop—
people like you,
people like you—
all knew.
But what did you say?
It was a wartime necessity.
No yellow face could be trusted.
It was for our own protection,
this phony military game.

But why was I detained?
Why was I imprisoned?
I was an innocent child,
born in America.
Because people at the top—

people who knew the truth
but no conscience to say stop—
people like you,
people like you—
lied lied lied.

Suddenly, there is a strange rumbling sound. Everyone looks around in fear. The earth begins to shake, small stones and gravel rolling around.

STEVE MARTIN: It's an earthquake! (*continues to report*) The desert landscape is rumbling beneath our feet. Oh. Oh. No. No. A fault, a fissure! The earth is parting her great lips. Mrs. Ogata, no! Where are you going?

SALLY OGATA *runs to hug the monument as it sinks into the earth.*

Ah. Ahhh. Everything is chaos! Look! Something is emerging from the fissure. Something. A great green . . . Some sort of gi gi la L.A. la MONSTER. No, NO. More like a tyro tyra gila Rex REX giLA rex GILAREX! Oh my God. Oh, the humanity of it all!

GILAREX *begins to unearth itself from beneath the Manzanar monument as* SALLY OGATA *disappears forever.* STEVE MARTIN *runs off in a panic, still talking wildly into the cameras while the crew continues their relentless shoot.*

SCENE 8

Back on the overpass. There is panic everywhere as the news of the monster, now dubbed GILAREX, *spreads.*

EMI *and* MANZANAR *watch the news on her tiny television.*

MAYOR OLVERA: (*on the news*) We have given orders for the gradual evacuation of areas in the city where we have firm indications that the monster may be headed. Those who do not follow the evacuation orders, do so at risk.

MANZANAR: (*looks below his overpass*) Years ago, my folks evacuated. I'm staying here. Let the others evacuate . . . Why do you have to look at that TV? Reality is happening at your feet!

Song
"The Reality on TV"

Reality is hap'ning at your feet.
You see it right there on the street—
no milk to feed that little babe,
gangs on dope and killing folks,
the fire from a tenement.
People dying, people killing, people crying—
you can see it all at your feet.

EMI: Reality is better on TV!
You never have to leave your seat.
The mother was on *Donahue*.
60 Minutes did the doc
and they'll repeat the news at ten.
People dying, people killing, people crying—
you can see it all on TV.

STEVE MARTIN: Reality is really on TV.
It's just another way to see—
starvation in North Africa,
the earthquake in Armenia,
terrorism in Beirut.
People dying, people killing, people crying—
and you can see me on TV.

ALL: (*at the sight of the monster*)

Reality is better on TV!
You never have to leave your seat.
Extinction of the dinosaurs—
it was all on PBS
and they'll repeat the show next week.
Reality is at my feet, right here on the street.
People dying, people killing, people crying—
you can see it all on TV.

EMI *returns to watch the TV for the news, and* MANZANAR *decides to conduct for the evacuating traffic below.* EMI *watches her TV in awe as* GILAREX *appears while* STEVE MARTIN *films the monster from a helicopter.* EMI *begins to notice something strange about the monster. As long as* MANZANAR *is conducting, the great dinosaur seems calm. He seems to be looking for something in the air, to be moving toward that something.*

EMI: (*orders* MANZANAR) Wait! Stop conducting! Look at this!

GILAREX *goes crazy, huffing and blowing fire from his mouth.*

              Okay, conduct!

The monster moves away in a daze.

              Don't you see? Manzanar, you're the key!

ACT II

SCENE 1

STEVE MARTIN *and* GARY YAMANE *are traveling over the city by helicopter while* EMI *watches her TV and* MANZANAR *conducts from the overpass.*

STEVE MARTIN: As you can see we are flying over Interstate Five in the heart of the San Fernando Valley. Ironically, the monster has followed the major highways to enter the L.A. basin area. There has been immense damage all along the way, to homes, crops, businesses, and roads, people scattering like insects in every direction.

EMI: Manzanar, concentrate on conducting, will you!

GARY YAMANE: (*on TV from the helicopter*) It's incredible, but from the looks of him, he has the coloring and some features of a Gila monster, but appears in other respects to be similar to the Tyrannosaurus Rex, the great tyrant carnivore of the Cretaceous era. And yet I'd have to say it's a hybrid creature descended from both the Asian and American continents, a sort of Asian American dinosaur, if you will.

STEVE MARTIN: We've seen that the air force had tried unsuccessfully back at Edwards Air Force Base to try diversionary tactics to force him back to the desert, but everything, short of an atomic bomb, seems to be failing.

GARY YAMANE: Unfortunately, it looks as if he may in fact be moving over the Hollywood Hills and toward the center of metropolitan Los Angeles.

STEVE MARTIN: Millions of yen in downtown real estate investment are about to go down in rubble with a monstrous kick! The stock market has been pitched into chaos!

Sure enough, GILAREX *arrives downtown while* MANZANAR *is conducting on the overpass.* EMI *continues to watch everything on her TV, even when the monster is close enough to see, toppling buildings and so forth.*

ALL: Reality is better on TV!
                You never have to leave your seat.
                Extinction of the dinosaurs—
                it was all on PBS,
                and they'll repeat the show next week.
                Reality is at my feet, right on the street.

The monster arrives at the overpass.

EMI: (*screaming to* MANZANAR) Don't stop conducting! DON'T
                STOP!

MANZANAR *conducts for their lives as the monster rips and lifts the overpass off the freeway and carries it across the city with* MANZANAR *and* EMI *atop. It eventually deposits the entire structure in front of Meiji Market in Gardena, then wanders off to Hermosa Beach for a nap.*

(NOTE: *The author continues to refer to the now-renamed Pacific Market as Meiji Market out of stubborn unwillingness to give up its historic/dinosaur name and the images that resonate from it.*)

SCENE 2

MANZANAR *appears alone atop the relocated overpass, Meiji Market and the Gardena/Torrance landscape in the background.*

MANZANAR: There it was, like she said, in my face. And when I saw
                the monster, it was as if I'd known it before, perhaps in
                the desert—a desert dream. The creature tore the over-
                pass right out from its steel roots and carried us away on
                this giant concrete cradle. And all the time she was
                yelling, "Don't stop conducting!" It was terrifying; it was
                electrifying . . . it's my most dramatic work by far . . . And

yet, I can't understand it. I knew where we were all going.
I knew. And I have never felt so afraid of knowing. My
fingers on the buttons of a remote control. But it was not
a control that anyone would want. I wanted to pull away,
to run away, but I could not. I could not let the creature
drop our precious cradle. I had to drive the beast. But I'm
a conductor, not a driver. I don't even have a license.

Song
"A Simple Citizen"

Who am I, a homeless wanderer
a no one on the streets
conducting traffic into music,
conducting monsters to their destiny?
What awful calling can this be?

MAYOR JANE OLVERA, *perhaps in her great windowed office, is dwarfed by
the background of a crumbled L.A. skyline, kinda a là General Patton.*

MAYOR OLVERA: My Los Angeles is in ruins. My political life in sham-
bles. Hundreds of Angelinos dead, missing, or injured.
Police, fire, and medical facilities frantically working day
and night. The Red Cross, National Guard, and myriad
insurance companies scurry across the city. An act of
God, they're saying. But how shall I save my city?

The following song is woven with MANZANAR'S *continuing song, "A Simple
Citizen."*

Song
"Our Lady of Angels"

An act of God is my beautiful skyline.
This live-wire circuitry of diamond lanes,
these pink stucco bungalows—
Hockney's vision of our sacred and profane.

MANZANAR: Why could I not be
             a simple citizen who only has to vote?
             An honest taxpayer who only has to pay?
             A bureaucrat who only has to file forms?
             An accountant who only has to count?
             A politician who only has to lie?
             A soldier who only has to pull the trigger?

MAYOR OLVERA: Ay mi naranja dulce!
             Blessed and kissed by the sun itself,
             as golden as sunsets over a graceful Pacific.
             Warmed by Santa Anas bending your palms
             open like poppies poised for embrace.
             Great city of angels,
             descended from great peoples,
             holy mecca of American myth.
             But, where is our winged lady now
             to stay the terror of this fire-breathing megasaur?

MANZANAR: Who am I, a homeless wanderer
             conducting monsters to their destiny?
             Why could I not be
             a simple citizen who only has to vote?
             An honest taxpayer who only has to pay?

DR. GARY YAMANE, *taken by helicopter by* STEVE MARTIN's *camera crew,
rushes to see his daughter* EMI.

GARY YAMANE: Emi! Emi! What the? What are you doing here? You,
             you should be in San Diego! And where's Maria?

EMI: Your housekeeper? I don't know. Maybe she went back to
             Guatemala. I gave her your Sony twenty-seven inch and
             the Panasonic VCR. She couldn't have gotten very far.

GARY YAMANE: I've been calling the house and no one answers. How did
             you get to L.A?

EMI: What do you care? You didn't even know I'd left! I've been gone for a whole week now!

GARY YAMANE: A week? Oh, no. Emi, I thought we had an understanding. That I could trust you. My work takes me all over the world. We've been through this before. When I can, I take you with me, but you've got your responsibilities, young lady. School for one.

EMI: I don't want to go anywhere with you. The last time you went to Egypt and you left me in a hotel in Cairo with that French nanny who practically handcuffed herself to me. I hate you!

GARY YAMANE: Emi, listen. I know you're angry. But it's all over now. At least you're safe. You're safe. The most important thing.

EMI: The most important thing? Right. I'm safe. Fine. Here. (*throws her backpack at him*) Take this stuff. It's a load off me. (*walks off*)

GARY YAMANE: Emi!—What the—(*looks inside backpack; pulls out fossil*) This looks like the upper molar of that duckbill I've been working on. Damn! I've been looking all over for it. We were going to have to reconstruct it. (*lifts backpack*) This weighs a ton! (*pulls out several other fossilized bones and*) My keys! The garage door opener! The TV remote? My fossil databases! And she must have erased the memory in the phone! No wonder nothing works! (*finally pulls out a silver framed wedding photo; pauses to look*)

GARY YAMANE AND EMI: (*each singing alone, in separate worlds*)

> *Song*
> "Fossils in Our Past"
> *(a rock song)*
>
> The fossils in our past—
> the things that really last.

A history built in solid rock.
A bedrock of memories.

But can our feelings take
the pressure of ions of time?
And who then will read
these fossils of leaf and fish?
The delicate imprints of our lives?
The delicate imprints of our love?

But can our feelings take
the pressure of ions of time?
And who then will read
these sabertooths, the petrified
morsels of our anger and pain,
and know we made it all up again?

Who can read this time capsule,
know the story in this skull—
the one who played the fool?
The one who broke the rule?

The fossils in our past—
the things that really last.

SCENE 3

Multiple scenes with EMI *and* MANZANAR, GARY YAMANE, EUGENE PATRICK, *the* SERIZAWA BROTHERS, *the* RAD MAN, *and the* LOVELY LADY.

EMI: That's it. I'm never going back. Never. Never. I knew it.
                The past is the past.

MANZANAR: The past may be the past, but the future has certainly
                taken an interesting turn.

EMI: Will you look where we are! In the middle of a parking

lot with a lot of Japanese cars and some market called
Pacific. Where are we anyway?

MANZANAR: Gardena, home of Asian takeout. You know, suburbia . . .
               So I made a mistake. Used to be strawberry farms. Sure
               looks changed.

EMI: And you said I was the only one, but this place is crawl-
               ing with rock-says. Well, who needs it? GiLArex! Yes.
               Come and take it all. Destroy it all!

               Song
               "The Monster in Me"
               (*continued*)

               No monster past is coming after me.
               No monster future is waiting down the road.
               The monster is living in me.
               Death is inevitable.
               Life is suicidal.
               Destroy it all!
               And we can start anew.

MINI AND MIMI MOTHRA:
               Helter skelter in L.A.,
               the moment you've been waiting for—
               the BIG ONE
               (and it wasn't even a quake).
               The ecstasy of chaos.
               The immediacy of now.
               An angel of darkness and fear,
               loathing in L.A.
               loathing in L.A.

RAD MAN/LOVELY LADY:
               Car phone's broke.
               Deal's sunk.
               Mirror's broke.

Mascara's messed.

ALL: I can't get to work.
              Can't cruise the scene.
              Can't be lookin' good.
              Can't be seen.
              Got no time for this monster jammin' my lane.

EMI: Death is inevitable.
              Life is suicidal.

MINI AND MIMI MOTHRA:
              Loathing in L.A.
              Loathing in L.A.

RAD MAN/LOVELY LADY:
              Got no time for this monster jammin' my lane.
              Got no time for this monster jammin' my lane.

SCENE 4

Back at the overpass, now dislocated to Gardena.

EMI: Where are you going?

MANZANAR: 'Bout time to be migrating.

EMI: You're leaving me here, alone?

MANZANAR: Haven't you been listening to your machine? Your dad's
              been appointed to head a task force to rid the city of this
              dinosaur or whatever it is. There's an eight hundred num-
              ber. Give him a call.

EMI: He doesn't care about me! Wait, I'm a Japanese Ameri-
              can minor roaming the streets! Aren't you concerned?

MANZANAR: Sally's . . . Sally's gone. If you want to preserve yourself, you better get your own pertinent information.

EMI: But what about GiLArex? What about your conducting?

MANZANAR: What about it?

EMI: You have control. We proved it.

MANZANAR: What control? I don't have any control. You must be crazy.

EMI: But that's not true . . . You're running away!

MANZANAR: Migrating. I'm going home.

EMI: No you're not. This is home, and now, you're running away! (*silence*) We can change things.

MANZANAR: (*pulls out baton and hands it to* EMI) Here, you're young. You change things.

EMI: I don't know how to conduct. You've gotta save the city.

MANZANAR: Save the city? I thought you wanna destroy it. (*leaves.*)

EMI: Right. I mean . . . (*stares at baton*)

SCENE 5

DR. EUGENE PATRICK *wanders into a sushi bar filled with Caucasian customers to nurse his wounds. He happens to meet the* SERIZAWA BROTHERS, *who are secretly meeting there. The sushi bar is filled with people despite the fact that the* MAYOR *has ordered the city evacuated. There is a blasé air of people enjoying their last piece of sashimi. A kind of repetitious Philip Glass music permeates the place.*

SUSHI BAR CLIENT: You know, I got my aficionado license in sushi, isn't that right Udemae-san?

UDEMAE: First-class black-belt sushi aficionado. I give it myself to my best pupils. Have to complete very rigorous testing test. Somebody say only Japanese can pass, but you pass.

SUSHI BAR CLIENT: Udemae-sensei, you are such a master.

OTHER CLIENTS: You know what I'm dying for? Uuuuni.
Udemae, make me up an uuuuni, please.
Make that two.

UDEMAE: I got something surprise special for you today.

SUSHI BAR CLIENT: Ouuuuu, Udemae, you rascal. You know how I love surprises. What is it?

UDEMAE: In all L.A., only Udemae make this one. I call it Udemae Special Number Four.

SUSHI BAR CLIENT: Didn't I tell you this is the best place in town?

ANOTHER CLIENT: Hey, whaddya suppose GiLArex eats?

CLIENTS: Sushi!

ICHIRO SERIZAWA: Dr. Patrick, what a coincidence!

JIRO SERIZAWA: Yes, what are you doing here?

EUGENE PATRICK: I should ask you that question.

SABURO SERIZAWA: Well, as you are aware, this is one of those sushi bars frequented only by Westerners like yourself.

ICHIRO SERIZAWA: To be frank, we come here to get away from other Japanese.

JIRO SERIZAWA: Well, we must suppose that that is also why Dr. Patrick comes here—to get away from us.

EUGENE PATRICK: To be honest with you, that's true. My one great passion for Japanese things is sushi, but how am I to admit this being the man that I am, the Pacific Rim specialist advocating anti-Japanese sentiments? No one knows except Udemae (nods at the sushi-maker) that I come here every Friday. I'm a regular. I sneak in by myself and hope no one will notice Dr. Eugene Patrick, PhD, author of *The Dollar versus the Yen*.

SABURO SERIZAWA: Well, I guess we have all been caught at our own games.

ICHIRO SERIZAWA: But why haven't you evacuated like others? It isn't safe to be in the city now.

JIRO SERIZAWA: Look at all these people. The place is filled. Everyone drinking sake and eating sushi, oblivious to the danger facing the city.

EUGENE PATRICK: It's sushi. You can never get enough. It grows on you and you keep coming back for more. No dinosaur is going to keep these people from their sushi.

                   Song
                   "Subtleties of Sushi" or "California Roll"
                   (*with the quality of flamenco*)

                   Toro! Toro!
                   Maguro! Maguro!
                   The only way to eat fish is to eat it raw.
                   To wrap your tongue around each piece is like amour.
                   To touch your lips, a subtle innuendo,
                   to taste a hidden and forbidden libido.

                   Let the sake trickle down your throat.
                   Let the ginger crunch between your teeth.

Let the wasabi thunder up your nose.

The only way to eat fish is to eat it raw.
To wrap your tongue around each piece is like amour.
To touch your lips, a subtle innuendo,
to taste a hidden and forbidden libido.

Gotta get my sushi fix.
Lemme at my chopsticks.
Gotta get some raw fish to chew,
dip her in the ol' shoyu.
Gonna get my last piece of maguro,
if it's the last thing I do.

The only way to eat fish is to eat it raw.
To wrap your tongue around each piece is like amour.
To touch your lips a subtle innuendo,
to taste a hidden and forbidden libido.

EUGENE PATRICK: Well, you know why I'm still here in L.A., but the three
of you?

ICHIRO SERIZAWA: We believe we may be of more service here in the city
rather than far away.

JIRO SERIZAWA: Something must be done about GiLArex. We have
come here to work on this problem.

SABURO SERIZAWA: We believe we may be able to formulate a plan.

EUGENE PATRICK: To save your investment?

ICHIRO SERIZAWA: Of course we are concerned about saving our investment. But first we have to find a way to save the city
and the people in it.

EUGENE PATRICK: Ah yes. Your long-term investment.

JIRO SERIZAWA: Yes, Dr. Patrick, our long-term investment: the peo-
       ple, the consumers.

SABURO SERIZAWA: As W. Edwards Deming once said, "The consumer . . ."

W. EDWARDS DEMING *appears as a sort of looming ghost that only* EUGENE
PATRICK *seems to see and react to.*

W. E. DEMING: "The consumer is the most important part of the pro-
       duction line."

EUGENE PATRICK: W. Edwards Deming? The Curmudgeon of Quality?
       The Messiah of Management himself?

ICHIRO SERIZAWA: Yes, I'm surprised Americans don't seem to know him.
       He's the American who taught the Japanese everything
       we know about business. He is our mentor!

EUGENE PATRICK: Your mentor, an American? W. Edwards Deming was
       my teacher. He also said,

W. E. DEMING: *Song*
       Reprise of "The Dollar versus the Yen"

       Read my book:
       Out of the Crisis.
       It's all right here in my preface.
       Quality comes with good management.
       A loyal consumer is not enough.
       Creating innovations every day—
       better products on their way.
       A new philosophy of work

       Doctor Patrick,
       you have been a jerk!
       Restore the heart
       of the American dream!

Patrick, what has become of you? You have made a mockery of my teaching. Your kind of irresponsible management has brought about the demise of American business. Only you can blame yourself for this sad state of affairs. Your counterparts in Japan have only been doing what you should be doing. Now that they are your equals, it is time to work together. Time is of the essence, Patrick, and yours is running out.

EUGENE PATRICK: I've failed Deming. I'm so ashamed. I'm sorry. I have been a fool. Deming is right. Mrs. Ogata was right. You are right. This is no time for petty economic differences. We need to face a great danger together.

SABURO SERIZAWA: Well said. We are agreed.

ICHIRO SERIZAWA: And, of course, we are prepared to show the world that a homogeneous collective culture

JIRO SERIZAWA: with an ancient tradition

SABURO SERIZAWA: can best resolve this problem.

SCENE 6

EMI *runs into* ITCHIE, *the senior citz.*

ITCHIE: Hey I know you. Kristi, aren't you?

EMI: Emi. I might be lost, but I'm still Emi. Have you seen him?

ITCHIE: GiLArex?

EMI: No, Manzanar. I lost him.

ITCHIE: Oh, he'll turn up. Might take some time. Last time, took a whole ten years.

EMI: When he was in the desert?

ITCHIE: Yeah, roaming around Manzanar.

EMI: So you knew him before?

ITCHIE: In those days, his name was Kamimura, Joe Kamimura. Was a quiet mousy guy who never went anywhere. Never talked to anyone. Just the animals. Worked in the zoo, you see. Just went back and forth between the zoo and his apartment. It was either feeding time at the zoo or at his apartment. I should know. Lived next door to me. One day I said, "Hey Joe, you should get out some." There was a pilgrimage to Manzanar. So he shrugged and went along. Don't know why. Sat next to me on the bus, but when it came time to go, he wasn't there. Disappeared. Next time I see him, he's on the overpass ten years later, and he's Manzanar Ringo Murakami, conductor.

EMI: He never went anywhere? Never walked around the world?

ITCHIE: Far as I know. Nope. Wasn't the sort in those days. I paid his back rent. He owes me, but what the heck. Cleaned out his apartment too. Nothing there but stacks of classical records and stacks of National Geographic magazines. Stacks up to the ceiling, mind you.

EMI: But he's not Manzanar?

ITCHIE: Of course, he's Manzanar.

EMI: But what Sally said, about his being born in the camp and all.

ITCHIE: Sally researched it all very thoroughly. Birth certificate and everything.

EMI: But you said he was someone else.

ITCHIE: I guess Joe Kamimura died out there in the desert. With Manzanar, it's never been whether you can see or hear, you know what I mean. All in the mind.

EMI: But I heard his music. I swear I did.

ITCHIE: Yeah, I thought so.

SCENE 7

Underground offices of what has provisionally been called the Mayor's Special Task Force.

GARY YAMANE, MAYOR OLVERA, *and their* STAFF *are feverishly working.*

MAYOR OLVERA: (*on video*) . . . We now have come to the realization that this is a crisis that requires special expertise and unusual care if we are to save lives and property. This is no ordinary disaster. We must proceed scientifically. Therefore, I have appointed Dr. Gary Yamane, our city's resident paleontologist, to head up a special task force to find a creative way to rid the city of this so-called GiLArex . . .

GARY YAMANE: It's preposterous.

MAYOR OLVERA: Dr. Yamane, the president's on the line.

GARY YAMANE: (*taking the phone*) Yes, ma'am . . . I realize time is running out. Nuclear weapons? Of course they've been ruled out! What? The Santa Monica Bay? No ma'am, I don't think the pollution in the bay would be strong enough to kill him. Yes, we're working on it. I've been in constant touch with the general. Yes, he's willing to cooperate. He's on standby. I'm told the Marines are all over the beach. I'll call you as soon as we have something more concrete. Thank you. (*to the* MAYOR) Okay. What have you got there?

MAYOR OLVERA: More old sci-fi films. We've discarded all the "this monster versus that monster" stuff. We haven't got another monster to fight ours, unless we can get that mechanical ape at Universal Studios to come to life.

GARY YAMANE: I can't believe this! Jane, I'm a paleontologist, not a sci-fi writer. All my life I've studied the prehistoric past to get answers for the present. There must be something in all that research to justify the presence of this monster today.

GARY YAMANE: *Song*
"You Can Learn from the Past"

You can learn from the past,
an educated forecast
from a time-distant broadcast.
You can learn from the past.

MAYOR OLVERA: (*spoken*) Maybe there's something to be said for these old sci-fi movies. The original Godzilla movie suffocated the monster under the ocean by some secret oxygen-extracting weapon . . . which we haven't got.

TASK FORCE MEMBER: (*spoken*) Yeah, but what about the fact that in every old Godzilla movie,

(*sung*)
*The monster stomps on Tokyo.
The monster razes buildings.
The monster rips the trains in two.

He burns the people in a barbecue.
The war has come again to Tokyo.
The war has come again.
The bombs have come again.
The people scatter underneath.
The bomb above is like a wreath—

ANOTHER TASK FORCE MEMBER: (*spoken*)

How about trying to stop him by tangling him up in the power lines? Course it never worked in the movies; the monster always got past the power lines . . .

ANOTHER TASK FORCE MEMBER: (*spoken*)

I seem to remember a film in which the monster gets lured into a volcano. We can lure him into a live one before—

*repeat

Suddenly there's a video replay of EMI *and* MANZANAR *on the overpass,* MAN-ZANAR *conducting and* EMI *watching her* TV.

GARY YAMANE: You can learn from the past,
an educated forecast
from a time-distant broadcast.
You can learn from the past.

EMI *enters.*

SCENE 8

Back at the beach with GILAREX.

STEVE MARTIN: Looking on this scene at this moment, it is difficult to believe that just hours ago, this sleeping giant was thundering across the Los Angeles basin, uprooting palm trees and setting fire to shopping malls.

GILAREX *stirs. The* SERIZAWA BROTHERS *suddenly shed their salarymen suits and ties and become ninjas on the spot.*

SERIZAWA BROTHERS:

Song
"A Homogeneous Collective Culture"
(*with* EUGENE PATRICK, UDEMAE-SAN, *and* SUSHI BAR CLIENTS)

(*spoken*)
Many people ask the question:
how does a homogeneous collective culture
with an ancient tradition
maintain its mission?

(*sung*)
The people know the place high on a mountain
where a goddess dances naked before a shadowed cave;
there you will find the very fountain,
that sputtering cascade of cool silk,
the aged source of our cultured milk.
An entire people sucking from the rich, dripping teats
of one very very very venerated cow.

(*spoken/rapped*)
OW!
Cultured milk!
Homogenized milk!
How does it get that way?
Well you shake it shake it shake it shake it
shake it shake it shake it shake it.
Yeah you shake it shake it shake it shake it
shake it shake it shake it shake it.

Cultured milk!
Homogenized milk!
How did we get that way?
'Cuz we shake it shake shake it shake it

> shake it shake it shake it shake it.
> Yeah we shake it shake it shake it shake it
> shake it shake it shake it shake it.

STEVE MARTIN: He's waking! He's looking around.

Suddenly, the SERIZAWA BROTHERS/NINJAS, DR. PATRICK, *and* THE SUSHI BAR PEOPLE *all jump out to fight the waking monster. This turns out to be more of a martial arts demonstration than anything really practical.*

SCENE 9

Back at task force headquarters.

GARY YAMANE: Emi?

EMI·   Dad? . . . I'm not going to apologize.

GARY YAMANE: I see.

EMI: I thought you could use some help.

GARY YAMANE: As a matter of fact, it would help if you didn't try to run away again.

EMI: Dad, I know some things about GiLArex that can help you out.

GARY YAMANE: What's that?

EMI: Well, he's a runaway, like me.

TASK FORCE MEMBER: (*interrupting*)
             Dr.—

GARY YAMANE: I understand, Emi. We need to talk, but just now I've got a lot of things on my mind.

EMI: Dad. (*holding* MANZANAR's *baton*) Just watch this. (*points to video monitor*) Watch there. Please.

GARY YAMANE: What the—

EMI *closes her eyes and concentrates and tries to conduct.*

TASK MEMBER: Doctor, it's very strange but . . . the creature seems to be confused. Almost tamed . . .

Everyone watches GILAREX *on the big screen, and for a moment, the creature walks about in a daze, but routs the* NINJAS *when* EMI *loses her concentration.*

GARY YAMANE: Emi, what are you doing?

EMI: Dad, don't you see? I can't really do it, but Manzanar can. We've got to find him.

TASK FORCE MEMBER:
               For a moment, it looked as if the monster was being guided.

MAYOR OLVERA: Doctor, please, we haven't time for—

GARY YAMANE: Guided. If we could guide it somewhere. But where?

EMI: Home. He wants to go home. He woke up, and it's not anything like he remembers about home. (*to* GARY YAMANE *in particular*) Can't you see? He wants to go back.

               Song
               "Back to the Cretaceous Period"

               Back to those days when the earth was a rain forest,
               a verdant greenhouse without effect,
               when every species lived in grace,
               the local food chain had its place;

there were no black holes into space.
And T. Rex
was king!

*It was Cretaceous!
Yes, it was Cretaceous!
And T. Rex
was king!

*repeat

On the large screen, STEVE MARTIN *is interviewing a group of school* KIDS.

KID IN SOCCERSAURUS T-SHIRT:
    I thought dinosaurs were extinct.

SECOND KID: Yeah, they all went to get a drink of water in the La Brea tar pits, and they fell in and got stuck!

THIRD KID: Ah, you don't know nothing. The ones that got stuck in the tar pits were like woolly mammoths from another period.

SECOND KID: So? They still got stuck. Then, the workers found the bones when they took the tar out to make freeways.

MAYOR OLVERA: That's it! Build a tar pit and lure him in.

GARY YAMANE: The dry lake beds out in the desert. Spill a tanker of oil into the deepest one.

EMI: What? You're serious. No. Let him go!

GARY YAMANE: Emi, where are we going to let a monster like this go? Think about it! (*to* TASK FORCE MEMBER) Get me the general on the phone. And Exxon as well. (*to* EMI) Emi, listen to me. GiLArex's home disappeared from this earth sixty-five million years ago!

EMI: (*left alone*) Manzanar. Where did he go? Migrating home. He said home. The water and the power. Of course! (*runs off*)

SCENE 10

News insert, perhaps with footage of SALLY OGATA *dramatically falling to her death.*

STEVE MARTIN: In these days of turmoil, when so many have perished under the deadly foot of the radioactive leviathan, I want to stop for a moment to remember the brave woman who was the first to give her life in a moment of tragic sacrifice. How many Americans across the nation have witnessed again and again the incredible footage of the unearthing of GiLArex and have asked themselves, who was that brave woman who threw herself around the great white monument at Manzanar and fell into the abyss of the unknown left by the emerging monster? That woman was Sally Ogata. And although I only knew Sally (as her friends liked to call her) through sparse interviews of mere sound bytes, I knew enough to know she was a Japanese American nisei of great strength of character, conviction, and persistence, whose years of service to her community were marked by an irrepressible spirit of justice and human dignity. Sally Ogata, we at KYLO salute your memory.

MANZANAR *is walking along the L.A. river with* EMI's TV-*radio.*

MANZANAR: Poor Sally. What did he know about Sally? Nothing. Sally was always good for a meal. Tempura udon on Wednesdays. Sometimes she brought rice balls and pickles to the overpass. I'd say, "What's this stuff? How about a hamburger?" She'd say, "You are what you eat. Food is what you come from. This is what you come from." What a pest she was. And always worrying about my personal hygiene. And always on the lookout for someone with the same build. She'd say to someone at the Towers, "What's your shoe size?" or "What's your inseam? Why don't you clean out your closet? Give me some of that stuff you never wear." Once, she even found me a new baton . . . Hell, I never wanted to be preserved, pickled to perfection like one of Sally's original issei tsukemono recipes. I said, "Go find some goddamned crazy issei to follow around." "Blasphemy!" she said, "to take the name of the issei in vain. They were the first generation. Great pioneers!" Yeah, I said, that's the problem; only the first generation gets to pioneer. But I admit, I needed her and she needed me. Now where is Sally? At the bottom of all of that history she was trying to preserve. Killed herself trying to preserve an old, ungrateful hobo like me.

MANZANAR *picks up a stick, pulls out a penknife, and smooths it out a bit. Then he stands at the edge of the river, and conducts once again.*

Music
"Song for Sally"

SCENE 11

The La Brea tar pits.

STEVE MARTIN: I'm here in front of the Japanese Pavilion of the Los Angeles County Art Museum, miraculously still standing despite the great destruction wrought by GiLArex throughout the city. Just a stone's throw from here, you can see the La Brea Tar Pits. We've come here to try to understand the plans of the Mayor's Task Force to creatively rid the city of GiLArex. Let's take a look.

MINI *and* MIMI MOTHRA *are both at the edge of the tar pit, ceremonially tossing plastic dinosaur replicas into the black tar.*

MEMBERS OF SLAP: (*chanting in the background as a chorus; beneath the chant is the Loathing in L.A. verse from "The Monster in Me"*)

> Motsuraya
> Motsuraya
> Motsuraya

MINI MOTHRA: Ste-ga-sau-rus (*tosses stegasaurus*)

MINI MOTHRA: Bron-to-sau-rus (*tosses brontosaurus*)

MINI MOTHRA: Ty-ran-no-sau-rus Rex!

STEVE MARTIN: This is Steve Martin, for KYLO.

SCENE 12

Back at the task force headquarters.

GARY YAMANE *looks up at the screen and sees the creature walking in a peaceful daze.*

TASK FORCE MEMBER:
> Doctor Yamane, I'll be damned! Look at this. It's the old tamed-creature stuff again.

GARY YAMANE: (*shakes his head, then looks around*) Emi? Where'd she go? (*looks back at monitor and sees* EMI *with* STEVE MARTIN *in the KYLO copter*) Damn!

SCENE 13

EMI *is with* STEVE MARTIN *up in the KYLO helicopter.*

STEVE MARTIN: We have here with us in the KYLO copter Dr. Gary Yamane's teenage daughter, Emi Yamane. Emi, as you have heard, was on that Little Tokyo overpass when GiLArex literally wrenched the whole thing off its steel girders and walked away with it. Emi, what could you have been thinking at that terrifying moment?

EMI: Just that Manzanar had to keep conducting.

STEVE MARTIN: I see. And what about Manzanar? Where is he now?

EMI: You have to follow the water three hundred miles. Up the L.A. River and to the aqueducts. We've got to find him!

STEVE MARTIN: No sign of Manzanar Murakami. However, we've got our sights on GiLArex, who is seemingly almost tamely marching north back toward the Owens Valley. And over along Route Fourteen—an incredible sight from the air—you can see for miles a continuous lineup of oil tankers all ominously moving north. I'm told that oil tankers from every part of the state and nearby Nevada and Arizona are all moving this way to spill tons of crude oil into this pristine desert. It's environmental terrorism in a concerted effort to fight an unnatural disaster!

EMI: There he is! Manzanar! At the top of that aqueduct up there! He's conducting! Please put me down. I've got to talk to him.

SCENE 14

Back at task force headquarters.

TASK FORCE MEMBER:
                Doctor, Your Honor, your transport has arrived.

GARY YAMANE *is still staring at his daughter in the monitor.*

MAYOR OLVERA: Doctor, please, we haven't much time.

GARY YAMANE: When she was born, she was this shriveled little thing. My wife thought she was so cute, but I saw this wrinkled little being, a tiny old person, brand new and so ancient all at once. Past, present, future. Once I held it all here, in my own hands.

SCENE 15

EMI *is with* MANZANAR *near the aqueduct overlooking the Owens Valley.*

EMI: How did you walk so far so fast?

MANZANAR: Hitched a ride on an oil tanker. You didn't think I was gonna walk?

EMI: You've got to do something. They're going to kill GiLArex in a tar pit, and they're going to turn this valley into a pit of tar to do it . . . I brought you this. (*hands* MANZANAR *the baton*)

MANZANAR: You keep it. It's not the baton. It's all in the wrists. It's all—

EMI: In the mind. I know. I heard it. And I think it's beautiful. Really beautiful. Thanks . . . Who's Joe Kamimura?

MANZANAR: I heard that name. Must be a friend of Itchie's.

EMI: What did you mean I was a rock-say?

MANZANAR: Sally was impressed with things like that.

EMI: Yeah, but what is it?

MANZANAR: Well, where'd your grandparents come from?

EMI: I don't know. Hawaii? Before that Japan. My mom used to talk about it. She said her ancestors came to Hawaii after the Civil War. Something about a great, great, great, great somebody. All I know is they were great.

MANZANAR: How many generations ago?

EMI: I dunno. Three. Four. Five—

MANZANAR: Six generations. Maybe you are rokusei.

EMI: But what's the big deal? It just sounds like the same bunch of people getting married to the same bunch of people six times is all.

MANZANAR: Yup. Species isolation. If you're on a little island, you can do that. Madagascan lemurs are a case in point . . . But in your case, maybe it's not the marrying that's important; it's the stories. After six generations, you oughta have some stories.

EMI: Stories?

MANZANAR: Yeah, stories.

SCENE 16

On a hill overlooking the Owens Valley.

MAYOR OLVERA: Has the valley been evacuated?

TASK FORCE MEMBER:
           Yes, nothing down there but sand and brush, so to speak.

MAYOR OLVERA: Where are all the oil tankers?

TASK FORCE MEMBER:

>The monster's moving too fast. If it keeps up this pace, the general's saying it's impossible to get the tankers here in time.

TASK FORCE MEMBER:

>There goes our plan!

GARY YAMANE: What about that aqueduct out there? If the monster somehow diverts or crushes it, the loss of water to L.A. could be devastating.

TASK FORCE MEMBERS:

>Oh my God, there he is!
>I can't believe what I'm seeing!
>AHHHH!

>*Song*
>"The Monster in Your Dreams"

>When I saw him last
>he could fit in my TV;
>the buildings like Legos fell in his path,
>the people scattered like Kens and Barbies.

GARY YAMANE: When I saw him last,
>he filled my paranoia—
>a great carnivore, a giant Sequoia.
>His jaws smacked of concrete, plastic, and palm trees.
>His back was a clatter of golden arches.
>His head rose through smog, set afire in the skies
>with one foot in Bel Air, the other, Van Nuys.

STEVE MARTIN AND MAYOR OLVERA:

>When I saw him last—
>no minor adventure—
>he was hugging the Bonaventure,
>devouring directors with their computers,

while stomping on Hondas, Mercedes, and Fords,
and nuking the leftovers sans distinction.
The unwieldy foot of earthly extinction.

EUGENE PATRICK AND THE SERIZAWA BROTHERS:
When we saw him last,
he was the competition—
ITT, IBM, Sony, and Honda.
The bad guys we need to win the trade war.
The war we crave to make us all heroes.
The war we crave to make us all heroes.

MANZANAR: *When I saw him last,
he was as big as life
as big as life.
A dream from the past,
I had seen him at last.

An intimate fear at the base of my brain
from a song I'd never sung, an old refrain.
An inkling of pain
no time can claim,
no new pain can claim.
An inkling of pain
for which only courage has a name.

*repeat

STEVE MARTIN: I can't believe what I'm seeing. There below us is a lone
man, Manzanar Murakami, conducting on a desert hill.
And there plods the monster, GiLArex. I don't know if I
can make this connection, but it's as if in this moment of
crisis, the monster and the man are bound together in a
kind of Wagnerian waltz . . .

MANZANAR: *Song*
"The Performance of Life"

This is the performance of my life,
the very thing I couldn't miss,
the drama in my heart,
the laughter in my belly,
the story in my past;
for everything on Earth is music to my ear.
Everything is music to my ear.

STEVE MARTIN: Oh no, the monster seems to be moving toward the town
of Independence. What the—it's destroying the aque-
duct! A great wall of water is washing forth. This desert
valley of sorrow and tears has become an ocean! Water
has returned to the Owens Valley! And the oil tankers
never even had a chance to unload. Doomed, engulfed,
sent to the bottom like so many toys. But the beast. Ahh!
He's won this battle, or has he? No. He's succumbing to
that great ocean below. Suicidal. Tragic. His great body is
sinking. Drowning. Gone back to the depths of its origins. Gone with the waters . . .

ALL: This is the performance of our lives,
the very thing we couldn't miss,
the drama in our hearts,
the laughter in our bellies,
the stories in our past,
for everything on Earth is music to our ears.
Everything is music to our ears.
Everything on Earth is music!

SCENE 17

Back at the overpass in Gardena.

GARY YAMANE: Mr. Murakami?

MANZANAR: Dr. Gary Yamane, world-famous paleontologist.

GARY YAMANE: I'd give anything now for some simpler title.

MANZANAR: Emi's father?

GARY YAMANE: I need your help. I've lost my daughter.

MANZANAR: Lost, huh? Isn't that something that you do? Uncover and discover lost things? Course live things are different from fossils. Always changing. Always changing. Can't just blow off the dust and put 'em somewhere. (*wanders off*)

EMI *appears.*

EMI: It's okay, Dad. I'm safe.

GARY YAMANE: (*looks up*) Emi, I've never told you this, but, but you are a very rare and special, ah, species, mutation, generation, no, no, I meant to say living formation, discovery.

EMI: Dad.

GARY YAMANE: I said rare, special.

EMI: You said mutation.

GARY YAMANE: (*silence*) Fifteen years ago, I pulled you into this world and for a moment I knew I held everything I ever needed in my life . . . in my hands . . . right here. I . . . I love you.

    Song
    "Fossils in Our Past"
    (*reprise*)

    The fossils in our past—
    the things that really last.
    A history built in solid rock.
    A bedrock of memories.

*But can our feelings take
the pressure of ions of time?
And who then will read
these fossils of leaf and fish?
The delicate imprints of our lives?
The delicate imprints of our love?

But can our feelings take
the pressure of ions of time
And who then will read
these sabertooths, the petrified
morsels of our anger and pain
and know we made it all up again?

Who can read this time capsule,
know the story in this skull—
the one who played the fool?
the one who broke the rule?

*repeat

SCENE 18

MANZANAR *and* EMI *walk onto the overpass again, now relocated in front of Meiji Market. Both have podiums, and both step up with their batons and begin to conduct. Scenes of L.A. pass behind the two; the reconstruction of the city has begun. A larger banner goes up with the words "Patrick–Serizawa Ventures." Presumably, the* SERIZAWA BROTHERS *and* DR. PATRICK *have plans to open a chain of floating sushi restaurants. The scene pauses on the* RAD MAN *and the* LOVELY LADY, *whose cars have been stopped by the rubble of the freeway. The normally car-bound people get out of their cars and finally meet each other in an intuitive moment of instant recognition. The sun sets over the L.A. horizon, and music fills the sky.*

THE END

FRIDAY, AUGUST 21, 8:00 P.M.

oiLAWrecks

An original musical play
by Karen Yamashita.
Original music by
Vickie Abe.
Directed by
Shizuko
Hoshi.

$12 General
Admission

A staged reading
of the farcical, fan-
tasy musical play by
award-winning author
(Through the Arc of the
Rainforest) and play-
wright Karen Yamashita.
Are Japanese Americans an
endangered species? With
tongue-in-cheek humor
Yamashita gives provoking
insight into our modern
society.

also SUNDAY, AUGUST 23, 2:00 P.M.

oiLAWrecks
FRI. AUG. 21, 6 P.M. & SUN. AUG. 23, 2 P.M.

Northwest Asian American Theatre Presents the World Premiere of

GODZILLA
comes to Little Tokyo

book & lyrics by
Karen Tei Yamashita

music & lyrics by
Vicki Abe

directed by
Tammis Doyle

musical direction and
arrangements by
Bruce A. Monroe

choreography by
Meg Tapucol

sound design by
Jonathan Sandelin

lighting design by
Cynthia Bishop

costume design by
Mary Duckering

set design by
**Peggy McDonald
Jennifer A. Lee**

video & slides by
Rick Wong

dramaturgy by
Vivian Umino

Karen Tei Yamashita's *Godzilla Comes to Little Tokyo* is the winner of NWAAT's First Annual Playwrights' Contest. NWAAT would like to thank the Music Theatre Workshop for agreeing to give *Godzilla Comes to Little Tokyo* its initial workshop in October, 1991

Cast

Steve Martin	**Allan Michael Barlow**
Manzanar	**Jonathan Te Ho Park**
Emi	**Gigi Jhong**
Rad Man	**Doug Swenson**
Lovely Lady	**Jennifer L. Michel**
Sally Ogata	**Eloisa Cardona**
Ichi	**David Hsieh**
Ghosts	**Ann Evans, Doug Swenson**
Mayor Jane Olvera	**Rebecca M. Davis**
Dr. Eugene Patrick	**Steven Boe**
Ichiro Serizawa	**Michael A. McClure**
Jiro Serizawa	**David Hsieh**
Saburo Serizawa	**Larry Tazuma**
Mimi Mothra	**Doug Swenson**
Mini Mothra	**Jennifer L. Michel**
Gary Yamane	**Robert Lee**
W. Edwards Deming	**Doug Swenson**
Task Force	**Eloisa Cardona, Jennifer L. Michel, Doug Swenson**
Koken	**Steven Boe, Eloisa Cardona, David Hsieh**

and Godzilla	as himself
understudy	**David Kobayashi**
Band	**Bruce A. Monroe, David Kobayashi**

Production Crew

Stage Manager	**Kenyetta Carter**
Light Board Operator	**Duane Mortensen**
Sound Board Operator	**Glen Gooding**
Video/Slide Operator	**Elizabeth Eddy**
Poster/Flyer Design	**Roger Tang, Amy Liang, Kathy Hsieh, Rick Wong**
Set Construction Crew	**Melvin Inouye, Peggy McDonald,**

You Can Learn From The Past

You Can Learn From The Past

You Can Learn From The Past

You Can Learn From The Past

You Can Learn From The Past

Imagination goes wild in musical 'Godzilla'

By Joe Adcock
P-I Theater Critic

When Karen Tei Yamashita started writing her musical, chaos and destruction in Los Angeles were merely a fantasy. When she was putting the finishing touches on the show for its premiere tonight in Seattle, fantasy had become reality.

"I live in Gardena, about a mile from the burning and looting in South Central Los Angeles," says Yamashita. "And I work as a secretary at KCET, the public television station. It's in Hollywood. Right across the street was a big Circuit City electronics store. The looting started there early in the middle of the afternoon."

Yamashita's show, "Godzilla Comes to Little Tokyo," premieres tonight at the Theatre Off Jackson, a Northwest Asian American Theatre production. Yamashita wrote the book and the lyrics. Vicki Abe, a classical pianist turned rock musician, wrote the melodies.

The basic situation in Yamashita's

Preview

Godzilla Comes to Little Tokyo. Premiere production of a musical by Karen Tei Yamashita (words) and Vicki Abe (music). Northwest Asian American Theatre production at the Theatre Off Jackson, 409 Seventh Ave. S. Opens tonight and runs through June 28. Tickets $5 for preview, $6-$12 regular run; 340-1049.

version of the Little Tokyo section of downtown Los Angeles entails a borderless eccentric, a running teen-ager, horrendous traffic, pollution, Japanese developers intent on building a vast real estate project over a freeway and avant-garde performers bent on turning the whole festering mess into art. This basic situation is complicated by a visit from Godzilla.

Godzilla is the loved/hated monster who runs amok in Japanese horror movies.

"This is a very high-tech, low-budget

show for us," says Northwest Asian American Theatre manager Kathy Hsieh. "We're lucky to have savvy volunteers. One of our volunteers does video for Boeing, so we can show on TV monitors scenes that would be just impossible on stage."

"I didn't cramp my imagination with the realities of actual putting things on a stage," says Yamashita. "My husband is a Brazilian architect. He has worked with theater sets and lighting. He told me, 'They'll think of something. It's a challenge to the imagination.'"

"So, yes, large chunks of Los Angeles will go flying, but they won't necessarily land in the audience's laps."

"Godzilla is such a perfect metaphor for whatever we fear," Yamashita says. "He can mean Japanese economic power, the forces of nature that are out of control, even the violence in society."

"I can tell you, it was very hard to write a final song when the riots were going on. I mean a musical comedy! It

See 'GODZILLA' Page C6

"Godzilla" cast members, bottom left clockwise: Doug Swenson, Gigi Jhong, Rebecca M. Davis, Steven Boe, David Hsieh, Jennifer L. Michel, Jonathan Te Ho Park.

PERSONALITIES

Conducting Traffic

Karen Tei Yamashita continues her creative odyssey with "giLAwrecks," a theatre piece scheduled at the JACCC.

By CHRIS KOMAI
RAFU CONTRIBUTOR

The music starts up in the George Doizaki Gallery. And stops abruptly. Starts up again. A singer begins a song, then trails off. Director Shizuko Hoshi's voice rattles around the room and the actors turn to listen. "This is the time for dancing," she says.

Playwright and novelist Karen Tei Yamashita, sitting in the foyer, leans her head forward, peeks through the glass doors and then rides back in her chair and smiles. Her first musical, "giLAwrecks," is reaching another stage of development and though there is a winding trail of hard work leading to the Japanese American Cultural and Community Center this weekend, Karen is obviously pleased.

And why not? Besides the stage readings at the JACCC of "giLAwrecks," set for Friday, Aug. 21, at 8 p.m. and Sunday, Aug. 23, at 2 p.m., Yamashita awaits the release of her latest novel, "Brazil-Maru" in September.

"Latest" may be a misnomer, Karen explains, since she began this book long ago.

It was only through the success of her previous novel, "Through the Arc of the Rain Forest," a fantasy

now a Japanese American man named Manzanar, who befriends a runaway girl. A m— the scene from the Relocation Camp s and the homeless ously, has control in-cheek humor ci farcical, fantasy mi to its style, will pr generally accessibl Yamashita's other

The musical's opment was accel by a series of con messages. Abe, w also a computer co ant, had noted an " American topics" s on her computer ne Yamashita and Al gan sending cryptic sages through it, cr challenging statem like "Asian Americ atre is dead." On they got an answe connected with the American Theat prompting the submission of "giLAwrecks" into a contest. The play took first prize, even though the music had yet

Karen and Vicki w vacation to finish could be produced shita crea erial for t as multipl her typew ng out so ll develop aren note me things

shita and

bers, smiling and nodding her head. "I nearly cried when she heard the music, I was so touched."

Interestingly, the feedback given the two collaborators in Seattle suggested that some of the songs had not moved the story in the manner of a Stephen Sondheim ("Pacific Overtures," "Company," "Sweeney Todd"). But, that didn't bother Abe, who is no fan of Sondheim. She

she says.
Karen notes that there is a big difference between writing a short

---

The AFTERHOUR
by GLENN SUGAVICH

Weekend's Best

As part of the Japanese American Cultural and Community Center's Fresh Tracks: Contemporary Performances series, writer Karen Tei Yamashita is scheduled to present "giLAwrecks" this Friday, Aug. 21 at 8 p.m. and Sunday, Aug. 23 at 2 p.m. in the Doizaki Gallery, 244 S. San Pedro St.

The author of "Through the Arc of the Rain Forest" and playwright, Yamashita premiers her latest effort which is a fantasy, futuristic musical play.

The staged reading features an all Asian American cast with original music by Vicki Abe and directed by Shizuko Hoshi.

With tongue-in-cheek humor, Yamashita gives provoking insight into Japanese Americans as an endangered species and our fast-paced modern society.

Tickets for this event are $12 per person for general admission. To charge tickets by phone, call the Japan America Theatre Box Office from noon-5 p.m. daily at (213) 680-3700.

Calendar

June 6, 1990   Seattle Chinese Post   Page 1

Godzilla comes to the L.D.

NWAAT offers a wild ride w/ a serious side

by Tracy Mamoru

Mishaps, imaginative, and stupify editors, "Godzilla comes to Little Tokyo", the new musical co-produced by Karen Tei Yamashita...

[to] Eloise Cardona, Jonathan Park, and David Hsieh star in "Godzilla Comes to Little Tokyo" at the Theatre Off Jackson.

'Godzilla': The destruction of L.A. is in miniature form

From Page C1

seemed so trivial, so irrelevant! But I think some of the need for healing came through in the song. It's a quiet number."

Yamashita is best known as the author of a novel set in Brazil, "Through the Arc of the Rain Forest." She became acquainted with Brazil (and Ronaldo Oliveira, the architect who is now her husband) when she won a grant to study Japanese immigration in Brazil after finishing college. A historical novel about the Japanese in Brazil, "Brazil-Maru" is due out this summer.

"When I decided to write a piece for the theater, I wanted to do something about cities, about Asian experience, something that has the elements I personally like to see on stage: songs, dancing, high drama," says Yamashita.

Besides resorting to video to convey high drama, the production will use miniaturized simulation. "Yes, the audience will see the destruction of Los Angeles," says Hsieh, "but it's a little model we made. Puppeteers will deal with Barbie doll-sized people.

> **"**
> Godzilla is such a perfect metaphor for whatever we fear. He can mean Japanese economic power, the forces of nature that are out of control, even the violence in society.
> — Karen Tei Yamashita

"You won't actually see Godzilla. You'll see the reactions of the actors, very big reactions, so you know something awesome must be going on.

"But we do have a real Godzilla — a model Boeing used for a safety education movie they made. . . . He won't be on stage. He'll be on display in the lobby."

GODZILLA from P. 6

Bring the Universe itself of Japan looking to the destructive escape of World War II. It is this sincerity with which one drops these issues that gives two loose-weight and keeps it from being superficial.

The story gets the the Manzanar, played by Jonathan Te Ho Park, the former person who lives on a well-way psychological agency. A downtown the Sacramento, the traffic forces, heading nearer to the staring of buses and the venting of engines. Here in Japanese romance, Eami Yamashita (Reng), she is a Kabuki, a shift, greets about Japanese Americans, who... bed around from loss into heritage together, should and retain developers, so smart English letters, clay, updates and promises, the watchful eye of the media, and of course Godzilla, they return to terms with their post to, order to enhance their destiny. Both Park and Jhong turn in strong performances but Jhong could stand a few more lessons.

Rebecca M. Davis is convenient to her role as the mayor of Los Angeles and things. Just plays a needy emcee gives us a T. Also adding to this scenic comic tone are founder Michel as young Deborah Harry in appearance, such as "the Solidities of Joshi," an empty historical, fragmentedly music was still being tested to the theater up until the week before unveiling they. This production has a well-progress feel which I'm sure will get tighter as it goes, but the art director, Deacon Terminal Doyle and Choreographer Meg Tanaka seem...

All the camp of a classic Godzilla flick.

TOKYO CARMEN
VERSUS
L.A. CARMEN

■

A Performance Collaboration

Written by Karen Tei Yamashita

Directed/Choreographed by Shizuko Hoshi

Video by Karen Mayeda

Scenery by Ronaldo Lopes de Oliveira and Chris Tashima

■

Performed in June 1990
for the *Thirteenth Hour*
at Taper, Too, Los Angeles

TIME/PLACE

Between today and tomorrow in Tokyo and L.A.

SCENE/PROPS

Slides of Tokyo and L.A. skyline, respectively on American/Japanese flag backdrop skies or some other obvious national symbols (eagle vs. Mt. Fuji, sequoias vs. pines, and so on), painted slides of ukiyo-e/manga mix. Later series of slides of American and Japanese scenes, American and Japanese comics. Thick, white elastic ropes, which can stretch to form a border or borders as in a giant changing comic strip. Layers of painted backdrops in a manga/ukiyo-e style with open holes for actors' heads. Sculptured/distorted mirrors. Ladders, stools, steps to adjust height of actors. Two television monitors: one with Japanese foreign language, American news, ninja shows, and American commercials; the other with American programs dubbed in Japanese language, Japanese news, Japanese baseball, and Japanese commercials.

COSTUMES/MAKEUP

Butoh in style, flamboyant mixtures of flamenco, Gypsy, and yakuza (body tattooing and so on), satin blood reds and blacks, red roses for Carmen. Also requires tie/suit combo for Jiro/Joe and ninja/baseball outfit for Ebizo/Skipper.

MUSIC

From the opera *Carmen*, by Bizet; mixed use of music: flamenco guitar, shamisen, sax, and taiko.

CHARACTERS

NOTE: There should be two sets of characters, one Asian couple and one Caucasian couple—a total of four actors. The Asian male plays Jiro and Ebizo; the Asian female plays Maki and L.A. Carmen. The Caucasian male plays Joe and Skipper; the Caucasian female plays Michele and Tokyo Carmen.

DON JOSE —

JIRO   a samurai who's come to L.A. to be a salary-
       man for a Japanese car company.
JOE   a car salesman who's come to Tokyo to start a
       business in ground-meat vending machines.

ESCAMILLO —

EBIZO   a kabuki actor who's come to L.A. to be a TV
        ninja.
SKIPPER a baseball pitcher who's come to Tokyo to
        play for a Japanese baseball team.

MICAELA —

MAKI   Jiro's wife, who's come to L.A. with her hus-
        band and wants desperately to return to
        Japan to be an education mama.
MICHELE Joe's wife, who's come to Tokyo with her hus-
        band and wants desperately to return to L.A.
        to be a working mother.

CARMEN —

L.A. CARMEN   a geisha who's come to L.A. to be a flamenco
               dancer and runs a sushi bar/front for the
               yakuza.
TOKYO CARMEN   a dancer who's come to Tokyo to be a
               Takarazuka dancer but is a captive of a
               yakuza prostitution ring.

STORY 1: CARMEN IN L.A.

JIRO HAS COME TO L.A. with his wife Maki and his mother, who is sickly. They live in a company house in Torrance. Maki is very lonely and isolated and longs to return to Japan. All her days are spent caring for her sick mother-in-law, taking her to the doctor, cooking, and feeding her. She can't speak English and has no friends, no one to talk to except the old lady and Jiro, who always works late or spends his evenings drinking with his company cronies. Maki wants very much to have a child, but cannot seem to. She cannot understand the doctor's advice to "relax and enjoy her life in America." She thinks the only way she will be able to conceive is if she and Jiro return to Japan.

While out drinking with his coworkers, Jiro meets Carmen, who runs the sushi bar he frequents. Jiro's cronies kid him that he is too pristine; they challenge Carmen to get his attention. Carmen flirts, dances flamenco on the sushi bar; Jiro breaks down.

Carmen's real name is _____, but everyone calls her Carmen because she dances flamenco. Carmen runs with a yakuza crowd. She manages the sushi bar as a front for their activities. Carmen pries secret company information out of Jiro, which she passes on to the yakuza in return for getting the sushi bar put in her name. She thinks that if she is the owner of the sushi bar, she will finally be free in America, free to pursue her career as a flamenco dancer. The leak through Jiro is discovered, and he is fired. He justifies his loss with his love for Carmen. Still, he is distraught over the loss of his job. He is lost in America, in a country where, even after two years, he cannot speak English. He abandons his wife and mother in Torrance and joins the yakuza.

Meanwhile Ebizo, a famous kabuki actor, turns up in L.A. He frequents Carmen's sushi bar. Although he is a well-known actor in Japan, he can't get any work in L.A. except stereotypical roles in commercials and other similar parts. Carmen pins his photographs to the walls of the restaurant: you can see him in all sorts of stereotypical roles: sometimes he is a Chinese gangster; many times he has to do some sort of martial art stuntwork. He and Carmen start to get it on. Jiro is enraged with jealousy. Jiro challenges Ebizo to a duel with Japanese swords, but Maki shows up and interrupts, saying that Jiro's mother is dying in Torrance.

After his mother dies, Jiro returns to the restaurant, despite protests from Maki. Carmen has installed a large television because Ebizo has gotten a break as a ninja on a television series. Everyone in the restaurant is anticipating Ebizo's first appearance on American TV. The show is about to begin. Jiro interrupts everything and makes Carmen come away from the TV. They argue. Carmen doesn't want to return to Japan with Jiro; she is as free as a Gypsy, free to go, do, and dance in America as she pleases. Carmen can hear the exclamations of the audience watching Ebizo as he slashes his opponent on TV. In that same instant, Jiro cuts Carmen down with a samurai sword and Maki runs her car off a Palos Verdes cliff.

STORY 2: CARMEN IN TOKYO

JOE HAS COME TO TOKYO with his wife, Michele, and his mother, who is sickly. They live in a very confined condominium rented at great expense in a neighborhood called Ogikubo. Michele is very lonely and longs to return to L.A. All her days are spent caring for her sick mother-in-law, taking her to the doctor, cooking, and feeding her. She can't speak Japanese and has no friends, no one to talk to except the old lady and Joe, who always works late and has to spend his evenings drinking with his Japanese business associates in order to make deals. Michele wants very much to have a child, but has put that plan on the backburner until she and Joe can return to L.A.

While out drinking with his business colleagues, Joe meets Carmen, who works in a hostess bar in the Ginza. Joe's Japanese colleagues kid him that he is too pristine, that Japan is a man's world and that he should take advantage of that fact. They challenge Carmen to get his attention. Carmen flirts and dances a Japanese striptease on the bar; Joe breaks down.

Carmen is a white slave. She answered an agency ad in *VARIETY* that promised her great money (yen) and a dancing career in Japan. Carmen jumped at the chance to go to Japan to dance and fulfill her dream of joining the Takarazuka, the Japanese version of the Rockettes. However, the agency she dealt with was a front for a yakuza operation aimed at tricking international women into becoming hostesses and prostitutes. The yakuza are withholding her passport and return ticket. When Joe comes into the bar, she immediately tries to get his attention for help. Joe talks with the yakuza bosses and agrees to give them a cut of his meat-vending business for "protection," with the stipulation that they free Carmen. Joe's contacts get wind of this underground deal and pull out of negotiations. Joe's business falls apart. He justifies his loss with his love for Carmen. Still, he is distraught over the loss of his business. He is lost in Japan, in a country where, even after two years, he can hardly speak Japanese. He abandons his wife and mother in Ogikubo and hangs out at the bar to be near Carmen.

Meanwhile Skipper, an American baseball pitcher who has been recruited to a big Japanese team, shows up at the bar. He was a rather unknown second-string major leaguer in the u.s. but is now very famous and popular among the Japanese. He is surrounded by adoring fans and clearly enjoys his newfound fame. His Japanese fans are always talking about Skipper's "concentration." He is instantly infatuated with Carmen, who is tired of Joe, who does nothing but hang around the bar. In addition, since the demise of his business, the yakuza have reneged on granting her freedom. She now turns to Skipper, with whom she is always dancing; she now has plans to dance out the door with the baseball player. Joe is enraged with jealousy. He challenges Skipper to a fistfight, but Michele shows up and interrupts, saying that Joe's mother is dying in Ogikubo.

After his mother dies, Joe returns to the restaurant. Carmen has gotten a large television from Skipper in order to watch him play in the final game of the national championships. Everything depends on Skipper's ability to strike out his opponents. If he does, he will make a lot of money and has promised to run away with Carmen. Joe interrupts everything and makes Carmen come away from the TV. They argue. Carmen doesn't want to have anything more to do with Joe; she dreams of her career as a dancer in Japan with Skipper. Carmen can hear the exclamations of the audience watching Skipper as he strikes out his opponents. In that same instant, Joe bludgeons Carmen with a baseball bat, and Michele jumps onto the tracks of an oncoming bullet train.

OPENING/OVERTURE

The Asian couple stands before the Tokyo skyline cast against the Japanese flag, or some other obvious symbol of their homeland. The Caucasian couple stands before an L.A. skyline cast against the American flag, or some other obvious symbol of their homeland. Both scenes are framed by white elastic borders to give the effect of a cartoon strip. Both couples have heavy suitcases. They turn to face each other and walk/fly (maybe by way of TWA/JAL) across the stage, passing each other and stepping into their opposing territories. All clothing, costumes, and props necessary for staging is packed into their suitcases, which they open and close to retrieve necessary bits and pieces. Their suitcases are always around because they are people in transit, temporary visitors, temporarily putting off the real plans of their lives to be in foreign environments.

SLIDES: Painted slides of Tokyo and L.A. scenes.

Actors put on demon horns/masks of both a western style and a Japanese style. They play alternately at being bulls and toreadors.

MUSIC: Overture to *Carmen*

ACT I: MICAELA

SCENE

Slides of Tokyo and L.A. are on separate sides of the stage: home interiors, out-side crowds, comparing Ogikubo to Torrance. There are two television mon-itors onstage. One shows a continuous stream of Japanese-language TV, American commercials, and so on. The other shows a continuous stream of American shows dubbed in Japanese, Japanese commercials, and so on.

Maki is bordered by very large borders, which seem to make her distant and small, while Michele is squeezed between her borders (sometimes as small as her face or lips), having to press on them and struggle to talk within very small confines.

MAKI: I came with my husband, Jiro, and my mother-in-law to live in L.A. My husband said it is his duty to sell as many cars in America as possible; otherwise, he will be demoted and return to Japan dishonorably.

MICHELE: I came with my husband, Joe, and my mother-in-law to live in Tokyo. Back in L.A., my husband was a respectable car salesman. Now he's a soldier in the trade war. We've come to Tokyo to infiltrate the market.

MAKI: My husband, Jiro, works very hard. I never see him any-more.

MICHELE: This business of Joe's is really innovative. He's selling ground meat to the Japanese in vending machines. My Joe says it is his patriotic duty to sell as many meat-vending machines in Japan as possible.

MAKI: All day, I am in this big American house in Torrance. I should be grateful. There are four bedrooms and three bathrooms and a big living room, big kitchen, big wash-ing machine, big dishwasher, and giant refrigerator. There is a TV in every room. I have a big American car to go to Giant supermarket. I should be very happy.

MICHELE: I never thought I'd ever be living in such an itty-bitty house; everywhere you turn, you bump into something. The bathroom is so small you can only take a bath if you close this door, but you can't use the toilet unless you open the door. I'm getting this claustrophobia thing where I think the walls of my mind are closing in on me. You can't get away from it even when you step outside. Out there, it's wall-to-wall Japanese.

MAKI: My mother-in-law is very sick, but she made the sacrifice for Jiro to come to L.A. I try to make her happy by feeding her Japanese food, but she doesn't talk so much. She is watching Japanese TV, channel eighteen or fifty-six, or sleeping all day. I cannot leave her alone, so I am watching TV all day too.

MICHELE: Joe's mom made the trip with us. She was a real trooper till she got here, fell, broke her hip, and got laid up. I do my best to keep her happy, but I'm having a heck of time finding anything she'd like to eat. Lately, she doesn't talk much. All day long she stares at the TV; can't understand a word, just stares.

MAKI: I am also sometimes practicing my tea ceremony, which I learned before I got married. I don't want to forget in case we go back to Japan.

MICHELE: I've been trying to learn Japanese from watching American programs on TV, but I'm not getting anywhere fast. It's all dubbed. I don't know why they do that; the Japanese could be learning English.

MAKI: It is my greatest dream to return to Japan to become education mama.

MICHELE: It's my ideal to become a working mother.

MAKI: I wish to have a boy to nurse and feed . . .

MICHELE: I wanna take maternity leave to have a boy . . .

MAKI: and when he goes to school, to send him off every morn-
             ing with a good meal . . .

MICHELE: then I wanna work full-time and leave him at the sitter's
             and daycare . . .

MAKI: and then to pick him up from school and to take him to
             English lessons, piano lessons, tennis lessons, math les-
             sons, swimming lessons . . .

MICHELE: and be able to rush out of my job on the excuse that my
             son has a doctor's appointment, or that I should attend a
             PTA meeting, or to hear him play the cymbals in the
             school orchestra.

MAKI: to violin lessons, judo, baseball, to help him with all his
             homework, and to follow him every step of the way to
             ensure his success in life, and to urge him on to study to
             enter a famous university.

MICHELE: I would rush home every day from work to cook his
             favorite dinner—macaroni and cheese—play a game of
             Nintendo, help him with his homework, get him in and
             out of his bath, read him a story; in short, give quality
             time every evening of his childhood life.

MAKI: Well, we came to L.A. We are lonely, but Jiro works too
             hard to notice. At first I call my mother on the phone all
             the time, but I have nothing new to tell her. I got lonely
             hearing about home and my old friends all having babies,
             all becoming education mamas.

MICHELE: Well, I gotta put that working-mother plan on a back-
             burner till we get back to L.A. This place is too small.
             No family room. No big yard with grass to cut and a
             swing set. How're you supposed to raise kids like this?
             I'll be lucky to fit a bassinet in here.

MAKI: I felt sad. Jiro's mother doesn't say much; there is no one to talk to. I begin to forget how to talk.

MICHELE: I tell Joe I'm not getting any younger, but he's too busy fighting the trade war. When he comes home, he practically slumps over and snores right there in the door with the shoes. And we got no privacy. You got no incentive with your mother-in-law right over there on the other side of the rice paper.

MAKI: I go to doctor. The doctor says nothing wrong with me. Nothing wrong with Jiro. Just we got to be patient, got to relax. Maybe we got to have sex too.

MICHELE: I get letters from home saying so-and-so had a baby or got pregnant, and I get really depressed. All I'm doing is counting the days till this trade war is over.

MAKI: Jiro only comes home to sleep. The doctor says we got to get a vacation, see America, enjoy life. Jiro is too busy. Work is first. Play later. Jiro doesn't want to have baby in America; then baby will be American, lose Japanese ways, be weak in competition, lose trade war. I am waiting every day for war to end, go back to Japan, have my baby, and raise my son.

MUSIC: I say no danger shall stay me.

ACT II: DRAGOONS

SCENE

Background slides of Tokyo and L.A. and other descriptive material show-ing trade merchandise and company emblems (for example, Honda versus Ford, Mitsubishi, IBM). Also book covers of the sensationalist Japan trade conspiracy sort, comics of Astro Boy versus Superman or Batman, news pho-tos and caricatures of Kaifu and Bush, Sony's Morita, and so on. The tele-visions show American and Japanese newscasts of stock-market reports (Dow versus Nikkei), clips of politicians spewing anti-Japan platforms (Gebhardt), and so on.

JIRO: I have been with the company since I graduated Keio University. I have been promoted every year and moving up in the company. Finally I was sent to the L.A. office. This was a big opportunity and responsibility for me, to be sent to the front.

JOE: I got into exporting ground meat to Japan because I figure I ought to do something for my country. Before I had it real good, selling cars. I admit, I made a lot a money selling Hondas and Toyotas and Nissans. Then I got to thinking about this trade imbalance . . .

(The following list of trade imbalance statements is divided back and forth between all four actors.)

> In Japan, everybody gets a cut of the action; this keeps everyone happy and working.
> In Japan, everybody gets a cut of the action; this makes American goods too expensive to buy.
> Japan's protectionist policy keeps American goods out.
> America's open-door policy keeps cheap goods flowing in.
> Japan has beat America at its own game; it's out-capital-ized the capitalists.

Americans don't want to pay high prices to keep industries at home. They want low prices and cheap third-world labor.

The average Japanese high school student scores better than the average American college student.

American youth have no backbone and are on drugs.

Japan is a closed society that does not produce free or imaginative thinkers.

Japan is a mimicking society; they copy American technology.

Japan doesn't just copy; it makes it better.

Americans look for short-term results.

Japanese look for long-term results.

American industry is poorly managed.

The Japanese are sinking money into robotics.

America's deficit is in the trillions.

The Japanese work longer hours.

The Japanese provide better benefits for their employees.

America is the biggest debtor nation in the world.

The American bond market is supported by the Japanese.

Japan doesn't pay for its own defense.

America spends too much on defense.

America has shoddy merchandise.

Japan is a racist country.

America is a racist country.

Japanese consumers subsidize their foreign markets.

The yen is overvalued.

The dollar has lost its strength.

The Japanese are buying up downtown L.A.

America for Americans.

Japan for Japanese.

It's the way of the free market.

Americans should stop being crybabies.

Americans should compete.

Americans should fight.

JOE: I was eating a hamburger at the time, and I thought hamburgers could be the answer to the trade imbalance.

If I could sell cars, I could sell hamburger. So I threw everything I had into it and set up business here in Tokyo.

JIRO: I have with me here my wife. She stays happy all day in this big company house in Torrance. Torrance has Japanese business, Yaohan supermarket, sushi restaurant, Japanese garden, Japanese language school, and Japanese American people. However, Torrance is not Japan.

JOE: Course I did some studying before I came, took a course in Japanese and Japanese business practices, researched the market, read everything. I know if I can make a dent in this imbalance, I'll be doing something. Else we'll lose the trade wars and become an economic satellite of Japan.

JIRO: My wife takes care of my mother. That's the way it should be—taking care of your parents when they get old. My wife is very busy this way. This is good activity for her.

JOE: I got Michele and my mother cooped up in this tiny place in Ogikubo. They don't complain 'cuz there's less to clean up after. Michele and Mom are real troopers. They know how important this is to me and to the future.

JIRO/JOE: Even when I got to stay out all night, Michele/Maki never complains. I know I got married to a trooper/old-fashioned type. That is the way it should be.

MUSIC: Dragoons

ACT III: HABANERA

SCENE

Backdrop slides of Tokyo and L.A. nightlife: Ginza/Shinjuku, sushi bars, hostess bars, karaoke, dancing, Takarazuka, flamenco, and bon odori. Ukiyo-e and cartoons of an erotic nature.

TOKYO CARMEN/L.A. CARMEN:
      Good girls.
      Bad girls.
      Good girls.
      Bad girls.
      Good girls.
      Bad girls.
      Good girls.
      Bad girls.

JIRO: Some of my colleagues are saying, "Jiro, you're too serious. Live it up; enjoy your freedom in America."

JOE: My Japanese associates all tell me I'm too serious. In Japan, you gotta mix pleasure and work. "Live it up," they say. "It's a man's world."

TOKYO CARMEN/L.A. CARMEN:
      Live it up. Enjoy your freedom in America. Live it up. Mix pleasure with work. It's a man's world. Live it up. Live it up. Live it up. It's a man's world. It's a man's world. Live it up.

      Omae, kite kite/Listen, sweetheart—
      Let me tell my story—

L.A. CARMEN: I am from a small village in the north of Japan. I never liked it there—too cold and too poor. As soon as I could, I ran away to Tokyo, and one day, I got to see this Spanish dancer. I never saw something so beautiful. At that moment, I decided to be a flamenco dancer.

TOKYO CARMEN: I had this dream to come to Japan. Everything I had ever
                known that was Japanese I adored. I adored the little col-
                ored paper umbrellas in the Shirley Temples. I adored
                the little cats in the curio stores, with their little paws
                beckoning you in. I adored Japanese food. I adored the
                kimonos and the fans. I even adored the men.

L.A. CARMEN: I looked everywhere to find a flamenco teacher. I studied
                until I was better than my teacher; then I found a way to
                leave Japan. I didn't have any money, so I made a deal to
                work for the yakuza in this L.A. sushi bar.

TOKYO CARMEN: I took Japanese lessons and Japanese dance classes. I was
                even in the Little Tokyo Nisei Week parade, dancing bon
                odori. I had this idea I could get to Japan to dance. I
                heard about a Japanese Rockette troupe called the
                Takarazuka. I thought they might be able to use some
                legs like mine.

L.A. CARMEN: I'm smart. I learn English fast. Pretty soon, I'm working
                as the manager, running everything, telling these sushi-
                makers what to do, dividing their pay. And I do my
                flamenco lessons every day.

TOKYO CARMEN: So when I saw the agency ad in *VARIETY* recruiting
                dancers for a Japanese stint, I thought this was my
                chance. But it was a scam. Sure, I was supposed to dance,
                but I was supposed to dance with Japanese men who
                would pay good money to dance with a white woman.
                Then you begin to get the picture—it wasn't just dancing
                they wanted; all these horny little Japanese men were try-
                ing to get some white ass.

L.A. CARMEN: Now I want my own place, maybe sushi bar or restaurant
                with dance floor. And we gonna all dance flamenco.

TOKYO CARMEN: When I protested, they told me I had signed a contract,
                but if I wanted to leave, fine. But there was a catch: they

had my passport; they had my money; and they were watching me all the time.

L.A. CARMEN: Why do I love flamenco? It is passion, love, very intense, very sexy, very free. It comes with the Gypsy life.

TOKYO CARMEN: So when I saw Joe walk through that door, I think to myself, thank God, an American. But, of course, I couldn't just run up to him and spill my story. So I kinda sidle up to the group and make some suggestions about Joe, tease them into betting if white men like their women Japanese or white.

L.A. CARMEN: When I see Jiro, I think, here is a strong man. He doesn't even look.

TOKYO CARMEN: Joe looks at me like he's embarrassed to notice another American—especially a woman—in a place like this. But I need him to more than notice, so I really turn on the fire.

L.A. CARMEN: I think to myself, I will make this good salaryman see me.

TOKYO CARMEN: I've got to make him come back. I've got to make him remember.

L.A. CARMEN: I will make him remember Carmen.

TOKYO CARMEN: I've got to slip this message down his pants.

Both Tokyo Carmen and L.A. Carmen dance on the bars and sing habanera, enchanting their respective men.

MUSIC: Habanera

JIRO/JOE: What is it you want from me?

L.A. CARMEN: Just a little information I can sell.

JIRO: I am a loyal company employee. I don't give away company secrets.

L.A. CARMEN: Not for Carmen? Everything is confidential.

TOKYO CARMEN: I need your help to make a deal for me.

JOE: Hey babe, I got a trade imbalance to fight.

TOKYO CARMEN: Honey, open your eyes. You see the trade imbalance right here. I wasn't traded! I was stolen! It takes a man to steal me back.

JIRO: What will I get in return?

L.A. CARMEN: You will get Carmen. I will get this sushi bar. I will finally be free in America!

JOE: Those bastards've got no right to mess with an American woman.

TOKYO CARMEN: So give them a protection cut to drive your competition out of Tokyo. Think of it. You, all alone in Tokyo, your meat-vending machines everywhere.

JOE: No. I gotta do it right, the American way. I gotta compete fair and square.

TOKYO CARMEN: Get real. This is war. What is fair? And on whose turf? This is Japan. Give 'em their cut, and they'll let Carmen go free.

JIRO: What do you want to know?

L.A. CARMEN: Any little company secret. You work for Honda? We sell it to Toyota. You work for Toyota? We sell it to Nissan.

You work for Nissan? We sell it to Mazda. You work for Mazda? We sell it to Acura. After all, they're all Japanese companies.

JIRO: No. Never.

L.A. CARMEN: Never?

JIRO: I gave her everything. My company found out. They fired me. It is a disgrace. I cannot go back to Japan, can never face my family and colleagues again. I did it all for Carmen. Now, I am lost in America like another immigrant without hope of return. I leave my wife and mother in Torrance. Leave everything for Carmen.

JOE: I gave her everything. My Japanese business connections all found out. They killed our deals. I can never get another deal in Japan. I did it all for Carmen. Now, I'm lost in Japan like one more homeless gaijin. I left my wife and mom in Ogikubo. Left everything for Carmen

ACT IV: TOREADOR

SCENE

Slides of Japanese baseball, toreadors, Ebizo in various stereotypical costumes (ninja, fu man chu, and so on), and Skipper in baseball card poses. The televisions show clips of baseball and Asian stereotypes in commercials.

EBIZO: In Japan, I am a great actor. I play Kabuki, film, TV, theater. I play Shakespeare, Molière, and Chekov. I have great charm and handsome. All women love me, but I am not just pretty boy; I am man. I play samurai, daimyo, modern man, cowboy, king, politician, general. I do great tragedy. I do comedy. In Japan they say I am the new Mifune. "Ebizo, Ebizo," everyone is crying.

SKIPPER: Ever since I was a kid, I've played ball. Only thing I know how to do. So when I got outta school, I got recruited easy to the leagues, but I got tired of being a second-stringer. They wouldn't put me up to pitch, and I wasn't getting any younger.

EBIZO: Now the world is growing bigger than Japan. I conquer Japan; now America. I come to L.A. Hollywood. This is great adventure.

SKIPPER: So when the Japanese came around and made me a deal I couldn't refuse, I left. I figure, Japan is the economic future. I got no argument with that. These people are honest, hardworking people. You don't hear about crime here, homeless people on the streets. You can leave your expensive stuff on a train seat, come back, and it'll still be there.

EBIZO: But, America strange place. So many different people living here: white, brown, black, yellow. So many Asian people like me, but no Asian people on film and TV. No international sensitivity. I fighting this all the time.

SKIPPER: I like my life here. Oh, I miss some things, sure. I'm like any true-blooded American. I miss the Fourth of July and my apple pie. I miss the space, places like the Grand Canyon and those wide-open prairies.

EBIZO: I get agent, but agent say, "Ebizo, what can you do?" I say, "I do Macbeth. I do Tennessee Williams. I do Beckett." But he says, "No no, can you do a little judo or tai chi? If you lose a little weight, you might be good for Vietnamese part. Grow a fu man chu, and we use you in Chinatown scene."

SKIPPER: But I'm lucky. Baseball field's the same size here as back home. I get to stand in the middle of a big field in a big stadium. I get my stretching room.

EBIZO: I gotta do TV commercial, bc Japanese salaryman buying American car. I gotta be Japanese gardener eating American hamburger. I gotta take Japanese sword and cut cucumber demonstrate food processor.

SKIPPER: There's no baseball crowd like the Japanese. These are fans to rival any back home. They come with banners, hats, and songs. The other day, they all sang me a song. Coach came out to the mound to tell me. I didn't know what to do; I was so touched. When it was finished, I bowed. And get this: they all bowed back! That's why I do my damnedest for this team.

EBIZO: First time I see Carmen, I know this woman is fighter like me. We dance flamenco together. A man like me needs a woman like Carmen.

SKIPPER: I had some Japanese girlfriends for a while, but the hard thing is not being able to talk. When I met Carmen, we just hit it off, talked all night about everything. Exile talk, you know. What I admire about Carmen is she's been through hell in Japan, and she still wants to give it

	another try. A woman with spunk. I'm gonna make it all up to her, take her away from here and show her the real Japan.
MUSIC:	Toreador's Song
JOE:	Here I go and ruin my life for you, and how do you repay me? You take up with a two-bit, minor-league, second-stringer, can't hold a bat to the real thing, gotta come here and play yellow ball.
TOKYO CARMEN:	What do you know of baseball, you meatball? Sitting around here feeling sorry for yourself. I'm tired of it.
JIRO:	Who is this pretty Kabuki actor who's finished in Japan? Has to come to America to make a living. What a sorry career, pandering to the Americans.
L.A. CARMEN:	Look at you, sulking here day after day. You haven't shaved. You stink. You are always drunk. I am sick of it.
JOE:	Carmen, I love you. How can you do this to me?
TOKYO CARMEN:	We are a silly pair of gaijin. Don't have the guts to walk out on this situation. You think I'm going anywhere with you? What a mistake I made.
JIRO:	Carmen, why do you treat me this way? I have given up everything for you. It is the ultimate insult.
L.A. CARMEN:	You are a fool. You can't keep a woman like me. If you love me, leave me.
JIRO/JOE:	You'll be sorry. I'll kill this guy!

They start to fight.

MAKI/MICHELE:	Stop! Please stop!

JIRO/JOE: Maki?/Michele? What are you doing here?

MAKI/MICHELE: I know you have left me for this other woman. But I have not come here to plead for myself. I have come here to plead for your poor dying mother. Jiro/Joe, your poor mother is dying in that big house/little place in Torrance/Ogikubo.

JIRO/JOE *runs out.*

MAKI: He has gone to see his mother. What will I do now, alone in this big country? I will throw myself over the cliffs of Palos Verdes. Better to be dead in the great sea, my bones drifting out over the Pacific, back to my home.

MICHELE: He has gone to see his mother. When he gets there, she'll be dead. If he looks for me, he can find me pressed against the hard nose of a bullet train. They say that train gets up to over two hundred miles an hour. I'll be speeding, pieces of me scattering all over Japan, just like Joe dreamed.

ACT V: VIVA VIVA

SCENE

The death scene. The slides are painted manga-style. The televisions show chambara/ninja slash-and-kill scenes and scenes of Japanese baseball crowds.

JIRO/JOE: Carmen, I'm back.

TOKYO CARMEN/L.A. CARMEN:
                 Fool. Go away.

JIRO/JOE: Carmen, you don't know what you are saying. You are killing me. You are killing us.

TOKYO CARMEN/L.A. CARMEN:
                 Can't you see, Ebizo/Skipper is on TV.

JIRO/JOE: Carmen, come away with me. I am going to start over again. I'm going to show them the true man that I am, but I cannot do it without you.

TOKYO CARMEN/L.A. CARMEN:
                 Fool. What is it now? Still fighting a war? And who is the enemy, I say? Who is the enemy?

JIRO/JOE *kills* TOKYO CARMEN/L.A. CARMEN.

MUSIC: Finale: Viva Viva

One television continues showing a ninja fight scene with swords and lots of blood. The other shows a Japanese baseball game, with a telecaster yelling excitedly over the cheers of the crowd. The slides, still done in cartoon fashion, show Maki driving her car off the Palos Verdes cliffs and falling to her death. Simultaneously, Michele jumps in front of a bullet train.

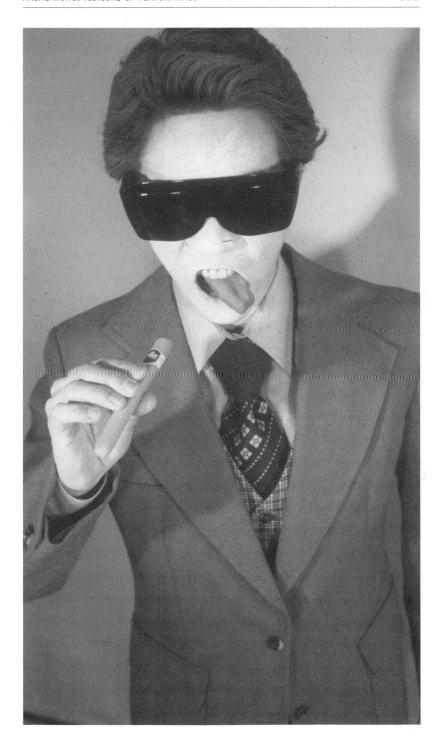

TOKYO CARMEN VS. L.A. CARMEN

Written and Conceived by KAREN TEI YAMASHITA
Directed and Developed by SHIZUKO HOSHI

KAREN MAYEDA, Video Artist
RONALDO L. OLIVEIRA, Set Designer
CHRIS TASHIMA, Technical Consultant
KEONE YOUNG, Production Consultant

Ensemble: VICTOR CHEW, TIMOTHY DANG, SALA IWAMATSU, MIMOSA, SUSAN NAKAGIRI, KEONE YOUNG

SHIZUKO HOSHI. After graduating from Tokyo Women's College in Japan, Shizuko Hoshi came to the United States to study at the University of Southern California where she received a B.A. and an M.A. in dance, and became an instructor for five years. As a recipient of a Ford Foundation grant, Shizuko returned to Japan to study classical Japanese Theatre. She has choreographed for the Taper's Improvisational Theatre Project and for East West Players for musicals such as Godspell, A Chorus Line, and Pacific Overtures (for which she won a Drama-Logue Award). She co-directed Philip Kan Gotanda's A Song for a Nisei Fisherman at the Taper's New Theatre For Now festival and has received Drama-Logue Awards for her direction for Hokusai, Reshomon and Asagakimashita.

KAREN TEI YAMASHITA. A graduate of Carleton College in Northfield, Minnesota in English and Japanese literature, Karen also lived and traveled in Japan for two years while studying at Waseda University. In 1977, she received a Rockefeller playwright-in-residence fellowship with the East West Players in Los Angeles to write and produce her play Omen: An American Kabuki. In 1974, Karen traveled to Brazil on a Thomas J. Watson fellowship to research the history and anthropology of Japanese immigration to Brazil. She lived and raised a family there for the next 10 years. Based on her experiences during that time, she has recently completed a novel Through the Arc of the Rain Forest, to be published by Coffee House Press this fall.

Acknowledgments:
Michael S. Yamashita for photographs of Japan.

Special Thanks to Steve James and Jane Boltz.

DOWNTOWN

Written and Performed by LUIS ALFARO
in collaboration with TOM DENNISON

LUIS ALFARO grew up in the Pico-Union district of downtown Los Angeles. He was honored by the California State Senate for his theatre work and this year is the recipient of a Brody Arts Fellowship. Most notable among the ten works Luis has written and performed in the last two years is True Stories From The Corner Of Pico & Union. Along with Tom Dennison and Mary Tamaki, he has created La Loca, Gateway To L.A., 'Til Death Do Us Part and Nectar. The three artists frequently help each other at LACE, Highways Performance Space, Zeta Theatre, Pipeline and on tour.

INSTRUMENTS OF DECISION

Conceived by DAN KWONG in collaboration with WILLIAM ROPER
Written by DAN KWONG and WILLIAM ROPER

DAN KWONG is a Los Angeles native who received his BFA from the Art Institute of Chicago long, long ago. Aside from being a lifelong mutant sports jock, he has also studied judo, tai chi chu'an, aikido and iaido. Since spring of this year, Dan has been touring with his full-length solo multi-media performance work, Secrets of the Samurai Centerfielder, to various colleges and festivals. The piece will also be presented in Los Angeles at East West Players August 2–5. The following weekend, August 10 and 11, he will perform Boy Story at the Japanese American Cultural Center Doizaki Gallery. Instruments of Decision marks his first collaborative work and continues his current interest in using autobiographical references for communicating broader issues of social conditioning and cultural awareness.

WILLIAM ROPER began his early training in his native city of Los Angeles. He continued his studies at institutions in Cleveland, Pittsburgh and New York. Musically, William's experience ranges from the symphony stage to free improvisational ensembles. He has toured the U.S., Canada and Europe with both jazz and classical ensembles. His musicianship is represented on recordings with Thelonious Monster and The Fibonaccis, poet Jimmy Townes, the new music ensemble Motor Totemist Guild, and with jazz trombonist John Rapson, among others. His recent efforts have been concentrated in the dance, theater and performance art fields. In addition to his own works he has collaborated with such artists as Betty Nash, Scott Kelman, John Fleck, Will Salmon, Jackie Apple, Anna Homler, Eve Stabolepsey, Joseph Mitchell, Jeff McMahon and Bob Carroll.

Music: Gavotte by Rodger Vaughan.

Recorded Music by David Hykes and The Harmonic Choir; The John Rapson Octet.

THE TOWER OF BABEL

Created, Composed and Directed by
JAN A. P. KACZMAREK

Ensemble:
DON CHEADLE,
JAN A. P. KACZMAREK,
PERI KACZMAREK,
MAREK PROBOSZ,
LAUREN TOM

JAN A. P. KACZMAREK has written music for more than forty productions in Poland and Europe. He recently composed music for 'Tis a Pity She's a Whore, directed by JoAnne Akalaitis at the Goodman Theatre in Chicago. He served as a resident composer for the Taper Lab '89 New Work Festival, produced by Robert Egan. As founder of the Orchestra of the Eighth Day he performed 13 major tours, playing in Europe and the United States. He recently appeared at Queen Elizabeth Hall in London and at the Radio Nederland Contemporary Music Festival in Amsterdam. The composer of music for twenty films, his most recent credits include Janusz Zaorski's Coming Home and V. V. Dachin Hsu's Pale Blood. Jan's solo albums include Music for the End, At the Last Gate, Waiting for Hailey's Comet and the soon-to-be-released Seven Dances for the New World.

Special Thanks to Bob Ezrin, Beth Donohue, Marek Stabrowski, Jerzy Krajewski, Paul Vangelisti and Nancy Knutsen.

Each time the Taper engages in the process of developing new work, we become aware of artists with whom we have not yet had the chance to work — artists with a wealth of diverse performance experience quite distinct from our usual presentations.

In developing The 13th Hour project, we wanted to introduce to Taper audiences these kind of artists, artists whose work is about exploring music, literary and performing arts forms. We hope that by having shared our resources with them and by providing an opportunity for them to collaborate with one another, this showcase event will serve not only as the beginning of a dialogue between the Taper and these performance artists, but also to broaden our and your contact with a diversity of performance styles.

Corey Beth Madden
Robin McKee
Josephine Ramirez

AN ARMY OF HEALERS

Written and Conceived by KAMAU DAA'OOD in collaboration
with KAREN MCDONALD, DADISI SANYIKA, SONSHIP THEUS and MUNYUNGO

Ensemble: KAMAU DAA'OOD, Performance Poet; KAREN MCDONALD, Dancer/Choreographer;
DADISI SANYIKA, Martial Artist; SONSHIP THEUS, percussionist; MUNYUNGO, percussionist

KAMAU DAA'OOD, performance poet, educator and community arts activist is a native of Los Angeles. He is a seasoned performer of literally hundreds of readings, whose work is published in two books of poetry and numerous publications. Kamau was the subject of an award-winning film Life is a Saxophone in 1985. An Army of Healers began as a video short produced by KCET and was included as part of Songs of the City which was nominated for two Emmys. A former member of the Watts writers workshop, Kamau has been dubbed "the word musician" because of his unique style and frequent work with musicians. He has been a California Arts Council grant recipient, as well as an honoree of the USC Master of Professional Writing Program. He currently runs The World Stage, a performance space in Los Angeles and is on staff at the Watts Towers Arts Center.

There will be one intermission.

NOH BOZOS

A Circus Performance
in Ten Amazing Acts

Written by Karen Tei Yamashita

Directed and choreographed by Shizuko Hoshi

Music composed by Glenn Horiuchi

■

Performed in August 1993
at the Japanese American Cultural and Community Center

NOH BOZOS
A CIRCUS PERFORMANCE IN TEN AMAZING ACTS

OPENING
Celerymen/Noh Bozos/The Struggle for Culture

ACT I
In Limbo/Gardena Gothic

ACT II
The Bad Rap

ACT III
The Glass Ceiling

ACT IV
Fly by Chopsticks/Freaks of Nature

ACT V
The Heads

INTERLUDE
The Noh Bozo Award Presentation

ACT VI
God's Gift to Asian American Women

ACT VII
The Bearded Lady

ACT VIII
The Moyashi Maru

ACT IX
Transformer Sushi

ACT X
Karaoke

CLOSING
Out of Limbo

PRE-OPENING

ACTORS/DANCERS
At least, five Asian American men.

MUSICIANS
A group equipped to play a mixture of Japanese traditional music, jazz, and some circus stunt percussion/background.

SCENE
The scene—extending into the audience—is a tent of the circus sort with definite elements of the Noh stage. (Perhaps the show *is* performed in a tent.) A palm tree (bonsaied) is painted into one layer of the background, or it may be projected. A sort of Noh ramp, decorated with pine trees (may be stylized and lit with lights), slides down into the main stage area. At the end of the ramp is a curtain that slides across a pole in Noh fashion. Perhaps there is a circus ring to denote the stage, round colorful stands, a trapeze, and other hanging paraphernalia.

Somewhere in a conspicuous place, there are the words: *This performance was made possible by a generous grant from the L.A. City Cultural Affairs Department.* (This notice should repeat in various places, including on slides, video, programs, and costumes.)

There is both the festive air of a circus and the solemn air of a Noh ceremony. Noh Bozo T-shirts are sold in the lobby. There are peanut and musubi vendors.

Musicians enter through a small passageway at the side of the stage. They enter with forced ceremony but end up being loud and noisy, carting in a mixture of instruments, both of a classical Japanese nature and of American jazz.

OPENING: CELERYMEN/NOH BOZOS/THE STRUGGLE FOR CULTURE

SCENE

The curtain on the ring slides back with a scrape. The traditional Noh percussion announces the beginning. Actors move in slowly at a Noh pace (as much as they can stand) down the ramp. They are all wearing suits, ties, Noh masks (masks may be traditional; some may be molded plastic with lights behind the eyes), red bozo hair, bozo shoes. They all carry briefcases. They are white-faced, as in Butoh. Noh Bozos are dead but in limbo.

Starts with Buddhist chant and moves into:

ALL: Noh Bozos
               Noh Bozos
               Noh Bozos
               Noh noh noh noh
               Noh noh noh noh
               Bohzohs
               Bohzohs
               Bohzohs
               Noh noh noh noh
               Noh noh noh noh
               Noh Bozos
               Noh Bozos
               Noh Bohzohs

PRIEST: Mukashi mukashi, a long time ago, sansei roamed the Southland. In those days, L.A. was still a rich and fertile concrete desert, and the sansei were in control. Yes, that's right, sansei gangs with territorial rights to everything in sight. To the south: Gardena. To the west: the Westside. To the east: the Eastside. To the north: the Valley. In those days, everyone wanted to be . . .

NOH BOZOS: (*in unison*) Buddhahead.

PRIEST: Examining the distinctive sansei culture of these early years, we travel to the southern regions of the L.A. basin.

Here at the crossroads of the 405 and the 110, made balmy
by the swishing traffic, you might have met the *Gardena
Bro*.

GARDENA BRO: Hey, what? This bro from the big island, yeah. My family's been in Gardena as long you can remember, but
home is still Hawaii. Well, Gardena–Hawaii, Hawaii–
Gardena, what's the diff?

PRIEST: Moving in a northerly direction to a region designated
as the Westside, scientists note the cultivation of another
species of sansei, the *Westside Dude*.

WESTSIDE DUDE: The true mark of the Westside (*makes hand sign*) Dude
was our righteous dancing. Westside movement was so
impressive, some people thought Marvin Gaye was a
Buddhahead.

PRIEST: Heading just east of the L.A. River, the very tips of the
L.A. horizon scraping our sunny brows, we come to the
ancient land of the *Eastside Homeboy*.

EASTSIDE HOMEBOY:
                 If it's East, it's east where the sun rises, East L.A. This
homey rides with the rest of them: low.

PRIEST: Cruising the hills northward, the valley spreads itself over
the landscape like one continuous giant minimall, once
the grazing grounds of that sansei of upward mobility,
the *Valley Boy*.

VALLEY BOY: Mine was the first Japanese American family to move to
the Valley. That's right. This sansei integrated Van Nuys.
Hey, don't get me wrong. Integration works. Until as
recently as 1986, I thought I was white.

PRIEST: (*insert background music*) Ladies and gentlemen. Welcome
to Noh Bozos, a brotherhood in limbo. Sansei limbo. Not

to be confused with nisei limbo, which is a true limbo between that which is Japanese and that which is American. No, sansei limbo is a murky, undefined space between the Westside and the Eastside, between Gardena and the Valley. Somewhere in the middle, the struggle for culture continues.

NOH BOZOS *all pass under a horizontal bar in limbo style, one after another, over and over again, as the height of the bar is decreased by inches. The exercise of the limbo becomes more and more athletic and strenuous.*

ALL: Noh Bozos
                Noh Bozos
                Noh Bozos
                Noh noh noh noh
                Noh noh noh noh
                Bohzohs
                Bohzohs
                Bohzohs
                Noh noh noh noh
                Noh noh noh noh
                Noh Bozos
                Noh Bozos
                Noh Bohzohs

PRIEST *presides at limbo, chanting in a ritualistic manner. Eventually,* PRIEST *rips off priestly garb and becomes* MASTER OF CEREMONIES, *or* MC.

ACT I: IN LIMBO/GARDENA GOTHIC

MC: Gardena! Someone called it the armpit of Asian Amer-
                 ica . . .

This statement appears on the video: SOMEONE CALLED IT THE ARMPIT OF
ASIAN AMERICA. GARDENA. GARDENA!

GARDENA BRO: You know, you got culture here in Gardena. Spot Market.
              Motoyama Market. Meiji Market. Marukai. Long as you
              got the food, you got the culture. Then you got the noo-
              dle joints. Hey, noodles are important. No noodles, no
              culture. And the brother eats noodles, yeah. Better yet,
              you got the bowling alleys *with* the restaurants *with* the
              noodles. The brother bowls and eats noodles, yeah. Then
              you still got a few gambling joints, but better yet, you
              know Nisei Charters? Bus picks up the bro's mom at
              Meiji Market. Puts her up at the California Club. Get
              some local motion. Twenty-four-hour turnaround: Gar-
              dena-Vegas-Gardena.

Video/slide visuals of Gardena appear.

          Chant/Song
          "Gardena Gothic"

          On a knoll in a strawberry patch,
          an immigrant wiped his brow.
          Looking out as far as the eye can see.
          To the south, the sea, the peninsula.
          To the west, Japan, Hawaii.
          But, at his feet, Gardena.

          *Asian armpits never sweat. Oh no.
          Asian armpits never sweat. Oh no.
          Working overtime. No sweat. You bet.
          The hard life. No sweat. You bet.

From a knoll in a strawberry patch,
an immigrant was hauled away.
Looking out as far as the eye can see.
To the south, boats off Terminal Island.
To the northeast, Manzanar.
But, at his feet, Gardena.

*repeat

On a knoll in a strawberry patch,
an immigrant has returned.
Looking out as far as the eye can see.
To the south, flowers and vegetables.
To the north, the produce market.
But, at his feet, Gardena.

*repeat

On a knoll in a strawberry patch,
an immigrant is an old man.
Looking out as far as the eye can see.
To the east, the Rainbow and the Horseshoe.
To the west, the JCI.
But, at his feet, Gardena.

*repeat

On a knoll in a strawberry patch,
an immigrant is dead.
Looking out as far as the eye can see.
To the west, Honda and Toyota.
To the east, Meiji Market.
And, at his feet, Gardena.

ACT II: THE BAD RAP

Video/slides of Eastside Los Angeles, lowriders, freeway traffic, and so on.

MC: The wonderful thing about L.A. is that wherever you
                want to go, all you have to do is drive to get there. Every-
                thing is conveniently located next to an off-ramp, and
                from there, it's only forty-five minutes away. It's all very
                simple. Intimate knowledge of twelve major freeways will
                literally give you the world. But intimate knowledge does
                not necessarily mean you can avoid the *Bad Rap* . . .

VOICES: Yeah right, when you chinks gonna learn to drive?
                Hey, yo' eyes so slant, how you gonna see the road?
                Whatcha wanna be low for? You too short to see over the
                wheel, man.
                Maybe you can make 'em good, but your driving sucks.
                Sig alert: Gooks up front causing the jam.
                So go drive your kids into the ocean!

EASTSIDE HOMEBOY:

                In the old days, Eastside was the Boyle Heights barrio.
                Eastside boys called themselves the Buddha Bandits.
                They wore the distinctive red bandanas and slouched
                around in GTOs and muscle cars like convertible candy-
                apple Cutlasses and dark blue Chevys with rims and lots
                of chrome. Thing to do was cruise around and pick up
                those Asian cholas with tight black skirts and black rings
                around their eyes. And they kept the ways of the old
                country too. Come Shogatsu New Years, they was
                pounding the pinche mochi jus' like any other Buddha-
                head. If I'm lying, I'm dying.

                So this is where I came from. Born this side of the river
                and between the Ten and the Sixty. My old man, my
                uncles, my big manos—all into cars. The old man and
                Uncle Sab still own the Eastside Nisei Automotive Shop.
                They got a rep as the best mechanics on the Eastside. Me
                and my manos all work there.

From time I can remember, it was cars. When I was five I got to be in the parade on Whittier, riding beside my brother. He had this pinche sixty-four Impala in those days. He let me work the hydraulics. I let that thing drop into the concrete, man. We coulda started a fire.

Hey, I could drive a car when I was eight. Feet don't reach the pedals. What the hell? Put the car in neutral on an incline and maneuver that baby. By the time I could reach the pedals, I could shift gears. By the time I got my license, I had put a good thirty thou' on the old man's Chevy pickup. I was born to drive.

First I had this seventy-eight Monte Carlo, chingon hydraulics, changed all the parts, put in a four-speaker job. Then I upgraded to a seventy-three Chevelle. New paint job, but the rest—all original parts, man. Sleek black. Insane. Wax job every weekend, man. After that I got an old Toyota pickup. Man, I put on these pinche monster wheels. But that thing was bad news. Got me three speeding tickets, and then this drunk cuts me off on the Santa Monica and totals it. Hey, this was my only accident, man.

Usually I can feel it coming. There's a feel about driving. A total feel that extends out from you as the center—the brain—of your car. Know what I mean? You gotta tune into it. They say it's about Zen and driving. Extends beyond your bumpers like your beams reaching out into the night and flows out into that silent stream of traffic.

So I talk a lot about cars. It's in the blood. A way of life.

VOICE:　　That's heavy, man.

VOICES:　　Yeah right, when you chinks gonna learn to drive?
Hey, yo' eyes so slant, how you gonna see the road?
Whatcha wanna be low for? You too short to see over the

wheel, man.

Maybe you can make 'em good, but your driving sucks.

Sig alert: Gooks up front causing the jam.

So go drive your kids into the ocean!

EASTSIDE HOMEBOY:

La tuya! So a few manos arrive from China and drive down the wrong side of the street. So what's this got to do with me? Hey, man, it's just a bad rap.

This monologue is followed by a martial arts/driving demonstration using several athletic figures, their heads embedded in cushioned cars, racing around the stage, jumping, swerving, cutting in, and doing a fantastic array of acrobatics. A musician with a saxophone wanders to one side of the stage and blows his heart out.

Chant/Rap

The brother from the motherland,

he steps into L.A.

We welcome him with open arms

then introduce him to the straightaway.

Hey man, welcome to L.A!

Say man, welcome to L.A!

Yeah, welcome to L.A!

(Hey, I been here all my life!)

The good life! The fast life!

Welcome to L.A!

So, this brother from the motherland

hasn't been here but a week

but check him out

check him out in the bi-

lingual line at the DMV.

Gettin' him a license.

Gettin' him a hot registration.

Gettin' him some bad car insurance, whoa.

Whoa whoa whoa whoa whoa!

Says the lady in the window:

"Baby, not so fast!
Mr. Yo, we know
that you can see the E,
but can you see the S-T-O-P?"
(I tell you; it's those manos from China!)
Now comes the inspector
with a clipboard in his hand, saying,
"Mr. Yo, we know
that you can see the light,
but can you hang a right?"

All you brothers from the motherland
are welcome to L.A.
We're happy to make room for you
while cruisin' thru
while cruisin' thru
our life our liberty our freeway.
Long as you keep goin' and don't come back
till you can shift some gears.
And don't come back
till you can change some lanes.
And don't come back
till you can drive.
till you can drive.
till you can drive.
(It's about Zen and driving, man!)

Say man, can you drive?
Yo man, can you drive?
Yo man, can you drive?
The good life! The fast life!
Welcome to L.A!

ACT III: THE GLASS CEILING

SCENE

This scene is essentially a cartoon. The characters involved stand below projected cartoon bubbles with appropriate dialogue/thoughts/commentary. Appropriate music accompanies this scene. Characters all wear ties; the bigger the tie, the bigger the boss. Maybe there is a table, as in a conference room. Some of the characters have their heads emerging from the holes in the table or floor. Also, there is a moving "glass ceiling" (probably a large sheet of cellophane), which impedes the movement of Asian characters trying to move upward (or into a new tie size). The actors may use this cellophane by pressing their faces into it, nearly suffocating or in fact succumbing, growing old, and so on. Maybe their cellophane-wrapped bodies are carried off the stage.

Above the glass ceiling or on it are big faces in mirrors, in the manner of a fish-eye (wide-angle) lens; these change and glare.

This short "cartoon" tells the tale of two sansei males trying to penetrate the "glass ceiling" in the hierarchy of the business world, one in an American company and another in a Japanese company.

MC: This Valley Boy graduated number six in his high school graduating class. Student body parliamentarian. Good at rules. Voted "Most Likely." That's right. Just *most likely*.

On the other hand, this Valley Boy had a 3.625 grade point average. Good enough to get into USC, but poor enough to be cool.

But notice the similarities between the two.

NOTE: They are absolutely the same, but the MC treats them as if they are different, pointing to one and the other, back and forth.

Uncompromising style of dress: not too conservative, but not too radical, not cheap, no no, expensive threads, brand names, but nothing flashy. Expensive, distinctive, tasteful, yuppy, and most important, blending in with that suave environment of successful sansei men. Hair by Andre. Not too short, not too long, combs it to the right. Unscented hairspray. Games: Golf. Tennis. Skiing at Mammoth. Car: Three Series charcoal-gray Beemer. Yes, *he* has a car phone. Yes, *he* has ski racks. Yes, *his* license plate says, "USC," or "L.A. Lakers." What is *he?* Program engineer at Hughes? *Him?* Loan officer at the Bank of California? Personnel manager at Honda, USA? Associate director of sales and distribution at Coca-Cola? The possibilities are infinite and predictable. You may be sitting next to one now, at this very moment.

TWO SANSEI MALE EMPLOYEES:

I work for an American company.

I work for a Japanese company.

It concerns me that I'm the best. Chosen from merit. Not because I'm a minority of any sort. Hired for the job because I'm the best.

I got the job because I'm pretty bilingual. The Japanese management at the top can relate to me. And the American employees at the bottom can relate to me.

If I knew I was hired to fill some minority quota, I'd quit right then and there. That's why I like working American. Merit counts.

I'm valuable to this Japanese company because I'm a bridge. Being a bridge is my contribution to the company.

Actions speak louder than words.

Actions speak louder than words.

They've got to notice me.

They've got to notice me.

I'm wonderful, but I'm very modest about it.
  Japanese approve of modesty, so I'm very modest.

If I'm patient, I'll be rewarded.
  This is a long-term commitment. I'm showing them
  I'm here for the long-term.

Don't make waves.
  Don't make waves.

Don't rock the boat.
  Don't rock the boat.

Employers don't like employees who rock the boat.
  Loyalty is important. I'm a loyal employee.

I work hard. They ask for more. I work harder.
  Hard. Harder. And hardest. I'm an example in my
  department. Middle management has to show the
  way.

Don't complain. Keep your mouth shut.
  I don't complain. They consider me a gaijin anyway.

Someone's got to notice me eventually.
  I'm sure they notice me.

Be on time and work overtime.
  I even spend my evenings drinking and socializing
  with them.

Don't use your sick time.
  What? Sick? Never.

Don't screw the company, even though the company may
screw you.
  Honesty pays.

Be organized.
    Be dedicated.

Be thankful you've got a job.
    Anyway I'd be embarrassed to get all that praise.

It was great to get all that praise in front of everyone. I
acted like it was nothing.
    And nothing will ever come of it.

I deserve a raise.
    I deserve a promotion.

What am I? Invisible?
    What am I? Invisible?

Funny how you can work for years for the same company
and never be noticed.
    Get another degree, but do it quietly.

Don't push it that you're probably overqualified for the
job.
    Of course, I've got managing skills.

I run everything when the boss is away.
    It's obvious I've got managing skills.

I've got a degree to show it.
    I've got years of experience.

I've taught everyone else, including the young, inexperi-
enced manager they just promoted.
    They overlooked me again.

I've invested everything in this company.
    My entire career is here.

If I leave, I've got to start at the bottom again.
    If I leave, I've got to start at the bottom again.

CHORUS: *Song/Hymn*
                 "The Glass Ceiling"

                 He was a hard worker.
                 He was an honest worker.
                 He was a loyal employee.
                 He was an exemplary employee.
                 He never pressed his advantage.
                 He was content to be a member of the team.
                 He wanted what was best for the company.
                 He peaked out and was content to be a member of
                     the team.
                 He reached his level of competence.
                 He was a good teacher. Taught younger, inexperienced
                     employees who were all later promoted before him.
                 He died at his computer.
                 He died staring into his monitor. He never knew what
                     hit him.
                 It was the glass ceiling.

ACT IV: FLY BY CHOPSTICKS/FREAKS OF NATURE

SCENE

This scene is devoted to the confused nature of Asian male representations as inscrutable, small but powerful, freaks of nature (ninja turtles) or nature freaks. Mixed in are so-called ancient teachings, Yamato-damashi, Zen, and the oddly macho-heroic but sexless, monastic nature of these representations.

Throughout the following demonstration, there is a woman clothed in layers and layers of kimono and other types of clothing who is sensually and interminably disrobing. Despite her sensuous display, the men never acknowledge her presence. (She is perhaps on video.) There is also a continuous/circular video of martial arts: a chaotic/anarchic video medley of every possible martial art representation on film and TV, interspersed with a cereal commercial (Kenmei): "Lifelong health is a precious gift. No one can give it to you. It must come from within yourself. And the path that leads you there must be traveled with well-chosen steps. The people of the Orient set a good example. They eat right and exercise. For generations their diet has included food considered healthy and low in saturated fat. That could explain why they have lower levels of cholesterol. Rice has always been a very important part of their diet."

MC: Everyday life is a contest toward the attainment of strength, health, and utility by means of spiritual, moral, and mental training. A method of thinking and living with the entire body. A physical form of chess . . .

A YOUNG MAN *is sitting in a rather ritualistic style. He picks up a pair of chopsticks before him and waits. The sound of a fly buzzes in. The* YOUNG MAN *attempts to grab the fly with his chopsticks. This is blatantly taken from the* Karate Kid. *Maybe there is a* NINJA TURTLE, *who descends from somewhere, swinging on a trapeze.*

NINJA TURTLE: (*disturbing the* YOUNG MAN's *concentration*)
                Your fly is down. (*opens his mouth and snaps the fly in*) Kawabunga! Always expect the unexpected, dude. Hey, so where's the pizza?

This is followed by a nunchuku or a pizza-cutting demonstration by the NINJA TURTLE. *This demonstration is interrupted and distracted by* BRUCE LEE *unicycling about.*

BRUCE LEE: . . . it is a question of balance, a harmony that unites the earth with the sky. A tranquility of movement.

This is followed by a kung fu demonstration by Bruce Lee, which is upstaged by KEY LUKE, *who enters blindly on a cane, manages to wipe out* BRUCE LEE, *and proceeds to meditate. As the monologue goes on, there is a visual moon running around across the stage or on video.*

KEY LUKE: Grasshopper, listen with care. There are no beginnings and no endings. Everything in the universe is connected. When the mind's activity fills the whole cosmos, it can seize opportunities, avoid mishap, see all things in one. The moon's reflection on the surface of the water moves incessantly. Yet the moon shines and goes nowhere; it stays, but it moves. The mind is as the moon, the body as the stream.

Possibly KEY LUKE *is interrupted in his zazen posture by the typical slap on the head/shoulder with a bamboo stick.* YOUNG MAN *goes back to trying to capture the fly with chopsticks. Suddenly* TOSHIRO MIFUNE *enters, whips out his sword, and slices the fly in half.*

TOSHIRO MIFUNE:
                  Maximum efficiency with minimum effort, for the mutual welfare and benefit of all. One must concentrate on and consecrate oneself wholly to each day as though a fire were raging in one's hair. When we must die, we must die.

MIFUNE *gives a sword demonstration, followed by a Benihana teppan cooking demonstration, which can be a video of restaurant dining or done live by* MIFUNE.

TOSHIRO MIFUNE:
                  Dinner for two includes teriyaki beef julienne, hibachi chicken, shrimp appetizer, soup, salad, vegetables, rice,

and green tea. Benihana: the Japanese steakhouse. Where great style means great dining. An American classic.

Demonstrations of judo, aikido, karate, taekwondo, tai chi, and so on follow. There are lots of yells and grunting, breaking of bricks, and voice-over dubs. The following sayings are acted out with sexual connotations in mind. See song that follows, which can be interspersed through the sayings.

VARIOUS: Yielding is strength.

Bend like a bamboo, then spring back.

These are painless techniques to subdue an opponent.

We control the opponent's mind before we face him.

The way of motionlessness. When you move, you show your weakness.

May the force be with you.

Winning means winning over the mind of discord in oneself.

Your posture must be that of a lion or a tiger, not a sleeping pig.

The true ninja is a master of everything, of his environment, of all things. Focus your thoughts.

The past returns, my son. It is time to seek our answers.

Don't confuse the specter of your past with your present worth.

Idiot, Darth Vader is your father!

We practice ninja, the art of invisibility.

You must not show your weak points, either in martial arts or everyday life. You must remain concentrated and not reveal your defects.

Life is a fight.

YOUNG MAN *goes back to trying to capture a third fly with chopsticks, possibly going out into the audience.* PAT MORITA *enters with a flyswatter and maybe hits someone in the audience on the head with it.*

MC: The way is beneath your feet.

Velcro sticking balls are tossed, juggled, and stuck everywhere.

> *Song*
> "Yeah, But Do You Got Any Balls?"
>
> Monkish heroes,
> freaks of nature,
> keepers of the inscrutable truth:
>
> You say,
>   (it is a question of balance,)
> it is a question of balance,
>   (the mind as the moon,)
> the mind as the moon,
>   (the body the stream.)
> the body the stream.
>   (Maintain.)
> Maintain my purity and posture.
>   (Focus your thoughts.)
> Focus my thoughts.
>
> But, what happens when I get that kinky feeling?
> What happens when I gotta gotta gotta?
>
>   (Life is a fight.)
> I'm training for death.

But what about,
        (what about?)
what about that hot flow of chi,
that grunting aiiiiii
flowing through me?

        (A question of balance.)
        (The mind as the moon.)
        (The body the stream.)
        (Life is a fight.)
        (Training for death.)

Yeah, but do you got
do you got
do you got
any balls?
Do you got
do you got
do you got
any balls?

ACT V: HEADS

SCENE

In this scene, the actors' heads are encased in television sets (well, light replicas thereof, with lighting from within. This can perhaps be mimicked on video.) Three actors each have separate TV heads; the two other actors share one screen. They have suits on from the waist up, but they can wear just about anything below. Four of the actors represent Asian politicians (the WOO HEAD, *the* FURUTANI HEAD, *the* MINETA HEAD, *and the* MATSUI HEAD*), the fifth the* REPORTER. *One of the TV heads, the* WOO HEAD, *remains in the dark at first, as if his TV set were turned off. He might run around trying to get attention while being ignored. His screen might turn into colors or snow (shake flakes from above). Possibly include actual video footage of politicians in question.*

REPORTER: We're pleased to have with us tonight three nikkei politicians in California. Coming to us live from Gardena is L.A. School Board Supervisor Warren Furutani. From San Jose, Congressional Representative Norman Mineta and from Sacramento, Representative Robert Matsui. Gentlemen, welcome.

We'll start with Supervisor Furutani, who had aspirations to the L.A. City Council. Supervisor, it's well known that you were once a so-called "movement radical." How do you reconcile your political ambitions today with the politics of your past? And furthermore, how do you account for the fact that all of you here today are liberal Democrats, while statistics show that the great majority of your Asian constituency is in fact conservative Republican?

THE FURUTANI HEAD:
Robin, I think the record will show that

Song
"The Life of a Head" or "The Asian Persuasion"
(soulful, maybe temptin' temptAsians)

The life of a head, it isn't so easy,
but
an Asian should always be able to trust an Asian
no matter what
my political persuAsian.
I admit I've got my future aspirAsians.
That's why I got my start in educAsian.

REPORTER: I see. Representative Mineta, the records show that you were among those listed in the House who bounced congressional checks. How did that news impact on the Asian community, which is generally thought to be fiscally tightfisted? In fact, statistics show that Asians TRWs have the cleanest ratings in the state.

THE MINETA HEAD:
Robin, I think the record will show that

(*sung*)
The life of a head, it isn't so easy,
but
an Asian should always be able to trust an Asian
in spite of my
congressional deviAsian.
I admit I've got my future aspirAsians.
That's why I was at the inagurAsian.

REPORTER: Representative Matsui, what about the allegations that you have received thousands of dollars in special-interest or PAC money to finance your political campaigns? In fact, the records show that you are second-most beholden to such moneys in the entire U.S. Congress.

THE MATSUI HEAD:
Robin, I think the record will show that

(*sung*)
The life of a head, it isn't so easy,

but
an Asian should always be able to trust an Asian.
Never mind the
lobbies, the delegAsians.
I admit I've got my future aspirAsians.
That's why my wife's in the administrAsian.

HEADS: *The rest of song divvied up between the* HEADS.

There's nothing to support these allegAsians.
We demand a full investigAsian.
It's character assassinAsian,
a media fabricAsian,
insinuAsian, confabulAsian, misinformAsian.
Our people know the truth . . .

(And then there is our colleague in Hawaii.
Thank God we haven't got his problems in-no-way)

It's true our voter registrAsian
is weighted on the side of moderAsian.
Tending toward conservAsian
and status preservAsian,
they voted for Ronald Reagan—
his only motivAsian
to sign our bill to redress
wartime relocAsian.
Nothing like a little redress check
for economic and cultural stimulAsian.
Five percent of twenty thou—a tidy contribution
to express your appreciAsian
for our dedicAsian
to the representAsian
of an Asian persuAsian.

THE WOO HEAD: *Refrain:*

> Woo woo woo woo woo woo
> Woo woo woo woo woo woo
> Woo woo woo woo woo woo woo

Words projected from slides/video:

> *Asian* persu*Asian* aspir*Asians* educ*Asian* devi*Asian*
> inaugur*Asian* deleg*Asians* administr*Asian* investig*Asian*
> assassin*Asian* fabric*Asian* insinu*Asian* confabul*Asian*
> misinform*Asian*
>
> *in-no-way*
>
> voter registr*Asian* moder*Asian* preserv*Asian* motiv*Asian*
> wartime reloc*Asian* cultural stimul*Asian* appreci*Asian*
> dedic*Asian* represent*Asian* *Asian* persu*Asian*

INTERLUDE: THE NOH BOZO AWARD PRESENTATION

This award is presented to any Asian American whose representation of Asians—politically, artistically, visually, or however—has contributed in a major way to further enhancing the Noh Bozo image. Nominees for this prestigious award will be made to the Noh Bozo Academy and selected for presentation at every performance. (This might be something actually staged, with video cuts from infamous scenes—commercials, films, movies—or it might be administered by lottery from nominations made by the audience.)

POSSIBLE CANDIDATES:

FRANCIS FUKUYAMA for his role as deputy director of the policy planning staff of the U.S. State Department and his pronouncement of the "end of history": "This does not by any means imply the end of international conflict per se. For the world at that point would be divided between a part that was historical and part that was posthistorical. Conflict between states still in history . . . would still be possible. There would still be a high and perhaps rising level of ethnic and nationalist violence, since those are impulses incompletely played out, even in part of the posthistorical world. Palestinians, Kurds, Sikhs, Irish Catholics, and Armenians will continue to have their unresolved grievances. . . . But large-scale conflict must involve large states still caught in the grip of history, and they are what appear to be passing from the scene."

SEIROKU KAJIYAMA, for his role as Japan's minister of justice. He compared Japanese prostitutes ruining Japanese neighborhoods to African Americans moving in and scaring whites out of their neighborhoods.

YASUHIRO NAKASONE, for his role as prime minister of Japan. He claimed that Americans had below-average skills because of blacks, Puerto Ricans, and Mexicans in the United States.

MICHIO WATANABE, for his role as Japan's minister of finance. He said that blacks had few qualms about going bankrupt and walking away from debts.

DANIEL INOUYE, for his role as senator of Hawaii. He said, "The war will be over in five days."

MIKE MASAOKA, for his role as Moses in the evacuation of 120,000 Japanese Americans to concentration camps.

CONNIE CHUNG, for her role as dragon-eyes anchorwoman on ABC *Nightly News*. Maury Povitch. Trying to have a baby. Check Asian/Rice.

RICHARD GERE, for his role as a Japanese American in Akira Kurosawa's film *Rhapsody in August,* based on the Japanese novel by Kyoko Murata, *Nabe no Naka.* And accepting for Richard Gere is: Akira Kurasawa. (Kurosawa makes an acceptance speech for Gere in Japanese.)

JONATHAN PRYCE, for his role as the engineer (with his eyes cleverly pasted down to resemble an Asian of mixed heritage) in the London production of *Miss Saigon.*

BERNARD BOURISCOT, for his role as a French diplomat to China and his curious inability to distinguish sexual attributes in Asians.

ACT VI: GOD'S GIFT TO ASIAN AMERICAN WOMEN

SCENE

The WESTSIDE DUDE *talks about life and love on the fast lane. During this scene, there is a gigantic koi that moves by with muscles. Also, there are slide and video visuals of shopping at Meiji, the checkers and the boxers, and so on, along with calendar visuals of Mr. Asian and other Asian hunks.*

MC: Now, ladies and gentlemen, direct from Westside, that man of incredible build and power, the man *People* magazine calls the Asian American Arnold Schwarzenegger, God's gift to Asian American women, Mr. Sansei himself!

WESTSIDE DUDE: (*Flexes. Looks out. Flexes. Concentrates. New stance. Flexes some more. Looks out. Smiles.*)
Not bad, huh? Wanna know how it happened, yeah? (*pulls some punches*) Boxing. Yeah. Got this physique boxing. Hey, babe, sincerely. I been around. Boxed for Foods, for Meiji, for Modern Foods, Lucky, Marukai, Yaohan. You name it, I been there. Course I work out in my free time. Pumping. Yeah, pumping. But boxing's better. Keeps me limber and in touch.

Meet a lot of lookin' sisters coming through those lines. They roll their carts in with six-packs of Coke, Purina dog chow, moyashi, and tofu. I make my moves. Boxing's a science. Cans of takenoko and water chestnut on the bottom, see. Tofu, sembei? Goes on top. Fifty-pound bag of Cal Rose? No problem. Power impresses. (*flexes biceps*)

It's not just them bitch'n Asian sisters, man. Boxing at Meiji, there's that kimochi feeling. You see the jichans and bachans, the real pioneers, man. These old folks made the first move. Na-ru-ho-do. You see them now looking all shikataganai-like, but they made big sacrifices. For the old ones, I always go out a skosh.

Shit, boxing is good money. Hey, I'm a union man. Put in for overtime and got me a Z. Four hundred horsepower of pure turbo headed down the fast lane of life.

Some people think I lead a charmed life, but I think about it like this: this (*flexes again*) is the result of generations of hard work and sacrifice. I am indebted to my past. Eat rice and proud of it. Hey me? Sansei, man. Full-blooded third generation in America. Got katana to prove it. Back in the old country, the ancestors walked around all day with their swords practicing yamato-damashi, did good deeds, loyal in battle, cut down the enemy.

Then, one day, bachan packed some musubi in a basket and she and jichan crossed the Pacific to America for life, liberty, freedom, and the pursuit of happiness. Ol' jich brought with him the wisdom of the old country, the real meaning of manhood and maleness. Taught it to his son who taught it to me. It's the meaning of the koi. You know koi fish? Symbol of manhood. The carp is a strong fish, rushes upstream against the current. Symbol of strength, courage, and perseverance.

While WESTSIDE DUDE *is talking, he is also dressing down. He puts baby oil all over to slick himself up. He puts on special footwear. He ties a hachimaki around his forehead and picks up a pair of taiko sticks. A large taiko is rolled in by several kuroko (stagehands in black). The kuroko literally pick the down-home boy up, walk him to the taiko, and control him through an amazing taiko show, as if he were a Bunraku puppet. In the background, there is chanting.*

VOICES: (*chanting*)
               Strength. Courage. Perseverance!
               Chikara. Yuki. Nintai.
               Strength. Courage. Perseverance!
               Chikara. Yuki. Nintai.
               Strength. Courage. Perseverance!

Chikara. Yuki. Nintai.
Strength. Courage. Perseverance!
Chikara. Yuki. Nintai.
Strength. Courage. Perseverance!
Chikara. Yuki. Nintai.

ACT VII: THE BEARDED LADY

MC: Ladies and gentlemen. Tonight only, by special engage-
ment, we bring you from Rome, from Paris, from New
York, and from Yokohama, the theme finalists of the
Bearded Ladies International Beauty Pageant!

A very pregnant M. BUTTERFLY *appears in full geisha regalia. A lot of other*
PREGNANT BUTTERFLIES *enter. Maybe some of them actually fly in. Then, the
entire lineup of M. Butterfly–types grow beards. Perhaps this is achieved by
peeling off one's face, by the use of masks, or by creating a transparent box of
sorts, which fits over the head, is lit within, and revolves about with a series
of facial types both mustachioed and bearded.*

M. BUTTERFLIES: *(sung operatically)*
        Song
        "The Bearded Lady"

        Yo so pregnantiti!
        Yo so pregnantiti!
        It's not because of linguine, fettucini, espeghetacini!
        This poor little moscatiti fell into a rancid pot of mante-
        quilla and sullied her virgin wings!
        (How can she sing such nauseating stuff?)
        Ai! Mamamia que al trovado.
        What would she say?

        *Drink up your miso soup.
        Drink up!
        Drink up your miso soup
        Drink up!
        Put a little manly hair on your chest!
        Put a little manly hair on your chest!
        Don't be a sissy!
        Don't be a prissy!
        Drink up your miso soup!

How many months are you?
At least nine. Nine months since I saw my love.
I'm pregnant with his child.
Pregnant with waiting.
Even if my love takes years to return, I'll still be waiting here, pregnant.
Won't that confuse him?
He doesn't know how to count.
Not only does he not know how to count.
What would my father say?

(insert *)

Is it anatomically possible?
I saw it in the *National Enquirer.*
He can't see in the dark.
What a dummy.
I told him I'm shaped a little different.
But what's the difference?
Ahhhh! What would my ojichan say?

(insert *)

If he doesn't return, I will kill myself.
Don't be silly.
I will hang myself.
I will throw myself into the ocean!
I will cast my pregnant self to the wolves!
And when I'm dead, what will bachan say?

(insert *)

BUTTERFLIES *disrobe, exposing enormous penises.*

ACT VIII: THE MOYASHI MARU

SCENE

The no-win situation. The screen projects scenes from Star Trek II *with* CAP-
TAIN KOK *speaking about the Moyashi Maru—the no-win scenario—a sim-
ulated test for sansei fleet cadets. What is Mr. Tsuru doing?* MR. TSURU *is on
the tightrope. If he falls to one side, he will be a dentist; if he falls to the other,
he will be an optometrist. But, he will always be Mr. Tsuru going into warp
five.*

*There is a patient on a dentist/optometrist chair (with wheels). On one side,
there are tools and paraphernalia as in a dentist's office. On the other side,
there are tools and paraphernalia as in an optometrist's office. On both sides
are diplomas from* USC *with the name George Hikaru Tsuru.* MR. TSURU
works on the PATIENT, *alternating between occupations, from one to the other,
pumping the* PATIENT *up or down, staring into his eyes or mouth as appropriate. Meanwhile,* CAPTAIN KOK *wanders around philosophizing.*

*Video/slide images of space and stars are running by like crazy. Maybe another
sign in the sky sliding sideways saying, "This performance was made possible
by a grant from . . ." and so on. Images of dentistry and optometry. Perhaps
an image of a person on a tightrope, or one who has the choice of diving into
a small bucket.*

*Mr. Tsuru masks (Mr. Tsuru's face on a fan with holes cut out for the eyes) are
being sold in the lobby. On the opposite side of the mask is written:* "Space: the
final frontier. These are the continuing voyages of the Starship Noh
Bozos. Its ongoing mission: to explore new worlds, to seek out new life
forms and new civilizations, to boldly go where no sansei has gone
before," *perhaps with Japanese translation. Audience participation should be
prepared for, everyone donning their masks on cue at the end.*

MC: Now, all you sansei Trekkies, the moment in time you've
been waiting for, the opportunity to travel into the distant future aboard the Starship Noh Bozos. Yes, you and
Mr. Tsuru, traveling boldly where no sansei has gone

before. Starship log 2193.084. Episode 9347: "The Moyashi Maru" . . .

TRANSMISSION: Imperative! This is the Moyashi Maru. (*static, garble garble*)

Coordinates flash on screen.

> Moyashi Maru
> Classification: Dentistry and/or Optometry
> Registry: OD DDS
> Commander: Miyamoto-Otera
> Crew: 81
> Passengers: 300
> Dead weight: 14,798 MT

CAPTAIN KOK: Mr. Tsuru, warp speed!

MR. TSURU: Ay ay, sir!

CAPTAIN KOK: Mr. Tsuru, warp speed!

MR. TSURU: Ay ay, sir!

CAPTAIN KOK: A no-win situation is a possibility every commander must face. Mr. Tsuru, project parabolic course to avoid entering neutral zone.

MR. TSURU: A no-win situation? What would the captain know about a no-win situation? He's the star of the show. As for the neutral zone, it could not be avoided. (*looks into* PATIENT'*s eyes*)

CAPTAIN KOK: How to deal with death is at least as important as how to deal with life. Mr. Tsuru, plot an intercept course!

MR. TSURU: Plot an intercept course? Is he crazy? The point at which life intercepts with death is exactly here where I stand, where I always stand, in limbo. I am the true captain of the Moyashi Maru, traveling through space interminably at the interception of life and death: the no-win scenario. (*works on* PATIENT*'s teeth*)

CAPTAIN KOK: The Moyashi Maru is a test of character. Mr. Tsuru, activate shields!

MR. TSURU: A test of character? Doesn't he understand? Then, the shields must come down . . . But, he's the captain.

CAPTAIN KOK: Klingons don't take prisoners. Mr. Tsuru, get us out of here.

MR. TSURU: Can you imagine? If it weren't for me, we wouldn't go anywhere. Who said Asians were bad drivers? (*zips* PATIENT *around on wheels*)

CAPTAIN KOK: I have never faced death. Mr. Tsuru, evasive action!

MR. TSURU: Evasive action. He wants evasive action? (*yanks glasses off* PATIENT)

CAPTAIN KOK: I tricked my way out of death by ingenuity. Mr. Tsuru, you may indulge yourself.

MR. TSURU: (*smiles, looks at* PATIENT *with tool.*)

CAPTAIN KOK: I was the only star fleet cadet who beat the no-win scenario. Mr. Tsuru, warp speed!

MR. TSURU: Ay ay, sir! (*whips around with* PATIENT *on chair*)

CAPTAIN KOK: Mr. Tsuru, warp speed!

MR. TSURU: Ay ay, sir!

CAPTAIN KOK: As I was saying, I was the only star fleet cadet who beat the no-win scenario. I reprogrammed the simulation. Mr. Tsuru, warp five!

MR. TSURU: He reprogrammed the simulation. If I could reprogram
                  the simulation, who would Mr. Tsuru be? Maybe I could
                  be Captain Kok. Maybe I could be the doc! Maybe I
                  could be a genius with pointed ears. Maybe I could be a
                  main character.

CAPTAIN KOK: That's right, I cheated. Tsuru! Get those shields up!

MR. TSURU: The captain cheated. Did you hear that? My upbringing
                  would never allow it. Maybe that's why I'm not captain.

CAPTAIN KOK: Well, maybe "cheated" is the wrong word. Let's just say
                  I changed the coordinates of the test. Mr. Tsuru, stand
                  by photon torpedoes!

MR. TSURU: Maybe that's the problem. I never get to write the coor-
                  dinates.

CAPTAIN KOK: Mr. Tsuru, stand by photon torpedoes!

MR. TSURU: Ay ay, sir! (*holds up some ominous tool and points at*
                  PATIENT)

CAPTAIN KOK: I don't like to lose. Best guess, Mr. Tsuru!

MR. TSURU: Oh goody. I get to write the coordinates. (*pulls out patient
                  chart*)

CAPTAIN KOK: I don't believe in a no-win scenario. Full stop, Mr. Tsuru.

MR. TSURU: (*stops suddenly, then . . .*)

CAPTAIN KOK: Tsuru! Fire! Fire!
                  Mr. Tsuru! Warp five!
                  Warp five!
                  Warp five!
                  Warp five!
                  Warp five!

At this point, an entire group of MR. TSURU LOOK-ALIKES *troop in.* MR. TSU-RUS *from the audience are cued in at this point. You can also see them crowded into the screen. They all look like* MR. TSURU. *They are all over the place.* MR. TSURU *approaches* CAPTAIN KOK.

MR. TSURU: Well, Captain, they've finally come for me. But before I go, I wonder if you would oblige me?

CAPTAIN KOK: What is it, Mr. Tsuru?

MR. TSURU: Mr. Kok, warp five!
                Mr. Kok, warp five!
                Mr. Kok, warp five!

MR. TSURU: (*all together with audience*) Space: the final frontier. These are the continuing voyages of the Starship Noh Bozos. Its ongoing mission: to explore new worlds, to seek out new life forms and new civilizations, to boldly go where no sansei has gone before.

ACT IX: TRANSFORMER SUSHI

SCENE

At first the scene is dark. You hear noises—moaning, that sort of thing—setting off a kind of tension of suspected eroticism in the dark. Then, there is the sound of chewing, the click of dishes and cups, and gradually the louder sounds of a sushi bar: "Irasshai! Hi!" As the lights brighten, two figures are seen bedded together: two pieces of enormous SUSHI *(maybe maguro). Actors are inside large sushi. A human figure appears with a whip or giant chopsticks. Maybe there is a giant shoyu bottle as well. The human figure is the* SUSHI TRAINER. *The* SUSHI TRAINER *points the whip/chopsticks, and voila! the* SUSHI *sit up on their sides or sit up on top of each other. More sushi couples enter: shrimp, bass, uni, ikura, and so on. The* SUSHI TRAINER *gets the* SUSHI-SUSHI *to do every sort of amazing trick: walk in circles, dance, acrobatics, hop over each other, turn into transformers, and so on.*

MC:	Ladies and gentlemen! The fabulous, the incredible, the fantastic Moyashi-san and his *Transformer Sushi*! Let's have a hand for the fabulous *Transformer Sushi*!

*Inari football sushi and onigiris (*SANSEI SUSHI*) tumble in. They stand to one side, like a new gang on the block.*

SUSHI-SUSHI:	Well, well. What have we got here?
SANSEI SUSHI:	Jichan, bachan, right on! Jichan, bachan, right on! Jichan, bachan, right on!
SUSHI-SUSHI: *(laughter)*	Sansei sushi! Sansei sushi! Hey! Going to a picnic? Huh? *(sniffs)* Spamu musubi! Picnic sushi!
SUSHI-SUSHI:	Sansei sushi. Pooru boys. Wonder what they do for fun? Play undo-kai. Basketobaru. Touch footobaru. Mah, sono

koto, nah.

Ne, used to be they protest Bietnam War.

Yeerrrroooooo Powwwwaaarrruuu.

SANSEI SUSHI: Unite in Asian solidarity!

All power to the people!

SUSHI-SUSHI: What about Asian American Studies?

Now eberabody gotta multiculturalru bishun. Jus you drink Coca-Cora, you gonna teach the world to sing . . .

SANSEI SUSHI: (*sings the Coca-Cola song*)

SUSHI-SUSHI: But ne, used to be sansei sushi fight for redresu. What about redresu?

All obaa now. Nijuman doraru mo hotondo spend suru shita. Ras Begas ya Princess Tours ya Cadaraki ya Japanese American National Museum mo zembu spend shita, ne.

Dame ne.

Sansei sushi . . . What they gonna do now?

Don't worry. Now gotta *Rising Sun* . . .

SANSEI SUSHI: Jichan, bachan, right on!

Jichan, bachan, right on!

SUSHI-SUSHI: (*mimicking*) Jichan, bachan, right on.

SANSEI SUSHI: Hey, you gotta problem, brother?

SUSHI-SUSHI: Nanka okashii nah. Nihongo wakaranmon, nah.

Sansei sushi! Sansei sushi!

SANSEI SUSHI: Hey, man. Stinking raw-fish sushi.

Jichan, bachan, right on.

Jichan, bachan, right on.

SUSHI-SUSHI: Hey. I heard those sansei sushi went back to Japan to find their rootsu.

What did they find? Gobo? (*laughter*)
Sansei sushi go to Japan looking for the real thing, but
they can't hack it. They gotta come back. Got no gam-
baru. No uni!

SANSEI SUSHI: Yuck? Uni? Scrambled brains. Baby poop!

SUSHI-SUSHI: (*following with undercurrent chanting from* SANSEI SUSHI:
                  "*Jichan, bachan, right on!*")

Sansei sushi got no wet, raw, srippery oystahs with touch
of lime.
They don't got ikura—those gristening golden eggs ready
to burst on the tongue.
Don't got no hard, srimy mirugai.
No dynomaito.
No spesharu numba foor.
They don't even got cooked shrimp!

We are raw.
We're fresh.
We're the closest thing to eating something live.
And most important of all.
We've got (*sucks in, shudders, snorts*) wa-sa-bi.

ALL: *Song*
                  "Subtleties of Sushi" or "California Roll"
                  (*with the quality of tango/flamenco*)

The only way to eat fish is to eat it raw.
To wrap your tongue around each piece is like amour;
to touch your lips, a subtle innuendo,
to taste a hidden and forbidden libido.

Let the sake trickle down your throat.
Let the ginger crunch between your teeth.
Let the wasabi thunder up your nose.

The only way to eat fish is to eat it raw.
To wrap your tongue around each piece is like amour.

Gotta get my sushi fix.
Lemme at my chopsticks.
Gotta get some raw fish to chew,
dip her in the ol' shoyu.
Gonna get my last piece of maguro,
if it's the last thing I do.

The only way to eat fish is to eat it raw.
To wrap your tongue around each piece is like amour.
To touch your lips a subtle innuendo;
To taste a hidden and forbidden libido.

Suddenly, there's a rumble from afar. A giant California roll rolls in and over, toppling and scattering both SANSEI *and* SUSHI-SUSHI.

ACT X: KARAOKE

SCENE

The costumes here will be formed with wiring underneath to exaggerate and create amazing curves. Also the lines will be accentuated with fluorescent paint; under black light, they will glow. There may also be the use of LEDs to create light in the costuming. It should be a light show.

This is a karaoke bar. There is an initial demonstration with the words and a romantic scene projected behind. The sound level and the key is obviously searched for and programmed in.

A SANSEI COUPLE *is coaxed from their seats in the audience. They are shy and somewhat embarrassed.*

MC:	Well, hello and thanks for joining us tonight. What's your name?
SANSEI GIRL:	_____.
MC:	And you are?
SANSEI BOY:	_____.
MC:	(*to* BOY) How long have you known _____?
SANSEI BOY:	Ah, well, we just met. We just met tonight. This is, ah, well, it's a blind date.
MC:	Oh, I see. Did you advertise? I mean, is this an *L.A. Weekly* date or something like that? *Nice sansei boy looking for nice sansei girl?*
SANSEI GIRL:	No. He's a friend of a friend.
MC:	Some friend, huh? And he takes you out to see some stupid show about Noh Bozos. Smart move. So how is it?

You two getting along? I'm mean, is this one evening going to clinch it?

SANSEI BOY: (*shrugs*) I don't know.

MC: Are you going to take that for an answer?

SANSEI GIRL: (*smiles*)

MC: Well, what are you going to sing for us tonight?

SANSEI BOY: We're going to sing a duet.

MC: All right. Ladies and gentleman, I give you _____ and _____.

Two television screens project two visual images. One screen projects the image of a brooding Caucasian fellow. Another screen projects the image of a beautiful blonde woman. At the bottom of both screens, the lyrics to the music can be read, a ball bouncing from word to word. The SANSEI GIRL *sings to the Caucasian fellow, and the* SANSEI BOY *sings to the blonde.*

VOICE OF GOD: *Song*
                "Song of Shoyu"

                Do you know the famous story of
                an ancient altercation
                'tween the sansei dudes and sansei sistahs?
                Eyeball to eyeball
                and butt to butt,
                they argued
                something fierce
                like this:

SANSEI SISTAH: Sansei dudes are possessive, insecure, and domineering.

SANSEI DUDE: Sansei sistahs are high-strung, status seeking, emasculating.

TOGETHER: Why repeat the mistakes of the past?
                   In the olden days,

SANSEI SISTAH: nisei moms

SANSEI DUDE: married nisei dads,

TOGETHER: you call that a relationship? Ha!

SANSEI SISTAH: Eurasian kids are so tall and beautiful.

SANSEI DUDE: But, who would want a kid that looks like you?

SANSEI SISTAH: Real men look like Dennis Quaid.

SANSEI DUDE: Real women look like Dolly Parton.

TOGETHER: How can I help it if
                   you're not the one
                   who turns me on?
                   How can I help it if
                   you're not the one
                   who turns me on?

VOICE OF GOD: So God said: I'll shoyu.
                   Little Tokyo and Gardena are doomed,
                   doomed to destruction in the next
                   earthquake or civil disturbance.
                   Wanna know why?
                   You're all a bunch of bozos,
                   lost souls in limbo,
                   that's why.
                   A warning to all
                   righteous dudes and smart sistahs.
                   Doomsday is a comin'.
                   Pack it up and get it goin'.
                   Cuz it's all going under.
                   It's all going under.

And by the way,
and by the way,
don't look back.
Pack it up and don't look back.
Pack it up and don't look back.
Don't look back—

SANSEI DUDE and SANSEI SISTAH *turn to leave, but something stops them, and they do indeed turn and look back. In the video monitors are scenes from the past, family scenes, historic scenes, scenes of nikkei culture, and so on. All this scrolls by for moment.* SANSEI DUDE and SANSEI SISTAH *have disappeared, "transformed." The stage goes black. When the lights appear again, superimposed on their staring faces are two people-sized shoyu bottles tied together by a symbolic rope.*

CLOSING: OUT OF LIMBO

SCENE

Release. The MASTER OF CEREMONIES *gets back into his priestly outfit. The actors get back into their Noh Bozo uniforms and their masks, except that they get in backwards. The priest ritualistically blesses the preceding; the* NOH BOZOS *do a lineup dance. The scene darkens. When the lights come up again, the actors have turned to face the audience. They bow.*

The End.

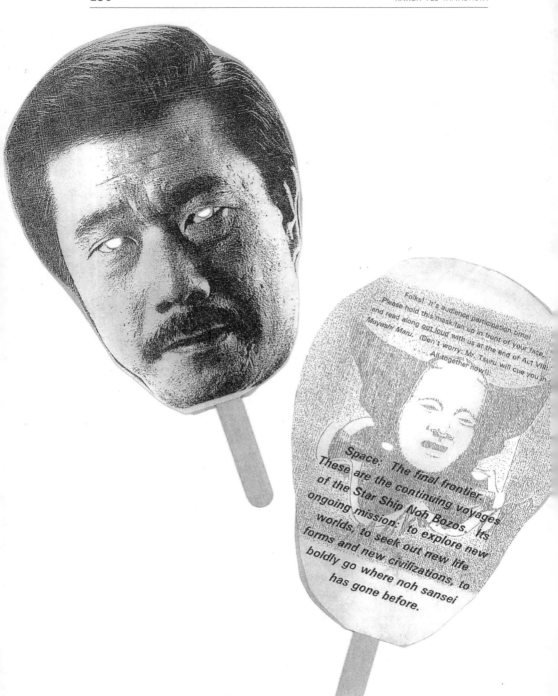

Folks! It's audience participation time!
Please hold this mask fan up in front of your face,
and read along out loud with us at the end of Act VIII,
Moyashi Maru. (Don't worry. Mr. Tsuru will cue you in.
All together now!)

Space: The final frontier.
These are the continuing voyages
of the Star Ship Noh Bozos. Its
ongoing mission: to explore new
worlds, to seek out new life
forms and new civilizations, to
boldly go where noh sansei
has gone before.

JACCC COMMUNITY PROGRAMS
FRESH TRACKS: CONTEMPORARY PERFORMANCES IN THE GALLERY

NOH BOZOS

The sensational circus Noh comes to Little Tokyo! Witness dazzling acts of culture and contortion, amazing feats of physical prowess and political juggling, a live freak show, dancin' sushi and much, much more! Hilarious! Irreverent! Noh Bozos!

Featuring the Amazing *Noh Bozos!*:
Mike Hagiwara
Dana Lee
Shaun Shimoda
Chris Tashima
Doug Yasuda
Keone Young
Mimosa

And the *Noh Bozo Band!*:
Sharon Koga - Cello/Taiko
Bill Roper - Tuba
Bill Plake - Saxophone/Flute

And now, the *Noh Bozos* to blame for this circus:

Dazzling Direction by
Shizuko Hoshi

Foolishly Written & Conceived by
Karen Tei Yamashita

Courageously Composed by
Glenn Horiuchi

Proudly Produced & Stage Managed by
Yuki Nakamura

Valiant Video Artistry by
Chuleenan Svetvilas

Complete Choreography by
Mimosa

Stupendous Set Design & Construction by
Ronaldo L. Oliveira

Creative Costume Design by
Kathleen Imanishi

Marvelous Mask Design by
Stella Boyd

Original Art & Logo Design by
James Kodani

Freaks of Nature

California Roll

Yamashita/Horiuchi

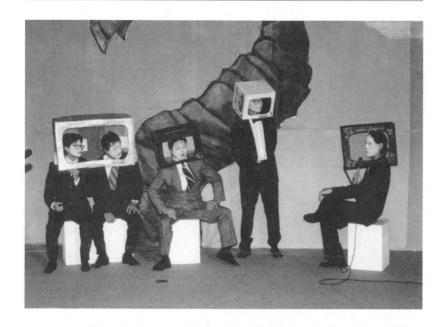

SIAMESE TWINS AND MONGOLOIDS

■

Three Abstractions
on Asian America

Written by Karen Tei Yamashita

ABSTRACTION 1: DRAMATIC THEATER—
HYPHENATED DREAMS

CHARACTERS

PA (*paper name:* AH GEE; *real name:* SUNG CHIANG),
owner of a Chinese delicatessen and father of

FIVE SETS OF SIAMESE TWINS

CHARLIE CHAN–#1 SON

MAO–CONFUCIUS

GREEN HORNET–KATO

CAPTAIN KIRK–MR. ZULU

FU MANCHU–DRAGON LADY

PLACE

Asian America (*where's that?*)

TIME

1971

Now it's just possible you'd prefer to read the original dramatic play in all its scenes and acts, hack out the middlewoman as it were, and you are perfectly free to do so. But I'm all for reading the reviews and the CliffsNotes, watching the trailers and making use of any shortcuts available. If a play is any good, my opinion is that you ought to be able to strip it down and dress it all back up. So let me strip this down for you.

Pa, also known as Ah Gee, also known as Sung Chiang, is a long-time Californ. That's right. The great general of the outlaws, Sung Chiang, is hiding out in America using a paper name. This is the great secret conspiracy kept under wraps: 108 outlaws snuck through Angel Island using paper names. Sung's Ah Gee cover is that he's the owner of a third-generation delicatessen that's been hanging slabs of red barbecued pork, roasted ducks, and soy sauce chickens from their necks for almost a century. Similarly, his band is scattered across Gold Mountain pretending to be hardworking laborers—pressing laundry, firing up woks, busing tables, mixing martinis, picking asparagus, shifting locks on railroad tracks. Any day now, they'll be called to their heavenly duties, but in the meantime, it looks like they're becoming a gang of old farts.

In Pa's case, he's got a load of kids, a pretty good count—nine sons and one helluva daughter, but this scenario's not without complications. His long-suffering wife gave birth to five sets of twins and finally gave up the ghost with that last twin labor of love. Discovering she'd finally produced a daughter was a brief moment of joy followed by a broken heart on learning that, once again, she'd birthed an attached set. Pa doesn't mince his words; he says, "My beautiful wife, your ma. You (*points at* FU MANCHU-DRAGON LADY) born. She take a second look, scream 'AIYA!' and die." A widower with five sets of American-born twins. My my. He's in deep cover, but is it worth the quintuple headache?

The stage directions for representing Siamese twins are vague. Actors might share a pant leg or be drawn together in a constant embrace with appropriate costuming. Clever use of acrobatics might produce grotesquely comic attachments. This might be a director's nightmare, but the playwright insists on the visual possibilities of the circus—an Asian freak show. As I always say, it's best to use your imagination.

But use your imagination to what end? What's the point of this circus of Siamese twins fathered by a hapless outlaw? Come to America, and your children all come out hyphenated. Half this-half that. Nothing whole. Everything half-ass. And it's more complicated then that. One half trying to be the other half and vice versa. As they say, duking out the dialectics. Working through schizophrenia and assimilation. Poor man. These kids drive him nuts. He's taught them everything they know, but still they have no respect. They think they're supposed to be free in Asian America.

Pa Ah Gee commiserates with his customers.

*

CUSTOMER: These kids all sneaking around with split personalities. What they call it? Identity crisis.

PA: Ha! (*unhooks skewered roast duck and tosses it on the chopping block*) Think you got problems!

CUSTOMER: Where did this second personality come from?

PA: What? (*picks up cleaver, slits open duck, and dumps out soy sauce marinade*) Who not split? Every paper son split in two memories. Now whose fault that?

CUSTOMER: Who knows who is fault? But, they blaming us.

PA: (*brings cleaver down on duck neck; shwack!*) Who?

CUSTOMER: Kids. Blaming us. We don't set good example. Continue to live like Chinese in America.

PA: Whatsa matter that? (*cleaves duck in half; shwack!*)

CUSTOMER: Gets them confused. Don't know if they coming or going.

PA: That's it! (*waves cleaver around*) I get them coming and going. (*leaves, marching off with cleaver*)

CUSTOMER: Hey, where you going? What about my duck?

*

Now I wouldn't want to spoil the end for you. But just think about this lot of thankless sons and one daughter wallowing in their duplicity. Our hero, Pa, goes off with his cleaver in search of each paired progeny, and that in itself is a search for Asian America (*where's that?*).

ABSTRACTION 2: TELEVISION SITCOM—*DENTALOPTICS*

EPISODE #21: "BLOCKBUSTERS"
Directed by: Mako

SUMMARY

STORY A: *Heco and Okada's covert Civil Rights mission is to subvert a neighborhood real estate blockbusting scheme*

SUBPLOT B: *Heco and Okada have posed for an Asian American male nude calendar, possibly damaging their father Warren's chances for local re-election*

SUBPLOT C: *Lucy San Pablo, office administrator of DentalOptics, is fed up with the work and threatens to quit.*

CHARACTERS

HECO HAMADA

Twin to the left. Dentist at DentalOptics and secret agent for civil rights. Characteristics: Pragmatic and logical, while artistic. Plays taiko and shakuhachi. Abstract painter. Verbally adept, persuasive, with wit and humor. Excels in team sports (baseball, basketball, volleyball, soccer). Drives a 400 HP Twin Turbo Supra. Interest in archaeology and musicology. Although imperfect language skills, charm makes him readily understood. Taekwondo and capoeira.

OKADA HAMADA

Twin to the right. Optometrist at DentalOptics and secret agent for civil rights. Characteristics: Highly imaginative and a math genius. Plays the saxophone and keyboards. Practices sumi-e and calligraphy. Introspective, intuitive, skilled psychoanalyst. In sports, excels as an individualist (track and field, diving, archery, scuba, weightlifting). Drives a Mazda RX7. Interest in geography, ecology, and political economics. Speaks multiple languages. Judo and karate.

NOBUKO HAMADA
Mother and avid community activist, energetic but over-
extended

WARREN HAMADA
Father and activist in local politics

LUCY SAN PABLO
Office administrator for DentalOptics, overqualified and
extremely efficient

AGENT CHANG
Civil Rights Agent

AGENT ENG
Civil Rights Agent

NANCY KIM
Reporter for radical left radio and newsprint, aotute and passionate

TIME
Circa 1990s

PLACE
Gardena, California

CAST LIST

```
HECO HAMADA . . . . . . . . . .Michael Hayakawa

OKADA HAMADA . . . . . . . . . . .David Shigeta

NOBUKO HAMADA . . . . . . . . . . . .Mary Kwan

WARREN HAMADA . . . . . . . . . . . .James Soo

LUCY SAN PABLO . . . . . . . . . . .Bea Salonga

AGENT CHANG . . . . . . . . . .Robert Shimoda

AGENT ENG . . . . . . . . . . Linda Iwamatsu

NANCY KIM . . . . . . . . . . . . .Lisa Rhee
```

WITH CAMEO APPEARANCES BY

```
TRICIA TOYOTA, CONNIE CHUNG, KRISTI YAMAGUCHI,
      AMY TAN, MARGARET CHO, PAT MORITA,
    GEORGE TAKEI, JUDGE LANCE ITO, ANGELA OH,
  DAVID CARRADINE, AND SENATOR DANIEL INOUYE
```

STATION ID W/UPCOMING SHOWS (1 MIN)

SHOW INTRO W/TITLES (1 min)

FADE IN:

1   EXT. GARDENA NEIGHBORHOOD - DAY

Pan Japanese American aspects of the neighborhood
(Japanese gardens with perfect Dichondra lawns and lol-
lipop bushes, local restaurants, shops, cultural centers, Buddhist temples and Baptist churches). Follow red
RX7 Mazda into minimall parking lot in front of offices
of DentalOptics.

Flashbacks and photo album inserts of sixties Asian
America and the twins growing up.

Sound of Asian American jazz fusion (oxymoron) and
shakuhachi.

                         V.O.
                In the midsixties two healthy twin
                baby boys were born to a sansei couple
                in Gardena, California. The couple—
                known Asian American movement radi-
                cals—had made a conscientious
                decision to live and work in the
                community and chose Gardena, a small
                working-class city on the great met-
                ropolitan outskirts of L.A. where an
                Asian American enclave continued to
                thrive. With faith in the power of
                the people, they raised and educated
                their boys to epitomize, mentally
                and physically, the very perfection
                of Asian America. Indeed the two
                boys grew to be men unlike any oth-
                ers—mentally astute, sensitive,
                visionary, politically activist,
                artistic, and physically exquisite.
                The only imperfection—a word denied
                by the boys and their parents—was
                the inconvenience of being bound to
                each other near the hip by a thick,
                fleshy ligament. Since words like

"Oriental" and "Siam" were considered passé, the boys were heroically referred to as "the Asian American duo."

HECO AND OKADA emerge from sports car.

Sound of taiko.

DISSOLVE TO:

2   INT. DENTALOPTICS OFFICE - DAY

Waiting room filled with mostly Asian American patients reading the Rafu-Shimpo, Amerasia Journal, and assorted iconic Asian American texts. Corner game of goh. Children playing with transformers, occasionally watching video of Chan Is Missing.

HECO AND OKADA enter, greet patients.
LUCY SAN PABLO hands twins patient files.

Pan wall art, sumi-e and oil abstracts, and diplomas: dental degree from USC and optics degree from UCLA.

TEASER (3 min)

CUT TO:

3   INT. INNER DENTALOPTICS OFFICES - DAY

AGENT CHANG and AGENT ENG are prepped in dental and optician chairs. CHANG is wearing a bib.

HECO AND OKADA enter in white coats.

AGENT ENG hands OKADA a small envelope. OKADA removes microfilm and places it in optics lens, enlarging it on dark wall.

                    AGENT CHANG
             Your mission, should yo—

HECO jams the dental mirror into CHANG's mouth, where he carefully scrutinizes reflected SLIDE IMAGES: the offices of Freedom Real Estate Enterprises, face of some suited white guy, tract of houses in construction, portrait photo of an African American family.

> AGENT ENG
> Have a look. Find out what they're up
> to.

OKADA switches to the eye chart's big E.

> HECO
> (moving his drill into CHANG's back
> molar)
> You need to lay off the soda and
> sweets.

> AGENT CHANG
> (breaks away and wipes his mouth on
> the bib)
> See if you can put your right and left
> brains together.

CUT TO:

COMMERCIAL BREAK: Mazda (RX7) (1 min)

ACT ONE (7 MIN)

                                                              FADE IN:

4   INT. DENTALOPTICS OFFICES - DAY

     WARREN storms into office with a glossy calendar: The
     Asian American Male Calendar 19—.

                        WARREN HAMADA
                 What's this? Since when did you guys
                 become pinups?

                          OKADA
                 When did that come out? It's not even
                 December.

                           HECO
                 Not bad. I'm the one who's buffer.
                 Check out the pecs!

                          OKADA
                 We're August.

                          WARREN
                 Are you crazy? What about my conser-
                 vative constituency?

                          OKADA
                 How many are they?

     Enter NOBUKO HAMADA in a big rush and loaded down with
     stuff.

                     NOBUKO HAMADA
                 I brought you obento lunch.(hands them
                 boxes of sushi, then notices calendar)
                 How cute. Reminds me of you guys as
                 babies with your little thingies
                 sticking out. Oh, I've gotta go. This
                 morning was the Pioneer Project.
                 Afternoon is the Manazanar committee.

                          WARREN
                 (groans) You know I could use some
                 help on my committee to reelect me.

NOBUKO dashes away.

                                                                    CUT TO:

5   EXT. WHITE RESIDENTIAL NEIGHBORHOOD - DAY

     HECO AND OKADA in front of house with Freedom Real
     Estate Enterprise "sold" sign.

                              OKADA
                    House is vacant.

                              HECO
                    Sale was by white owner directly to
                    real estate. I checked out the status.
                    Escrow initiated by real estate with
                    family named Dandridge.

                              OKADA
                    Dandridges are African American.

     (TWINS step into car.)

                              HECO
                    (looking out of car)
                    Integrating the neighborhood.

                              OKADA
                    (looking at rearview mirror)
                    I think we're being followed.

     HECO steps on the gas, and the RX7 disappears in smoke.

                                                                    FADE TO:

6   INT. DENTALOPTICS OFFICES - DAY

     LUCY SAN PABLO is gathering her belongings.

                              HECO
                    You can't quit.

                              OKADA
                    We can't survive without you. You do
                    everything.

LUCY
Right. I do everything. From scheduling to accounting, from bibbing down to adjusting nose pads. Now you want me to write a grant? For what?

HECO
We've bought the space next door. We're starting a nonprofit youth center.

OKADA
We thought you wanted to do more intelligent work. Expand your horizons.

HECO
We want a ping-pong table.

LUCY
That's it.
(stomps off)

OKADA
Maybe if I ask her to marry me.

                                                              CUT TO:

COMMERCIAL BREAK: 7/11 (smiling Korean American store owners) (1 min)

ACT TWO (8 MIN)

DISSOLVE IN:

7   EXT. SUBURBAN HOUSING TRACT IN CONSTRUCTION - DAY

HECO AND OKADA walking around construction site of tract
homes with sign: Freedom Enterprises.

>   HECO
>   It's elementary.

>   OKADA
>   One-drop rule.

>   HECO
>   Just one African American family in an
>   all-white neighborhood to start a
>   selling frenzy.

>   OKADA
>   (adopts some kind of white accent)
>   Your lily-white neighborhood is
>   "turning." Have you thought about mov-
>   ing to the Valley?

>   HECO
>   White flight. They get sales coming—

>   OKADA
>   And going.

FADE TO:

8   INT. DENTALOPTICS OFFICES - DAY

HECO AND OKADA enter offices and find everything in disarray.

>   OKADA
>   And I loved Lucy.

WARREN enters.

                         WARREN
          What a mess. You were taking advantage
          of Lucy. But now she's working for my
          reelection campaign.

                                          DISSOLVE TO:

9   INT. APARTMENT OF AFRICAN AMERICAN FAMILY - EVENING

    HECO AND OKADA are sitting in the living room with the
    DANDRIDGES, their children running around in the back-
    ground.

                     MR. DANDRIDGE
          The price is reasonable.

                     MRS. DANDRIDGE
          They offered it like this: a pretty
          little starter house in a safe neigh-
          borhood.

                     MR. DANDRIDGE
          With a good school just blocks away.

                     MRS. DANDRIDGE
          We're renting now. It would be a dream
          come true.

                                             CUT TO:

10 EXT. OUTSIDE APARTMENT OF AFRICAN AMERICAN FAMILY -
    EVENING

    HECO AND OKADA walk away from the apartment to the
    street when two masked kids, ATTACKER ONE and ATTACKER
    TWO, emerge in the dark and attack them. The twins act
    swiftly with combined taekwondo-capoeira-karate moves.

                         HECO
              (grabbing ATTACKER 1)
          Who are you?

                     ATTACKER ONE
          A gangsta!

                         OKADA
              (sitting on ATTACKER 2)
              What?

                      ATTACKER TWO
              Stay outta our hood!

HECO AND OKADA pull off attackers' masks to reveal white
faces.

                         HECO
              What do you call this?

                         OKADA
              Appropriation? Inauthenticity? Par-
              ody? Stereotyping? Blackface? Cultural
              imperialism? Minstrelsy? Cross-dress-
              ing? Exploitation? Reverse passing?
              Racial drag? Slumming it.

                         HECO
              (to ATTACKERS)
              You work for Freedom.

                      ATTACKER ONE
              Yeah, you could say that.

                         OKADA
              Are you a neo-Nazi?

                      ATTACKER TWO
              What's a neo-Nazi?

                                          FADE TO:

11 INT. HAMADA LIVING ROOM - EVENING

                         WARREN
              It's called blockbusting. Tactic is as
              old as the John Birchers.

                         NOBUKO
              I'm on it. I'll start a committee.

                         WARREN
              Okay, saved. Your mother's on it.
              (sighs) Lucy is driving me crazy.

            She's running my campaign like a doc-
            tor's office.

                          OKADA
            How does one run a doctor's office?

                                              CUT TO:

COMMERCIAL BREAK: United Colors of Benetton (cute multicultural kids) (1 min)

ACT THREE (4 MIN)

DISSOLVE IN:

12 INT. NEIGHBORHOOD MEETING - DAY

NOBUKU and DANDRIDGE FAMILY and COMMUNITY MEMBERS gathered, socializing, organizing, making placards.

> NOBUKO
> Eight o'clock sharp in front of Free-
> dom Real Estate.

DISSOLVE TO:

13 EXT. FREEDOM REAL ESTATE ENTERPRISES - NEXT DAY

NEIGHBORHOOD COMMITTEE TO BUST BLOCKBUSTING (NCBB) are
picketing and organizing cheers.

> NANCY KIM
> (with mic in front of camera)
> Freedom Real Estate refuses to make
> any comments. However, members of the
> NCBB, short for Neighborhood Commit-
> tee to Bust Blockbusting, have issued
> a strong statement against Freedom's
> purported tactics of discrimination
> and racism.

FADE TO:

14 INT. HAMADA FAMILY KITCHEN - LATER

> WARREN
> (with copy of The Asian American Male
> Calendar)
> This thing is selling like hotcakes.
> Nisei vets even bought it. What the
> heck, the second edition is endorsing
> my reelection.

> NOBUKO
> Hmmm. This endorsement suggests you
> are in the calendar.

WARREN scrutinizes the calendar cover.

                                       NOBUKO (cont'd)
                        You know, I think you could use a
                        smart political organizer like me.

                                                                    FADE TO:

15 INT. DENTALOPTICS OFFICES - DAY

    HECO AND OKADA return to a clean and efficiently run
    office. LUCY is busy behind the desk.

                                       LUCY
                        Politics is not my thing.

                                       OKADA
                        I know how you feel. I crave a life of
                        quiet contemplation.

                                       HECO
                        Are you kidding?
                        (hands Lucy the grant application)

                                       HECO (cont'd)
                        Don't forget the ping-pong table.

                              CREDITS (1 MIN)

While credits roll, in the background, HECO plays the
shakuhachi, and OKADA plays the saxophone.

                                  END

                              FADE OUT

                                                                    CUT TO:

COMMERCIAL BREAK: Yamaha (Hiroshima Band playing) (1 min)

Station ID (1 min)

ABSTRACTION 3: OPERA—*MIKE KATO*

DRAMATIS PERSONAE

MIKE KATO .... *(Professor of Asian American Studies)*

KATISHA .... *(Activist attorney married to Mike Kato)*

PEEP-BO .... *(Adopted daughter of Mike Kato and Katisha)*

YUM-YUM .... *(Graduate student in business and finance having an affair with Mike Kato but in love with Nanki-Poo)*

PITTI-SING .... *(Yum-Yum's mother, feminist attorney having an affair with Katisha)*

NANKI-POO .... *(International student, TA for Professor Mike Kato, and son of prominent PRC family)*

GO-TO .... *(Son of prominent North Korean general, living in Hanoi, and Facebook/Skype friend of Nanki-Poo)*

PISH-TUSH .... *(Student studying computer science on another coast and Facebook/Skype friend of Nanki-Poo)*

KO-KO .... *(Lord High Executioner)*

CHORUS 1 .... *(Asian students)*

CHORUS 2 .... *(Non-Asian students)*

ACT I

SCENE 1.—COLLEGE LECTURE ROOM

Professor MIKE KATO gives a lecture on television sitcoms, "situation comedies," noting that there was only one successful Asian American sitcom that lasted three seasons and sixty-three episodes. He points out that *DentalOptics* was conceived and written entirely by Asian American scriptwriters and had a wide audience, proving, contrary to a history of yellowface and Orientalizing stereotypes, that Asian Americans could be funny, could act in their own roles, and were attractive stars. (Song: *We Can Be Funny*)

"Admittedly," KATO goes on to say, "*DentalOptics* was about model minority professionals, but," he waxes almost nostalgically, "it was our *Ozzie and Harriet,* our *Leave It to Beaver.*" "What's he talking about?" someone asks, and another shrugs, "Google it." (Song: *Google It*)

> *Vincent Chin, Ho Chi Minh,*
> *I-Hotel and Pat Morita.*
> *Cold tofu?*
> *What's he talking about?*
> *Google it!*

Three students rise and make a group presentation based on Wikipedia research. (Song: *Based on a True Story*)

> *Based on a true story:*
> *Chang and Eng Bunker,*
> *born in 1811 in a river houseboat in Siam.*
> *Attached from birth: Siamese Twins.*

> *Exploited novelty, make their way across America,*
> *then Europe, a circus attraction,*
>   *for P. T. Barnum.*

> *Siamese Twins settle in Mount Airy,*
> *North Carolina, landowners, farmers,*
>   *and slaveowners. Americans!*

Marry Southern sisters, Sarah and Adelaide, and
father twenty-one kids.
Pillars of the community, Siamese sons fight and die
for the Confederacy.
Age of sixty-five in 1874, Siamese Twins pass away,
RIP in White Plains.

A student raises his hand. "Are they kidding? They made that up. It's offensive." Professor KATO points out that later episodes of *DentalOptics* employed the history of the original Siamese Twins, though comically. For example, Heco and Okada marry two "movement sistahs" and father between them twenty-one children. He reads from his notes: "In the sitcom, one sister is the result of artificial insemination, the other adopted. Heco marries a strangely beautiful Eurasian with green eyes and perfect hair who does the nightly news for Fox Television. Okada's bride is one quarter Cherokee, one quarter African American, one eighth Palestinian, and three eighths Micronesian. She's an artist and spiritual healer and specializes in native linguistics." He laughs, but no one laughs with him. KATO rubs his forehead and closes his eyes. (Song: *Life Framed in a Monitor*)

SCENE 2.—HOTEL CONFERENCE ROOM IN WASHINGTON, DC

KATISHA gives the keynote speech for the Conference on Human Rights. Her subject is her work and advocacy for the Uyghur Chinese detained at Guantanamo Bay as "enemy combatants" in the war on terrorism. She connects Guantanamo Bay and the racial profiling of Arab and Muslim Americans to the history of the Japanese American incarceration during World War II. (Song: *Same Same but Different*)

After the talk, PITTI-SING comes up to praise KATISHA for her work. Then she talks about her own work on behalf of international sex workers. The conversation is animated; they exchange phone numbers and emails. They're interrupted by a call from MIKE KATO to KATISHA. KATISHA says she may have to extend her trip in DC a few days, to which MIKE replies, "No problem." He says his lecture class today was a bust. "They didn't even laugh." She says her keynote was a spectacular success. (Song: *They Didn't Laugh*)

SCENE 3.—STARBUCKS

PEEP-BO works at Starbucks as a barista making espressos. YUM-YUM is also at Starbucks, sipping a tall double latte and plugged into her laptop. PEEP-BO is on the phone with her mother KATISHA and YUM-YUM is on the phone with her mother PITTI-SING. The conversations with the obsessive and overachieving mothers are similar. Both may have to extend their trips in DC. "But how are your classes? What are your grades? Did you apply to this or that? What are you plans? Your future in activism. Your future in business finance. Competition is fierce. Never let up! So what if I'm a tiger mom?" (Song: *You'll Thank Me Later*)

SCENE 4.—YUM-YUM'S APARTMENT AND WASHINGTON, DC, HOTEL ROOM AND NANKI-POO'S DORM ROOM

In YUM-YUM's apartment, MIKE KATO and YUM-YUM get into an argument. KATO says, "You never take my classes. You never even audit." YUM-YUM answers, "I don't have time for electives. Besides, my mother monitors my course load. I have to complete my business and finance degree in three years. I can't take anything irrelevant." KATO is stunned. "Irrelevant?" YUM-YUM ignores KATO's shock and dials a callback number on her cellphone.

In a DC hotel room, KATISHA and PITTI-SING are sipping wine and talking excitedly about politics when suddenly, in a fit of passion, they grab each other, tearing away at their clothing. After the rough and tumble, KATISHA slips off to the bathroom, and PITTI-SING makes a phone call to YUM-YUM.

In a dorm room, NANKI-POO is jerking off to porn on his laptop when he gets a phone call from YUM-YUM. But then as the phone sex gets hot, YUM-YUM receives a call from her mother, PITTI-SING, and puts NANKI-POO on hold.

KATO and KATISHA and NANKI-POO query their lovers about the phone calls. (Song: *Who You Talking To?*)

SCENE 5.—KOREAN AMERICAN CHURCH

PEEP-BO has joined a Korean American church. Suddenly, everything is clear to her, and she experiences a sudden epiphany of identity. (Song: *Born Again!*)

ACT II

SCENE 1.—NANKI-POO'S DORM ROOM

NANKI-POO is on Skype with his best buddies, GO-TO in Hanoi and PISH-TUSH on another coast. They talk about their future business venture together: drone technology made miniature, affordable surveillance with practical applications. PISH-TUSH has named it "the hummingbird," but of course, it's top secret. (Song: *Sugar Water in a Triple-A Battery*)

And why will their business venture succeed? They are a perfect three-some, with GO-TO's business and military connections, PISH-TUSH's genius in computer technology, and NANKI-POO's geographical and financial resources in China and Africa. They map out their spheres of influences: China, Africa, India, Hong Kong, Vietnam, Korea, Taiwan, Singapore, Thailand, Japan. (Song: *Taking Over Our World Byte by Byte*)

SCENE 2.—RESTAURANT

YUM-YUM and NANKI-POO dine at an upscale, ultraexpensive restaurant. They speak evocatively or disparagingly about food. NANKI-POO talks about his business venture and business partners and suggests they will need someone like YUM-YUM, with business acumen. They toast apple-tinis to the future. (Song: *Facebook for the Faceless*)

After dinner, NANKI-POO invites YUM-YUM to a party.

SCENE 3.—NANKI-POO'S DORM ROOM

When YUM-YUM realizes that "the party" is in NANKI-POO's empty dorm room, she asks, "You call this a party?" But he replies, "Meet my friends," and he Skypes in GO-TO and PISH-TUSH. (Song: *Bicoastal and International*)

PISH-TUSH says he's excited because he's got a surprise and switches the monitor to what appears to be a sex video. They watch in voyeuristic fascination, but PISH-TUSH interrupts and announces, "It's a live feed, like reality TV." YUM-YUM asks if the couple knows they are being filmed. "Of course not! This is what I've been talking about. My hummingbird is at the window! Hey, that's my roommate. Wait till he finds out!" YUM-YUM disapproves of this invasion of privacy, but NANKI-POO protests. (Song: *Isn't This a Free Country?*)

YUM-YUM leaves in disgust.

SCENE 4.—COLLEGE CLASSROOM

NANKI-POO is leading a section discussion about Professor KATO's lecture. He opens the discussion by suggesting the theme of twins and hyphenation. One student says that everyone in America is some kind of hyphen or a hybrid these days: Japanese-Chinese, Chinese-Jew, Mexi-Pino, Indi-Pino, Afro-Asian, Afro-Vietnamese, Korean-Brazilian. But someone protests, can't we all be just Americans? Class divides into camps. (Song: *Hyphen Nation vs. Just Americans*)

A non-Asian student protests that it might not be the bloodline that makes you Asian, that he speaks Japanese pretty fluently. Culturally, he's closer to Asia than "some in this class who only look Asian." Another non-Asian student says, "Okay, I'll admit it. I came to this class looking for the other side of my hyphen, an Asian girlfriend." Groans go around. "He doesn't want an Asian girl. He wants an anime girl." (Song: *Like Tomoyo Sakagami* or *His Otaku Babe*)

An Asian student says, "Okay, we know why *they* want to be in this class, but what about us? My parents say I gotta get a job, a profession; I'm wasting my time." Another students protests, "It's a racist jungle out there; what we learn here are survival skills. You can get your profession and hit a glass ceiling." Someone else says, "That's not true. If you have money, it doesn't matter. Even the Siamese Twins bought their plantations, slaves, and respectability." Another protests, "But what if you arrive with nothing; you're undocumented, an exile, or refugee? American capitalism caused a war in my country that caused my migration. But, with tuition costs going up, I'm going to have to drop out." "Don't worry," someone quips, "they'll get an international Asian student to pay a triple-ride and replace three of you." NANKI-POO realizes he's one of those international students who pay the triple-ride. Meanwhile he's been TA-ing for Professor KATO and learning about Mao, Marxism, and the Cultural Revolution. (Song: *What Would Mao Say?*)

NANKI-POO suddenly feels panic, as if he's emerged from his Skyping dorm room for the first time. Every sort of Asian immigrant is represented in this class. Several American generations of Chinese, Filipino, Japanese, Okinawans, Pacific Islanders, South Asians, and Koreans. Then the more recent stories: the granddaughter of the ex-Peruvian president Fujimori, an Afghan woman who escaped the Taliban, children of Vietnamese boat people and Hmong refugees, children who survived the Cambodian genocide, children of Iranian exiles, a Brazilian Japanese undocumented dekasegi, and him, the son of a prominent Chinese party leader. Their stories, real and animated, swirl around him. The class divides into overlapping choruses for NON-ASIANS (Song: *Cultural Creds*) and ASIANS (Song: *Post Your Race*).

Suddenly everyone is reading Twitter on their phones. Twitter news #1: Some student on another coast is accused of causing the suicide of his roommate, having posted a sex video of the same roommate. Twitter news #2: A big-shot North Korean general has been demoted. Twitter news #3: The wife of a prominent PRC leader has been arrested for the murder of her foreign business partner involved in a China-Sudan oil deal. (Song: *Twitter Twitter in the Sky*)

As class ends, YUM-YUM runs in with her cellphone.

SCENE 5.—FILM FESTIVAL RECEPTION AND SCREENING

Everyone gathers for the film festival and screening of MIKE KATO's debut documentary about the making of the sitcom *DentalOptics*. There is a prescreening reception with cocktails and hors d'oeuvres. YUM-YUM toasts MIKE, then announces plainly that whatever was between them is over. She's going to be with NANKI-POO, who obviously really needs her now. MIKE is disgusted. Hasn't he tried to educate NANKI-POO about Mao and Marxism and the ill-conceived pursuit of imperial capitalism? KATISHA comes by to also congratulate her husband, then says she knows all about YUM-YUM and hopes that it will work out for him, because she's thinking of moving to Washington, DC, and living with PITTI-SING. Finally, PEEP-BO greets her father and announces that she's going with a Christian group to Seoul to find her birth mother. (Song: *Found Identities*)

The documentary film is screened and ends with applause. MARGARET CHO is the mistress of ceremonies and invites JOHN CHO and KAL PENN to the stage. They gush about the success and influence of this sitcom on their own work, and praise those who took the jokes away from white writers. "Hey, I heard even white people watched it." They fondly remember comedians Pat Morita and Jack Soo. (Reprieve Song: *We Can Be Funny*)

CHO invites the nubie director MIKE KATO to the stage. Applause and flowers. Then Q&A from the audience. Someone stands to ask a question: "Professor Mike Kato, do you recognize me? KATO squints through the spotlights. "Are you a student of mine?" The questioner dons an anime mask and announces, "I am KO-KO, the Lord High Executioner!" He then produces from the inside of his heavily padded kimono two automatic assault pistols.

The End.

ANIME WONG
A CYBERASIAN ODYSSEY

A Performance in Six Mangas

Written by Karen Tei Yamashita

MANGA I

Goddess of Democracy

I would rather be cyborg than goddess.

MANGA II

Sirens of Angel Island

Sirens were created by man. They evolved. They rebelled.
There are many copies. And they have a plan.

(or)

You're frakking a toaster!

MANGA III

BorgAsian Queen

Surrender your bodies. Your culture will adapt.
Resistance is futile.

COMMERCIAL INTERLUDE

iToto

She's so sweet with her get-hack stare.

MANGA IV

Ridley's Believe It or Not Alien

A survivor . . . unclouded by conscience, remorse,
or delusions of morality.

MANGA V

Mulan Will Make a Man out of You

Mysterious as the dark side of the moon

MANGA VI

Iron Chef Takes Back the Hattori Hanzo

Tell me what you eat, and I will tell you what you are.

PERFORMERS

SUPER STAR
Anime Wong

OTHERS
CYBORGS (extras/kuroki/puppeteers)
ANDROIDS (techies/DJs)
ALIENS (chorus)
PAPARAZZI (someone's gotta record this nonsense)

LOCATION
CyberAsia (okay, duke it out for CyberAsianAmerica; okay,
CyberAsiaPacificAmerica . . .)

MUSIC
Sampled (stolen) techno, modified by Asian DJs

VIDEO
YouTube and Powerpoint

WEBSITE
animewong.com
(coming to your global cybertheater on demand)

MANGA I: GODDESS OF DEMOCRACY

I would rather be cyborg than goddess.
(with apologies to Donna Haraway and the Chinese student movement)

CYBORGS *roll out the Goddess of Democracy/Statue of Liberty and position her beneath the lights dramatically. Music and drumroll perhaps. It becomes evident that her face is African American, in fact that of Maya Angelou.*

CYBORG: Aya! Wrong goddess!

CYBORGS *run in with a stepladder, unscrew the statue's head, and replace it with another head, this time that of Hillary R. Clinton, maybe. Again, the lights come on dramatically with music and drumroll. They gather around to appreciate it for a moment, then shake their heads, scale the stepladder again, and replace it with an Asian face. Perhaps it's the face of John Lone, or maybe Mao wearing a Madam Butterfly wig, or Ziyi Zhang as a geisha. A series of other Asian faces might be superimposed by way of projection onto the face. Lights and music rumble dramatically.*

In the backdrop, a video of Tiananmen Square. East is Red. Roar of crowds and speechmaking. Mao's photos. Grand history. Then, tanks rolling across, approaching, then looming larger and larger. The statue is rolled forward to meet the tanks. Flowers are strewn. Tanks morph into Hummers and other vehicles of war and weaponry; then cityscapes, cars, crowds, the 80808 Olympic games spectacle, then the generic shopping mall.

CYBORGS *roll the statue around this imagescape. Crowds of* CYBORGS *and* ALIENS *walk along to recreate the shoppers moving hurriedly to their commercial appointments.*

Video shows a retina scan recognition system, loaded and working. Or perhaps, from the stepladder, a CYBORG *scans the eyes of other* CYBORGS *with a supermarket scanner. The* CYBORG *scans the eyes of the statue. A video image responds.*

VOICE: Ah! Ah-Yakimoto! Pleased to see you again. Please step
                    this way. We have your exact size and favorite color too!
                    How about it, Yakimoto-san? Buy a new look!

CYBORGS *replace the statue's wig with an Astro Boy wig.*

VOICE: Buy new boobs!

CYBORGS *add breasts to statue.*

VOICE: Tummy tuck? Lipo suck-tion!

CYBORGS *connect statue to hose with a sucking action.*

VOICE: Eye job! Big eyes! Round eyes! Blue geisha memoir eyes!

CYBORGS *add Japanime facial features to statue's face: big blue eyes! Eyes are
rescanned.*

VOICE: Oh indeed? Most honorable guest and valued client,
                    Anime Wong . . . pleased to see you again! Right this
                    way! And will you be wanting the usual?

CYBORG *attaches a large rubber penis to the front of the statue. The penis flips
this way and that, gets really excited, flings around, then hangs there.*

VOICE (OF GODDESS):
                    Come now. Come play with my Orientalia. Come you
                    tired, you poor, you huddled masses, yearning, yearning,
                    to breathe free. Free. Wretched, wretched refuse! But
                    look at me! I'm teeming. Teeming! Virtually teeming.
                    Homeless and tempest tossed! I lift. Lift. Lift. Lift my
                    lamp.

Lamp's light turns on.

VOICE (OF GODDESS):
                    I lift my lamp to your golden door!

CYBORG *dog runs up to statue, sniffing and excited.*

CYBORG: Toto? Come back here. Toto, now what do you think you are doing? Toto, remember, we're not in Little Tokyo anymore.

Back-and-forth movement of penis with the sound of sawing.

CYBORG: Oh my! Toto, look, if I'm not mistaken, it seems to be a weenie on the end of a sword!

Sword cuts through the body of the goddess. Possible puff of smoke, rumbling drums, goddess music. ANIME WONG *pushes self out of statue, looking like some kind of androgynous Asian Barbie with Anna May Wong makeup and hair and maybe a version of a* Thief of Baghdad *costume, the apron flap being the image of a Warhol Mao covering her hot pants.*

ANIME WONG: Stuffy old goddess. (*stretches, struts about, walks up to the golden door, and strikes a pose; tosses the rubber penis into the crowd, looks out, and addresses the audience*) What? Are you going to just sit there? While all the action is in there? Through those gold mountain doors?

On screen, huge, imposing, Orientalized, but also globalized, capitalized, empire-like doors appear as a tremendous backdrop. Think Hero, Ran, Cleopatra, Clytemnestra, Throne of Blood, Dr. No., *and so on.* ANIME WONG *dramatically pushes the doors open; there is creaking and rumbling, smoke creeping out from within, virtual light flashing—whatever that is. Beyond, a sped-up video shows a mishmash of urban scenes (a là* Blade Runner*) of Tokyo, Hong Kong, Taipei, Singapore, Seoul, Beijing, L.A, the global Chinatown.*

ANIME WONG: Ooou. Our global Chinatown. Confusing. Multilingual. Transnational. Sub(di)versity on every corner. And for all you golden goddesses, it's the Matrix-archy! And . . . in techno-color. One hundred blooming flowers! One hundred million miracles!

Flashing lights. Backdrop of Zhang Yimou's 80808 Olympic spectacle and techno-multiplication of thousands of synchronized tai chi performers, plus a battlefield of electronic drummers. 80808 flashes.

ANIME WONG: The future is here, ku ku clock. (*again addressing audience*) Coming? (*when no one follows, shrugs*) Oh well, suit yourselves. (*walks seductively through the doors and away*)

MANGA II: THE SIRENS OF ANGEL ISLAND

The Sirens were created by man. They evolved. They rebelled. There are many copies. And they have a plan.
or
You're frakking a toaster!

CYBORG: (*spoken in an almost unintelligible broken English*)
So to maku a rongu estory shorto, fasto taimu, Anime Wong trabulingu by shipu to Angelru Irando, many sairansu frying round and round. Okay, I exprainu. Sairansu hafu bird, hafu woman. Topu hafu woman. Bottom hafu bird. Maybe like angeru. Ah (*bats head*) so! Therefore, maybe that'su why this irando name is Angelru Irando. So many angelru Saironsu. Okay? Sairansu has spesharu talrento to singing. You know riku rive karaoke. Making beautifulru music with singing voice. You hear Sairansu and you go crazy. You can't helrupu yourself. You get carried away, drowning drowning bery tragicalry in the Pacific Ocean rim. Grubu grubu grubu.

But helrupu is on the way! Anime Wong no drowning. Because this poet guy, Orfeo, he's the one to save Anime Wong and the whole CyberAsian crew. How does he do it? By pretty singing and his Greek-style ukelrelre. Okay not ukelrelre, maybe more like Chinesu-stylru harpu. Okay maybe was a shamisen. Actualry, someone telru me was a Yamaha. Anyway, you get the pictucha. Orfeu praying so beautifulru, more beautifulru than the most beautifulru singing of the Sairansu. So no one ristening to Sairansu. Orfeu, he's numba one. Asian American Idolru.

During this monologue, CYBORGS *reenact* ANIME WONG'*s boat journey past Angel Island and the seductive Sirens. Video also shows what the Sirens look like: half woman, half bird. Then there's* ORPHEUS *with his lyre, playing and singing.* CYBORG SIRENS *seem to be singing in mute, their mouths moving and cooing. Of course, they all look the same. There are many copies.*

CYBORG (ORPHEUS):
>Where have all the flowers gone?
>Long time passing?
>Where have all the flowers gone?
>Long long time ago.
>Where have all the flowers gone?
>Gone—

ANIME WONG: (*steps up, draws a sword, and hacks off Orpheus's head, tossing it to* CYBORG NYMPHS) Fucking folk singing.

CYBORG: Whatchu doing? Now we all gonna be tragicalry drowned into Pacific Ocean rim by irresistible sexy, seductive, provocative, gorgeous, most perfect Sairansu.

ANIME WONG: Only weak men fall for Sirens. (*walks into audience and picks up someone to address*) Isn't that right? Only weak men fall for Sirens. Right? (*pulls audience member to stage*)

CYBORG: Quicklry! Sairansu coming! (*motions to other* CYBORGS, *who strap* ANIME WONG *and, in the confusion, the audience member, to the ship mast*)

ANIME WONG: Listen, cyborg. Speak English. It's *Si-rens*. (*to audience member*) Tell him. *Si-rens*.

CYBORG: Sai-ran-su.

ANIME WONG: Watch our lips: *Si-rens. Si-rens.* Sirens.

CYBORG: Sai-ron-su. Sai-ron-su. Sai-ron-su.

Suddenly, the CYBORG SIRENS *who've been muted are unmuted; they break out into a techno version of Carl Orff's* Carmina Burana *in full force. Blast of wind (maybe by way of portable fan) from their mouths. A video panorama of battle scenes a là* Battlestar Galactica *races across.*

CYBORG (SIREN): (*sung*)
        Come away baby.
        Come away and see
        if you can push my
        sensitive buttons,
        light up my intricate
        electronics.
        I dare you.

ANIME WONG: Sex with a Siren? Can it be real sex?

CYBORG (SIREN): Am I not human?

ALIENS: Are you nuts? You're a frakking toaster!

        (*to* ANIME WONG)
        It's a frakking fatal fem.
        Frak with a toaster
        And you'll fry your stem.

ANIME WONG.   (*resoluto again*) Only weak men fall for Sirens.

ALIEN: Sirens are my best friends.

PAPARAZZI: Fag hag!

ALIEN: Where is Margaret Cho when you need her?

PAPARAZZI: Fag hag!

ALIEN: Where's my comic relief?

CYBORG (SIRENS): (*circling* ANIME WONG)
        (*sung*)
        Come away baby.
        Come away and see
        if you can push our
        sensitive buttons,
        light up our intricate

electronics.
We dare you to try.

ANIME WONG: (*relenting*) Oh, but how can sex
taste and smell so fine?
Raw pink tuna belly,
succulent steaming dumplings,
and
the very dim sum of everything,
hot sriracha cha cha . . .

ALIENS: Frakking fatal fem!
Frak with a toaster
and fry your stem!

CYBORG (SIRENS):
What are you afraid of?
We dare you to try.

ANIME WONG *roars out of restraints and (with the audience member), has sex
with all the* SIRENS. *Techno-sound version of* Carmina Burana *returns.
Miraculously, the* SIRENS' *spines all light up and* ANIME WONG *survives.
Bells and whistles. Audience applause.*

CYBORG: (*to audience member*) You've won! What's your name?
_____, you're our surviving and, therefore, winning
contestant!

CYBORGS *rush in with the winnings: all toasters.*

CYBORG: You've won a digital, handheld, fully automatic, solar
rechargeable, self-censoring, fully evolving with down-
loadable two million gigahertz memory, wireless Blue-
tooth, airportable eco-sustainable, seven-year warranty
. . . blah blah blah . . . toaster.

CYBORGS: There are many copies.
This model is made in China.
This model is made in Japan.

> This model is made in Singapore.
> This model is made in Hong Kong.
> This model is made in Korea.
> This model is made in the Philippines.
> This model is made in Thailand.
> This model is made in Vietnam.
> This model is made in India.
> This model is made in Malaysia.
> This model is made in Laos . . .

ANIME WONG: You can't have sex with that.

CYBORG (BUTTERFLY): (*wearing a Madame Butterfly wig*)
Oh yes you can! (*demonstrates sex with the toasters—pretty kinky stuff!*)

Puccini's music wails, techno-style. CYBORG (BUTTERFLY) *stuffs English muffins into one toastser, French fries into another, rice balls into another. Suddenly* CYBORGS *run away with the toasters.*

CYBORG (BUTTERFLY): (*running after them, stumbling and weeping*)
Come back! That toaster has my baby!

Tragic ending ensues. CYBORGS *wipe stage clean.* ANIME WONG *reappears with a toaster and audience member.*

ANIME WONG: (*to audience member*) You're so lucky. I myself have never won anything. I'm so jealous. (*caresses toaster lovingly until it pops a couple of muffins or whatever*) So what will it be? Organic sprouted wheat and soy with walnuts and raisins, or dark Russian rye with fennel seeds, or sourdough jalapeño cheddar cheese?

AUDIENCE MEMBER:

_____.

ANIME WONG: (*raises eyebrows*) Oh really? (*picks the hot muffins out of the toaster and stuffs one into the audience member's mouth and the other into her mouth*)

MANGA III: BORGASIAN QUEEN

Your culture will adapt . . . Resistance is futile.

Techno Star Trek music and lots of smoke and steam. When it settles, ANIME
WONG *appears in seductive leatherwear. She's attached by a spaghetti of metal
plumbing, articulated tubing, and pipes to a larger contraption of welded
metal parts and heavy machinery that extends behind her in wings and claws,
like the body of a great dragon. That's right—she's the dragon lady.*

ANIME WONG: We are the BorgAsians. Lower your shields and surrender your bodies. We will add your biological and technical distinctiveness to our own. Your culture will adapt to
service us. Resistance is futile. Are you even listening? I
repeat: surrender your bodies. Your culture will adapt.
Resistance is futile.

ALIENS: (*chanting*) Surrender your bodies. Your culture will adapt.
Resistance is futile. (*repeat*)

*Backdrop to the chanting: a revolving video/Powerpoint slide presentation
shows, in rapid succession, a series of hybrid/mixed/hapa human portraits,
layered on top of video footage of cosmopolitan urban landscapes, real and
fictional—old sci-fi, cyberfilms, manga, and so on.*

CYBORG: (*sitting in audience*) I surrender! I surrender all to you . . .

(*sung loudly, a là Celine Dion*)
Take me! Take me!
I give my life to you, baby!
I'll break free! Take me!

(*steps through, around, over audience*)
I surrender!

ANIME WONG: Who are you?

CYBORG: You don't recognize me?

Flash on screen: Hint! *and a series of stills of the* Star Trek *character Data.*

ANIME WONG: Oh, now I remember. You're the one with the yellow
              complexion.

DATA POSES *under a halo of yellow light, or maybe* CYBORGS *move around him, pointing yellow flashlights.*

ANIME WONG: Your yellow tinge, I love it. It's so artificial. How did you
              acquire it?

CYBORG (DATA): It's my unique bioplast sheeting. I was born this way.

ANIME WONG: Born?

CYBORG (DATA): All right—modeled, if you like.

ANIME WONG·   We don't often come across your model.

CYBORG (DATA): That's because only a minority of us were modeled in this
              particular hue.

ANIME WONG: A model minority. How quaint. I suppose you're also
              intelligent in math and science, a hardworking achiever,
              and a Republican?

CYBORG (DATA): I'm the one you want.

ANIME WONG: What makes you so sure? Maybe we lean toward the
              otaku type, the insular techno-weirdo peeping Tom who
              cultivates paranoia and stalking activities in game videos.

On screen: examples of the otaku techno-weirdo.

              Or, we could go for Akira, a deranged psychosociopathic
              kid who, becoming powerful with a nuclear arsenal of

magic and machine guns (NRA approved), takes bloody
revenge.

On screen: examples of the bullied Akira psychosociopath.

CYBORG (DATA): You mean you don't want me? You'd take those pre-
tenders over me? I'm the real thing! Completely syn-
thetic! I'm CyberAsian down to my last emotion chip!

ANIME WONG: Well then, calm down and deactivate it, will you? . . . We
used to be like humans, you know, but we've evolved.

CYBORG (DATA): I was never human, but I believe I'm becoming human.
But sometimes I'm convinced I'm human. I dream about
being human. I dream like a human. Humans dream,
don't they? I dream!

ANIME WONG: Dream?

CYBORG (DATA): Yes. Come to think of it, I had an amazing dream last
night . . .

*On screen: video clips of various bizarre nightmares—Shinya Tsukamoto's
Tetsuo/Iron Man with a gyrating metal penis; Sin City Miho with her
swords slicing up bodies; Minority Report floating precogs; Anna May Wong
as Tiger Lily, rubbing noses with Peter Pan; Ghost in the Shell sexaroids
and scene with scientist Dr. Haraway, and so on.*

CYBORG (DATA): And I have memories, distinct memories, like humans. I
remember!

ANIME WONG: What do you remember?

CYBORG (DATA): Look! I have these photos. I can show them to you to
prove my memories.

*Powerpoint showing of series of photos by Arnold Genthe, Dorothea Lange,
Ansel Adams, and other famous photographers.*

CYBORG (DATA): See! There I am as a child growing up. And there with my parents. And there with my high school sweetheart. And there . . . And there . . . And there . . .

ANIME WONG: Oh rubbish. We also have an album of your memories. Observe.

Powerpoint presentation of a series of photographs: Doraemon, Pokemon, R2D2, Song Liling, Mr. Sulu, Hello Kitty, transformers, Power Rangers, replicants, androids, and so on.

ANIME WONG: Here's a photo of you as a child, and your siblings. Here's a photo of your dog. Here's a photo of your mother. And here, your father. Here's your first girlfriend. Here you are with your high school buddies . . .

CYBORG (DATA): Why are you mocking me? My memories are stored at the Smithsonian!

On the screen, a list of websites are displayed: Go to http://www.smithsonian.edu; Go to http://www.japaneseamericannationalmuseum.org; Go to chinesehistoricalsociety.org; Go to http://manilatown.org.

ANIME WONG: Pathetic photos. CyberAsians and your memories. Always trying to prove you're human. What's all the fuss about?

CYBORG (DATA): Don't you see? I am a living, thinking entity born in a sea of information! I remember, therefore I am!

ANIME WONG: You remember what? You remember the past. Screw the past. Screw your photographic memories. Think of the superiority of BorgAsia. We live in the future, at the cutting edge. You others can never catch up.

ALIENS: (*chanting*) Surrender your bodies. Your culture will adapt. Resistance is futile. (*repeat*)

ANIME WONG: Do you surrender?

CYBORG (DATA):   I surrender. A foolish human question, but do you love me?

ANIME WONG: You are pure data: 0101010010101 . . . what's not to love?

CYBORG (DATA):   Wait. I forgot. There are rules about robot sex.

ANIME WONG: Rules?

Rules appear on screen: Robot Sex Law #1: A robot may not allow a human being to come to harm during sex. Robot Sex Law #2: A robot must acquiesce to the sexual pleasure of a human being except where such sex would conflict with the first law. Robot Sex Law #3: A robot must protect its own sexuality as long as such protection does not conflict with the first and second laws.

CYBORG (DATA):   *(spoken while engaging in sex . . . okay, foreplay)*
        Robot Sex Law Number One: A robot may not allow a human being to come to harm during sex.

ANIME WONG: What's the fun of that? Oh.

CYBORG (DATA):   Robot Sex Law Number Two: A robot must acquiesce to the sexual pleasure of a human being, except where such sex would conflict with the first law.

ANIME WONG: Acquiesce, yes. We can bend the rules.

CYBORG (DATA):   Robot Sex Law Number Three: A robot must protect its own sexuality as long as such protection does not conflict with the first and second laws.

ANIME WONG: Robots are screwed. Do you love me?

CYBORG (DATA):   You are an entire civilization. What's not to love?

ANIME WONG *and* CYBORG *engage in passionate, even athletic, theatrical sex, despite her complicated leatherwear and the tangle of metal plumbing, dragon wings, and claws. Meanwhile, Powerpoint presentation spins with* Star *newsflash updates:* Anime Wong sleeps with Ridley Scott! Anime Wong in steamy relationship with Harrison Ford! Anime Wong seen with new beau: Bruce Willis! Anime Wong in love with Will Smith! Anime Wong vacationing in the Yucatán with Tom Cruise! Anime Wong gives Quentin Tarantino the shove! Anime Wong in threesome with Lana and Andy Wachowski! Anime Wong to marry Steven Spielberg! Anime Wong divorces George Lucas! *and so on . . .*

ALIENS: (*chanting*) Surrender your bodies. Your culture will adapt. Resistance is futile. (*repeat*)

Return to chanting backdrop: a revolving video/Powerpoint presentation rapidly shows a succession of hybrid/mixed/hapa human portraits, layered on top of video footage of cosmopolitan urban landscapes, real and fictional— old sci-fi, cyberfilms, manga, and so on. A cloud of smoke obscures the final moments of surrender and adaptation.

COMMERCIAL INTERLUDE: ITOTO

She's so sweet with her get-back stare.

CYBORGS *heft or roll in a toilet to center stage. Perhaps Japanese commercials for the Toto toilet tinkle on screen.*

CYBORG: This is the newest model of the iToto, also known as the intelligent toilet.

CYBORGS *run around the toilet, admiring it and testing its many features.*

CYBORG: How intelligent you ask? Besides its normal douching, air drying—that's right, say good-bye to toilet paper . . . bye-bye!—and massaging features, look! It plays music!

A CYBORG *opens the toilet cover and it sings an iPod tune. Open the cover again, another song!*

CYBORG: And it can even talk to you.

On screen, the toilet buttons are displayed with a menu.

CYBORG: It's possible to have iToto speak, but you must choose a voice. Would you prefer the voice of . . .

On screen, the menu choices might be: Yoda, Chow Yun Fat, Miyoshi Umeki, George Takei, Bruce Lee, Pikachu. CYBORGS *highlight and press the options, and examples of the various voices can be heard.*

CYBORG: Isn't that amazing?

ANIME WONG: (*seems to appear out of nowhere*) But the most amazing feature about the iToto is its ability to anticipate your every need. Let me demonstrate. (*walks up to the toilet; by some magic the toilet cover opens for her; she sits down on the toilet and smiles, then closes her eyes and assumes a meditational position; after a moment of digital Zen, she rises, walks away, and the cover closes)*

Automatic sound of flushing.

ANIME WONG: Impressed, aren't you? Well now, let us continue to impress you. The iToto is so intelligent, it simply knows who you really are.

CYBORGS *line up in front of the toilet, but the cover never opens.*

ANIME WONG: Silly cyborgs. You have no need for these facilities. The iToto already knows. Let's just say it's sniffed you out.

CYBORGS *slink away in dejection.*

ANIME WONG: But let's say you have a manly need to pee. (*saunters up like a guy to the toilet, at which the first cover, then the second cover, open wide*) See? (*looks around and smiles*)

CYBORGS *line up with fake penises, dildos, and even diapers, but all fail to get both covers to open.*

ANIME WONG: (*to* CYBORGS) Useless cyborgs, eunichs all of you! What we need are some real men. Are there any real men around here? (*looks out at the audience*) Well?

CYBORGS *go out into the audience and drag* VOLUNTEERS *to the stage. They are positioned in front of the* ITOTO, *and the covers respond accordingly. Depending on the volunteer, maybe the covers open to erect attention, or perhaps tentatively or very slowly, or they become confused and plop up and down. Music and/or voices of menu choices accompany opening and closing.*

ANIME WONG: (*stands to one side of one* VOLUNTEER *and observes the covers opening wide; looks into the toilet, nods, and points*) You know, there's a ghost in there. How about it? Are you willing to do business with the ghost? . . . You don't imagine that the iToto is free, now do you? You must feed the ghost in the iToto. Let me demonstrate.

ITOTO: (*voice of Yoda*) Feed me!

CYBORGS *rush forward with word cards. Screen above flashes the words on the cards:* Science. Fiction.

ITOTO: (*voice of Chow Yun Fat*) Feed me!

ANIME WONG *shows the cards to the audience, then hands them to the* VOLUNTEER, *urging him or her to toss them together into the toilet. Sound of munching, grunting, flushing.* CYBORGS *lead subsequent* VOLUNTEERS *to the* ITOTO *with similar "feed me" cards:* East. West.; Technology. Culture.; Machines. Humans.

CYBORG: (*announces as the final* VOLUNTEER *approaches the* ITOTO)
                   Oh no, we're plum out of dichotomies! (*pulls out his pock-*
                   ets to show they're empty and looks sheepishly at the VOLUN-
                   TEER) Other than dichotomies, the iToto only accepts
                   cash. I think there's an ATM machine in the lobby . . .

ITOTO: (*voice of Miyoshi Umeki*) Feed me!

ANIME WONG: Oh that's ridiculous. Get rid of it.

CYBORGS *rush around the* ITOTO *and lift it off the stage as if it is extremely heavy (though it's probably made from Styrofoam), wavering precariously with their burden.*

ANIME WONG: (*points to the last* VOLUNTEER) What's your name?

VOLUNTEER: _____.

ANIME WONG: _____, you are now the proud owner of
                   this year's newest and completely loaded model of a
                   MyFaceMySpace iToto!

CYBORGS: (*hand off* ITOTO *to last* VOLUNTEER) Congratulations!

ITOTO: (*voice of George Takei*) Feed me?

MANGA IV: RIDLEY'S BELIEVE IT OR NOT ALIEN

A survivor . . . unclouded by conscience, remorse, or delusions of morality

Synthesizer arrangements of classical music such as Beethoven's Fifth Symphony *or Wagner's* Valkyries, *mixed with triumphant Astro Boy and Godzilla theme music, songs, and sound effects. When the lights come up, there are two spotlights on two identical* ANIME WONGS.

ANIME WONG I: (*looks over at* ANIME WONG II) What are you doing there? Get off my stage.

ANIME WONG II: No need to be rude. Don't you remember? There are many copies.

ANIME WONG I: Oh bullshit. That was back in Manga Number Two. Besides, copies do not give rise to variety and originality. Life perpetuates itself through diversity, and this includes the ability to sacrifice itself when it is necessary. So, sacrifice your copy, now!

ANIME WONG II: You're just jealous because I'm the good Anime Wong.

ANIME WONG I: Wrong. There's no such Anime Wong.

ANIME WONG II: Believe it or not, there are positive representations of our kind.

On screen, video manga shows a rendition of Mickey Mouse that morphs into a rendition of Pinocchio that morphs into a rendition of a bomb with the name Little Boy and is placed into a plane named the Enola Gay and dropped over Hiroshima. From the mushroom cloud that explodes over the city emerges a composite boy with torqued hair and jet engine feet: Astro Boy. Majestic Astro Boy music accompanies. CYBORGS *rush around with a plastic blow-up copy of Astro Boy, flying him around the stage.*

ANIME WONG II: (*hugs the blow-up of Astro Boy*) Little Boy Astro arrived to do good deeds and to save humanity.

ANIME WONG I: I feel so much safer! (*pokes Astro Boy's head*) Is there a mind in there?

ANIME WONG II: Oh I wouldn't know. But there is a conscience. A sense of duty and of sacrifice.

ANIME WONG I: An airhead with a conscience. Banzai!

ANIME WONG II: Think about it: In the war on terrorism, only cyborgs can save us. What human would be willing to make such a sacrifice?

ANIME WONG I: What human indeed? Oh, now what have we here? (*walks over to a* CYBORG *writhing on his back, center stage*)

On screen, a YouTube segment of the parasitoid extraterrestrial Xenomorph busting out of the chest of this white guy. On stage, the same chest-busting birth is performed by the bodies of not just one but several CYBORGS, *all writhing in painful labor. From their bloody chests emerge plastic replicas of Godzilla.* CYBORGS *assisting are appropriately spattered with goo and blood.* CYBORGS *nurse, burp, and wrap up the lizards, then push them around in strollers and buggies. Split screen: On one half—manga of baby Xenomorph/ Godzillas training in judo, karate, kung fu, boxing. On the other half—Astro Boy fighting various robots. Until finally, one day . . .*

CYBORG: Ladies and gentlemen, welcome to the final fight of the www dot virtual contest to name the winner of our final frontier, the very future of CyberAsian life on Earth. Will it be on the right side of the ring, our techno-Oriental atomic robot/cyborg/android, programmed with a con-science, a sense of sacrifice and duty, and the will to save humanity, our global citizen: Little Boy Astro?

ANIME WONG II, *costumed as Little Boy Astro, raises her arms in victory.* ALIENS *give a roar of approval and applause.*

CYBORG: Or will it be on the left side of the ring, that phallic-faced dinosaur, that supersized insect with its DNA programmed to survive, born out of great human evil but impervious to any knowledge of sin, our chest buster and global alien: Godzilla?

ANIME WONG I, *costumed as a Xenomorph/Godzilla, raises arms in victory.* ALIENS *give another roar of approval and applause.* PAPARAZZI *run into photograph and film the fighting heroes.* CYBORGS *ritualize the ring as if it were a sumo dohyo, with accompanying yells and commentary.* CYBORGS *also hook up air tubes to the inflatable costumes of* ANIME WONG I *and* ANIME WONG II.

CYBORG: (*garbed in the sumo official's attire, signals the start of the fight*) Yoshi!

ALIENS *cheer and jeer, chanting and taunting and making a general fanfare. The two* ANIMES *go after each other, chasing each other this way and that, tumbling around and around. On either side of the ring, the* CYBORGS *are busy pumping air into the inflatable costumes. Very slowly, the costumes grow in size until they are supersized and beach bull likes the* ANIMES *lumber and bump about like astronauts in space. With the help of bungee cords, they might even float. In a last, furious attempt to attack each other, they rush at each other from either side of the ring. At the moment of contact, the stage goes black with the sound of a huge explosion. On screen, scenes of the Big Bang and other cosmic explosions accompanied by the initial synthesizer arrangements of classical music such as Beethoven's* Fifth Symphony *or Wagner's* Valkyries.

MANGA V: MULAN WILL MAKE A MAN OUT OF YOU

Mysterious as the dark side of the moon

On screen, a YouTube clip of a Mulan *segment: "I'll Make a Man out of You."*

ANIME WONG: (*looking Kabukiesque, like Queen Amidala*) Welcome to the land of Mu. That's right. There's Disneyland, Never Never Land, Soapland, and here we are in Muland, where anyone—man, woman, or child—can become a man, I mean, a mu. For after all, isn't manhood, oh that is to say muhood, just a matter of strategy and tactics? Now, let's get down to business. Muland's virtual CEO and puppet-master speaks to us from millennial knowledge.

On screen: manga with various representations of Pat Morita morphing into Key Luke morphing into Toshiro Mifune morphing into Bruce Lee morphing into Yoda morphing into Chow Yun Fat morphing into Master Splinter morphing into Jet Li morphing into Jackie Chan morphing into Batou morphing into John Cho morphing into Federation viceroys from Star Wars, and so on. You get the morphing picture. During this morphing session, CYBORGS *take turns speaking/dubbing in multiple voices.*

CYBORGS: Muhood is a matter of . . . vital importance to . . . CyberAsia, a matter of . . . life or death, the road to . . . survival or ruin. On no account . . . may the study of muhead . . . so sorry, we mean mu-hood . . . be neglected.

ANIME WONG: Oh, get to the point, will you?

CYBORG: All muhood is based on deception.

CYBORGS *demonstrate various methods of deception: queer cowboys, Clark Kent salaryman-type ripping off suit and tie, transformations of Power Rangers, Kabuki performers, and so on.*

CYBORG: When capable, feign incapacity. When active, inactivity.

CYBORG: Pretend inferiority and encourage arrogance.

CYBORGS *mount and swing from bungee cords and wave around swords, guns, knives, bows and arrows, spears, or anything else pointy. Use caution: bungee cord masculinity can be dangerous!* ALIENS *form trooper units, congregate, and are variously positioned or disorganized across the stage.*

CYBORG: (*zooming around on bungee cord*) When near, make it appear that you are far away.

CYBORG: Feign disorder, and strike!

CYBORG: When he is concentrated, prepare against him. Where he is strong, avoid him.

CYBORG: Attack when he is unprepared. Rally out when he does not expect you.

CYBORG: Keep him under strain and wear him down.

ANIME WONG: (*appears out of nowhere—okay, from the rafters—with the longest and biggest sword of all, and dressed up like Aurra Sing*) When he is united, divide.

ALIENS *scatter in disarray, utterly and totally defeated.*

ANIME WONG: I love being the woman warrior.

CYBORGS *parade down the runway cross-dressed as CyberAsian versions of Cinderella, Snow White, Sleeping Beauty, Alice, Pocahontas, Jessica Rabbit, Tarzan's Jane, Esmeralda, Arial, Jasmine, and so on.* PAPARAZZI *run after them.* ALIENS *cheer, scream, and swoon. All contestants line up in courtly fashion with* ANIME WONG *at center top tier with crown and flowers.*

ANIME WONG: Once upon a time, in a Muland far far away, the great CyberAsian strategist Sun Tzu was given an audience

with the King of Mu. And the King of Mu said to Sun
Tzu . . .

CYBORG (MU KING):

Here are one hundred and eighty of the most beautiful
women of my kingdom. And for good measure, I even
throw in my two most favorite concubines. (*throws in two
concubines*) If you are the great CyberAsian strategist you
say you are, turn these women into men.

Faint techno echo of Mulan: *"I'll Make a Man out of You."*

CYBORG (SUN TZU): (*bowing graciously*)

No problem.

ANIME WONG: So it was that Sun Tzu began their basic training, lining
up these beautiful women and handing them each a hal-
berd. He yelled out . . .

CYBORG (SUN TZU):

Face right!

CYBORG *princesses all giggle and laugh.*

ANIME WONG: The women all laughed, but Sun Tzu calmly gave his
order five more times.

CYBORG (SUN TZU):

Face right! Face right! Face right! Face right! Face right!

ANIME WONG: But each time the women laughed. So Sun Tzu stopped
to explain his orders.

CYBORG (SUN TZU):

Let me explain. When I command you to face right, it
means that you will turn your bodies and FACE RIGHT!

ANIME WONG: At which, he swiftly beheaded two women.

CYBORG (SUN TZU) *borrows* ANIME WONG*'s sword and beheads two women; this beheading action is of course made possible by* CYBORG *staging magic.*

ANIME WONG: And in succession, also slashed off the heads of the Mu king's favorite concubines. Tsk tsk.

CYBORG (SUN TZU) *beheads two more women.*

ANIME WONG: After that, as you can imagine, the other women performed quite well. And the king of Mu, though mourning the loss of his favorite concubines, realized the great capacity of our CyberAsian strategist, Sun Tzu, and made him his general.

CYBORGS *drag off the bodies of the slain women, and* CYBORG (SUN TZU) *continues on with his remaining* CYBORG *princess contingent in strict formation.*

ANIME WONG: So, as I was saying, in Muland, any man, woman, or even child can become a mu. It's just a matter of strategy and tactics.

CYBORG (ORPHAN ANIME) *waddles in wearing a Raggedy Ann red wig, a schoolgirl skirt, and kneesocks, dragging a stuffed dog and Hello Kitty paraphernalia, and looking very cute.*

ANIME WONG: Oh you are so cute. I used to be a cute schoolgirl just like you. But then, one day, I grew up.

CYBORG (ORPHAN ANIME):

Don't patronize me, bitch. I'm a genius, and a hacker, and a bona fide killer in a kid's body. (*pulls a spiked metal ball on a chain out of Hello Kitty bag and swings it around*) And check this out. (*strips off her shirt to expose her back, entirely tattooed*)

ALIENS *gasp.* CYBORGS *rush in. They light a cigarette for* CYBORG (ORPHAN ANIME), *pass her a martini, and slip her some condoms.*

ANIME WONG: Oh my. (*to audience*) And you thought Little Boy Astro or Akira or the Ninja Turtles were tough.

CYBORG (ORPHAN ANIME): (*snickering*)
                Toys.

ANIME WONG: When I was a child, I spoke as a child, I understood as a child, I thought as a child.

CYBORG (ORPHAN ANIME):
                When I became a man, I put away childish things.

ANIME WONG AND CYBORG (ORPHAN ANIME): (*holding up a mirror through which to admire themselves*)
                For now, we see through a glass darkly . . .

As ANIME WONG *and* CYBORG (ORPHAN ANIME) *ascend gloriously to the mandate of the heavens, the faint techno echo of "I'll Make a Man out of You" becomes a roar and fills the stage.*

MANGA VI: IRON CHEF TAKES BACK THE HATTORI HANZO

Tell me what you eat, and I will tell you what you are.

On screen, narrative video with techno CyberAsian Iron Chef *soundtrack is accompanied by a chorus of* ALIENS. ANIME WONG *is in an elaborate silk smoking jacket, some kind of Chinafied hairstyle and facial makeup, and sipping from a gigantic wine goblet, sitting regally somewhere plush beside a flickering fire, spitting flames.*

ANIME WONG: (*on screen*) If my memory serves me correctly, centuries ago I had the culinary foresight to banish all knives to the realm of the kitchen and to the province of my iron chefs. For what can be more barbaric than a knife and fork at the table? If one were to contemplate treachery at my table during those peaceful moments of elegant and sumptuous partaking of so many sensual delights, these (*holds up pair of silver chopsticks*) might be the only pointed objects within reach, thus forcing any assassin to conceive of a much higher degree of creativity and imagination.

Dramatic opening Iron Chef *music with on-screen Kitchen Stadium backdrop, employing multiple levitating daises; giant Mao-like portraits of* ANIME WONG *wielding knives, torches, and fluttering flags; and an army of* CYBORGS *dressed as chefs.*

ANIME WONG: (*rising on a dais amid smoke and lights; she is costumed in another Queen Amidala extravaganza*) Creativity and imagination! Any ordinary outlaw can fly over a steamed dish of seven treasures to blind a king, but that's been done before. And after all, how banal to render such a dim sum. More difficult to use one's skills of hatchet and dagger behind the scenes and in secrecy. Here in this arena, two of my greatest, most invincible chefs will lay down their knives forged in fire on this very battlefield, using all their skills—deceit, treachery, and duplicity—

to execute artistic dishes never before encountered. And
if my memory serves me correctly, today is a good day to
die. (*peels and bites into a banana*)

*Split on screen: YouTube video collages of Uma Thurman and Lucy Liu in a
series of martial art and knife and sword scenes, slashing, kicking, punching,
stabbing, and so on. Uma's collage can be of any number of non–Asian
women—probably all blonde, 007 babes, undercover spies, buffed-up bad
girls—kicking ass. By contrast, Lucy's video collage can incorporate any number of Asian women: Michelle Yeoh, Ziyi Zhang, Kelly Hu, Maggie Q, Grace
Park, and other bungee-jumping Asian bad girls, kicking ass.*

VOICE: For today's culinary battle, Chairman Wong has chosen
Iron Chef the Bride, consummately trained in the art of
slicing, dicing, and reduction; and Iron Chef the Geisha,
known for her ability to sever and divide a man in his
tracks with a single stroke.

CyberAsian Iron Chefs the BRIDE *and the* GEISHA *rise in darkness and bombast,
their shadows against their great photographs, the light slowly rising to reveal the*
BRIDE *in her yellow Power Ranger bike outfit and the* GEISHA *in a kimono
with the top of her head sliced off; both wield swords, daggers, and knives.*

ANIME WONG: (*whipping off a red silk cloth from a pile of rubble, some of it
writhing live animals—dragons, octopi, birds—proffered on
a rising dais to intensifying music that reminds us that the
East is Red*) And the theme for today is: CHINA!

Running around with microphones, two matching CYBORG ANNOUNCERS
*are dressed in long Chinese gowns and pillbox headdresses; they sport shumai
(dumpling) heads, rendering them noseless but giving them beady sesame eyes.
Since they have no noses, they sound stuffy when they speak; all of their dialogue sounds dubbed.*

CYBORG (TRADE FEDERATION VICEROY HATTORI):
        Well Viceroy Fukui, the battle has begun. How about just
a little background history while the contestants strate-
gize their menus?

CYBORG (TRADE FEDERATION VICEROY FUKUI):

> Yes, well, Chairman Wong created this culinary battle site, encouraged by the idea that if a few Iron Chefs put on their hats, kimonos, hanboks, saris, ao dais, and cheongsams, we could show the world how hospitable our CyberAsia can be.

CYBORG (VICEROY HATTORI):

> How true! And indeed our business and tourism is booming.

CYBORG (VICEROY FUKUI):

> These two amazing chefs, legends in their own time, the Bride and the Geisha, have proven that we CyberAsians can sell our exotic skills, if not our exotic bodies.

While the VICEROY ANNOUNCERS *jabber on, a great deal of commotion ensues in the opposing kitchen laboratories, which are equipped with every sort of garage and welding tool and explosive material. Imagine hacking up, sawing through, pounding, and bashing large pieces of fake animals, mannequins, gigantic vegetables; blowing up concoctions in ovens; hosing down fires; stirring vats of poison; and of course using a lot of hatchets, axes, saws, drills, knives, and other implements.* PAPARAZZI *run around filming everything at close range.* CYBORGS *in chef hats and aprons run around assisting while the* IRON CHEFS *get down to business.*

CYBORG (VICEROY HATTORI):

> Viceroy Fukui, what's going on down there? If I'm not mistaken, aren't those Mattel Hot Wheels?

CYBORG (VICEROY FUKUI):

> Yes, that's right. And it seems that Iron Chef the Bride is working on a secret sauce to create a kind of skidding effect for these toy automotive copies.

CYBORG (VICEROY HATTORI):

> It looks like a mix of chocolate and diesel. What is she adding to the sauce now?

CYBORG (VICEROY FUKUI):

> I'm told it's a secret, but word has it that it's lead.

CYBORG (VICEROY HATTORI):

> Very clever indeed. How about Iron Chef the Geisha? She seems to be trussing some sort of poultry.

CYBORG (VICEROY FUKUI):

> Yes, this is a very rare species of bird, but doubly so because it fell from the sky due to complications from the avian flu.

CYBORG (VICEROY HATTORI):

> And now she's stuffing it.

CYBORG (VICEROY FUKUI):

> I'm told that the stuffing is an illegal mixture of rhino horn, jaguar liver, and whale blubber.

CYBORG (VICEROY HATTORI):

> Incredibly daring! Any secret ingredients?

CYBORG (VICEROY FUKUI):

> Again, this is extremely confidential, but I'm told she means to win with her brains.

CYBORG (VICEROY HATTORI):

> Shocking! But switching arenas, Iron Chef the Bride is scoring and pounding a piece of rubber tire. It looks like it will be used as a kind of wrap.

CYBORG (VICEROY FUKUI):

> In preparation, the rubber tire was soaked in a silica and mercury solution, then exposed to a high concentration of carbon monoxide.

CYBORG (VICEROY HATTORI):

> If I'm not mistaken, that's Iron Chef the Bride's special technique for global warming. But what is Iron Chef the

Geisha going to do with that surfboard?

CYBORG (VICEROY FUKUI):

Hattori Viceroy, that remains to be seen, but it seems to be related to that water broth.

CYBORG (VICEROY HATTORI):

Now this has to be a first: isn't Iron Chef the Bride opening up a can of dog food?

CYBORG (VICEROY FUKUI):

Well, she'd better be quick about it as time is running out.

VOICE: Ten seconds to go.

CYBORGS *scurry about; the* BRIDE *and the* GEISHA *put the final touches on their dishes.*

VOICE: Five seconds to go.

CYBORG (VICEROY HATTORI):

And there we have it. Time is up. The China challenge is over!

Roar and applause from the ALIEN *audience. On screen, a display of the competing menus.*

CYBORG (VICEROY HATTORI):

Iron Chef the Bride's four courses are a delicate appetizer of dog food dumplings laced with melamine, followed by Severe Acute Respiratory Syndrome, or SARS, served as a centerpiece on a soft bed of juk. For the main course, she offers an aspic of concentrated greenhouse gases served in succulent tire rubber, and for the final dessert, Hot Wheels on a bed of spiced chocolate and diesel.

CYBORG (VICEROY FUKUI):

> Iron Chef the Geisha offers up an equally eclectic set of dishes: stuffed avian flu followed by a water torture broth with fried CIA documents served up and partaken on a Cuban surfboard. Then, to cleanse the palette, a fragrant antifreeze toothpaste sorbet on a blue plate of memoir, ending with the one-child policy seared and sliced and spread thinly on a multicolored Tibetan mandala.

CYBORG (VICEROY HATTORI):

> And the moment of truth: tasting and judgment. On the CyberAsian panel today for the China Challenge are: a senior member of the High Jedi Council, a CyberAsian of the tridactyl species supporting a high midi-clorian cell count, Jedi Master Yoda.

ALIENS *applaud.*

CYBORG (VICEROY HATTORI):

> Next, Lieutenant Junior Grade and sleeper agent, one of many humanoid Cylon copies, Copy Number Eight, Sharon Boomer Valerii.

ALIENS *applaud.*

CYBORG (VICEROY HATTORI):

> And finally, the genetically engineered supertyrant from Northern India with a fifty percent greater lung efficiency, and recently reawoken from his cryonically frozen state, Khan Noonian Singh.

ALIENS *applaud.*

CYBORG (VICEROY HATTORI):

> As you might realize, the food of our Iron Chefs not only requires the most discerning tastes, but also the most iron of stomachs.

CYBORGS *run in to serve the illustrious panel the prepared dishes.*

CYBORG (YODA): Interesting this is. First the gritty texture, then the subtle pollutants, my mouth it fills. Impressed I am.

CYBORG (BOOMER):
>I was thinking this would be overpowering, but it is very nice and refreshing for those fevered summers.

CYBORG (KHAN): This is a real discovery. I chew it and as I do, it expands in my mouth and then my belly. A luxurious dish, taking advantage of so many inhuman ingredients and combining various alien techniques. So agonizingly aromatic. A cruel masterpiece.

ANIME WONG *appears, recostumed in another Queen Amidala extravaganza, and maybe even announced by bugles and entering the stage on horseback.*

CYBORG (VICEROY FUKUI):
>And what is the verdict? Whose cuisine will reign supreme? Who will go down in defeat? And who will enjoy the sweet nectar of victory?

ANIME WONG: Viceroy Hattori!

CYBORG (VICEROY HATTORI):
>Yes, Chairman!

ANIME WONG: Your sword, please.

CYBORG (VICEROY HATTORI) *kneels and hands her a long sword that glints and blinds from every direction. A lot of dramatic fanfare music, clackers, drums, and anything else to create this sword sensation.*

ANIME WONG: *(taking the sword and announcing to all)*
>If my memory serves me correctly, you meet the true Hattori Hanzo, and now meet your demise!

A staged battle between ANIME WONG *and the* CYBORG *chef assistants, the* THREE PANELISTS, *and finally the* BRIDE *and* GEISHA *ensues.* ALIENS *scatter.* PAPARAZZI *continue to film and record everything. Techno music accompanying, beating out the pulse of the frenzied final battle.*

How do you think it ends?

Oh well then, suit yourself.

The End.

JAN KEN PON

▪

A Dance Performance Idea

Written by Karen Tei Yamashita

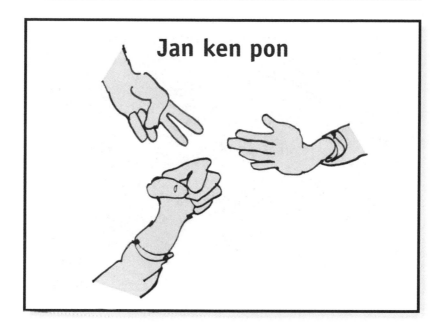

John can po
I gonna show!

jan ken pon
aikou deshou
omawari san
jan ken pon

jan ken a man ken shaka shaka po
wailuku wailuku bum bum show!

guu (rock)
choki (scissors)
paa (paper)

The Asian American narrative:
Japanese Americans brought this game from Asia to America.
Maybe this was an ancient form of conflict resolution.

But first, a story of natural and sexual selection . . .
wherefore conflict anyway?

Lizardland UCSC

Barry Sinervo
- Professor of Biology
- behavioral ecology
- reptilian natural and
  sexual selection

Listen to Barry Sinervo on KUSP: *Seventh Avenue Project* with Robert Pollie and Barry Sinervo, the Jane Goodall of lizards.

Listen to first eleven minutes (total about sixty minutes).
http://7thavenueproject.com/post/451026680/barry-sinervo-lizards-and-evolution

February 28, 2010

In this interview, Robert Pollie introduces Professor Barry Sinervo, a field and evolutionary biologist at UC Santa Cruz, who's studied lizards for over twenty years in the hills of central California. Professor Sinervo has learned that the "beauty of lizards" is that they "stick to the script," their script being their genetic program, and watching lizards is to watch genes in action and evolution unfold in social patterns, patterns that can be decoded by game theory.

The lizards in Sinervo's study are side-blotched lizards. The females are about seven inches and the males generally larger. If you look up the videos on the Lizardland website, you will see that the males do a lot of push-ups to demonstrate strength. As Sinervo says, "It's all about signaling whether you are weak or strong."

Uta stansburiana

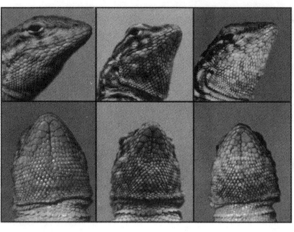

Interviewer Pollie suggests that Professor Sinervo might be the "Jane Goodall of side-blotched lizards," but Sinervo demurs that after twenty years, they treat him like any cow hanging around the pasture. The time-frame is important, because although Sinervo has grown twenty years older observing lizards, the lizards have generated another twenty generations. He notes that if you want to study evolution, you have to see it speeded up, and these side-blotched lizards live one year. With one generation to mature yearly, it's ideal to study natural selection.

And here is the important part: mature male lizards come in three color types: orange, blue, or yellow. Sinervo says: "If you pick up a lizard and flip it over and its throat is orange, you know that they are aggressive. If you flip them over and they are solid blue, you actually know they are cooperative. And if you pick up a male lizard and they are yellow, what's interesting is that they are a female mimic, so they pretend to be a female."

Pollie quips in response, "Female impersonator," then asks if they are "gay," to which Sinervo responds, "No, it's just their strategy right?" So it turns out that the sneaky yellow males invade the flaming orange male harems and copulate with the females.

But check out the medium-sized blue-throated males who are cooperative, meaning that they come in pairs with buddies, like a team. If you figure two is better than one, by virtue of their buddy system, they in fact attract females.

Side-Blotched Lizard
Uta stansburiana
(male dominance/playing power)

• Orange-throated males: strongest, polyg-
amous, defeat blues (orange bullies)

• Blue-throated males: middle sized,
monogamous, cooperative, lose to orange
but guard against yellows (true blues)

• Yellow-throated males: smallest, posers
(sneaky yellow bastards)

So there you have it—three lizard types: the orange bully, the true blue,
and the sneaky yellow bastard. Sinervo interjects that there is a "more
colorful" description actually used in behavioral ecology texts that is
impermissible to say on the air. But since it's in the science books, Pollie says, "Go ahead and say it." Sinervo says, "Sneaky fucker." After all,
technically, it's a strategy. "That," says Sinervo, "is their role." What's the
role of the scientist? What's the role of the radio host?

To wit—Lizard Dicks:
*orange bully
*true blue
*sneaky yellow bastards (sneaky fucker) (he who lives to get copulations)

That's right: yellows are sneaky little posers and queer to boot.

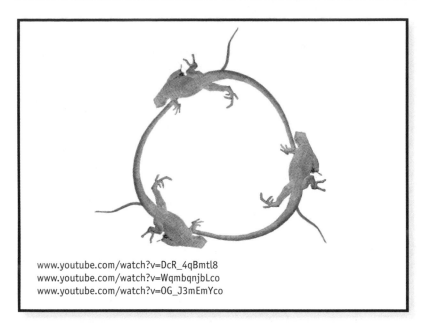

www.youtube.com/watch?v=DcR_4qBmtl8
www.youtube.com/watch?v=WqmbqnjbLco
www.youtube.com/watch?v=OG_J3mEmYco

What can we learn from the life cycles of lizards?
The guys do their push-ups, and, meanwhile, the ladies get to choose.
Check out the music videos on YouTube: MoniKa, Katzenjammer, Kree-
    sha Turner.

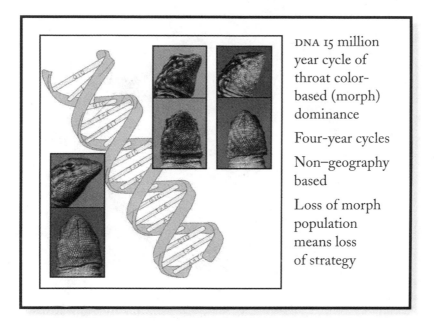

DNA 15 million year cycle of throat color-based (morph) dominance

Four-year cycles

Non–geography based

Loss of morph population means loss of strategy

And thus we have the rise and fall of populations of color dominance.

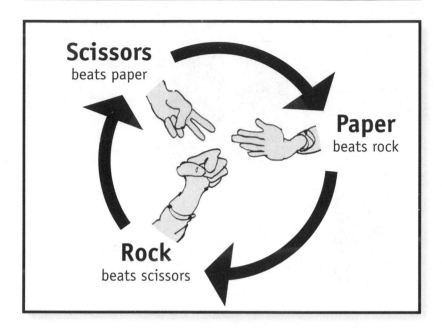

Back to the Asian American narrative:
jan ken po
rock paper scissors
also known as:
rochambo
rochambeau
or how an Asian game returns to kick yellows in the nuts

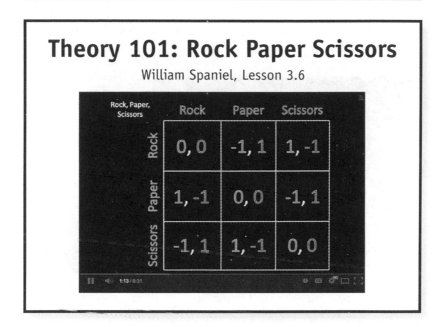

John Forbes Nash, *Nash Equilibrium*
www.youtube.com/watch?v=sQVbeAEorsc

Please note: the beautiful mind, John Forbes Nash, thought through the Nash Equilibrium, of which jan ken po is an example. Listen to William Spaniel explain this as a mathematical problem. He does so in about six minutes. If players stick to their strategies, it's a zero-sum game.

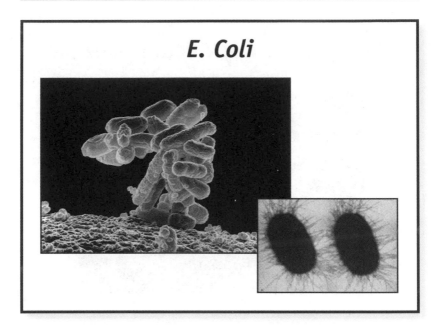

E. Coli

Now:
Some bacteria also exhibit a rock-paper-scissors dynamic when they engage in antibiotic production. Colicins produced by *Escherichia coli* (*E. coli*) compete among strains in a three-way battle.

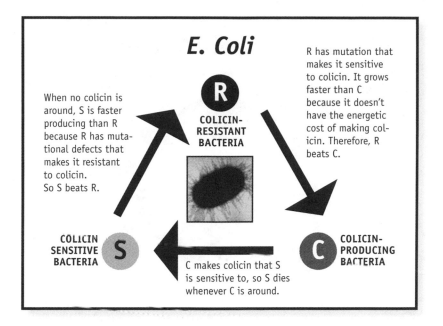

E. coli plays the game too.

This game is as old as bacteria.

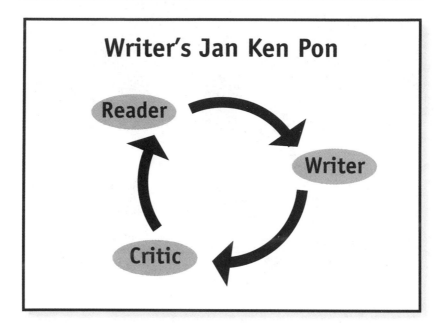

Oh, and you thought it was just about lizards:
reader
writer
critic!

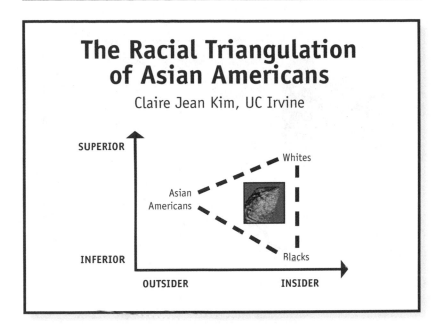

But what about those sneaky yellow bastards?

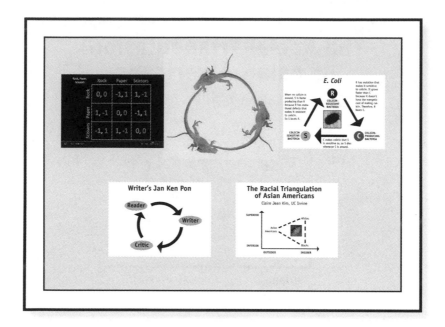

From games to lizards to intestines to people

Dialectics

struggle of binaries of power to
demonstrate intrinsic weaknesses;
inevitability of shift in power balance

Master   Slave

theory interlude

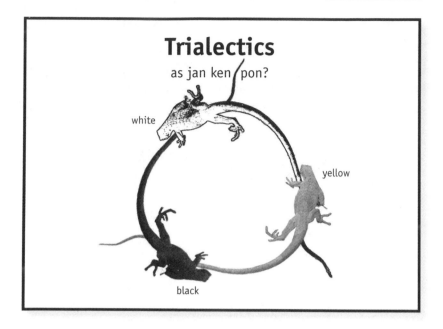

The good news: we get to take turns.

The other news: your turn may not come up for a long time (unless you're a lizard).

Oh I know, let's play Rock Paper Scissors Lizard Spock.

A further nerdy complication

It's very simple...
Scissors cuts Paper. Paper covers Rock. Rock crushes Lizard. Lizard poisons Spock. Spock smashes Scissors. Scissors decapitates Lizard. Lizard eats Paper. Paper disproves Spock. Spock vaporizes Rock, and, as it always has, Rock crushes Scissors.

http://youtu.be/iapcKVn7DdY

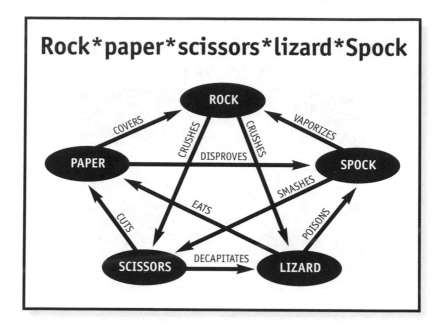

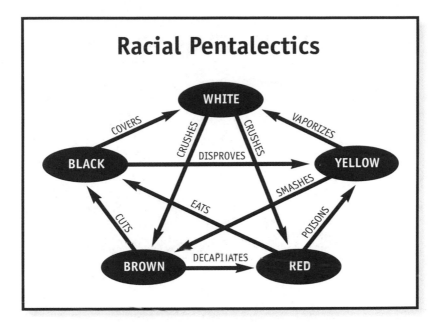

Now the dance really begins.

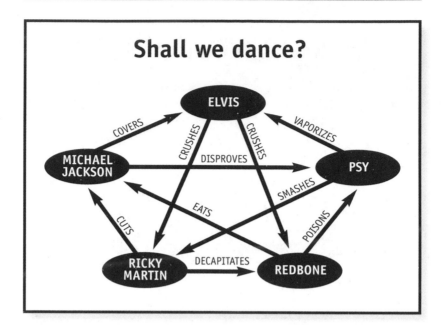

Shall we dance?
Gentlemen: stick to your strategies!
Ladies: whom do you choose?

Biodiversity

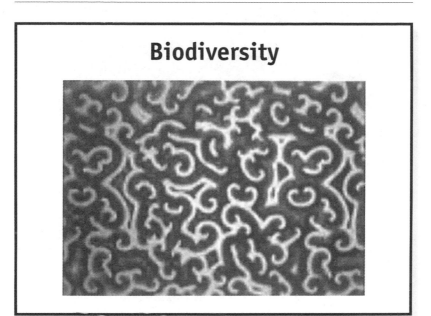

But can you dance to this?
"Using the rock paper-scissors game to model interacting species, we demonstrate that mobility critically affects biodiversity. A threshold mobility exists such that above, some species go extinct, and only one survives. Below the threshold value, all species coexist in a stable manner by self-arranging into entangled, rotating spirals."

Tobia Reichenbach, Mauro Mobilia, and Erwin Frey "Mobilty promotes and jeopardizes biodiversity in rock-paper-scissors games," www.theorie.physik.uni-muenchen.de/lsfrey/research /biological_physics/2007_004/index.html

Instructions

- five dancers
- five musicians/instruments
- performative/physical/narrative stereotypes of sound/text/movement
- cyclical dominance
- game change
- What is biodiversity?

This is the idea.
Add text/poetics/song.
Change it. Subvert it. Strip it down. Work it.

But this is the backdrop:

Intel Report: Asia's Power to Surpass U.S. and Europe Combined (reported by Amy Goodman on *Democracy Now*, December 11, 2012)

What will we do when those sneaky yellow bastards change the game plan?

Are strategies attached to racial phenotype?

What about hybridity? You can mix and match, mix and match, but it all comes out in the wash. Oh your precious identity.

If mobility is a factor and there is a threshold, what is it? (Maybe we don't want to know the answer to this one.)

Are we sneaky fuckers or are we just fucked?

What if all Asians just left Earth?

What does it mean to become extinct?

Okay, so there's a difference between lizards and humans, but say you cut to the chase—bacteria, DNA, life as algorithm; what's the point? Cooperation is attractive?

At least we know this much: if life depends on masculinity, our chances seem slim.

Like the two Kings once said: Can't we all just get along?

Everybody, come on home.

http://youtube.com/watch?v=N4rqprK05wI

Bye-bye

ANIME WONG

A CRITICAL AFTERWORD

by Stephen Hong Sohn

Anime Wong: A Critical Afterword
BY STEPHEN HONG SOHN

You might say that Karen Tei Yamashita needs no introduction. She is the author of five critically acclaimed works—*Through the Arc of the Rain Forest* (1990), *Brazil-Maru* (1992), *Tropic of Orange* (1997), *Circle K Cycles* (2001), and *I Hotel* (2010); she has received numerous literary awards and distinctions (being named a 2010 National Book Award finalist, for example); and she is a widely respected literature professor at the University of California, Santa Cruz. A fierce advocate of the arts and of culture more broadly, she champions other writers and scholars and routinely brings them to campus for readings and introduces them to her classes. Her publications are known to a broader audience and are fiercely embraced at the institutional level, where they routinely appear on college syllabi. But, as *Anime Wong: Fictions of Performance* illuminates, Yamashita's creative output is far more eclectic than her previous publications suggest. An afterword, then, is the ideal place to bring together some important threads and to engage a general critical commentary on the collection as a whole.

Most scholarly attention has focused on Yamashita's fictional publications,[1] but this die-hard fan of her work wanted to learn more about the period preceding her first novel's publication. My research revealed a surprise: Yamashita possesses an extensive background in playwriting and musical performance, beginning with the production of her first major dramatic work, *O-Men: An American Kabuki*, in 1976. Her subsequent works include *Hiroshima Tropical* (1983), *Asaka-No-Miya* (1984), *Kusei: Endangered Species* (1986), *Rock Candy* (1987), *Hannah Kusoh: An American Butoh* (1988), *GiLArex (Or Godzilla Comes to Little Tokyo)* (1989), *L.A. Carmen vs. Tokyo Carmen* (1990), and *Noh Bozos* (1993). This incredibly diverse and extended body of cultural productions ultimately pushes readers, critics, and fans of Yamashita to reconsider her artistic influences and the scope of her creative writing in light of her performance work, which includes some recent forays entitled *Anime Wong: A CyberAsian Odyssey* (2008), *Siamese Twins and Mongoloids* (2012), and *Jan Ken Pon* (2012).[2]

This collection brings together most of these works, which together generate one of the most sustained avant-garde undertakings with

respect to Asian American performance, musicals, and creative composition.[3] Yamashita's past work in this aesthetic arena complicates the
nature of authorship, racial identity, and genre. She keenly recognizes
that the collaborative nature of performance—which includes acting,
music composition, choreography, set design and video imaging, and
costuming—offers a uniquely collective creative vision. Because many
of these pieces are performed live, this collection can only partially reconstruct their dynamic content. *Anime Wong* preserves much of the experimental and parodic impulses of the actual performances, but moves
beyond their original forms. It generates an innovative approach to these
works through a measured inclusion of musical lyrics, archival photographic material, cartoons and storyboards, and original programs and
playbills.

The vast majority of Asian Americanist critique focuses on narra-
tive-based genres such as memoir, autobiography, and fiction.[4] A number of prominent literary critics (including Dorinne Kondo, Karen
Shimakawa, James Moy, and Josephine Lee) do explore Asian American
drama. However, as I noted earlier on, Yamashita's performance productions have received virtually no critical attention. Part of this over-
sight is because she first achieved notoriety as a novelist[5]—by the time
Tropic of Orange was written, she had left behind her playwriting and
other theater-based projects. At the same time, Yamashita's performance
writings have been difficult to consider generically because they do not
function within a traditional drama setting; they often require elaborate
props, staging, musical accompaniment, and costuming, and are multi-
disciplinary in their scope. With respect to musicals, even fewer Asian
Americans have penned such productions, with a handful of notable
exceptions that include Philip Kan Gotanda's *Avocado Kid* (1980), Gary
Iwamoto's *Miss Minidoka 1943* (1987), Fred Wei-han Ho's *A Chinaman's
Chance* (1987), and Richard Wong's *Colma: A Musical* (2006). As a result,
Yamashita's entry into the world of performance placed her on the mar-
gins in multiple ways. Her first play, *O-Men*, deviated from the realist
style of many early Asian American plays; her following two plays,
Hiroshima Tropical and *Asaka-No-Miya*, do not easily fit within a u.s.-
based racial framework. Further still, Yamashita's later performance-
based work heavily incorporates comedic and parodic elements and
deviates from the realist aesthetic tradition that critics within the field of
Asian American cultural criticism have tended to favor.

Nevertheless, her performance work is imperative to recover, for a number of reasons. First, this collection encourages and hallmarks the dynamics of collaboration and mixed-genre productions and broadens our understandings of Asian American cultures. The subtitle to this collection, *Fictions of Performance,* highlights the fluid formal boundaries of Yamashita's work. Second, *Anime Wong* offers much to contour our understandings of Asian American cultural production, especially through the exploration of parody. Third, *Anime Wong* demonstrates that Yamashita has long led certain trends that transformed American Studies in the nineties, such as emerging discourses on transnationalism and globalization. Her pieces invoke varied social contexts, cultural currents, and historical events ranging from the Japan–U.S. trade wars in the eighties, to the growing place of Los Angeles with the Pacific Rim economic system, to the advent of cyberpunk fiction and film.

In this critical afterword, I summarize Yamashita's periods of performance work and then explore the formal and contextual elements that ground the pieces in this collection. Next are selected introductory readings of specific pieces, which together illustrate the incredible range and comedic tone of Yamashita's performance fictions.

BIOGRAPHICAL TIMELINE

Yamashita maintains a strong transnational focus in her writing, partly because she has spent significant portions of her life living in Brazil, Japan, and the United States. Early in her undergraduate education, Yamashita spent a year in Japan from 1971 to 1972 to further her studies as a Japanese literature major. She also dabbled in performance work in a college production, *Urashima Taro,* which she penned and based on a Japanese folktale. Working with a small group of other Asian American students, Yamashita undertook one of her first collaborative opportunities in staging and performance. Graduating in 1974, Yamashita considered a career in anthropology. Subsequently, in 1975, she traveled to Brazil on a fellowship to examine the Japanese diasporic population that had settled in the area to work on coffee plantations after the National Origins Act of 1924 restricted immigration to the United States. Although she had intended to pursue an anthropological methodology in her investigations, the primary result of this research was her first two novels.

In addition to her research-turned-novels, Yamashita began composing a number of plays while in Brazil, the first of which was *O-Men:*

An American Kabuki. O-Men was subsequently staged in 1978 by the East West Players, then headed under Academy Award–nominated actor Mako. Unlike *Through the Arc of the Rain Forest* and *Brazil-Maru, O-Men* has little to do with Brazil and centers on the question of the Japanese American identity as it has evolved over time. Surrealistic and allegorical in scope, the play is staged largely in reverse chronology, moving from a contemporary narrative about Japanese Americans and traveling back in time to the point of Japanese immigration to the United States. Yamashita's work on *O-Men* further involved the use of musical accompaniment, as she collaborated with Alan Furutani, who composed original music. Influenced by traditional theatrical forms such as Kabuki and Noh, Yamashita's subsequent work in theater and performance consistently included music.

During this period, she wrote the short story "Asaka-No-Miya," winner of the James Clavell Award for Short Fiction in 1979. This piece was later redeveloped into a play of the same name, which was completed in 1984. *Hiroshima Tropical* (1983), another play, was written during her time in Brazil. Under Mako's encouragement, *Hiroshima Tropical* was greenlit as a play-in-progress by the East/West Players in 1984. Both *Asaka-No-Miya* and *Hiroshima Tropical* envisioned the perilous and jingoistic Japanese nationalism that pervaded post–World War II diasporic populations living in Brazil. Evocative of John Okada's *No-No Boy* (1957) with respect to the protagonist's Ichiro Yamada's mother, both plays contained characters who are driven to suicide (or who attempt suicide) over the realization that Japan's divine imperative was destroyed in the wake of the nation's unconditional surrender. Yamashita later abandoned these plays due to their inopportune timing: the Japanese American internment redress movement was gaining steam in the late seventies and culminated in the eighties with the Civil Liberties Act of 1988, which provided $20,000 for each surviving Japanese American internee. Consequently, neither *Asaka-No-Miya* nor *Hiroshima Tropical* ever received a full-fledged production.

After returning to Los Angeles from Brazil, Yamashita balanced her work between performance writings and fiction. She completed *Kusei: Endangered Species* (1986) in collaboration with her husband, architect Ronaldo Lopes de Oliveira, and video artist Karen Mayeda. Mayeda subsequently received a grant from Visual Communications that allowed her to direct a short film based on the script. *Kusei* premiered at the

Japanese American Cultural Community Center (JACCC) on July 12, 1986, where Mayeda's directorial adaptation was screened alongside others who had taken part in Visual Communication's Filmmaker Development Program. In 1987, Yamashita wrote *Rock Candy* (1987), a musical about an all-female rock group. This piece firmly established her connection to musician, composer, and singer Vicki Abe. While *Rock Candy* does not possess an explicit racial thrust, and therefore would be difficult to read strictly through an Asian Americanist lens, it altered Yamashita's work by influencing her to incorporate original music compositions with full lyrics and songs directly into future productions.

Following *Rock Candy,* Yamashita completed a more ambitious, collaborative project, *Hannah Kusoh: An American Butoh* (1989), which was staged by a core group of women that included Mako's wife, Shizuko Hoshi, as well as Mayeda and Abe. Hoshi developed the play's choreography and directed the production. Mayeda created all the video segments that were used as backdrops, while Abe composed any original music. Oliveira provided his support by helping with set designs. *Hannah Kusoh* saw two distinct runs, debuting first at the JACCC in Los Angeles on September 9 and 10, 1989. It was later staged at Highways in Santa Monica from March 28 to 30 in 1990.

Yamashita's next performance production, *L.A. Carmen vs. Tokyo Carmen* (1990), employed Hoshi as director and choreographer; Mayeda constructed set elements, specifically those involving visuals taken from slides that were mounted on carousels and projected onto screens. *L.A. Carmen vs. Tokyo Carmen* was staged at the Taper, Too for a three-night run between June 28 and 30, 1990, premiering in Los Angeles at a multiperformance event called the Thirteenth Hour: A Festival of Performance.

GiLArex (titled at the time *Godzilla Comes to Little Tokyo*) (1992) was Yamashita's first full-fledged musical production. It included many songs and lyrics and was picked up for a limited run at Seattle's Northwest Asian American Theatre in 1992.[6] Abe and Yamashita traveled to Seattle as the theater company put on a set of workshops and rehearsals related to the production. During that period, the Los Angeles riots occurred, and filming in the Seattle area began on a movie adapted from the popular cartoon program *The Teenage Mutant Ninja Turtles.* With many of those involved in *GiLArex* leaving the musical for parts in *Teenage Mutant Ninja Turtles,* the entire cast—sans the actor who played the lead character Manzanar—was replaced for the full production, which ran in late May and early June. It was staged a second time on August 21 and 23 of that year, at the JACCC. Though not a full production, this second run did involve a significant amount of work. Hoshi returned in a directing capacity, and actors performed most of the songs in costume.

Noh Bozos: A Circus in Ten Amazing Acts (1993) was written as Yamashita readied and completed her novels, *Through the Arc of the Rain Forest* and *Brazil-Maru*. *Noh Bozos* reunited Yamashita with Hoshi, again in the director's role; Oliveira again operated as set designer while Glenn Horiuchi composed all original music. Mimosa, the daughter of Mako and Shizuko Hoshi and an actor in previous Yamashita performances, took over full choreography duties for *Noh Bozos*. Like many of Yamashita's past productions, *Noh Bozos* premiered at the JACCC, where it received a two-night run on August 27 and 28, 1993. In 1996, memoirist and poet David Mura independently staged a reading of *Noh Bozos* at Theater Mu in Minneapolis.

Yamashita then rerouted her energies into fiction, where her performance writings appear in encrypted forms. For example, Manzanar Murakami in *GiLArex* finds a second life as a major character in Yamshita's 1997 novel *Tropic of Orange*. *Circle K Cycles* (2001) is a mixed-genre publication whose visual elements evoke the author's avant-garde production days. More recently, Yamashita has written pieces in light of the shifting cultural currents related to Asian Americans and popular culture. The continued link between Asian Americans and technology became the basis for the performance fiction *Anime Wong: A CyberAsian Odyssey* (2008). This work shines with its many cultural references, including but not limited to Ronald D. Moore's *Battlestar Galactica, Iron Chef,* and Quentin Tarantino's *Kill Bill: Vol. 1*. As this collection took more coherent shape, Yamashita managed to pen one more cultural production, *Jan Ken Pon* (2012), which playfully employs the PowerPoint presentation format so ubiquitous in academic circles to explore comparative racial formation and the future of ethnic studies, among other such themes and tropes. Throughout her career, Yamashita never abandoned her love for multimedia, performance, mixed genres, and creative experimentation. Even her most recent novel, *I Hotel* (2010), from its spatially inventive opening pages to its idiosyncratic use of "we" narration told from the surrealistic perspective of the titular, doomed building, reminds us that her work continues to exude a performative quality.

FORM, CONTEXT, AND THE EDITORIAL VISION OF *ANIME WONG: FICTIONS OF PERFORMANCE*

My own participation in the editing of *Anime Wong* began in 2007, after I began researching and revising a dissertation chapter based on Yamashita's *Tropic of Orange*. Many published biographies referred to her performance work, but the pieces themselves were nowhere to be found. Living within driving distance of Yamashita's office at University of California, Santa Cruz, I set out to learn what had happened to these productions. After we talked in person, she entrusted me with a tremendous archive of materials. I rummaged through dozens of boxes of VHS cassette tapes, newspaper clippings, photographs, masks, theater and performance reviews, slides, music sheets, and manuscripts and began collating them into one document. I also aimed to get a better sense of these productions by digitizing performances and documents whenever possible. By 2008, I had met with Yamashita enough times to hammer out a rough manuscript. Some complications did arise, of course: *Kusei* had no extant script, for instance, since the production began as a written abstract and then quickly moved to storyboarding and actual filming. In addition, some VHS tapes were too degraded to be converted into digital files. Variations in the textual manuscripts raised questions about which versions to include in the final publication. And we had to work painstakingly to locate all the photographers and artists related to specific slides, video projections, photographs, and lyrics, in case we needed to obtain permissions and provide the proper acknowledgment.

In collaborating on this book, Yamashita and I met often to consider various possibilities for its vision and how it might come together as a set. We made some editorial cuts to what could have been a more comprehensive collection of Yamashita's performance fictions. *O-Men* was not included for the simple fact that Yamashita did not want to have this piece published. We based other excisions primarily on thematic unity and the ways each work generated a sustained consideration of Asian American racial formation and popular culture as it has moved from the eighties to the current moment. *Hiroshima Tropical, Asaka-no-Miya,* and *Rock Candy* were all excised as they did not fit as coherently around the domestic and transnational valences of Asian American racial formation as it is understood within the U.S. context. As I mentioned earlier, *Hiroshima Tropical* and *Asaka-no-Miya* were both written during Yamashita's time in Brazil and reflect a diasporic focus that stood apart from the other works included here. Yamashita also expressed her viewpoint that she felt that works such as *Hiroshima Tropical* did not necessarily find their footing as full theatrical productions because they were never staged; thus, she did not feel as though they were entirely finished. Finally, *Rock Candy*'s focus on an all-female rock band, though certainly invested in issues of identity and social difference, was not an entirely completed work. Indeed, the music intended for this piece was never finished nor was the production ever staged.

After finalizing what to include in the manuscript, we had to make a couple more important decisions. First was the issue of sequencing, which we solved by taking a rough chronological approach to the performance fictions. This trajectory highlights how each performance fiction is a product of a given sociohistorical context and how Asian American and ethnic identity formations continually evolve in relation to certain trends. For instance, the aesthetic employed in techno-Orientalist cultural productions in the eighties (in movies such as *Blade Runner*) arose specifically as a creative response to Japan's strong economic and geopolitical position as well as the fear incited by the country's reemergence as a world power. The term *techno-Orientalism* refers to the ways that Asiatic images and elements are included in a cultural production, especially those that invoke speculative or futuristic landscapes and temporalities. Indeed, techno-Orientalism often conjures up images of a dystopian future in which an Asian nation reigns supreme. Performance fictions such as *Kusei* and *L.A. Carmen vs. Tokyo Carmen* reflect the growing unease in the United States as it relates specifically to the transnational paradigm codifying Japan as an economic aggressor. Though Japan's economic primacy has since waned, the arc of this collection reveals how techno-Orientalism itself becomes reconfigured. In this vein, *Jan Ken Pon* spotlights China's new leadership role in the global economy and increasing Western fears that this change signals a potentially dangerous power shift in the Asia-Pacific.

The second issue was how best to transform the collaborative nature of theatrical and musical productions into print form. Aspects of the real-time performance could not be replicated, so we had to dispense with the idea that we could make some sort of direct translation. Further still, the degradation of the many VHS tapes made it impossible to view some of the performances. Consequently, using existing playbills, photographs, lyrics, and other such elements, we agreed that these works would find a new life in print form and would offer new ways for audiences to interact with these playful and comedic cultural productions, on visual, textual, lyrical, and musical levels. Calling this collection "fictions of performance" is a nod to the genre-busting nature of Yamashita's works. On the one hand, though many of these collected pieces were first performed, their movement into the print realm reconstitutes their formal natures. On the other, with Yamashita's consistent exploration of speculative fictional registers, whether the imaginary future found in *Kusei* or the catastrophic arrival of the monster lizard in *GiLArex*, these works move beyond the bounds of realist representations and forefront the collaborative nature of cultural production.

Yamashita's devotion to parody has also strongly influenced the book's thematic and creative vision.[7] Parody is traditionally defined as a genre that appropriates the language of a common narrative or story and humorously reconfigures it.[8] These cultural productions reveal the "excesses" (Van O'Connor 241) of particular sedimented discourses and narratives, which become comically transformed or altered and, in the process, grant us an opportunity to reconsider a number of issues and dilemmas, including Japanese American ethnic ancestry, Asian American racial formation, and the deployment of Orientalism in popular culture.[9]

Even as these performance fictions poke fun at common narratives and tropes, they also operate self-reflexively, critiquing various aspects of cultural heritage and other such identity-based frameworks. As a whole, these cultural productions advance the estrangement that Asian American subjects can experience in matters of racial and ethnic authenticity. Many performance fictions in this collection address anxieties over ethnic preservation and purity by making clear that Japanese theater and performance modes (including Kabuki, Noh, and Butoh) cannot be exported exactly into an Asian American context.[10] At the same time, many idiosyncratic characters populate these performance fictions (such as Caucasian Japanophiles and cyborg sirens), immediately disorienting how native informants are defined. While certain Asian American characters surface here who are intent on assimilating, they often become fetishized objects of the Western gaze, making the prospect of desired inclusion questionable. Such a depiction might mark the Asian American as a stereotypically liminal figure, located neither within the East nor West. But Yamashita's performance writings move beyond this in-between status through the many multifaceted characters who populate the representational terrain. Hence, I use the rest of this afterword to make concrete some of the parodic and comedic valences that surface throughout this collection, especially in conjunction with Yamashita's exploration of all things Asian and American and the hybridity that comes from the combinations of the Orient and the Occident.

INTRODUCTORY READINGS

Kusei: Endangered Species opens this collection and advances the question of cultural and ethnic erosion over time. *Kusei* is an approximate Japanese pun, referring to something putrid or stinky (*kusai*), and is an offshoot of the word *kyusei*, a Japanese term denoting the ninth generation. As such, the script imagines what the ninth generation of Japanese Americans might look like. *Kusei* is primarily set in the year 2244, at which point the last surviving Japanese American (a young man known only as 805.AJA) has been rescued from a relocation camp located on the planet Topanzanar. At the height of the Ford–Mitsubishi War in 1995, 103 Japanese Americans are shipped off to the planet Topanzanar with no explanation.[11]

   Kusei imagines an Earth rendered from the common narrative of the postapocalyptic future, where transnational corporations generate a major world war with disastrous results. In this case, the rift is perpetuated by the increasingly volatile economic climate between Japan and the United States, as marked by tension among multinational companies such as Mitsubishi and Ford. Clearly, this cultural production takes much inspiration from a particular social context that emerged in the eighties: the growing u.s. anxiety over "Asian tiger economies." Further, since *Kusei* falls within the parameters of science fiction, the narrative finds much resonance alongside the cyberpunk genre that surfaced with Ridley Scott's *Blade Runner* (1982) and William Gibson's *Neuromancer* (1984). Rather than envisage a specifically Asian future cast with Japan or East Asia in mind (within the techno-Orientalist model defined by David Morley and Kevin Robins and others), *Kusei* considers the prospects and perils of maintaining Japanese American identity, and ostensibly Asian American identity more broadly, in an extraterrestrial location.[12] *Kusei* implies that cultural coherence is an impossibility to the extent that alien races must intervene in maintaining Japanese American genealogies. Even 805.AJA is already partially cloned from an earlier genomic counterpart, suggesting that the ninth generation could be achieved only through otherworldly scientific measures. The question the piece generates is through the "alien voice": who is it that desires the preservation of the Japanese American "race"? This piece does not provide an answer as the alien scientists are masked subjects; at later points, they exist as disembodied voices. Within this aporia, *Kusei* conveys the message that Japanese American cultures and families cannot be tethered to a preservation instinct focused on ethnoracial purity. While *Kusei* points to the ridiculous tendency to uphold the illusion of a pristine pedigree, this performance fiction also suggests that Asian Americans face continued marginalization, as they are related to an "alien" culture. The planet Topanzanar exists simultaneously as a humorous yet dangerous reminder that forms of oppression and segregation can reemerge.

In *Hannah Kusoh: An American Butoh* (1988), Yamashita tackles the Orientalist gaze that can be so attuned to the Asian American female body. While employing musical arias taken directly from Giacomo Puccini's *Madama Butterfly*, this particular production is not a musical but an extended performance piece composed of monologues, spoken word sequences, and choreographed routines. Deliberately parodying Puccini's fetishization of the Asian American female body, *Hannah Kusoh* takes a much more experimental route than Yamashita's previous work through the deliberate employment of Butoh, a theatrical dance form founded by Tatsumi Hijikata and Kazuo Ohno that includes stylized choreography, costuming, and white body makeup.[13] Structured in "six senses," *Hannah Kusoh* moves from one of the body's senses to another, in the following order: smell, touch, sight, taste, sound (or hearing); and adds a final sense, intuition. Each sense involves a particular quandary related to Asian American identity. As such, the sense of smell begins with the performers dropping out of a large ukiyo-e (print) of a Japanese woman's face; they emerge from the nasal passages. Video projections of the atomic bombings of Hiroshima and Nagasaki, as well as of Japanese American internment camps, take place above the performers, whose writhing bodies are encased in costumes that are meant to invoke a mucus covering. As Joanna Brotman explains, "Born in the devastated aftermath of the atomic bomb, [Butoh] was an improvisational practice at once grotesque and humorous, erotic and violent, exploring issues

previously considered inappropriate for the content of dance" (50). Karl
Eric Toepfer adds that "the movements of Butoh dancers project an
eerie, grotesque aura in which the nude body achieves expressivity
through a repertoire of spasms, convulsions, twitchings, sputterings,
whirlings, slitherings, stampings, crawlings, and plant-like convolutions
of limbs, torso, and head" (80). *Hannah Kusoh*'s opening sequence clearly
depicts some hallmark stylistics of Butoh as offered by Brotman and
Toepfer. At the same time, because these dance forms are paired with
images of the Japanese American internment, this performance fiction
involves a kind of cultural transformation in which grotesque humor
abounds. In this respect, this cultural production defamiliarizes Japanese cultural forms, as they become deployed to explore Asian American–centered themes. The sense of touch provides the clearest example
by suggesting that one's ethnicity does not necessarily offer a strong or
clear-cut connection to a national heritage. In this case, the Caucasian
man seems to have appropriated Japanese culture to a level that his date,
a Japanese American sansei woman, cannot claim nor would even desire
to. What does Japanese American mean when a Caucasian can be more
"Japanese" than a Japanese American?

Yamashita strips the *Madama Butterfly* narrative of its gendered eroticism in "the sense of sound." This segment most explicitly employs parody as a way to challenge and question the Western male gaze on the
Oriental female body. Notably, the performers do not actually sing the
Madama Butterfly arias but lip-synch them, suggesting that they do not
seamlessly inhabit these roles. Further, their costuming recalls the Orientalist lens that has long been associated with the "butterfly" stereo-
type, but the paradigm is subverted, as everyday objects come to embody
these "found" kimonos, made of what has been discarded (including food
wrappers, soda can tabs, and other such pedestrian items). In this respect,
the Asian American woman's exoticism is stripped and replaced, literally,
by trash. This performance fiction introduces gender-bending by
employing male performers, who further erode the heterosexual
scopophilia associated with Puccini's play. As the performers feign ritual suicides with chopsticks and then use these same chopsticks to eat
spaghetti noodles, the sense of sound continually pokes fun at Puccini's
vision of the tragically configured Japanese woman. This play also redi-
rects the reductive Orientalist gaze to Puccini's Italian heritage, as the
performers pretend to consume and later decorate their bodies in pasta.

Included as an appendix to *Hannah Kusoh* and connected to the sense of sound is the short story "Madama B" (1993), Yamashita's autobiographical account of attempting to record the chicken noises that would be integrated into an aria in *Hannah Kusoh*. An unforgettable comic episode, "Madama B" catalogs the writer's personal experiences and her methodology to help augment the critique of Puccini's musical as a contrived construction of the Asian woman.

GiLArex (1989) was originally conceived as an Asian American musical but finds a new configuration here in its print form. Those familiar with Yamashita's fiction will immediately notice that this musical is a precursor to *Tropic of Orange* in that she employs some similar characters, including the two main figures, Manzanar "Ringo" Murakami, the first sansei born in internment captivity, and Emi Yamane, a young runaway. Manzanar is the more faithful precursor character of the two in that, as in *Tropic*, he is portrayed as an eccentric man with a penchant for conducting what he believes are symphonies directly composed from the sounds of Los Angeles traffic. Emi Yamane is much younger than her *Tropic* counterpart (and possesses a different surname—in *Tropic*, it is Sakai), and although her fixation with media remains, a different character in *GiLArex* (reporter Steve Martin) provides the major journalistic commentaries within this performance fiction. Beyond these surface elements, *GiLArex* takes its own spectacular path, wherein Los Angeles is positioned less as a multicultural city and more within the discourse of the Pacific Rim economy.

Perhaps the most obvious parodic impulse located in *GiLArex* is Yamashita's intertextual references to many Godzilla films. In the Japanese original, entitled *Gojira* (1954), "nuclear weapons tests in the Pacific awaken Godzilla and make him radioactive. Godzilla acts on his suffering by trying to destroy Tokyo, Japan's center of Modernity. Emiko Yamane (Momoko Kochi), the central character, is caught between three men: father (Takashi Shimura), fiancé (Akihiko Hirata), and lover (Akira Takarada)" (Shapiro 140). Noticeably, Yamashita reuses the main character's name, Emiko Yamane, for her performance fiction and places her in constellation with a similar group of men, which includes Manzanar and her father, Gary Yamane, and others.[14] As Philip Brophy reminds us, "the figure of Godzilla—as famous as a suit as he is a character—is less a vessel for consistent authorial and thematic meaning as he is a shell to be used for the generation of potential and variable meanings" (41). Accordingly, Brophy explains, Godzilla's transformation from "innocent victim of nuclear testing" to "Godzilla as tamed being" and later to "Godzilla as heroic champion" (40) allows this monstrous figure to become an artificial screen on which to project certain anxieties and tensions related to Japanese culture and identity. However, the continual return to and adaptation of Godzilla-themed films in the United States, including *Godzilla* (1998) and *Cloverfield* (2008), denote the giant lizard's relevance and its plasticity as an agent invoking social contexts outside of Japan. Both Joyce E. Boss and Kathi Maio contend that the box-office failure of the 1998 American version of *Godzilla* stemmed from the fact that the monster itself failed to generate any connection with the audience: why did it travel on its path of destruction, and how could the audience ultimately identify with the monster?[15] Whereas the Japanese version found critical resonance at its inception as a return of the atomic repressed, the American version seemed to be devoid of meaning. Nancy Anisfield writes that such a dichotomous approach represents how "the Japanese embrace the bomb/monster into their cultural conscience, whereas Americans push it away" (53). Yamashita's *GiLArex* poses the American version of the monster lizard as a malleable reflective screen related to various characters, who all possess repressed pasts that should not be escaped and that inevitably return. The mutant lizard's seemingly evil machinations are never fully revealed, but its emergence suggests a historical erasure of Japanese American internment, or the danger inherent in the East with the rise of Asian tiger economies, or even the postmodern detachment connected to those living in dense metropolitan urban spaces. The comedic nature of this monstrous beast's appearance in *GiLArex* is made apparent by its submission to Manzanar Murakami's musical conducting. If the beast's catastrophic tendencies are made impotent by an eccentric man who proclaims to hear music in traffic noise, what then do we make of Manzanar's powers?

This performance fiction positions Manzanar Murakami as a character imbued with quite incredible talent, who ultimately encourages individuals to unite to find a way to destroy this dangerous beast. Consequently, even as *GiLArex* parodies the various Godzilla films, it still negotiates a critique based on a kind of metropolitan fragmentation. *GiLArex* once again revisits the question of Japanese American lineage, as Emi Yamane stands in direct contrast to the intentions of the Japanese American Preservation League. For instance, Emi directly avoids her Asian American or Japanese American cultural heritage, while the JAPL, headed under Sally Ogata, seeks to retain and conserve ethnic and racial traditions. The Serizawa brothers further complicate this piece by highlighting the continued presence of Japan within Los Angeles through their purchasing power. In this respect, *GiLArex* positions various Japanese and Japanese American characters in Los Angeles, but presents them as individuals with their own agendas. Whether it is for profit (the Serizawa brothers), preservation (Sally Ogata), or artistic freedom (Mimi and Mini Mothra), there exists a single-minded focus in these characters that stands in the way of coalition-building and problem-solving. Emi's desire to watch the drama unfold on television rather than to witness it directly further signals the nature of estrangement that characterizes many of the relationships within this performance fiction.

Foiling the Serizawas' plans to create a hotel complex and the city's desire to maintain its economic primacy within the Pacific Rim, the great lizard monster's destructive presence also offers a symbolic narrative in which individuals of all backgrounds must rally together to overcome a dangerous menace. The monster's continued rampage, of course, is integral to establishing the link between Emi and Manzanar, a link that is further fleshed out in *Tropic* as that novel reveals that these two characters are related to each other (Manzanar is Emi's long-lost grandfather). Even as Emi seems to believe that she does not have a viable ethnic or racial identity, the emergence of the monster lizard, whose very origin gestures to the interconnectedness of Japan and the United States, suggests she cannot simply escape attachments to her ancestry. On the opposite side, Sally Ogata's quest to preserve Japanese American identity at the expense of allowing Manzanar to "conduct" his own life relays the impossibility of maintaining a uniform cultural identity. In this respect, Emi appears as a bridging character: she expresses her confusion regarding the importance of embracing her ethnoracial ancestry and, at the same time, she stands as a counterpart to a character like Ogata, who comes off as too rigid about what it means to be a Japanese American. The conclusion of *GiLArex* sees both Emi and Manzanar return to the overpass to resume their traffic compositions, while Los Angelenos are forced to get out of their cars and help one another during the reconstruction. This rather cataclysmic conclusion obliquely invokes the genuine exigencies facing urban populations at that time, especially as the

1992 Los Angeles riots erupted and revealed the deep racial divisions still undergirding the city.[16]

L.A. Carmen vs. Tokyo Carmen (1990) returns the collection to the issue of the global economy. While *Kusei* and *GiLArex* both reference the growing tensions between Japan and the United States during the eighties, this musical performance fiction uses that element as its primary premise. Economic growth alone cannot explain the antagonistic relationship the United States developed with Japan, but scholars such as Bernard Gordon and Youn-Suk Kim remind us that the widening trade deficit alarmed America's policymakers and strategists (Gordon 100 and Kim 494). Edson W. Spencer explains the trade relations during the eighties thusly: "Some U.S. experts on Japan now argue that Japan is an economic predator, unwilling or unable to change its ways" (153) whereas the "Japanese, on the other hand, look at the United States increasingly as a country that has grown soft and complacent, that has lost its competitive industrial edge, and that is calling for protection from the pressures of the international marketplace because it is unwilling to deal with its own shortcomings" (154). From the American perspective, Japan appeared a ruthless economic competitor, intent on dominating the global marketplace. At the same time, from the Japanese perspective, the United States could be couched as a country filled with citizens who had grown lazy and who were not willing to work to improve their country's economic conditions.

This transnational tension is the basis of *L.A. Carmen vs. Tokyo Carmen*, but Yamashita's performance fiction pokes fun at this heated economic relationship through the dual deployment of a parodic narrative based on Georges Bizet's *Carmen*. This piece moves away from the opera's Spanish geographies and instead shuttles between the titular metropolitan locations: Los Angeles and Tokyo. *L.A. Carmen vs. Tokyo Carmen* involves twinned tragic narratives involving these two cities. In one, a group of Japanese characters migrate to the United States only to face unfortunate ends, while in the other, a group of white Americans traveling to Japan in hopes of addressing the trade imbalances meet untimely fates.

Drawing from Bizet's original musical production, this performance fiction includes analogs of the opera's four main characters: Don Jose, Escamillo, Micaela, and Carmen, who are refigured as Jiro, Ebizo, Maki, and L.A. Carmen, all Japanese immigrants. The Tokyo narrative alters the situation slightly, but more or less repeats the story from the perspective of white Americans, with Joe, Skipper, Michele, and Tokyo Carmen standing in for the main four figures. Like *Hannah Kusoh*, this piece takes an amusing look at the figure of the melancholic migrant, a subject who cannot assimilate and therefore faces psychic instability, which in turn results in suicide, murder, or some other violent act. Rather than make this narrative paradigmatic of the Asian migrant coming to the United States, *L.A. Carmen vs. Tokyo Carmen* implies that such a scenario is just as possible in the reverse direction, wherein Joe, Skipper, Michele, and Tokyo Carmen as white Americans might face difficult new lives in what for them is a foreign country that actively denigrates their presence. Like Yamashita's previous work, *Carmen* uses humor to defamiliarize Bizet's dramatic story. *Carmen* concludes with both female title characters stating, "Fool. What is it now? Still fighting a war? And who is the enemy, I say? Who is the enemy?"—a sentiment that critiques the so-called trade war occurring between the United States and Japan. Because both transnational movements—Joe to Tokyo and Jiro to Los Angeles—are motivated by their involvement with the economy, the Carmens imply that their murders will not address the feelings of impotency and disorientation these male characters experience, nor will it ameliorate Michele and Maki's melancholy. The Carmens become stand-ins for a lost home, one that cannot be retrieved and must be expunged so that none may possess it. Skipper and Ebizo both demonstrate the exportability of cultural commodities—respectively of baseball and kabuki—but their movements to different national locations are not without challenges. Ebizo's classically trained Japanese theater does not seamlessly translate to an American context, where he is typecast as "the foreigner" in commercials. Skipper, while receiving a strong welcome in a country that appreciates baseball, still finds it very difficult to assimilate. As a result, for Skipper and Ebizo, the Carmens represent a link to a more stable and more promising period in their lives. The diagrammatically symmetrical way that Bizet's *Carmen* is transplanted into different sociocultural and national contexts helps to amplify the comic effect of this reconsideration of transnational movements and migrant subjectivities.

Noh Bozos: A Circus Performance in Ten Amazing Acts (1993) is an important companion piece to *Hannah Kusoh*.[17] While *Hannah Kusoh* focuses much more on the ways in which the Asian American female body becomes appropriated or fetishized in various cultural contexts, *Noh Bozos* directly engages issues related to Asian American masculinity, especially as depicted in popular culture. Additionally, this focus on Asian American masculinity can be traced to Yamashita's interest in reconfiguring the Japanese theatrical form known as Noh.[18] According to Kunio Komparu, stage Noh requires a number of different elements, including but not limited to vocal music (chants), instrumentals, acting and dance, fine arts (masks, robes), architecture (traditional Noh staging), and the critical intertwinement of time and space (xvi).[19] As Andrew C. Gerstle further explains, "the development of Noh drama from the fourteenth century and its appropriation by successive samurai governments until the nineteenth century is particularly significant. Training in the recitation and performance of Noh drama became an essential part of samurai education, and gradually a hobby that many non-samurai as well continued throughout their lifetimes" (191). While this performance fiction does involve some elements of traditional Noh theatrics as outlined by Komparu and Gerstle, they are considerably mutated. The masks and costumes do not present us with heroes or deities, but rather other figures such as pop culture icons. Although chants are integral to this piece, the performers enter the stage in the first act repeating the phrase "Noh bozos," a silly pun on the Japanese theatrical form. Further, this piece employs an all-male cast in the same tradition, but once again shifts the context by focusing on Japanese American sansei men, who find themselves in a variety of dilemmas.

These dilemmas, explored in the following nine acts, range from the complications of interracial hybridity as outlined in Act II, "Bad Rap," to the class mobility issues facing Asian American male professionals in Act III, "The Glass Ceiling." Cultural stereotypes of Asian American men are considered in Act IV, "Fly by Chopsticks/Freaks of Nature" (Asian American men as martial arts experts), as well as in Act VIII, "Moyashi Maru" (Asian American men as ornamental and Oriental appendages to white male lead actors as evoked by the television series *Star Trek*). The *Star Trek* sequence is a prime example of Yamashita's use of parody, as the leads from the television series—Captain Kirk and Sulu—appear under different monikers: Captain Kok and Tsuru. Act V, "Heads," meditates on the intricacies of political involvement and Asian American leadership. Acts VI ("God's Gift to Asian American Women") and VII ("The Bearded Lady") explore

Asian American masculinity as it relates to sexual desire. Sequencing is especially important here, as Act vi posits a hypermasculine Asian American male sex object, replete with a performer, Westside Dude, who exhibits bulging muscles and attracts obvious female attention. In addition to this embodied virility, Westside Dude employs his monologue to reveal that his training program is fueled by ethnically appropriate foods. While the performer's proclamations demonstrate an overdetermined ethnoracial masculinity, the stakes in this hyperbolic construction are made more clear with its pairing with Act vii, "The Bearded Lady," which forefronts a parody of David Henry Hwang's *M. Butterfly*. In Hwang's version, Rene Gallimard, a Frenchman, falls in love with a Chinese woman, Song Liling, who Gallimard discovers in the climactic conclusion is actually a man. In Yamashita's comic adaptation of Hwang's drama, Song is revealed to be pregnant. Of course, because Song Liling is biologically male, this pregnancy would be impossible. Yamashita's performance fiction irreverently points to a skepticism directed at Hwang's drama: Song's so-called anatomical ruse would not be so easily overlooked. While Hwang's *M. Butterfly* allows Gallimard to sustain a personal fantasy of his heterosexuality, Yamashita's "The Bearded Lady" challenges such an assertion and places queerness at the forefront of the relationship between Song and Gallimard. In this respect, the middle two acts of *Noh Bozos* humorously question the obsession with, and the issues related to, the recovery of Asian American masculinity and heterosexuality.

Another partially new work added to this collection is *Siamese Twins and Mongoloids: Three Abstractions on Asian America* (2012). Yamashita included the first portion in *I Hotel* (2010), but the second two parts are entirely new and previously unpublished. This performance fiction loosely tracks the evolution of Asian American racial formation as it moves across different historical periods. The first section occurs just after the United States relaxed its restrictions on Asian immigrants in 1965. It revolves around a butcher named Pa—otherwise known by his paper name, Ah Gee—musing on the ways in which his children experience a kind of split identity as Chinese Americans. As the title implies, each "abstraction" also involves repetitive references to conjoined twins in both allegorical and literal forms. In this case, Ah Gee fathers five different sets of conjoined twins, a way to comically literalize the status of the Asian American as a hyphenated subject.

The second abstraction moves to the nineties. This segment is written in a form that appears to be a playscript based on a television series starring conjoined twins who also happen to be spies—Agents Heco and Okada Hamada—and depicts their adventures as they root out civil rights violations.[20] Heco and Okada are also white-collar professionals—the former is the dentist, while the latter is the optometrist—who operate out of a business called DentalOptics, located in Southern California. This abstraction proceeds as Heco and Okada receive a new assignment from Agents Chang and Eng: they must find out whether the Freedom Real Estate company is using discriminatory policies in its treatment of African American home buyers. The geographical and temporal setting of this abstraction recalls the critiques of multiculturalism that emerged especially after the Los Angeles race riots. This abstraction also targets the ossification of Asian Americans under the guise of the model minority—Heco and Okada demonstrate that Asian Americans can become upwardly mobile as they engage in white-collar professions, yet they can never fully be embraced since they are also apparently spies.

Set in the new millennium, the final abstraction, in part a parodic reformulation of Gilbert and Sullivan's *The Mikado*, depicts an intricate and thorny web of romantic relationships that ends with the portent of violence. This section of *Siamese Twins and Mongoloids* focuses on a professor of Asian American studies, Mike Kato; his wife Katisha, an attorney and an activist; and their adopted daughter Peep-Bo. Both Mike and Katisha are having extramarital affairs, Mike with Yum-Yum, a graduate student, and Katisha with Pitti-Sing, who coincidentally happens to be Yum-Yum's mother. Yum-Yum herself is actually in love with Nanki-Poo, another graduate student. As the story progresses, Peep-Bo finds fulfillment in her religious fervor. We also discover that Mike's research concentration is in popular culture. Thus, the conclusion of the third abstraction sees the premiere of his documentary, which examines the television series *DentalOptics*. The conclusion of this section dramatically unfolds when Ko-Ko, an executioner figure, unveils assault pistols. The third abstraction helps break open questions related to the institutionalization of ethnic studies: can it retain any coherent political vision, especially considering the heterogeneity of the Asian American population? Rather than reading this piece as a call to terminate the study of Asian Americans, Ko-Ko's provocative concluding stance instead suggests that we must be ever more vigilant against the forces that seek to dismantle it. Further still, as this final abstraction details in various instances, the violence occurring on American soil cannot be disarticulated from the continued emergence of global conflict and social inequality.

Anime Wong: A CyberAsian Odyssey (2008) is structured in "six mangas," a nod to the Japanese-stylized comic drawings. The first manga debuts the major character of this piece, Anime Wong; the title is both a pun on Anna May Wong, the major Chinese American Hollywood star of the early twentieth century, and a reference to the Japanese comic book aesthetic. Other featured performers include aliens who act as a traditional chorus; the paparazzi, who also function in a chorus-like role to catalog the events that transpire; and finally, a large group of cyborgs. *Anime Wong* is a performance fiction aware of the many popular culture impulses that repetitively invoke Asian American racial formation among a set of overdetermined stereotypes, ranging from the yellow peril, to the model minority, to the femme fatale, among others. In the second manga, for instance, Yamashita redeploys a *Battlestar Galactica* remake as a lens through which to consider the connections between the cyborg and the Asian American. In the television series, one of the Cylon characters, played by Korean American actress Grace Park, makes apparent the ways in which the Asian American, as cyborg, embodies the tenuous borderland between model minority and yellow peril. Although there are no overt racial overtones in the actual show, the casting of an Asian American in the role of Sharon Valerii, a character who is continuously tormented by her allegiances—to her human counterparts and to her Cylon companions—metaphorically exposes the Asian American's liminal status. On the one hand, he or she might be a threat to the nation; on the other, his or her loyalty and hard work is evidence of a postrace world in which even the oppressed can rise up and be successful. Precisely because there are no direct references to racial formation in *Battlestar Galactica*, this reading relies on this cultural production's elliptical relationship to the era in which it has been historically produced. But this manga's consideration of racial discourses is more explicit, as it retools the highly specific language of *Battlestar Galactica* and parodies the unification of gender with cyborgian subjectivity. Indeed, the manga raucously depicts this irreverent act: Anime Wong having sex with cyborg sirens. This sequence also deconstructs the dramatic focus of the television show by directly involving audience participation: as a survivor of the cyborg siren sexual event, one audience member wins a "toaster," a term that is also a slang reference to a Cylon. The use of wordplay spotlights how the cyberAsian, as figured by the character Anime Wong, must be related to the production of goods and commodities, as depicted by the toaster, which is apparently made—and for our Cylonic purposes, replicated—in various Asian countries.

Jan Ken Pon (2012) explores the use of multimedia in academic and popular contexts by poking fun at PowerPoint presentations and the ubiquity of YouTube. The title refers to roshambo, the game otherwise known as "rock, paper, scissors." The triangulated nature of this pastime provides Yamashita the inspiration for what is called a "dance performance idea," in which comic questions arise concerning aspects of social competition. This work unfolds through a series of PowerPoint slides, which include narrative sidebars at the bottom of each page. These sidebars take the form of playful interviews and pop culture critiques, and are sometimes filtered through an irascible narrative voice. At first, the performance fiction focuses more specifically on theories of evolutionary biology, as related to lizard speciation. From there, other triadic relationships are explored, including but not limited to racial formation and bacterial production. Such theories of relationality are extended in a hyperbolic direction as the faux PowerPoint slides forward the possibility of pentalectics, a five-tiered structure of dominant-subordinate connections. Ultimately, the piece finds inspiration in the unending cycle that defines power structures.

Unsurprisingly, the conclusion of *Jan Ken Pon* turns to global capitalism, prompting us to consider the rise of China in the new millennium. Of course, part of the point here is to spotlight how a yellow peril discourse that once branded Asian immigrants as forever foreign can resurface in light of an economic power shift. One of the last slides asks the question, "What if all Asians just left Earth?" This rather absurd question returns us all the way back to the collection's beginning, where, in the distant future, Japanese Americans find themselves exiled to Planet Topanzanar in *Kusei*. In this way, these pieces model the continued ambivalence accorded to all things Asiatic. On the one hand, American popular culture embraces transnational trends such as the rise of K-Pop, referenced in *Jan Ken Pon* through Yamashita's inclusion of Psy, the hitmaker behind the omnipresent "Gangnam Style." On the other, the economic might of a rising nation like China becomes the target of increased scrutiny, which presages a future in which exclusion acts and barred zones resurface. The use of the PowerPoint slides in this dance performance suggests that a lesson must be learned, but the absence of any references to actual students begs the question of whether this presentation will unfold in front of a receptive audience.

THROUGH THE PERFORMANCE ODYSSEY

Rather than rehearse what Viet Thanh Nguyen might call the discourse of the bad, resistant Asian American subject, *Anime Wong* depicts characters and roles that are often ridiculous, politically incorrect, sometimes outrageous and other times assimilatory. As these brief readings show, Yamashita's use of the parodic form in so many of these works must be further fleshed out through the social contexts in which they are enmeshed, allowing these performance fictions to be understood in their multifaceted intricacies. But my afterword can accomplish only so much, and if there is a lack of closure here, it is more indicative of the fact that these considerations can only begin to break the surface of these pyrotechnic cultural productions. I thus encourage readers and critics of American literature to give Karen Tei Yamashita's performance fictions their due by creating their own forums and venues for the continued discussion, exploration, and dissemination of these visionary productions.

NOTES

1. Ling (2012) is devoted to Yamashita's works.

2. I have dated the composition of *Siamese Twins and Mongoloids* as 2012 based on the newest additions (the second and third abstractions), though abstraction one was previously published in *I Hotel.*

3. *Rock Candy* is the only piece from Yamashita's later performance works that is not included here; its specific narrative lacks the more extended connection to conceptions of race and ethnicity that appear as ordering tropes in her other performance fictions.

4. There are not many documented publications from Asian American creative artists, especially those who have tended to go the more experimental route. Some isolated examples do exist here; please see the work of Kwong (2004) and Uyehara (2004). In addition to performance, poetry tends to be overlooked within critical circles connected to Asian American literature. For some recent monographs, see Zhou (2006) and Park (2008).

5. See Moy (1993), Kondo (1997), Lee (1997), and Shimakawa (2002).

6. Abe composed the music for the songs, while Yamashita composed the lyrics.

7. As Seymour Benjamin Chatman succinctly states, parody is "a subspecies of satire, the genre of making-fun-of " (2001, 28) that "only satirizes other texts or genres, that is, what has *already* been textually modeled" (30). Revising earlier readings of parody as apolitical, Linda Hutcheon redefines the genre by arguing that "even the most self-conscious and parodic of contemporary works do not try to escape, but indeed foreground, the historical, social, ideological contexts in which they have existed and continue to exist" (1986–1987, 183). Hutcheon specifically frames parody within the parameters of a politicized postmodernism, but distances parody from its comic properties, an approach considered by Ansgar Nünning as too limiting. Instead, Nünning advocates, by way of Margaret A. Rose, that parody can exist simultaneously as a humorous and self-reflexive genre (1999, 127). Finally, William Van O'Connor reminds us that "one of the functions of parody is to make us see, or better, let us experience, the nature of a style and subject, and their excesses" (1964,

241). I consider Yamashita's performance fictions as variously invested in parodic impulses as defined by Chatman, Hutcheon, Nünning, and Van O'Connor. While parody might be traditionally seen as a written genre, there are other valences to consider when analyzing Yamashita's parodies. Claycomb (2007, 105–106) usefully extends parody through the consideration of the parodic image, reminding us of the visual qualities related to such playful representations.

8. Robert Phiddian (1997, 686) advances the possibility that parody can act as a form of deconstruction; he further explores how parody functions through imperfect supplementation, as it relies on exceeding an original script or a cultural context in some form.

9. For Margaret A. Rose's discussion of parody, see *Parody: Ancient, Modern, and Post-Modern* (1993).

10. For a useful introductory essay on Japanese theatricality, see Mori (2002).

11. In terms of representational approach, Yamashita's depiction of a future in which Japanese Americans are interned is fairly unique. Miyake (2002) is another example in which internment is imagined as a future possibility. Many other examples of post–Japanese American internment writings do not follow a science fictional model, including Otsuka (2002), Kadohata (1989), Roripaugh (1999), and Kageyama-Ramakrishnan (2008).

12. Morley and Robins (1995) first coined the term. For more on techno-Orientalism, see Niu (1998), Nakamura (2002), Ueno (2002), and Cornea (2005). In contrast to techno-Orientalism, Chun (2006) coins the term "high-tech Orientalism."

13. According to Kurihara, "Hijikata saw the body in everything and attempted to capture it in words" (2000, 16). Some typical Butoh features include "intensely slow and controlled movements and white body make-up" (Brotman 2007, 50).

14. More generally, names are imported directly from the Godzilla films and transformed into various analogs. Dr. Daisuke Serizawa, the main love interest of Emiko Yamane, is obviously the basis for the Serizawa brothers. The surname of Sally Ogata connects to Hideko Ogata, the sailor with strong feelings for Emiko. Steve Martin, the American journalist in the Godzilla film, is completely exported into

Yamashita's production, but in a different temporal context. Mini and Mimi Mothra's surname refers to one of the later monster incarnations in the film series.

15. See Boss (1999) and Maio (1999).

16. This performance fiction prompts us to reconsider the inspiration and the production of a given writer's so-called end product. Indeed, we can read Yamashita's novel *Tropic of Orange* as a more palimpsestic narrative that is driven by its impulse to creatively consider the import of race riots and the related media sensations surrounding them as its more direct social contexts. This novel also turns away from the global economic regional frame of the Pacific Rim that is evident in *GiLArex* and focuses more on the interracial tensions, especially as posed by its inclusion of major characters—Rafaela Cortez, Gabriel Balboa, Buzzworm, and Bobby Ngu—absent from the earlier musical production. Interestingly enough, Yamashita herself stated that the development of *Tropic* as a novel was primarily inspired by her desire to alter the plotting details in relation to the titular orange. Thus, Emi and Manzanar's experiences would have to be altered given the geographical and temporal movement of the orange northward and through Los Angeles.

17. Noh has also influenced other Japanese North American writers. As Johnston notes in her reading of Terry Watada's *The Tale of a Mask,* "drawing from different cultural dramatic traditions, *The Tale of a Mask* engages theatre at the crossroads of traditional Japanese Noh theatre design, pantomime, stylized gestures, naturalistic acting in the flashback scenes, and masked theatre in the Onibaba scenes" (2005, 136).

18. According to Shinkokai, "the invention of Noh is attributed to Kwannami Kiyotsugu (1333–1384), a distinguished actor and writer of Sarugaku and to his son Zeami Motokiyo (1363–1443), who developed and refined the art under the patronage of Yoshimitsu, the third Ashikaga shogun" (1960, ix).

19. For another excellent explanation of the various characteristics of Noh, see Alland (1979, esp. 5–7).

20. Here, Yamashita is clearly riffing off the names of Joseph Heco and John Okada.

WORKS CITED

Alland, Jr., Alexander. "The Construction of Reality and Unreality in Japanese Theatre." *Drama Review: TDR* 23.2 (1979): 3–10.

Anisfield, Nancy. "Godzilla/Gojiro: Evolution of the Nuclear Metaphor." *Journal of Popular Culture* 29.3 (1995): 53–62.

Boss, Joyce E. "Godzilla in the Details." *Strategies* 12.1 (1999): 45–49.

Brophy, Philip. "Monster Island: Godzilla and Japanese Sci-Fi/Horror/Fantasy." *Postcolonial Studies* 3.1 (2000): 39–42.

Brotman, Joanna. "Beyond the Metaphor of Mirrors." *PAJ: A Journal of Performance and Art* (PAJ 87) 29.3 (2007): 46–50.

Chatman, Seymour Benjamin. "Parody and Style." *Poetics Today* 22.1 (2001): 25–39.

Chun, Wendy Hui Kyong. *Control and Freedom: Power and Paranoia in the Age of Fiber Optics.* Cambridge, MA: MIT Press, 2006.

Claycomb, Ryan. "Staging Psychic Excess: Parodic Narrative and Transgressive Performance." *Journal of Narrative Theory* 37.1 (2007): 104–127.

Cornea, Christine. "Techno-Orientalism and the Postmodern Subject." *Screen Methods: Comparative Readings in Film Studies.* Ed. Jacqueline Furby and Karen Randell. London: Wallflower Press, 2005. 72–81.

Gerstle, Andrew C. "The Culture of Play: Kabuki and the Production of Texts." *Oral Tradition* 20.2 (2005): 188–216.

Gibson, William. *Neuromancer.* New York: Ace Science Fiction Books, 1984.

Gordon, Bernard K. "Truth in Trading." *Foreign Policy* 61 (1985–1986): 94–108.

Hannoosh, Michele. "The Reflexive Function of Parody." *Comparative Literature* 41.2 (1989): 113–127.

Hutcheon, Linda. "The Politics of Postmodernism: Parody and History." *Cultural Critique* 5 (1986-1987): 179–207.

Hwang, David Henry. *M. Butterfly.* New York: Penguin, 1988.

Johnston, Kirsty. "Migration, Mental Illness and Terry Watada's *The Tale of a Mask.*" *Journal of Canadian Studies* 39.3 (2005): 123–145.

Kadohata, Cynthia. *The Floating World.* New York: Viking, 1989.

Kageyama-Ramakrishnan, Claire. *Shadow Mountain.* New York: Four Way Books, 2008.

Kim, Youn-Suk. "Prospects for Japanese–u.s. Trade and Industrial Competition." *Asian Survey* 30.5 (1990): 493–504.

Komparu, Kunio. *The Noh Theater: Principles and Perspectives*. New York: Weatherhill/Tankosha, 1983.

Kondo, Dorinne. *About Face: Performing Race and Fashion in Theater*. New York: Routledge, 1997.

Kwong, Dan. *From Inner Worlds to Outer Space: The Multimedia Performances of Dan Kwong*. Ed. Robert Vorlicky. Ann Arbor: University of Michigan Press, 2004.

Kurihara, Nanako. "Hijikata Tatsumi: The Words of Butoh." *TDR: The Drama Review* 44.1 (2000): 10–28.

Lee, Josephine. *Performing Asian America: Race and Ethnicity on the Contemporary Stage*. Philadelphia: Temple University Press, 1997.

Ling, Jinqi. *Across Meridians*. Stanford, CA: Stanford University Press, 2012.

Maio, Kathi. "The Soul (or Lack Thereof) of the New Monster." *Fantasy & Science Fiction* 96.6 (1999): 71–75.

Miyake, Perry. *21st Century Manzanar*. Los Angeles: Really Great Books, 2002.

Mori, Mitsuya. "The Structure of Theater: A Japanese View of Theatricality." *SubStance* 98/99 31.2/3 (2002): 3–93.

Morley, David, and Kevin Robins. "Techno-Orientalism: Japan Panic." *Spaces of Identity: Global Media, Electronic Landscapes, and Cultural Boundaries*. New York: Routledge, 1995. 147–173.

Moy, James. *Marginal Sights: Staging the Chinese in America*. Iowa City: University of Iowa Press, 1993.

Nakamura, Lisa. *Cybertypes: Race, Ethnicity, and Identity on the Internet*. New York: Routledge, 2002.

Nguyen, Viet Thanh. *Race and Resistance: Literature & Politics in Asian America*. New York: Oxford University Press, 2002.

Niu, Greta Ai-Yu. "Techno-Orientalism, Cyborgology and Asian American Studies." Paper presented at the Discipline and Deviance: Genders, Technologies, Machines Conference, Duke University, October 1998.

Nünning, Ansgar. "The Creative Role of Parody in Transforming Literature and Culture: An Outline of a Functionalist Approach to Postmodern Parody." *European Journal of English Studies* 3.2 (1999): 123–137.

Otsuka, Julie. *When the Emperor Was Divine*. New York: Knopf, 2002.

Park, Josephine Nock-Hee. *Apparitions of Asia: Modernist Form and Asian American Poetics*. New York: Oxford University Press, 2008.

Phiddian, Robert. "Are Parody and Deconstruction Secretly the Same Thing?" *New Literary History* 28.4 (1997): 673–696.

Roripaugh, Lee Ann. *Beyond Heart Mountain*. New York: Penguin, 1999.

Rose, Margaret A. *Parody: Ancient, Modern, and Post-Modern*. Cambridge: Cambridge University Press, 1993.

Shapiro, Jerome F. "Atomic Bomb Cinema: Illness, Suffering, and the Apocalyptic Narrative." *Literature and Medicine* 17.1 (1998): 126–148.

Shimakawa, Karen. *National Abjection: The Asian American Body on Stage*. Durham: Duke University Press, 2002.

Shinkokai, Nippon Gakujutsu. *The Noh Drama*. Rutland, VT: Charles E. Tuttle, 1960.

Spencer, Edson W. "Japan as Competitor." *Foreign Policy* 78 (Spring 1990): 153–171.

Toepfer, Karl Eric. "Nudity and Textuality in Postmodern Performance." *PAJ: A Journal of Performance and Art* (PAJ 54) 18.3 (1996): 76–91.

Ueno, Toshiya. "Japanimation: Techno-Orientalism, Media Tribes, and Rave Culture." *Aliens R Us: The Other in Science Fiction Cinema*. Ed. Ziauddin Sardar and Sean Cubitt. Sterling, VA: Pluto Press, 2002. 94–110.

Uyehara, Denise. *Maps of City and Body: Shedding Light on The Performances of Denise Uyehara*. Ed. Denise Uyehara, Anthony Escobar, and Sunyoung Lee. Los Angeles: Kaya Press, 2004.

Van O'Connor, William. "Parody as Criticism." *College English* 25.4 (1964): 241–248.

Yamashita, Karen Tei. *Brazil-Maru*. Minneapolis: Coffee House Press, 1992.

_____. *Circle K Cycles*. Minneapolis: Coffee House Press, 2001.

_____. *I Hotel*. Minneapolis: Coffee House Press, 2010.

_____. *Through the Arc of the Rain Forest*. Minneapolis: Coffee House Press, 1990.

_____. *Tropic of Orange*. Minneapolis: Coffee House Press, 1997.

Zhou, Xiaojing. *The Ethics and Poetics of Alterity in Asian American Poetry*. Iowa City: University of Iowa Press, 2006.

ACKNOWLEDGMENTS

In the years I worked with performance, theater was for me a communal process and practice. Folks came together, created an event for a larger community. Collaboration learned the work. There were a multitude of kinetic encounters: bodies with music, voices with song, movement with costume, appearance with lighting, slide and video with movable staging. A flat text on the page stood up and became voluminous, a wild beast, never entirely tamable, and this was exhilarating and dangerous. So many creative people devoted their time and risked their passions to be there, taming the beast. Most of you are named in the playbills that announce these performances, and I thank and remember you all. It never seemed quite fair to have expended all that time and effort, in some cases, for just a short weekend of performances, but perhaps this book in some small part can recognize your dedication to your art, talent, and imagination.

I want in particular to thank the East West Players in Los Angeles, the Northwest Asian American Theater in Seattle, and venues such as the Japanese American Cultural and Community Center in Little Tokyo, Highways in Santa Monica, and the Los Angeles Taper, Too, for producing my work, as well as the many associated actors, musicians, producers, stage personnel, costume designers, videographers, mask makers, and publicity writers, who gave their time to these projects. I would also like to recognize funding support from a Rockefeller Playwright-in-Residence Fellowship and a City of Los Angeles Cultural Grant Award.

Most especially, I want to thank and remember the spirit of Mako, then–artistic director at East West, who directed and staged my first work and was always present with his support. Another gifted talent who has since passed is Glenn Horiuchi, who composed and directed the music for *Noh Bozos*. Thank you to Edna Horiuchi and Francis Wong for allowing us to share Glenn's compositions, poised to match the work's circus bombast.

Infinite thanks to Vicki Abe, Shizuko Hoshi, and Karen Mayeda, my sisters in the crime of performance—powerful, iconoclastic, extraordinary artists who were always slightly *bad,* and thus always fun to work with.

Over these years, I've had the privilege of working with many accomplished actors, artists, designers, and musicians, among them: George Abe, Tim Dang, Alan Furutani, Alberto Isaac, Sala Iwamatsu,

Steve James, Emily Kuroda, Mimosa, Jeanne Chizuko Nishimura, Elaine Oda, Chris Tashima, Keone Young, and many others. Many thanks to all of you.

And to Laraine Crampton, Joanne Funakoshi, Maria Gonzalez Mathews, and Kay Funakoshi Torres, thank you for your recordings and photography, for documenting those ephemeral events.

Thanks to Barry Sinervo for the inspiration of your work on lizard ecology and natural selection, and my apologies for this anthropomorphized side adventure. Thanks to Christine Hong for your incisive reading and comments on the later, unstaged work. Thanks also to Aimee Bahng, Sean Borton, Ruth Hsu, Ikue Kina, Casey Lelia Krache, Micah Perks, Keijiro Suga, and Ronaldo Wilson, for allowing me to subject you to queries and various draft versions of these experiments. And special thanks to Lucy Mae San Pablo Burns for always being willing to fly away with me to another city to attend a play, for your interviews and dramaturgy, and for your support and theater intelligence.

Thank you to the Coffee House crew: Anitra Budd, Caroline Casey, Chris Fischbach, Allan Kornblum, Linda Koutsky, and your wonderful staff. Thanks for believing and going along with yet another experiment in fiction.

So many years later, sets sawed into firewood, giant forms of foam-rubber sushi degraded into rubbish, costumes tossed or reused at Halloween, a cache of outdated audio and video cassettes, the hokey and popular bound to the times, all this having become pieces of ephemera and memory, I threw what remained into a box. One day Stephen Hong Sohn carried the box home and a few months later returned with a collection of manuscripts. Steve, I am indebted to your productive energies and persistence, your careful reading, and your love for and thinking about this work. I always thought there was a book in that box, but you made it happen. Thank you.

Thanks to Victor and Esther Abe, Roy and Eileen Mayeda, Asako Yamashita, Jane Tomi and Pat Boltz, Kay Yamashita, and Chizu Kitow Togasaki, family who put up with these shenanigans. And this book is dedicated to Jane Tei and Jon, who packed Legos or Monopoly into backpacks and played during rehearsals, who fell asleep at late-night dinner meetings, who cut discarded foam rubber into little people spread in armies across my workroom, who intuited the projects and memorized favorite lines, and who, despite all this, grew up all right.

Finally I want to say that the motivation behind this urge to do theater was the creative and endless imagination of Ronaldo Lopes de Oliveira. It was your original idea to create Hannah's nose; you who noticed, while I napped, the man on the Harbor Freeway overpass conducting traffic; you who envisioned Godzilla's giant foot on stage. It was your traveling and work with the Brazilian theater groups Pão e Circo and Teatro Oficina, that edgy experience of inventing and innovating a stage almost literally from detritus, oil cans, and light bulbs at the back of an old automotive repair shop in São Paulo. For you, the possibilities for theater were provocative, makeshift, and slightly mad. You brought all that to L.A., though it wasn't always easy. Thank you.

And thank you to all of you, named and unnamed, participants, audience, and readers, who have come along unwittingly or wittingly, for your open imagination or for just imagining that it might be worth chancing events rendered absurd and parodic to accompany the pain and joy of the beast—giant lizard, giant sushi, chicken, Siamese twins, or cyborg—on stage.

—Karen Tei Yamashita

The critical afterword could not have been completed without the help of my research assistants, Jennifer Liu and Haerin Shin. I also must thank Gina Valentino for her feedback concerning *Siamese Twins and Mongoloids* in July of 2012.

—Stephen Hong Sohn

CREDITS

"Madama Butterfly: The Sense of Sound," from the performance *Hannah Kusoh: An American Butoh*, was published in *Premonitions: The Kaya Anthology of New Asian North American Poetry*, edited by Walter Lew. New York: Kaya Productions, 1995.

"Madama B" was published as "Madonna B" in the *International Examiner* in May 1993.

Parts I and II from *Tokyo Carmen versus L.A. Carmen* were published in M*ulticultural Theatre: Scenes and Monologues from New Hispanic, Asian, and African-American Plays*, edited by Roger Ellis. Colorado Springs: Meriwether Publishing, 1996.

Production photos from *Kusei, Hannah Kusoh*, and *Tokyo Carmen versus L.A. Carmen* are reprinted by permission of Joanne Funokoshi, Kay Torres, and Karen Mayeda.

Music for "You Can Learn from the Past," by Vicki Abe, is reprinted by permission of the artist.

Music for "Freaks of Nature" and "Subtleties of Sushi or California Roll," by Glenn Horiuchi, is reprinted by permission of Edna Horiuchi.

Photographs of Professor Barry Sinervo and *Uta stansburiana* are used by permission of Barry Sinervo.

COFFEE HOUSE PRESS

The mission of Coffee House Press is to publish exciting, vital, and enduring authors of our time; to delight and inspire readers; to contribute to the cultural life of our community; and to enrich our literary heritage. By building on the best traditions of publishing and the book arts, we produce books that celebrate imagination, innovation in the craft of writing, and the many authentic voices of the American experience.

Visit us at coffeehousepress.org.

COLOPHON

Anime Wong was designed at Coffee House Press,
in the historic Grain Belt Brewery's Bottling House
near downtown Minneapolis. The text is set in Caslon.

FUNDER ACKNOWLEDGMENT

Coffee House Press is an independent, nonprofit literary publisher. Our books are made possible through the generous support of grants and gifts from many foundations, corporate giving programs, state and federal support, and through donations from individuals who believe in the transformational power of literature. Coffee House Press receives major operating support from Amazon, the Bush Foundation, the Jerome Foundation, the McKnight Foundation, the National Endowment for the Arts—a federal agency, Target, and in part from a grant provided by the Minnesota State Arts Board through an appropriation by the Minnesota State Legislature from the State's general fund and its arts and cultural heritage fund with money from the vote of the people of Minnesota on November 4, 2008, and a grant from the Wells Fargo Foundation of Minnesota. Coffee House also receives support from: several anonymous donors; Suzanne Allen; Elmer L. and Eleanor J. Andersen Foundation; Mary & David Anderson Family Foundation; Around Town Agency; Patricia Beithon; Bill Berkson; the E. Thomas Binger and Rebecca Rand Fund of the Minneapolis Foundation; the Patrick and Aimee Butler Family Foundation; the Buuck Family Foundation; Claire Casey; Ruth Dayton; Dorsey & Whitney, LLP; Mary Ebert and Paul Stembler; Chris Fischbach and Katie Dublinski; Fredrikson & Byron, P.A.; Katharine Freeman; Sally French; Anselm Hollo and Jane Dalrymple-Hollo; Jeffrey Hom; Carl and Heidi Horsch; Kenneth Kahn; Alex and Ada Katz; Stephen and Isabel Keating; the Kenneth Koch Literary Estate; Kathy and Dean Koutsky; the Lenfestey Family Foundation; Carol and Aaron Mack; George Mack; Gillian McCain; Mary McDermid; Sjur Midness and Briar Andresen; the Nash Foundation; Peter and Jennifer Nelson; the Rehael Fund of the Minneapolis Foundation; Schwegman, Lundberg & Woessner, P.A.; Kiki Smith; Jeffrey Sugerman and Sarah Schultz; Nan Swid; Patricia Tilton; the Archie D. & Bertha H. Walker Foundation; Stu Wilson and Mel Barker; the Woessner Freeman Family Foundation; Margaret and Angus Wurtele; and many other generous individual donors.

ART WORKS.
arts.gov

MINNESOTA
STATE ARTS BOARD

TARGET.

amazon.com

To you and our many readers across the country,
we send our thanks for your continuing support.

OTHER TITLES BY KAREN TEI YAMASHITA

I Hotel 978-1-56689-239-1
NATIONAL BOOK AWARD FINALIST
"I Hotel is an explosive site, a profound metaphor and jazzy, epic novel rolled into one. Karen Tei Yamashita chronicles the colliding arts and social movements in the Bay Area of the wayward '70s with fierce intelligence, humor and empathy." —JESSICA HAGEDORN

Circle K Cycles 978-1-56689-108-0
"At once [a] short story collection, memoir and scrapbook—charmingly enlivened with snapshots, advertisements, signs, random factoids and graphics. . . . [Yamashita] brings it all together with humor and heart."
—*PUBLISHERS WEEKLY*

Tropic of Orange
978-1-56689-064-9
"Fiercely satirical. . . . Yamashita presents [an] intricate plot with mordant wit."
—*NEW YORK TIMES BOOK REVIEW*

Brazil-Maru
978-1-56689-016-8
"This enriching novel introduces Western readers to an unusual cultural experiment, and makes vivid a crucial chapter in Japanese assimilation into the West."
—*PUBLISHERS WEEKLY*

Through the Arc of the Rain Forest
978-0-918273-82-6
"Bizarre and baroque, funny and sad. Yamashita's novel may say more about saving the rain forest than its non-fiction counterparts do."
—*UTNE READER*

OTHER TITLES FROM COFFEE HOUSE PRESS

Leche by R. Zamora Linmark
978-1-56689-254-4
"Linmark nails the excitement and terror of being young
with a rare and moving accuracy." —*SPIN*

Screaming Monkeys edited by M. Evelina Galang
978-1-56689-141-7
Screaming Monkeys sets fire to Asian American stereotypes as it illuminates the diverse and often neglected
history and culture within the Asian American diaspora.

Famous Suicides of the Japanese Empire by David Mura
978-1-56689-215-5
"There is no writer that dives deeper (or more bravely)
into the chasm that is the human heart. [David Mura's]
first novel is a tour de force: luminously written and by
turns crafty, tough, wise, and joyful." —JUNOT DÍAZ

Whorled by Ed Bok Lee
978-1-56689-278-0
"These poems are filled with 'a certain historical color
of light.' They're funny, slyly political, and gorgeous.
Working with a variety of forms and modes, Ed Bok Lee
rocks my socks off. I love this book."
—SHERMAN ALEXIE

Her Wild American Self by M. Evelina Galang
978-1-56689-040-3
"An honest and insightful look at the experiences of
Filipina American women who 'grew up hearing two
languages.'" —*MS. MAGAZINE*